MIDNIGHT MASS

At the altar, Father O'Connor genuflected devoutly. His white head was bowed low and he held a Host with thumb and forefinger of both hands.

Before he could rise from his knee, a tremor jolted the church and the cat roared a jungle cry of outrage that joined with the quake to announce that the evil had returned.

The cat opened its mouth to roar again.

Wide.

Too wide.

The jaws came unhinged and from deep within its throat another pair of eyes appeared and an earsplitting shriek split the air, now bone cold and filled with wisps of acrid smoke. From the animal's gaping jaws a new face emerged, like the birthing of a disgusting baby, tugging the cat inside out with a howl of pain.

A grotesque little beast with wrinkled, stubby legs stood where the cat had been. It was blue and naked, with a concave face and piglike nose, puffing vapor with the foul smell of raw sewage.

"Happy birthday, Lucius," it screeched. "Happy, happy birthday."

CAMPFIRE STORY

ROBERT Y. KLINE

CHARTER/DIAMOND BOOKS, NEW YORK

CAMPFIRE STORY

A Charter/Diamond Book / published by arrangement
with the author

PRINTING HISTORY
Charter/Diamond edition / December 1990

ISBN: 1-55773-424-0

Charter/Diamond Books are published by The Berkley Publishing
Group, 200 Madison Avenue, New York, New York 10016.
The name "CHARTER/DIAMOND" and its logo are trademarks
belonging to Charter Communications, Inc.

PRINTED IN THE UNITED STATES OF AMERICA

10 9 8 7 6 5 4 3 2 1

CAMPFIRE STORY

1

"YOU'RE SCARED, AIN'T YOU?" Wally Fenner said to the boy behind him. He chuckled, turned, and barreled through the darkness, swinging the wrecking bar into the thick brush and letting the branches whip back into Scott Stein's face.

"No, I'm not scared," Stein croaked as a leafy branch lashed him across the tender skin of his neck. "Why should I be scared?"

He stopped to rub the rising welt and Billy Harman stumbled blindly into his back. "For Christ's sake, Steiny, what are you stopping for?"

"He's scared shitless," Fenner called back over his shoulder.

"I am not."

"You are too." Fenner wheezed a mirthless chuckle. "I think you just crapped your pants."

"That's your breath blowing back in your face," Stein said, secretly pleased with himself for slipping in a rare lick at the burly boy whose shadowy outline moved through the trees in front of him.

Scott didn't often take liberties with Wally Fenner's temper but this night was special. Tonight he had been invited to join the two older boys in a harmless bit of mischief and it pumped him full of spirit if not courage.

"Did you ever kill anything before?" Billy Harman asked. He spoke with the detached nonchalance of one who regularly flirts with danger.

"Sure, lots of times," Stein lied.

"Like what?"

"What's the big deal anyway?" the younger boy asked.

"Will you two keep quiet," Wally Fenner hissed back at them as they reached a small clearing.

They stood at the edge of a vigorous cornfield, bristling with stalks that pierced the night like rows of vigilant soldiers. The sky was dark as pitch and misting lightly, enough to lay an annoying film on Stein's glasses. He took them off and wiped them on his shirttail.

"What do we do now?" he whispered.

"We wait," Fenner told him. He jerked his thumb toward the ramshackle structure silhouetted on the other side of the cornfield. A pair of dirty yellow windows glowed like cat's eyes from the lower floor of the old farmhouse. "He ain't gone out yet."

In a gesture like a salute, Stein shielded his glasses from the mist and squinted across the dark spikes of corn. The world around him was a dull montage of black on grey and shrouded in a chilling fog that squeezed its boundaries. He shivered and wished that he had worn his jacket like his mother had advised. "Who's not gone yet?"

Fenner huffed impatiently. "Old man McKechnie, for cris-sake. His truck's still parked there."

Stein followed Fenner's glance across the field and saw the shadow of a pickup poking around the corner of the shed.

"What if he don't go nowhere tonight," Billy Harman wondered.

"Haw, haw! That'd be a first." Wally Fenner grinned and the other two boys saw the gleam of teeth across his moon face. "I think Gilly's would go out of business if old man McKech-nie missed a single night."

"That's right," Scott Stein piped. He realized that his words were pitched too high and he reached down to his toes for full-throated maturity. "My dad does Mr. Gillespie's books and I heard him tell my mom that old man McKechnie is good for ten percent of the bar's business."

He was proud to contribute to the font of the older boys' knowledge but they seemed unimpressed.

Fenner glanced at the murky squares of light across the cornfield. "Hurry up and get thirsty you old lush," he mumbled impatiently.

He leaned the heavy wrecking bar against a tree and lowered himself to the ground as if preparing for a long vigil. Billy Harman, acting on Wally's cue, propped his gleaming machete against the same tree and sat cross-legged facing him. Scott Stein scanned the dark clearing for a dry spot and, finding none, hooked his thumbs over the belt to his jeans and leaned reluctantly against the damp bark of an oak tree.

Stein was short and slight, even for his thirteen years, and with his stylish blond hair he might have been a pretty preteen about to burst into the bloom of feminine adolescence. Even when he tried to posture mannishly with his thumbs hooked on his wide belt and his pelvis boldly thrust out, he looked more like a seductive teenybopper than a latent Marlboro man.

In tonight's company, the difference was even more dramatic. Billy Harman, at fourteen, was older and bigger than Stein. He had lank blond hair that looked lifeless and dirty no matter how recently washed and his sallow face was a cratered map of maltreated pimples, the genesis of which, Wally Fenner assured him, was a preoccupation with his groin.

"Do you still pull your puddin a lot?" Fenner asked matter-of-factly.

"Naw," Stein squeaked.

"I don't mean you, dickhead. You probably ain't got enough to grab onto. I'm talking to Harman. What about it, Billy," Wally goaded. "Do you flog your dong, whack your carrot, hammer your hamhock?"

"So what if I do," Billy answered defensively.

"It'll make your face break out in goobers," Fenner warned. "And when you get older your teeth will all fall out."

Billy Harman ran the tip of his tongue into a gaping hole in a back molar.

"Look at Steiny," Fenner went on. "He don't whack off and look at how pretty he is."

It irked the hell out of Billy Harman the way Wally hammered away with his timeworn jokes, but what could he do? Just as Billy was older and bigger than Scott Stein, Wally

Fenner was older and bigger than Billy Harman and he was also a bully. It didn't pay to cross him.

Billy tried to change the subject. "Where's he keep the chickens?"

"He sticks 'em in that shed at night." Wally jerked a thumb at the fragile building.

"I thought that chickens lived in a chicken coop," Stein argued.

Fenner shrugged his meaty shoulders in the darkness. "Well, why don't you just go on over there and knock on old man McKechnie's door and tell the old bastard that he don't know nothin' about raisin' chickens."

Stein blushed crimson and was thankful for the darkness. "How many are we going to kill?" he asked, trying to recover his dignity with a show of bravado.

"I'll eat a coupla the suckers all by myself," Fenner bragged. "Six of 'em oughta be plenty."

"I can't wait to see the other guys' faces when we show up with fresh killed chickens and they're still scrounging out of cans of pork and beans." Billy Harman worked at a boiling bump on his chin as he spoke.

"Me too," Stein chirped. "I'm going to—"

"Shut up!" Fenner ordered sharply.

He rose from the damp ground and squinted across the dark field. Tendrils of mist were impaled on the tips of the corn spikes and a yellowed glow flooded the cluttered yard before being snapped off by the sudden slam of a door.

"There he goes," Fenner said.

Billy Harman pulled to his feet and stood alongside Wally Fenner. In silhouette, he looked like a narrow slice of the bigger boy's shadow. He gripped the knurled handle of the machete and Fenner wrapped his hand around the cold metal wrecking bar. Scott Stein gulped with excitement and pushed away from the base of the tree.

The pickup coughed and spat its objections to being forced out on such a damp night, but it finally mellowed to the farmer's practiced touch and bumped indignantly down the dirt driveway. When the pinpoints of red finally vanished into the mist, Wally Fenner pumped his fist up and down and stepped from the clearing.

"Let's kill us some chickens," he roared, and he plunged into the field, lumbering between corn rows toward the farmyard shed. With each step he took a wide swipe with the wrecking bar, wreaking havoc on the defenseless pods unfortunate enough to be caught in his path.

The metal rod was Fenner's traditional instrument of mischief, one he had used to cut many a destructive swath through windshields, mailboxes, and plate-glass windows. It was his personal trademark, something to set him apart from the less distinctive hell-raisers of Hensleyville. He thought of it in the same way that he thought of Police Chief Ben Littlejohn's low-slung holster or old man McKechnie's twelve-gauge that he always kept tucked under the seat of the old pickup. Stopping near the edge of the cornfield, he decapitated a last unlucky stalk before stepping boldly through the mist to the door of the shed.

Up close the outbuilding was even more decrepit than it appeared from the clearing; the distance, the darkness, and the mist having cloaked it in a veil of pastoral respectability. It was wide planks banged together with random nails, weathered paint, no windows, and an ill-fitting door that hung drunkenly from rusting hinges. Incredibly, a shiny bicycle lock speared a metal hasp, securing the flimsy door to one of the vertical planks.

Scott Stein broke from the cornfield and pulled up to Fenner's side. "It's locked," he said, puffing with exertion.

"No shit, Steiny," Fenner moaned.

"We wouldn't want those chickens beating the door down, would we?" Billy Harman chided. "I hear they're mean suckers."

Scott Stein blushed in the darkness.

Wally Fenner stepped to the door of the shed and rattled the lock. It jangled like chains in an empty attic, making the shed seem hollow and deserted. It sent a queasy chill through the Stein boy.

"You're gonna be on guard duty, Steiny. You stand outside here and watch for anybody comin' while me and Billy go inside and kill us some dinner." He hesitated as if struck by a sudden thought. "Unless you want to go in and do it yourself while we wait out here."

The younger boy swallowed hard and his Adam's apple bobbed up and down like a yoyo in his slender throat. He felt cold and suddenly miserable. The fun dissolved like the mist and it all seemed wrong, portentous, much more meaningful than the simple act of dispatching a half-dozen chickens so that they would impress the rest of the Hensleyville Eagles at the campout the following night. Stein shivered and hugged himself.

"Haw, haw! Lookit the killer. He's crappin' his goddamn pants." Still chuckling, Fenner turned and rammed the steel bar between the hasp and the door and he lunged his ample frame against it.

Long wood screws screamed in outrage as they were ripped from the weather-beaten planks, pulling away and dropping off like ugly scales from festered skin. The lock fell to the ground and the door creaked partly open. A bitter stench flowed through the dark crack and rode on the mist, firmly convincing Scott Stein that guard duty was indeed an honorable calling.

"I don't hear no chickens in there," Billy Harman said. He leaned forward into the foul air to peer inside but Fenner blocked the doorway.

"Maybe they're asleep."

"After all that racket?"

"Maybe they had a tough day." Fenner held the door with one hand and took Harman's arm with the other. "Who wants to eat chicken tomorrow night?"

"I do, Wally."

"Then let's go." Without warning, he swung open the door and pushed Billy ahead into the stinking blackness, then he stepped in behind him and pulled the door shut, blocking out the cornfield, the mist, and any semblance of light.

Scott Stein watched the door close and slumped against the corner of the shed, wishing with all his young heart that he was somewhere else.

"I can't see diddly squat," Billy Harman complained. He lingered just inside the door, groping like a blind man whose dog had just deserted him. His hand fumbled against the wall to his right and touched something soft. He jerked it away, then tentatively reached back. It was a cloth, maybe chamois, hanging on a nail that was banged into a stud. He let out a slow breath and felt farther along. He touched something hard. A rake. "It stinks in here," he complained.

"Don't breathe."

"I still don't hear no chickens. Anyway, how are we gonna kill them if we can't even see them?"

"Shit," Fenner muttered. "Steiny got the flashlight."

He banged on the door and edged it open a crack. A thin strip of misty grey broke the total darkness. "Hey, Steiny," he called, "gimme the flashlight."

He stuck his arm through the narrow slit, palm up like a surgeon awaiting the slap of a scalpel. Outside the shed, the sharp rap on the wood shook the young boy from his reverie and he did Fenner's bidding, slapping the silver cylinder into his waiting hand. The disembodied arm withdrew and the door closed behind it.

Scott Stein's heart skipped. Feeling dizzy, he leaned back against the wall of the shed but quickly pulled away. The wood felt damp and cold, colder than it ought to be, cold like the milky marble of a snow-capped tombstone, but it was the middle of the summer.

He looked around anxiously. The misty night disturbed him. It sucked the color and vitality from normally friendly things. Giant oaks, great for perching tree forts and climbing, became clawing creatures stretching their scaly limbs into the dank night air. Disciplined rows of corn whose fruit would one day drip with golden butter thrust their fingers into the blackness, challenging the foolish to pass their way. And then there was the shed, a stuffy little barn for storing spades and gas cans, but now it assumed the fearsome presence of a shabby crypt.

Scott Stein's heart fluttered against his rib cage like a hummingbird. He could be draped over a gum-caked chair at the movies right now. There was a Clint Eastwood at the Rialta. That's where he told his mother he was going. Or would the movie already be over?

Probably.

OK, he'd be at Baker's Square on the edge of town glomming down a sensuous piece of French Silk pie and washing it down with a vanilla shake. Better yet, he could be home in bed with the sheet pulled up to his chin and the tiny night-light glowing safe haven from beside the door, not a bad place for a thirteen-year-old boy to be on a wet and dark night.

But Scott wasn't home tonight because he had been chosen. Wally Fenner—the oldest, the biggest, the meanest—had personally chosen Scott Stein—the youngest, the smallest, the meekest—to share in tonight's adventure.

"What are you guys bringing to cook on the campout?"

"Hamburgers."

"Me too."

"I don't know. Hot dogs probably."

"Tube steak? Yecccch!"

"How about steak?"

"Costs too much."

"Chicken?"

"Maybe."

"I know where we can get us some chicken for free."

"Yeah! Where?"

"Old man McKechnie's. But we gotta kill 'em."

"He's crazy."

"Naw, he's just an old drunk."

"Do you gotta strangle them?"

"It's called wringing their necks, stupid."

"Ooooooh!"

"But we don't gotta do that. We cut their heads off."

"Yecccch!"

"What do we use?"

"I got a machete. It's my dad's."

"Who wants to go?"

"Me. I got the machete, remember?"

"Who else?"

There were no volunteers.

"What a bunch of pussies. How about you, Steiny? You wanna go with us and kill some chickens?"

"Su-sure, Wally."

So here he was.

A thin blanket of fog curled over the tops of the corn. Like a diaphanous wave, it crept toward the trembling sentry and encircled him, binding him together with the corn and the shed and the night. Willing or not, he was part of it.

Wally Fenner smiled at Billy Harman's discomfort but the other boy didn't see the thick lips spread across the yellow teeth. It was too dark. Dead dark. The kind of dark that greets a dead man's eyes when they snap open and he finds himself wrapped inside a cocoon of grey metal and buried under six feet of wormy earth.

"Turn on the flashlight will you, Wally. Let's kill these chickens and get the hell out of here."

"What chickens are you talking about, Billy? I don't hear no chickens."

Billy Harman felt the hairs in the small of his back rise and tingle. "C'mon, Wally, cut the crap, will you. Let's just get this over with."

"You wanna know something funny, Billy? I don't really like chicken all that much after all. I'd rather have tube steak any day."

"Then what are we doing—"

"C'mon over here, Billy."

"Where are you? I can't see you."

"I'm right over here."

Billy yelped when he felt Wally's hand take him by the elbow and the machete slipped from his grip and clanged to the dirt floor.

"There ain't no chickens here, Billy." Wally made it sound like something that any fool should know. "We got something even better."

Billy felt himself being tugged across the damp shed by more than Wally Fenner's steady pull. There was also the tethered power of an evil undertow and he felt an exquisite stab of fear.

"Gimme your hand, Billy."

The boy stood stiffly.

"Don't be so goddamned scared. Gimme your hand."

Reluctantly, Billy did.

"Reach down here."

Billy allowed his hand to be led through the darkness, pulled slowly down and to the right. "Wh-what's in here, Wally?"

"It's just a little farther, Billy. Don't be afraid," the older boy soothed.

But Billy was afraid, nightmare fear, the kind that filled his belly with fire and begot dark dreams and sweaty sheets and a heart that pounded like a jackhammer. Suddenly his hand brushed against something hard and he wheezed a sharp intake of breath and jerked away as if he'd touched a fiery ember. It wasn't the hardness of steel or stone or even of wood. It was hard yet soft; inert yet very much alive.

"Wh-what's in here, Wally, goddammit." He stammered like a schoolboy at a recital. "What are you trying to do?"

Wally Fenner didn't answer the panicked plea. Instead he began to croak a throaty chuckle that rumbled in his deep chest and stood the hairs on Billy Harman's neck on end. The chuckle spiraled higher and the grip on Billy's reluctant hand tightened, and when the laughter crossed the fragile border of sanity, Wally Fenner jerked viciously at Billy Harman's hand and planted his splayed fingers on something wet and furry and decidedly evil.

Billy screamed and his heart exploded in his chest and Wally snapped the beam of the flashlight on the bored face of a filthy goat.

"Holy shit," Billy panted and he reeled backward and crashed into the wall of the shed, shaking its fragile frame and scattering hand tools across the earthen floor.

Across from him Wally Fenner tumbled against the opposite wall, the rocking vibrations of his wheezing laughter rattling the structure like an earth tremor.

Billy was near tears but lacked the strength to cry. "Why did you do that?" he blubbered.

But Wally Fenner couldn't answer. The flashlight shook up and down and sprayed the shed like a laser show as he slid helplessly down the wall in a giggling puddle. With tear-filled eyes, he waved the yellow beam back and forth, centering it occasionally on Billy Harman's blood-drained face before lapsing into another convulsive bout.

"You oughta—hee, hee—you oughta—hee, hee, hee—see

yourself. You look like—hee, hee—you look like you saw a—hee, hee, hee—like you saw a goddamn ghost."

For silent moments broken sporadically by Wally's fitful snorts, the two boys sat across from each other on the damp floor of the shed and pulled together their composure. Wally wiped his eyes with a red-haired knuckle and the bouts of giggles finally faded to little more than a dull ache in his side. Billy Harman leaned against the opposite wall with his head thrown back, eyes closed as if in prayer, fingers laced together around his knees. The pounding in his chest slowed to a drumbeat, his breathing withered to regular gasps of the pungent air, the blood flowed back to his pimply face, and he finally found the strength for anger.

"That was a shitty trick, Wally."

"It's only a goddamn goat for chrissake." A leftover giggle erupted from the big redhead but he quickly stifled it. "You shoulda seen your face."

"It was still a shitty trick," Billy repeated. "Shit, Wally, you scared the hell out of me."

Billy stood and tested his legs and seemed surprised to discover that they still worked. He brushed the dirt from the seat of his jeans and blew the dust from his hands. "You went to a hell of a lot of trouble just to scare the crap out of me."

Wally Fenner pushed himself back to his feet. Shining the light across the floor, he stooped and picked up the grounded machete. He tested the edge with his thumb and whistled softly. "Geez, Billy, you could shave with this sucker if only you shaved."

Billy either missed or chose to ignore the insult. "My dad brought it back from somewhere down there in South America. They use them to cut down bananas or sugar beets or something like that."

"Geez, you could cut off a monkey's nuts with it," Wally said. He brushed his chubby fingers across the ebony hilt, caressing it as one would a fickle talisman whose power and proclivity were yet to be learned. The beam played on the blade and sent splashes of reflected light bouncing off the walls.

"It sure would have done a neat job on the chickens," Billy said. He had recovered from the fright and tried to put the episode into perspective. He'd been had but good by the older boy, and after all was said and done, it really was a neat joke even if it was at his expense. And it would help to cement his relationship with Wally Fenner because Wally would tell and retell the story until the facts finally became as unrecognizable as a rumor the second time around. Why not accept it?

"What chickens?" Wally asked.

The two boys laughed together and Billy Harman's dark mood lifted. "So," he asked expansively, "what do we do now, go over to the 7-Eleven and pick up some dead chicken?"

The flashlight hung aimlessly from Wally Fenner's hand, drawing erratic lines and circles on the dirt floor. "And some tube steaks," Wally added with unusual bonhomie.

Absently, he began to flick the yellow beam from corner to corner. It stopped for a moment on a tangle of leather straps and buckles and some sort of a harness. On the wall behind Billy Harman hung a trove of much-abused hardware that hadn't felt the caress of oil or any other type of care since the day it was purchased. At least it hadn't been cared for since that day so long ago when Rose McKechnie rattled out her last weary breath and smiled contentedly, finally at peace with the sickness that had long ravished her young body. Ian McKechnie never recovered from the painful blow and Ian's loss became Gilly's gain.

The beam jumped to the ceiling and worked its way back and forth, spotlighting rough-hewn planks nailed carelessly to two-by-six joists. A cluttered workbench spanned the rear wall of the shed. On the wall above it hung a discarded pair of white enamel kitchen cabinets, the door to one of them hanging crazily from a single hinge. A calendar selling seed was tacked high on the wall, 1974. The floor was hard-packed earth littered with bits of straw, dropped screws, bolts and nails, and mounds of fragrant goat droppings.

"We oughta at least help ourselves to something as long as we're in here," Wally said.

He skirted the yellow beam under the workbench. A red and yellow gas can with a plastic spout. A pile of greasy rags. Lawn mower parts. A tire, black and bald with cord showing through. More goat droppings swept or kicked there.

Billy Harman scoffed. "The goat shit's probably worth more than most of this other stuff."

Fenner turned the beam on Billy's face and the boy squinted and his pupils shrunk to pinpoints. "You know what's supposed to be real lucky?" There was genuine enthusiasm in Wally's voice.

"Goat shit?"

"Wrong end. Try a horn."

"A goat horn," Billy said with a trace of derision. "Since when is that supposed to bring good luck?"

"I heard about it somewhere. I dunno where. Maybe it was in one of those weird books that Looshis brings to the Eagles' meetings."

Harman became interested. "How are you supposed to get it off?"

Wally swung the beam lower. The goat stood against the wall, its whiskered jaws working soundlessly on some unseen delight as it went about its business unimpressed by the noisy intrusion.

"Jerk it off," Wally answered.

They both laughed at the crude pun. "I can see the headlines now," Billy said. "Vandals jerk off old man McKechnie's goat."

Wally Fenner seemed to like that because the beam bounced up and down the wall, finding then losing the munching goat with each swinging pass.

"I don't think it'll come off so easy," Billy ventured. He stepped across the shed and laid a tentative finger on the horny growth.

Wally played the beam on the gleaming blade of the machete. "Then we'll just have to cut it off." He allowed his thumb to respect the edge one more time. "Our biology teacher says that it's made of the same kind of stuff that fingernails are made from."

Billy stared at the grizzled white head. "Then it won't hurt him none?"

"Beats the shit out of me. Who cares anyway? Do you wanna be the one to do it?" Wally offered. "Maybe it'll bring you good luck."

"Naw. You go ahead, Wally. It was your idea."

With the flashlight in his right hand aimed at the goat's face, Wally gripped one of the horns with his left and pulled the animal toward the center of the floor. It looked up at him in mild confusion but offered little resistance. Wally released the horn and brought the flashlight down to within inches of the goat's head.

"I'll give it a cut right about here."

His finger entered the beam of light and tapped at a spot about an inch from the goat's white skull.

Billy nodded in the darkness. He was anxious to get this over with. He thought of Scott Stein standing guard outside and realized that he wouldn't mind trading places with the younger boy.

Wally pushed the flashlight toward him. "Here, you hold this steady while I knock that sucker off."

Billy took the butt of the flashlight. It was wet with Wally's sweat and he wiped it against his jeans.

"You think I oughta saw through it or should I just give it one quick whack?" Wally asked.

"Just do it, will you?"

"Sure thing, Billy. You hold the light real steady right there so I can see that spot real good."

Wally tapped the horn on the right side of the goat's head with the dull edge of the blade and the animal flinched.

"This goat's a pansy." The redheaded boy laughed. "I'm just gonna give the stinkin' thing a little horn trim and he's gettin' jumpy as a cat."

"Just do it, Wally."

"Sure, Billy. You hold the light right there. A little bit closer. Move it around to the left a little. Yeah, yeah. That's perfect," he breathed.

Billy's eyes were glued to the spot when he heard Wally's sharp intake of breath and the sudden whoosh of the machete through the damp air. His stomach flipped when he heard the sickening crunch and saw the fountain of blood that geysered forth and soaked his shirt. His head spun dizzily and he blew his dinner an instant after the severed head hit the floor.

2

HENSLEYVILLE, NAMED AFTER the early settler Adolph Hensley who, at various times in his career, was reported to be a sailor, a gambler, an explorer, and a farmer—and at each endeavor a dismal failure—was a quarter mile short of being a perfect square. Bounded on all four sides by ruler-straight farm roads, the town was the mecca for commerce and entertainment for five hundred square miles of rolling farmland in what some tourist brochures describe as the Amish Country. It's true that many of those good people lived in the area, as evidenced by the horse-drawn buggies and the wide-brimmed hats, but they played no significant role in the functioning of Hensleyville, that being the domain of the merchants and the mechanics who sold the feed and fixed the tractors of those who opted to use the danged contraptions.

WELCOME TO HENSLEYVILLE
POPULATION 2916

The green and white road sign that grew from the weeds across from Elmer Fridley's Exxon station hadn't been updated in more than seven years but that hardly mattered. A handful of people more or less would go largely unnoticed unless of course the handful included the likes of the owner of the John Deere dealership or Timmy Gillespie who owned one of the town's two bars.

Police Chief Ben Littlejohn maintained law and order with one full-time policeman but he spent more time writing up farm accidents than he did crushing crime. The closest that Hensleyville ever came to major league notoriety was four years earlier when nine-year-old Melinda Zooker disappeared and was eventually found at the bottom of the flooded Blue Rock quarry. She was bound in chains but was otherwise unmarked. It never was conclusively proven that she didn't do herself in.

She was a strange little girl.

The mystery and its memory still haunted the dreams of small children on murky nights when timbers creaked and the wind sang mournful tunes and rattled bedroom windows.

There was a public library in Hensleyville, fairly well stocked thanks to the tireless efforts toward heartland literacy by a portly spinster named Emma Guilden who also directed 4-H activities for the entire county. There was a movie theater, the Rialta, that closed on Sunday in respect of the Sabbath, and there were two bars of which Gilly's was the most popular because he had the foresight to be the first to install a color TV years earlier. Gilly's was also better situated, being on Main Street smack in the center of town, directly across from Town Hall, which made it a natural spot to begin and end the scores of Hensleyville functions, official and otherwise, that occurred there. The event currently taking place was one of the exceptions.

"Knock it off, Fenner, or I'll deck you."

Except for the gym instructor at the consolidated high school, Pete Bishop was the only adult whose bite Wally Fenner feared more than his bark.

"Sure thing, Mr. Bishop. Anything you say, sir."

He let Jeff Zack slip out of the punishing headlock but not before applying a final squeeze that made the boy's eyes bulge like a beached sucker.

Pete Bishop was built like a boxcar, squat and thick and physically imposing to those who were intimidated by that sort of thing and that included Wally Fenner, which was exactly the way Peter Bishop intended it to be. It felt good, the surge of respect that greeted his command. It made him a leader. What did it matter that most of the adults in Hensleyville thought he was a smacked ass and snickered at his manner. It was more than enough for Pete Bishop that the kids of the town snapped to when he barked an order. Of course he could do without some of the more libelous rumors concerning his private life and his sexual preference. But let them talk. Let them say whatever the hell they wanted to. The kids would stick with him. They'd back him up.

The rumors were baseless anyway, the vicious work of idle tongues who couldn't understand how a single man could find such reward in associating with a noisy group of adolescent schoolboys. So let them talk. He didn't see any of them stepping forward and volunteering to run the boys' club. Anyway, the whole idea to form the club was his from the start and he liked that too. It made him proud. The Hensleyville Eagles were Pete Bishop's creation, and if some gutless parent didn't like the way he ran the club, then they could pull their kid out of it. Who needed them? These thoughts were always at the back of his mind but never more so than before one of the club's overnights.

He pointed at a curly-haired boy with fair skin and a meadow of freckles across his nose. "Lockwood, pile those backpacks over there against that wall."

"Sure, Mr. Bishop," came the polite reply, and Chris Lockwood swept a wide circle around the hall and slid the scattered backpacks across the smooth floorboards.

The club was meeting in the Explorer Room at Town Hall, twelve hundred square feet of polished oak floor that commemorated Adolph Hensley's dubious exploits in and around the Susquehanna River valley in an earlier century. Town Hall was the third oldest building in Hensleyville, right behind the original Hensley homestead—now a patched-up, three-story boardinghouse that only passed the fire code by virtue of its proper bloodlines—and the First Methodist Church where Mallory Whitney reigned supreme. The hall was the geographical center of town, not because the city planners had cleverly chosen to do so—the hall was there before the town—but because the town lines were drawn a decade after the building was erected.

Pete Bishop's creation, the Hensleyville Eagles, was an all

boys' club whose adolescent membership shot pool, wrestled, played basketball, camped out—who basically participated in the more manly activities that weren't made available by the other young people's social organizations. Mal Whitney's church once sponsored a Boy Scout troop but it died from a combination of neglect and Mallory's proclivity to preach at every opportunity. Pete Bishop, a local bachelor who owned a small construction company that specialized in pole barns, moved in to fill the breach and the Hensleyville Eagles were born.''

This Friday afternoon in July he was herding the seven boys and their gear together for the weekend overnight. There would have been a few more along for the trip but Zeb Miller and his family left for a summer vacation down on the Chesapeake, the Hopkins boy couldn't get off work at Hemp's lumberyard, and Timmy Ellis came down with a case of strep throat the night before.

"All right, you guys, toe that white line. Dress right and cover down."

Pete had the Eagles stand in military parade rest along a white stripe that he had painted across the room. Folding chairs lined two of the walls and paintings of famous presidents hung at regular intervals. The floor at one end of the room was elevated ten inches where a wooden podium with a brass lamp stood a lonely vigil. Light streamed in through multipaneled windows high on the walls. The room smelled faintly of disinfectant and sweat.

Pete Bishop strode up and down in front of the line of campers in a final inspection. His thumbs were hooked behind his back and his square jowls quivered with each heavy footfall. Wearing camouflage slacks with a knifelike crease and a khaki shirt, he looked very military. This impressed the boys even if their parents did snicker behind his back and mutter that the closest that Pete Bishop ever came to serving his country was when he worked on summer corn detasseling crews as a teenager.

"Something strike you funny, Harman?" he barked. He paced in front of the boy and thrust his jaw in Billy's face.

Billy Harman had been laughing dutifully at something

Wally Fenner had whispered to him. It was about last night's episode at old man McKechnie's farm.

"No, sir, Mr. Bishop. Nothing's funny."

"Then why are you laughing, Harman? Only idiots laugh at nothing. Are you an idiot, Harman? What do you think this is, the 4-H Club, the Cub Scouts? Step out front and center."

Billy shot an accusing glance at Wally Fenner and took two rigid steps forward.

"Give me twenty quick ones, Harman."

That's not so bad, Billy thought. He'd been given fifty push-ups for what had seemed lesser offenses. He dropped to the varnished floor and pumped them out, ignoring the burning in his triceps on the final few.

"Does anybody else feel like giggling like a little school-girl?" Bishop wanted to know. He stood directly in front of the line of boys with his legs spread wide, his hands locked behind his back, his jaw powerfully thrust out in front of him in imitation of every drill sergeant who he had ever seen on the Late Show. Timmy Gillespie, the owner of Gilly's, always referred to him as "Patton" though not to his face. But for all Pete cared, it wouldn't have mattered. He would have been flattered by the comparison.

"OK, let's talk about the hike," he growled. "If any of you guys think this is going to be a stroll through the park, you better listen up."

There was only one rookie among the gathered Eagles and that was Lucius Cady. The rest of the boys had a pretty good idea what to expect and they looked forward to it in a perverse sort of way.

Making a man out of you, Pete Bishop called it. *Teaching you pain. Cutting your mama's apron strings.*

As far as the Eagles were concerned, the hike was no big deal. It was a stroll through the woods, kind of fun really, and that's why they put up with Pete and his funny ways. Otherwise, why would they do it? But if Pete Bishop thought that a simple hike through the woods was tough and macho, who were they to bust his bubble?

"I don't want any stragglers out there. If any of you don't

figure that you can keep up with the rest, you'd better step out of line right now."

Wally Fenner snickered at the absurdity of Bishop's order, but Pete didn't notice or chose not to.

"Anybody whose tender little feet are going to get blisters might as well pack up his things right now and go to the movies tonight. I don't have any time for that." He shot a glance at Scott Stein and the fragile boy met his gaze with angry determination.

"And we don't need any wise guys either. Anybody who has enough energy to try to be a big shot is going to handle firewood duty all by himself. That ought to burn off some of the piss and vinegar."

He was staring at Lenny Brothers during the last admonition. Lenny stared back like a West Point cadet although a tremor of a latent smirk twitched at the corner of his mouth.

"Good hiking shoes," Bishop went on, "are the tank treads of the serious camper."

Billy Harman gritted his teeth and stifled a yawn. He was sure that if Bishop saw it it would have been good for fifty quick ones and his arms still burned.

Pete Bishop paced down the line and checked each camper's foot gear. Except for Lucius Cady, they all met muster. Lucius wore a bedraggled pair of high-top Keds and Pete shook his head in disgust but said nothing.

Bishop didn't know quite what to make of the Cady boy. Like everybody else in Hensleyville, he knew that the boy lived with his father in a beat-up shack in Covey's Woods near Muddy Creek. What the hell, Pete figured, if the kid walked all the way back and forth from there in the grubby tennis shoes he could probably handle the hike.

The kid's old man was about as close to a real character as the small town could boast. He showed up in town on occasion, always on foot, and he'd pick up some provisions with as few words as possible before throwing the sack over his shoulder and heading back down the road. And he always had a kind of gleam in his eyes, not the kind that rings of breeding and intelligence but the kind that reeks of madness. There wasn't a one who could recall Festus Cady ever causing a speck of trouble in Hensleyville but the townspeople gave him a wide berth nonetheless.

Some of the father's traits must have passed on to Lucius, especially the tendency to be quiet and shy and mind his own business. That's why Pete Bishop and the rest of the Eagles were more than a little bit surprised back in the spring when young Lucius Cady answered the call for new members that the publisher of *The County Herald* had placed in his paper gratis as a public service.

"Rain gear." Bishop pronounced the words with reverence, as if they called for group genuflection. "Did everybody bring his poncho?"

They all mumbled something in response but their voices rang together like carillon bells and Bishop didn't care anyway. Screw them. If they forgot to bring rain gear they got wet. Served them right.

Lucius Cady's eyes widened apprehensively as if he was about to fail yet another inspection but Bishop moved on.

"You're all responsible for bringing your own meat. We'll find all the vegetables we need on the trail. Nature provides plenty of good things to eat, things that your mother won't find in the A & P."

Lenny Brothers wrinkled his nose and Bishop noticed.

"What did you bring, Brothers?"

"Hamburger, Mr. Bishop," Lenny barked back like a skin-headed recruit at Parris Island.

"Lockwood?"

"A piece of steak, Mr. Bishop."

Bishop shook his head and rolled his eyes. "A piece of steak," he said mockingly. "Fenner, what did you bring?"

"Well, we almost had us some chickens but we changed our mind. Me and Billy and good ol' Steiny here got us some tube steak."

Bishop was certain that Fenner's story went deeper but he didn't pursue it. Lucius Cady tried to melt into nothingness as the stocky man's eyes bore into him.

"Cady, what did you bring, possum?"

A flash of resentment came and went but the boy met his gaze. Lucius was the youngest boy in the club. His thirteenth birthday was a few days away and twelve was the arbitrary minimum age for membership. His hair was straight and blond with sudden streaks of darkness and it was cut like a Dutch boy straight across in front and back, probably by Festus himself because no barber would be responsible for such a butchering. His eyes, dark and brooding, were shaped like tilted almonds giving him a look of Eastern mystery, almost Oriental. The look on his face at the moment was a mixture of fear and determination.

"Me and my pa don't never eat possum, Mr. Bishop."

As Pete Bishop had intended, his unkind comment had drawn guarded smirks from the line of Eagles but Lucius Cady's simple response dampened the humor.

"OK so you don't eat possum." Bishop felt strangely irritated by the boy's directness. "What did you bring?"

Lucius stared at the polished floorboards and worked the toe of his sneaker at a dark knot. "Me and my pa don't use much meat."

"What are you trying to tell me, Cady? Did you forget to bring your food along?"

"Didn't forget," the boy answered matter-of-factly. "I don't need to bring nothin'. I know how to eat in the woods."

"I bet you do," Bishop said with a wry smile. "But the Eagles isn't some undisciplined group of kids out for a walk in the woods. We're learning to get along here, Cady. That's all part of surviving. We have to pull together. That's what this is all about."

Wally Fenner caught Billy Harman's eye and snickered at the timeworn lecture.

"Mr. Bishop." Chris Lockwood took a step forward from the line. "I have plenty of steak. Too much really. Lucius can help me cook it. There's enough for both of us."

Bishop stepped close to the curly-haired boy, his barrel chest only inches from Lockwood's nose. With his feet planted wide and his fists on his hips, Pete Bishop glared at the top of Chris's head. "I don't remember asking for any volunteers, Lockwood."

Cady turned to Chris with a saddened look on his young face. Chris stared impassively at the leader's crisp brown shirt, concentrating on a bone button at a level with his freckled nose. The other boys exchanged bemused glances.

They all liked Chris Lockwood. He was a good kid, one who joined in their horseplay but always managed to be somewhere else when the joking began to take on an edge of cruelty. He didn't preach—he just chose not to participate. And he was able to take jokes on himself although he never dished them out. Chris Lockwood was all right but the other boys thought that the Cady kid was something else.

"Spooky little shit," Wally Fenner had called him when he showed up for that first meeting back in the spring. And since then, Lucius Cady had done little to gain their acceptance, opting instead to watch from the sidelines as an amused spectator while the rest of the Hensleyville Eagles roughhoused around the Explorer Room and shouted insults at one another. It made them wonder why he had bothered to join the club in the first place. But Lucius religiously showed up for every meeting, always one of the first to arrive and always the last to participate. He normally showed no emotion, but the slight curl of his lips while he watched the Eagles' antics indicated at least some level of entertainment. And who knows, maybe that's all that it took to make it worthwhile for the shy little boy. If being an outsider in the aerie of Eagles bothered Lucius Cady, he didn't show it.

Even when Wally Fenner and Billy Harman teased him, he'd turn his sad eyes on them and give them that mysterious look that took the fun out of their sport. Except for the time that they caught him reading the book, the weird one that talked about the devil and had a scary picture of a goat on the cover. They teased him unmercifully that time, especially Wally Fenner.

Pete Bishop did nothing to stop them. In fact, he had pretended not to notice but he was obviously enjoying it, hovering nearby and cocking his head to the side so he wouldn't miss a single mean-spirited word. And now Mr. Bishop was at him again, and the others, all except Chris Lockwood, seemed to be enjoying his discomfort.

Lucius Cady stood at one end of the row and hung his head. Chris Lockwood stood stiffly at the other end. Between the two, Fenner, Zack, Stein, Harman, and Brothers smiled in anticipation of one of Pete Bishop's famous tirades. They weren't disappointed.

Bishop stepped three paces back to catch a better angle where all the boys could see him. A snaky blue vein wriggled on his forehead and Lenny Brothers thought of a good line but was smart enough to tuck it safely away with other witty things wisely left unsaid. Fenner elbowed Billy Harman in the ribs hoping for a reaction that would refocus Bishop's outrage while Wally stared innocently at the ceiling. Billy grunted but Pete Bishop chose not to notice, preferring to direct his wrath at the strange Cady boy and his unsolicited defender.

Hands on hips, face beet-red, jowls quaking in anger, Pete Bishop laid a look of dislike on Lucius Cady that would wring tears from most twelve-year-olds, but Lucius seemed to absorb the hate with little effort, as if such malevolent displays were more the norm than the exception. A portion of the hate might even have been deflected back like a light beam off a mirror and it gave Bishop a slight jolt before he renewed his lecture.

"You're in the Hensleyville Eagles, Mr. Cady, in case you didn't know it. We're not the Boy Scouts or the Indian Guides or the 4-H Club. We don't have uniforms or nice oaths or cute little hand shakes."

The others had heard this one before and they spread their legs a bit more comfortably and rocked lightly on their heels, but Chris Lockwood didn't join them. He stood stiffly at attention and glared with as much anger as his friendly face could muster, but the resulting expression looked more like disbelief than rage.

Lucius Cady met the burning eyes of the Eagles' leader with no show of emotion. He was afraid to let his feelings show. It wasn't that he was frightened of Pete Bishop. He wasn't. It was exactly the opposite.

He was frightened *for* him.

What if Lucius lost control and one of the bad spells happened. That's what his pa always called them, spells. They always started with a bad feeling, like the way Pete Bishop was making him feel right now. Anger, hate, revenge. The shy, young boy didn't often harbor such emotions but when he did, unusual things sometimes happened. He didn't want anything to happen here, not in front of his new friends. He had to clear his mind of the anger. Looking over Pete Bishop's square shoulder into the doleful eyes of a powder-wigged George Washington, he tried to recall the words of the Declaration of Independence.

When in the course of human events, it becomes necessary for one people to . . .

Pete Bishop's voice filled the room but his words had lost their meaning. "We're not a bunch of starry-eyed do-gooders collecting old newspapers and helping old ladies across the street, Cady."

That was a new line and Wally Fenner snickered and Pete Bishop shot him a murderous glance but Bishop didn't miss a beat.

"We're the Hensleyville Eagles, Cady, and you damn well better remember it. We have one motto, Cady. Survival! That's what this is all about, Cady. Survival." He turned to Chris Lockwood at the other end of the line. "You won't be sharing your big steak with anybody, Mr. Lockwood. If Mr. Cady here thinks that he's so good alone in the woods, then I aim to give him a chance to prove it."

He turned back to Lucius who was mentally fumbling with the next line of the Declaration. "We'll see just how much your crazy old man taught you about living in the woods, boy."

At the mention of his father, Lucius lost his fix on the Declaration. Where did his father fit in to this, he wondered.

Pete Bishop's face flamed and the blue vein squirmed from the heat. "I hear stories about your old man running around the woods like a wild animal, cutting totems into trees and shouting crazy things at the moon. If that's how he taught you to catch a meal, it's no wonder the two of you don't eat much meat."

Fenner and Billy Harman laughed out loud at that one and Pete Bishop let them, but the rest of the boys didn't seem to catch the humor.

"Don't say things like that about my father."

Lucius Cady rarely spoke and when he did one usually had to strain one's ears to pluck the reedy words from the air but not this time. This time the voice was young and high of pitch but it rang of indignation and it filled the farthest corners of the Explorer Room. The Eagles all looked at Lucius as if seeing the boy for the first time.

"Weird," Fenner whispered for all to hear.

Pete Bishop's face boiled like a beet and he glared down at the towheaded boy. "What did you say, Cady? Are you telling me what to do, boy?" He took two angry strides that brought him chest to nose with Lucius Cady. "Are you telling me that I can't say whatever I want to say about your crazy old man?"

From the start, Pete Bishop didn't like the idea of having anything to do with kin of Festus Cady. He was a crazy man and everybody in town knew it. He was dirty. Ever since his wife walked into town a dozen years ago and hopped on a Trailways, he had lived like a hermit in a stinking shack in the woods. Bishop wanted nothing to do with Festus or his boy. Maybe if the kid got mad enough he'd quit. Good riddance!

"Your old man's a loony, kid. Can you understand that?"

Lucius clenched his small fists until his knuckles whitened and his elbows shook. His jaw muscles flexed corners on his smooth face. With his eyes fixed on the portrait on the wall he began again.

When in the course of human events . . .

"The two of you live like a couple of wild animals out at that shack of yours in Covey's Woods. Your old man ought to be ashamed of himself. Doesn't he have a job—"

. . . it becomes necessary . . .

Lucius's eyes were tightly closed and he didn't realize that he was talking aloud.

. . . for one people to dissolve the political bands . . .

Pete Bishop looked down on Lucius Cady's golden head. The thick blond hair parted at the crown and exploded like a sunflower. He couldn't see the boy's almond eyes but he could picture them squinting tightly, fighting back tears of pain and shame. He couldn't have been more wrong.

"Doesn't your old man have any pride?"

At Bishop's last unkindness, the Declaration of Independence suddenly lost all meaning to Lucius Cady and his eyes stared at the dark brown shirt with an intensity that would have shaken Pete Bishop had he seen it. The man's harsh words burned in Lucius's ears and his world grew hazy with wavy lines of mist that seemed to creep from the floorboards and encircle the ranting leader.

Lucius could have let it continue, let it take over, but he didn't. With a force of will that sent a searing pain through his own head, Lucius Cady quelled his appetite for vengeance. The mist subsided and the Explorer Room returned to normal.

"You and your crazy old man give me a royal pain in the ass, Cady."

No sooner had the words left his mouth than Pete Bishop shrieked in pain and grabbed both cheeks of his ample buttocks. Like a man being branded by a blazing iron, he yelped and began to hop around the room like a madman.

Then the pain was gone. It was like it had never happened.

Pete Bishop tentatively touched the seat of his camouflaged pants, searching for a flame that wasn't there. Six of the Hensleyville Eagles gaped at their leader as if he was demented. The seventh looked at him sadly and chewed worriedly at his lip.

A funny smell, biting, cloyed at their nostrils, then vanished.

Without a glance at Lucius Cady, Pete Bishop regained his dignity and stood before the ragged line of campers. "We're going," he croaked. "Grab your gear and move out."

The boys retrieved their backpacks from against the wall and helped each other struggle into them. Lenny Brothers helped Wally Fenner slip his arms into the canvas straps. "This thing's heavy," he observed. "What do you have in it?"

"Goat steak," Wally answered with sarcasm, and he strode from Town Hall to Pete Bishop's waiting van.

Lenny Brothers shrugged and followed.

3

THE HEAVY-DUTY van handled Pete Bishop and the seven Eagles in comfort with plenty of room left at the rear to pile their gear.

"You'd better believe it's American," Pete proclaimed proudly in response to a query from one of the boys. "It's not one of your damn rice wagons or some poofy French car."

The last crack was directed at Scott Stein whose father drove a middle-aged Mercedes. Fortunately for Pete, the boys' knowledge of European manufacturers went no deeper than his own. Either that or they just didn't care.

Without any argument, Wally Fenner assumed possession of the copilot's seat to the right of the driver. The rest of the boys sat three across on the back two bench seats; Jeff Zack, Billy Harman, and Lenny Brothers in the middle, Chris Lockwood, Lucius Cady, and Scott Stein in the rear.

The seven boys represented the broadest range of families in the tight little town, all the way from the Cady boy who, with his father, eked out bare survival in a shack in Covey's Woods, to Chris Lockwood who lived with his widowed father in a spacious brick colonial that looked down on the town from its hilltop perch. Though opulent by Hensleyville standards, the home would have attracted little more than an approving nod in any one of a thousand other suburbs. Between the Cadys and the Lockwoods existed the rest of Hensleyville's inhabitants who were adequately represented by the other five boys.

If net worth was to be estimated by the luxury of camping gear, Lucius Cady would have maintained his solid lock on the lower rung but Scott Stein would have catapulted to the top. He wore heavy hiking boots that smelled of rich new leather, burr-resistant walking pants bristling with snaps and pockets, and a lightweight bush jacket with reinforced shoulders to withstand the abrasive abuse of the blue nylon backpack. If Lucius Cady was the pauper, Scott Stein was indeed the prince.

Pete Bishop looked over his shoulder and did a final head count. Satisfied, he rolled out of the Town Hall parking lot, took a right on Main Street, and pointed the nose of the van through the tended fields toward the wooded hills of the Susquehanna River valley. As he passed Elmer Fridley's Exxon station at the edge of town, Pete shifted his weight in the deep bucket seat and cautiously checked his wallet, gently rubbing the spot that had earlier exploded in pain.

Nothing. It was as if it had never happened.

He looked in the rearview mirror and caught a glimpse of Lucius Cady's empty eyes. They told him nothing either. Uncommonly silent, Pete leaned on the gas pedal and sped down the empty road.

But the driver's sulking mood didn't infect the other seven passengers. Before they were past Ed Bochman's scrubby cornfield, Lenny Brothers and Billy Harman were already wrestling in the center seat and Wally Fenner was shouting insults diagonally across the van at Scott Stein who had been leaning away from Lucius Cady and staring dreamily out the window.

"Pipe down," Bishop shouted over the din, but his tone lacked conviction. "Save your energy. You're going to need it."

Fenner twisted in his seat. He put on a mock scowl and glared toward the back of the van. "You heard what Mr. Bishop said, Looshis." Wally Fenner had a way of pronouncing the boy's name that made it sound like a kind of droopy marshmallow. "Keep the racket down back there."

Pete Bishop pretended not to hear but his tight smile gave him away. Lucius continued to stare straight ahead and paid no attention to either of them.

"There once was a boy name of Cady," Fenner began.

Billy Harman picked up the cue. "Who had a butt like a lady."

That won everyone's approval except for Lucius and Chris Lockwood. "Why don't you guys knock it off," Chris tried.

Lucius gave Chris a grateful look. "That's OK," he said quietly. "They don't bother me none."

"But instead of big tits," Zack contributed.

"He had hundreds of zits," Brothers added.

The boys looked from one to another hoping for renewed inspiration, but they had exhausted their poetic bent, and tiring of the sport, they resumed their wrestling, but this time Bishop ignored it and covered the next twelve miles lost in his own thoughts. At the edge of the valley, where the fields began to roll toward the distant hills and stands of evergreens began to infiltrate the geometric plantings, Bishop swung off the blacktop and rolled onto a pebbled lane that flowed upward with the contours of the land. Like a black arrow, it pointed into the mountain pass and vanished into the sun-drenched hills.

"Are we gonna have to hike very far today, Mr. Bishop?" Fenner asked as they spun higher and the flat boredom was replaced by lush green foliage.

Bishop glared at the boy with heavy lidded eyes. "You can sleep in the van if you want to, Fenner. The rest of us are going to hike."

"Oh, no, Mr. Bishop. You got it all wrong. I love to hike. It's Looshis that I'm worried about. I mean he got those cheesy shoes on and he ain't got nothin' to eat and all that."

Fenner shook his head sadly and shot a pitiful glance toward the rear seat. Lucius Cady met his eye and held it with a look of cold indifference that sent a chill through the older boy, but before he had a chance to dwell on it the van bounced off the road again and hooked into a lane that looked too narrow for a compact car let alone Bishop's van.

Leafy branches swept noisily at the windows and the tires groaned over ruts and rocks until the van finally burst from the shrubbery and rolled to a stop in a small clearing sheltered by an umbrella of ancient maples.

"Everybody out," Bishop shouted. "Fun time's over. Grab your gear and stack it in front of the van."

"Sure thing, Mr. Bishop, sir," Wally Fenner said. "We got us some serious hiking to do."

Pete Bishop curled his lip and shook his head resignedly. "You're a real leader, Fenner."

"Gee, thanks, Mr. Bishop. Hearing you say that really means a lot to me."

Bishop shook his head again and slammed the doors to the van, testing them to be sure they were locked. Kind of stupid, he thought. If anybody happened to stumble across the van in this remote location, they'd have no problem taking their good old time breaking the windows and doing whatever else they had in mind. But Pete didn't expect any such problems. As far as he knew, nobody even knew that the clearing was there. He had stumbled onto it completely by accident while scouting for a new camping location. Besides, this was Hensleyville, not York or Lancaster or one of the other big towns where some of the lower forms of life actually would steal someone else's property.

With a shrill whistle and a wave of his arm, Bishop lined the boys up in front of the van where he gave last-minute warnings about a broad range of offenses that he categorized under the general heading of grabass. "Anybody pulls any grabass is going to pull firewood duty along with it, understand?"

Unseen, Wally Fenner grabbed a handful of Billy Harman's pants and they both choked back a laugh.

"Put on your packs," Pete shouted. "Help the guy next to you tighten his straps. I don't want anybody dropping out or complaining about a loose pack."

Chris Lockwood lifted his pack and slipped his arms through the loops. He was struggling to hump it higher on his back when the load suddenly lightened. Turning, he looked into Lucius Cady's shy face.

"Thanks," Chris said, but Lucius only nodded and walked to where he had dropped his own worn pack.

Pete Bishop watched the preparations with the withering patience of a drill instructor on the first day of boot camp. He was the picture of packaged belligerence with his camouflage pants from the Army-Navy store tucked into high-top hiking boots and a pair of aviator sunglasses encircling his sweat-speckled head. A web belt bulging with pouches encircled his waist and a bone-handled knife in a leather sheath lay across his right hip.

"We're moving out," he shouted. "And we're doing double time. You guys liked to screw around in the van so I figure you must have a lot of energy to burn up. Well, here's your chance to prove it. Anybody who thinks they're going to dog it is going to give me a hundred and I don't care what your daddys have to say about it." He flicked a glance at both Cady and Stein as he issued the warning.

Bishop wasn't joking. The boys double-timed for the better part of an hour until he finally let them rest by a small lake that marked the halfway point of their march. At first they had treated the extra effort as a joke, laughing and goosing and making it even tougher on the weaker boys like Lucius and Scott. Wally Fenner was particularly brutal, physically and mentally assaulting Lucius on the sweaty trek through the woods. Before they were a quarter mile from the van, he took up a post next to the jogging column and began shouting cadence at Bishop's request.

"Hup, hup, hup, hup."

The footfalls of the column scattered pebbles, snapped twigs, and sent up plumes of dust in their passing.

"Hup, hup, hup, hup."

Wally positioned himself next to Lucius and he barked the tempo in the smaller boy's ear.

"Hup, hup, hup, hup. What's the matter, Looshis? Didn't your pa cook you possum for breakfast?"

Lucius kept an even pace, his eyes straight ahead and fixed on Scott Stein's bobbing backpack. The pace at the time was slow and even, as yet not too great a burden. Pete Bishop led the column, and for a big man, he moved through the woods with the grace of a black bear, loping effortlessly, planting one foot in front of the other with his pack snugged against his shoulders and his bone-handled knife slapping against his hip.

The midafternoon sun leaked through the branches of the evergreens and painted the line of boys with splashes and streaks. Jeff Zack was the last boy in the column, not a coveted spot since it breathed the leaders' dust. Chris Lockwood was in front of Zack, about ten feet behind Lucius Cady who had Wally Fenner jogging annoyingly at his shoulder.

"Hup, hup, hup, hup."

The other boys picked up the chant, planting their left foot in the dust with each "hup." Like an ungainly centipede rocking from side to side, the column snaked through the trees. Wally Fenner edged closer to Lucius and nudged him roughly to the side. The smaller boy stumbled but caught himself before falling.

"Golly, I'm sorry, Looshis," Fenner apologized dramatically. Then a silly grin crossed his face as a new idea came to him.

"Loo-shis, Loo-shis, Loo-shis, Loo-shis," he chanted.

The annoying persistence of "hup, hup, hup, hup" had finally matured to monotony and the boys were pleased with the new cadence that Wally had come up with. With "loo" to the left foot and "shis" to the right, the ragged column stomped doggedly through the sun-dappled forest.

"Loo-shis, Loo-shis, Loo-shis, Loo-shis."

Only Chris Lockwood and Lucius himself failed to pick up on the new chant but both maintained the steady pace. Five minutes later, even the new mantra began to grate on their nerves and Bishop switched to a double-time tempo that he learned while watching Marine movies on late-night TV.

"I got a girl in Hens-ley-ville."

The boys snatched the new beat from the air. "I got a girl in Hens-ley-ville," they sang out.

Bishop responded, "She won't do it but her sister will."

Knowing smiles on beardless faces repeated the second line. Even Chris Lockwood picked it up. Lucius didn't but he smiled shyly at the impropriety of it.

"Sound off."

"One, two."

"Sound off."

"Three, four."

The backpacks became heavier, the straps looser, the path steeper, but Bishop showed no signs of slowing the labored

pace. It was made bearable only by the ongoing competition of
creating the next ditty. Billy Harman drew panting laughs with
his entry.

"I know a man whose name is Pete."

The others echoed the line.

"He's got great big smelly feet."

The boys giggled and Pete Bishop flashed a pained grin back
at the column.

Wally Fenner, encouraged by Billy's success, decided to
give it a try. "I know a boy named Looshis Cady."

"I know a boy named Looshis Cady," the others responded.

"He got a crotch just like a lady."

The boys' gasping laughs muffled their echoed response but
it didn't matter because Pete Bishop had his right fist raised in
a signal to halt and the puffing column gratefully slogged to a
stop.

"Haw, haw." Wally Fenner poked a playful shot at Lucius's
shoulder and this time the boy did trip. He fell to the mossy
earth in the gnarled roots of a tree. Chris coasted to a stop
beside the fallen boy and he shot an angry glance at Lucius's
tormentor.

"Why are you always picking on him, Wally? He hasn't
done anything to you."

"Haw, haw," was all that Wally could think of at the
moment and he jogged lazily ahead to join the rest of the group
who were starting to shuck their packs and flex their aching
shoulders.

Chris turned to the younger boy. "Don't pay any attention to
Wally, Lucius. I think he got dropped on his head when he was
a baby."

Lucius looked up at Chris, his expression thankful, his eyes
sad. Chris extended his hand and pulled the slight boy to his
feet. He felt almost weightless. With Chris's help, Lucius
shrugged his pack off and dropped it by the tree, then he
scuffed at the dirt with the toe of his sneaker as if embarrassed
by the attention.

Chris never had a real conversation with the Cady boy. As
far as he knew none of the others had either. Lucius would just
show up at the weekly meetings and stake out his patch of

space and he'd even surrender that if the rough and tumble
came too close. He'd fold his arms across his chest and stand
by the big round post in the Explorer Room of Town Hall and
stare at the goings-on with his sad eyes as if he were watching
a circus tent being raised, but he never volunteered to help nor
did he ask to join. Chris had tried a few times to draw the boy
into the group but his attempts were met with shy shakes of the
head and downcast eyes. Shoot, Chris thought at the time,
maybe he just likes to watch.

"Are you OK?"

Lucius nodded. "I ain't hurt none."

"Wally's kind of a bully but he's really not such a bad guy."
After he had said it, Chris realized how stupid it sounded.
Whether or not Wally Fenner was a bad guy was surely related
to who was on the butt end of his perverse attempts at humor.
Since the first day that he showed up at the Eagles' meeting,
Lucius Cady had been an easy target.

"I mean he doesn't really mean any harm. He just doesn't
know any better," Chris continued, as if not knowing any
better was an excuse for Wally's brutish streak.

"Maybe somebody oughta teach him," the young boy
ventured.

The statement struck Chris as strange, not only because it
came from the normally dormant lips of Lucius Cady but
because it was uttered without the slightest trace of anger or
vindictiveness. It was spoken as a statement of fact.

"I guess so," Chris agreed, then his face lit with a sudden
thought. "You know I was serious back there at Town Hall
when I said that I had extra steak." He shook his head and
smiled. "My dad packed enough food to feed me and a small
bear. How about it?"

Lucius looked down at the bulging root and scuffed the moss
with the toe of his sneaker. "I—I guess so," he muttered. Then
he met Chris's eye and forced a smile but it only made his sad
face seem even more forlorn.

"That's great," Chris told him. He was about to continue the
record-breaking conversation when Lucius suddenly turned
and stared into the woods. Chris started to speak but he stopped

when he noticed the slight quaking movements of the boy's shoulders.

Fifteen minutes later, they were back on the trail with Pete Bishop setting a merciless pace. The column stretched and groaned elastically behind him, and when they finally arrived at the campsite a half hour later, all thoughts of grabass had been sweated out of them. Still panting like racehorses, the boys were assembled and brought stiffly to attention.

The worst heat of the day was already behind them but sweat ran freely from every face. Even the soft breeze that floated from the tree-lined lake did little to ease their discomfort. Aside from their own oxygen-gulping gasps, the only sound was the silvery lapping of the water's final reach. Pete Bishop changed all that as his shouted command shattered the beauty like a vile obscenity, a hack of yellow phlegm on the soft petal of a wildflower.

"Stand tall goddammit." He paced up and down the line, pivoting at each end, but his eyes stayed locked on the bedraggled row of boys in front of him. Rivulets of sweat ran freely over his jowls and a dark triangle stained his shirt where his chest and stomach met. His jaw muscles quivered and his small eyes blazed. He stopped in front of Jeff Zack who was the last to stagger into the camp.

"You guys make me sick, you know that?" This not shouted but uttered in fervent contempt. "Where would you be if this was war, Zack?" He put his hands on his hips and leaned in to the youngster.

"I—I—"

Not waiting for the answer, Pete Bishop moved down the line to Wally Fenner. "Look at you, Fenner," he spat. "You're a disgrace. Fat, sloppy, out of shape. You're a goddamn mess."

Wally Fenner smiled sheepishly and bit back a grin. "I'll try harder, Mr. Bishop," he said.

Billy Harman snorted and hid it with a fake sneeze.

"I wouldn't trust this bunch to mind my goddamn cat," Bishop muttered.

Wally snorted at that line and Bishop shot him a killing look. Then the Eagles' leader dropped his hands loosely to his sides and looked up and down the ragged line with undisguised disgust. He shook his head ruefully. "We might as well start setting up camp. Let's see if you can do that right."

Pete had selected a flat spot atop a slight rise. It was next to a sparkling lake that filled a gorge in the foothills of the low mountain range. There was no wide clearing as such, only level ground nestled between widely spaced trees. The area was grassy and pebbled. Comfortable.

Pete Bishop paced to the most open spot and X'ed the ground with his toe. "Here's where we'll build the cook fire," he said. "Pitch your tents around here and leave at least ten feet between them." He swung his arm in a wide sweep that would place the tents in a semicircle behind the fire and facing toward the lake.

"Fenner, you pitch at the far end." He pointed toward a dead tree stump to his left. "Zack, Brothers, Stein, Harman, Cady, Lockwood." He ticked off the campers' names and indicated spots from left to right with the far end next to a rounded boulder that hunched its elephantine back through the rocky earth.

The boys watched and waited for further instructions until finally Pete Bishop's eyes bulged and the wriggly vein returned to his forehead. "Well, what are you waiting for? Move it!" he bellowed.

As if snapped out of a trance, the boys tore into their packs and began to rummage through them. Scott Stein dumped his on the ground and pulled out a blazing red package that made Pete Bishop wince. Jeff Zack had a small mountain tent in faded blue and the others had a variety of shapes and sizes in the more traditional browns and greens.

All except Lucius Cady.

While the others unfolded their tents, stretched ropes, and counted tent pegs, Lucius stuffed his hands in the pockets of his jeans and stood head down, staring at the lake, working the toe of his tattered sneaker into the pebbles. Pete Bishop began to set up his own tent across from the group when he looked up and noticed the idle boy. He had been squatting at the crest of the slope, clearing a smooth spot in the dirt with the flat blade of a folding shovel. Dropping the tool softly to the ground, he rose slowly, not taking his accusing eye off Lucius Cady's back.

"Don't tell me," he said in a tone that turned all seven heads. They looked up in unison and saw their leader glaring angrily across the campsite.

"Cady," he said with a disdainful curl to his lips, "where's your tent?"

Lucius pushed his hands deeper into his pockets but he thrust out his small chin to show Pete Bishop a full measure of Cady family pride. "I sleep out-of-doors lots of times, Mr. Bishop. Don't need no tent on a nice night. And even when it ain't so nice, there's plenty of ways to keep warm and dry if a person knows how to take care." He looked down and kicked at a pebble. "I do it all the time."

Pete Bishop glared across the campsite with his hands on his hips looking more surprised than annoyed. "Cady, just what *did* you bring? You got no tent, no food, no hiking shoes—did you bring a poncho?"

Lucius shook his head.

"A change of clothes?"

"I brought a blanket and some traps."

"Possum traps?" Pete wondered.

"Food traps," the boy answered simply.

The other campers watched the exchange like spectators at a tennis match. "I bet he brung a b'ar trap," Wally Fenner said loudly in exaggerated mountain talk. That earned him a laugh from most of the others.

Chris Lockwood brushed a drop of sweat from his forehead and walked to Lucius's side. "I have a two-man tent, Mr. Bishop. Lucius can sleep with me."

"Ooooooooh," Wally whistled. "Now they're sleeping together."

That drew a round of giddy eye rolling and knowing giggles. Pete Bishop stared at Lucius for an eternity, saying nothing, letting his silence convey his irritation. With a deep breath he dropped back down into a crouch and picked up his shovel. "Nobody sleeps outside on one of my campouts," he said without looking up. "I don't care if you think you're Daniel Boone. He's all yours, Lockwood. I want nothing more to do with him." Pete Bishop went back to scratching at the gravel and the other boys eventually resumed their own work.

Chris Lockwood forced an excited smile. "This is great, Lucius. I can use the help pitching the tent and there's plenty of room for both of us."

Lucius nodded shyly and squeezed out his own tight grin but his eyes were wet with frustration. Wordlessly the two boys erected the tent while the happy chatter of the other campers sparkled around them.

The next hour was consumed with the busy confusion of digging latrines, gathering wood, hauling water, and pitching tents. Pete Bishop shouted the orders and assigned the various jobs while the boys scurried from chore to chore, tripping over tent poles and spilling buckets while trying to look busy, have fun, and keep out of Pete Bishop's line of sight when a new order was about to be barked.

But eventually the camp was organized to Pete's satisfaction. The arc of tents, red, blue, brown, and green, curled around the fire site, that being a circle of melon-sized rocks planted around a shallow dugout with dry wood stacked like Lincoln Logs around a steeple of kindling. To the rear of the tents, deeper into the trees, two pits had been dug; one for garbage and the other for the boyishly joyful task of straddling and squatting while being pelted with insults and clods of dirt.

The final personal touches were now being added to the campers' premises—a rebel flag flying from a pole in front of Wally Fenner's tent, a rectangular border of stones embracing Jeff Zack's domain, a coon tail dangling from Chris Lockwood's front tent pole.

"Well, how's it look?" he asked expansively as he tightened the last rope in the notch of the angled tent peg.

Lucius Cady was busy performing a similar task on the opposite rope until the post was perfectly vertical. He rose and dusted off his hands, then he walked to the front to examine their handiwork. "She looks straight enough," he said after a critical examination.

Chris Lockwood came around and stood by the smaller boy's side. "I think you're right," he said with a gleam in his eyes and pride in his voice. He wrapped a comradely arm around

Lucius Cady's slim shoulders. "Thanks a lot for your help, Lucius."

Lucius smiled and kicked a clump of grass.

The sun was leaning toward the horizon, a jagged graph of trees atop a ridge on the other side of the lake. A refreshing breeze wafted over the lapping water, evaporating their sweat and gluing the dust of their activities to dirt-stained bodies.

"You guys are filthy," Bishop admonished. "I'd be ashamed to be seen in public with any of you."

Fenner gave Billy Harman an elbow in the ribs. "Must be time for the beauty contest."

Billy smirked and nodded.

Pete Bishop jerked his thumb toward the lake. "That water's not just for looking at. You guys are cruddy and I'm not going to eat my dinner next to somebody who smells like a goat."

Wally and Billy exchanged glances and furtive grins.

"I want you guys so clean that you squeak. You got fifteen minutes," Bishop warned.

"Mr. Bishop."

"What do you want, Stein?"

"Can we wear our bathing suits this time? I brought mine along."

Bishop shook his head in exasperation. "Do you wear a bathing suit at home when you take a bath, Stein?"

"No, sir."

"Then what's the big deal about wearing one here?"

Scott Stein blushed and he felt his face catch fire. "I—I don't know."

"It's his pecker," Wally Fenner volunteered loudly. "It's only about this big." He stuck out his little finger and most of the boys laughed.

"And when he gets in the cold water it disappears completely," Billy Harman added.

Scott Stein was crimson and his eyes were wet. Pete Bishop stopped the speculation. "That's enough. No bathing suits. Everybody in the water."

The boys wandered slowly toward their tents.

"Now!" he barked.

The campers disappeared into their tents like gophers

popping into their holes and they emerged moments later stripped down to their grimy skin. Wally Fenner flexed his muscles and yelped a war whoop, then he barreled down the slope and belly flopped into the crystal water, shrieking like a tomcat as the chill struck his warm skin. Harman, Zack, and Brothers screamed down close behind him, shattering whatever tranquillity remained. Lucius and Chris Lockwood trotted at their heels.

Finally Scott Stein poked his head from the opening in the red tent, then he emerged with a terry-cloth towel draped over his arm and hanging down in front of him. Pete Bishop walked over to the young boy and laid his arm across the boy's bare back and squeezed his shoulder with a beefy hand. "Don't worry about it, kid," he said, and Scott turned red once again and pulled away from Pete's fingers. He walked self-consciously down the slope and Pete Bishop swallowed hard and watched until the boy's slim hips disappeared beneath the silver water.

"I know a boy named Looshis Cady."

Wally Fenner started the chant and Billy Harman picked up on it. "He's got a crotch just like a lady."

This was followed by shrieks and catcalls as the boys leapt and dove like dolphins in the water. Lenny Brothers screamed for everybody's attention.

"Imitation, imitation. Tell me what this looks like."

He plunged his head underwater and grabbed his ankles so that only his moon-white cheeks bobbed on the surface like doughy rolls. Bursting back into the air, he shook his head like a wet dog and looked around him for approval.

"Well?"

"Fenner's face," Billy Harman ventured warily. He was safely out of Wally's reach.

Before Lenny could solve his own riddle, Wally broke into another verse. "I know a guy named Scotty Stein."

Billy Harman and Jeff Zack echoed the words.

"He wishes he had one as big as mine." Wally leapt into the air and his ample equipment slapped against his stomach.

Pete Bishop watched intently from the top of the hill. "Five more minutes," he finally shouted.

Wally Fenner lumbered from the water and began the long trudge up the slope. "I was the first one to go in, Mr. Bishop," he said as he passed the leader. "I'm clean already." To prove his point he extended his left arm and placed his right hand on his hip and twirled like a fashion queen.

Bishop wrinkled his nose and rolled his eyes. "Dry off," he ordered.

One by one the others emerged, some running, some trudging slowly up the incline. Pete inspected each one for cleanliness as they passed. Scott Stein was the last to leave the water and he quickly gathered his towel from the shoreline. With his back to the campsite he wrapped and tied it around his waist before walking up the hill. A look of disappointment flashed across Pete Bishop's face as he passed.

Lucius Cady passed Bishop's inspection without comment, then he ducked his head and crawled into the tent only to shoot out an instant later. "My pack's gone," he told Chris. "It was all the way in the back. My traps are still in there but somebody took my pack." He said it as if he had almost expected it.

"Hey looky, looky, looky." Wally Fenner pranced like a chimp in front of his tent clad only in blue jeans, holding Lucius's scruffy backpack over his head.

"He ain't got no food and he ain't got no poncho. Let's see what he *did* bring."

As the others watched, Wally undid the buckles and dug his hands into Lucius Cady's meager belongings.

"Yecccchhh!"

He hauled out a threadbare army blanket and dangled it between thumb and forefinger as if it was infectious.

"You'll get cooties," Billy Harman warned.

"Or bedbugs," Lenny Brothers added.

Wally dropped the offending cloth to the ground and jumped back from it. To the amusement of the others, he dug once again into the canvas bag, this time working his hand from side to side before pulling out a shiny white stone resting in the center of his upturned palm. He stared at it in amazement.

"No shirt, no pants, no poncho, no tent, no meat." He dropped the empty bag to the ground. "I guess you don't need none of those things if you got yourself a shiny white stone. Haw, haw!"

The stone was the shape of an egg only somewhat larger, milky white with pale blue marbling, and it shone with the shimmering gloss of a wet pearl.

"What you got here, Looshis? You plannin' on eatin' this here stone or wearin' it? Haw, haw!" He flipped it from hand to hand like a baseball.

Lucius walked purposefully across the campsite and stopped in front of Fenner. Without a word he stooped and picked up his blanket. While Wally Fenner smirked and the others stared, Lucius folded it into a square, then he picked up the pack and stuffed the blanket neatly inside.

"Give me that stone, Wally." If Lucius doubted that Wally Fenner would hand over the white stone, no such concern edged his voice.

"Gimme that stone," Wally echoed. "Is that a nice way to ask for something? Didn't your paw teach you no better manners than that, Looshis?"

Pete Bishop watched the exchange from the edge of the campsite, leaning lazily against a tree with his arms folded across his chest. Chris Lockwood had taken a halting step toward Lucius to help him if necessary but he stopped. Like the others, he watched the confrontation more out of curiosity than concern, as one watches a proud David challenge a cloddish Goliath.

Wally Fenner extended his hand toward Lucius with the oval stone resting gently in the cup of his palm. "Here's your stone, Looshis."

Wally's planned prank was much too obvious. Lucius would make a grab for the stone and Wally would jerk his hand away and they would all have another good laugh at the boy's expense. But Lucius didn't grab. Instead, he held the backpack in outstretched arms, inviting Wally to drop the stone into the opening. The maneuver spoiled Wally's joke and now he felt and looked foolish. The other boys sensed his discomfort and they all enjoyed it.

Every one of the Hensleyville Eagles had, to one degree or the other, been at the butt end of a Wally Fenner prank at least once; and how they wished that they had the guts or even the presence of mind to turn the tables on him. Now this strange Cady boy, the youngest and smallest among them, had won at least a minor victory. He had landed a stinging jab and that was encouraging, even though Goliath would no doubt end the bout with a devastating blow.

But Wally recovered quickly. Craning his neck, he looked into the open pack and grimaced. "Yeccccch! You want me to put a pretty stone like this in that grungy thing?" He backed off and began flipping it from hand to hand again. "I couldn't do that, Looshis." He flipped the stone over his shoulder and caught it behind his back. "Fact is, I don't think you oughta even be allowed to have somethin' as purty as this. Look at this beauty." He held the stone at eye level and studied it closely. "You think something as purty as this oughta be kept in that dirty old shack where you and your old man live? It ain't right, Looshis. It ain't right at all."

Something about the stone appealed to Wally and he suddenly decided that he wanted it. "I'll give it a better home, Looshis." He flipped the stone one more time, then he stuffed it into the pocket of his jeans.

The standoff that the boys expected had finally arrived. It was a strange tableau, a clutter of young boys in various stages of undress, all of them stiff and silent, the only movement the flick of eyes back and forth among them. Hints of smiles played across two faces, Wally Fenner's and Pete Bishop's, but the others seemed to suddenly lose their appetite for Wally's style of entertainment.

"Give it to me," Lucius demanded.

"There you go again with those bad manners, Looshis. If you don't learn to—"

"I'm only going to say this one more time, Wally. Give me that stone."

Lucius Cady's words resounded like a thunderclap, stunning those in its range with their intensity. The almond eyes in the boy's sad face no longer pleaded shyly. They gleamed like anthracite and fixed Wally Fenner in their icy grip. It was only a lopsided and childish confrontation but it smelled of greater danger.

Chris wanted to stop it. Lucius was no match for Wally Fenner and Chris didn't want to see him get hurt. And since he was on good terms with all of the Eagles, Wally Fenner included, Chris thought that he had a chance to stop the dispute before it went any further. "Why don't you just give the stone back to Lucius, Wally. Nobody wants any trouble. We're up here to have fun."

He stepped forward and put a hand on Lucius's shoulder and was stunned by the vehemence with which the small boy shook him off.

"I'll handle this," Lucius warned, and Chris shrugged and backed off.

Wally Fenner was no longer enjoying the sport. He imagined that he looked like an oaf to the others, towering over the Cady kid like King Kong and making a big deal out of a stupid rock. But the kid had challenged him in front of the rest and that was the part that bothered him. If he gave the stone back, it would look like the kid had called his bluff. If he didn't give it back, he would look like a silly bully picking on someone half his size. Pete Bishop sensed his consternation and stood apart with his arms crossed in front of his chest, grinning at Fenner's predicament.

Lucius stepped closer to Wally and held open the backpack. "Give me the stone, Wally. Drop it in here. I warned you."

This was too much for Wally. Not only was the Cady kid making him look like a fool, now he was actually threatening him. If he walked away now, he'd never live it down, not with this bunch.

"Just supposin' that I don't want to give your stone back, Looshis. What's gonna happen to me? Are you gonna rough me up or something like that? Haw, haw!" He scanned the faces of the other boys for their approval, but they turned away in embarrassment.

Lucius dropped his arm to his side and let the backpack drag on the ground. For a moment Wally thought that the boy had finally given up, that he was about to slink away as so many others had done before him. But Lucius made no move to leave. Standing stiffly in front of the bully, he brought the heels of his hands to his face and pressed them deeply into the sockets of his eyes, as one does when trying to stifle a migraine or hold back a flood of tears. Lucius stood like that for what seemed an eternity, a lonely little boy biting back his frustration, unable to cope with the meanness and the insensitivity of the Hensleyville Eagles.

The boys felt removed from the strange scene, watching it as if it were happening somewhere else, somewhere far away. None of them felt the urge to drop a humorous joke or shoot a careless line across the campsite. The birds and the waves and the wind must have felt the same because their ever-present melody became obvious only when it stopped.

The silence became total.

Wally fidgeted nervously, uncomfortable under the questioning stare of his fellow campers and the eerie presence of Lucius Cady. He couldn't just haul off and smack the kid. What would stop this? Would Lucius finally tire of it and leave? Would Billy Harman toss out an insult and break the veil of stony silence? Would Pete Bishop shout an order? But none of these things happened. Instead he heard a hollow buzzing, faint at first, maybe no more than a ringing in his own ears. His nose wrinkled at an acrid tang that crept from the ground and his thigh began to tingle. Then it got warm.

The stone!

The patch of skin next to Cady's stone began to burn, uncomfortable at first like a splash of hot coffee, then it screamed with the shock of a branding iron. Wally shrieked in pain and dug into his pocket. He pulled the stone out and flung it aside, fearful that he had burned his skin from his fingers. It landed at Lucius's feet and rocked on its oval side until Lucius stooped, picked it up, and carefully dusted it off.

Without a backward glance at Fenner or the other campers, Lucius dropped the stone into his backpack and walked slowly to Chris Lockwood's tent. He was inside for over a minute before the campsite once again rang out with the hoots of adolescent laughter, but Wally Fenner chose to retreat to his own tent and nurse his wounds. But there were no wounds, only a heavy weight in his chest where his heart beat fearfully against his ribs. His thigh and fingers were unmarked.

4

THEY WERE SCATTERED around the campsite, leaning against trees, squatting on rocks, sitting cross-legged in front of their tents. The pungent aroma of hot fat dripping on glowing embers hung in the air at nose level and the scrape of knife against metal mess kit grated like music to their ears. The sun was a blazing ball pondering its fate as it began to sink into the spiky line of trees on the horizon.

Pete Bishop, his back against a stump, gnawed the final trace of flavor from the skeleton of a pork chop and his lips shone with the filmy residue of grease. Wally Fenner squatted nearby, applying a hemorrhage of catsup to a fire-blackened hot dog. Scott Stein and Lenny Brothers chewed experimentally at a ganglia of fibrous roots that Bishop had dug up along the trail, their sour expressions betraying their feelings about the succulence of nature's bounty.

Chris Lockwood and Lucius Cady had smoothed a spot in front of their tent and they sat together quietly, watching the grandeur of the setting sun as they chewed on the tender strip steak. Chris had more than enough meat and Lucius ate his portion from the top of Chris's mess kit. He passed up an offer to share Chris's knife, apparently comfortable enough holding the warm morsel in his fingers.

None of the others sat close to the pair as if, by some unspoken signal, it was decided to leave them to themselves. That suited Chris and Lucius just fine and they were more than content to enjoy the welcome time out from the grapple and chatter of their campmates.

Since the painful episode with the stone, Wally Fenner hadn't chanced a sidelong glance at the strange young boy. Even Pete Bishop had chosen to disregard his earlier ultimatum that Chris not share his steak. Lucius slipped the last of the meat between his lips and licked his greasy fingers. Chris sipped at the last dregs of his iced tea, by this time warm and bitter, that sloshed around the bottom of his canteen. Then he pulled a granola bar from his shirt pocket, snapped it in two, and offered the larger piece to his tent mate. Lucius declined with a timid shake of his blond head.

Chris dropped a piece in his shirt pocket and took a bite from the other. "That must be a real special stone," he said. He didn't mean to be nosy but the episode with Wally Fenner had sparked his curiosity.

Lucius looked up and nodded slightly but he offered no explanation. He wiped his greasy fingers on the knees of his blue jeans. He seemed distracted and he was wondering just how much he should reveal to his new friend. He had never spoken of these things to an outsider. Even his father spoke about it in reluctant grunts and nods whenever the subject came up. But neither had Lucius ever felt such a warmth as he did in the friendly glow of Chris Lockwood. The boy moved him in a way that he had never experienced, and for the first time in his life, Lucius knew what it meant to have a friend.

"It's a special stone because it keeps the evil away," he finally blurted and with the admission came a pang of regret that he had already said too much, as if the show of trust in Chris Lockwood would become a burden, one that shouldn't be inflicted on a new friend.

"Can I see it?" Chris asked.

The sad boy with the mysterious eyes raised his head slowly and met Chris's eager gaze. What should a friend do, he wondered. Should he oblige the boy who has treated him with such kindness? That might make Chris feel good—at least for the present. Or should he deny the request and risk his disapproval? Lucius feared the disapproval. What if it angered his new friend. Would Chris turn away from him, become just like the rest of them, snub him, ignore him, or, even worse, join them in their constant ridicule? He thought not but could he risk it? On the other hand, no one had ever benefited from having a knowledge of the Cadys' ways.

Lucius hedged. "Maybe later," he said without conviction. "The stone's already put away in my sack in the tent."

It was lame but Chris sensed the boy's reluctance and accepted the excuse. He had already pried further than was his style and he decided that, for the time being, he wouldn't pursue it any further.

"Chris," Lucius said.

Chris looked at the younger boy's eyes and tumbled into the pools of their sadness.

"Thank you for being my friend." Lucius's eyes swam and his reedy voice broke. "Someday I'm going to help you. I promise."

He reached out his small hand and Chris took it in his own and when he looked into Lucius's face he somehow knew that what the boy said was true.

"It was really weird, Mr. Bishop." Wally Fenner sucked the last drops from a Dr. Pepper, then crushed the can in his hand. He studied the wrinkled aluminum with the kind of awe that was usually reserved for a three-minute mile.

"What are you talking about, Fenner?"

"That stone of Looshis's. Sucker really burned." To prove his point, he blew across the tips of his fingers. "Do you think he put some kinda spell on it?"

Bishop shook his head. "You're as crazy as he is. There's no such thing as spells, Fenner."

Wally looked insulted. "Then what burned my fingers, huh? Tell me that." A sudden grin of victory crossed his face. "And what made you jump like a goosed frog back at the meeting hall?"

Pete Bishop's small eyes bored into the stocky camper. "A cramp, Fenner. I got a cramp in my hip. Is there anything so mysterious about that?"

Wally shrugged and grinned knowingly. "No, sir, Mr. Bishop, sir. If you said that you had a cramp, then I guess that's what you musta had." He turned to leave, then threw a parting line over his shoulder. "I heard of people casting spells but this is the first time I ever heard of anybody casting cramps. Haw, haw!"

He scurried out of reach before Bishop could react to his insubordination.

The sun finally sunk behind the ridge but it was another two hours before the last shards of daylight seeped from the evening sky. Mealtime cleanup orders were dispensed with military precision and the campers grudgingly executed their assignments. Jeff Zack and Billy Harman buried the garbage, Stein and Brothers policed the area for any trace of civilization that wouldn't have been found on the spot a millennium earlier. Chris and Lucius scouted the surrounding woods for fallen limbs that would keep the fire glowing through the night. Wally Fenner excused himself from the labor, claiming that he suffered from a terminal case of the trail vegetable squirts.

By darkness, the fire blazed like a beacon and painted the campers' faces with licks of brilliant orange and streaks of shadow. Its glow flickered on the trees and changed their profile from kindly provider to ghostly fiend. The moon hovered high above it all, its prying eyes searching out the secrets of the forest. The water lapped monotonously at the shoreline as chirps and muted hoots chilled the air. A shower of sparks exploded from a wet log and a cloud of eye-stinging smoke erupted in its wake.

The campers sat in a loose ring around the fire, enjoying the memories as their eyes and ears and noses absorbed the familiar ambiance of campout.

"Do you guys think there's any bears out there?" Pete Bishop asked no one in particular. It was S.O.P. to banter scary prospects across a roaring campfire.

"There's a lot worse than that," Billy Harman warned. "We're not too far from the ol' Blue Rock quarry."

Scott Stein shifted uneasily. "What's the big deal about the Blue Rock quarry?"

"Jeez, Steiny, don't you know anything? That's where they found Melly Zooker."

At the dead girl's name there was a momentary cessation of breathing.

"Where is it?"

"What?"

"The quarry, stupid."

"About a mile from here. Back there through the trees." Billy jerked his thumb toward the shadows. "They never caught the guy that did it either," he reminded them.

"Wow!" Jeff Zack breathed.

"A lot of people think that she committed suicide," Chris Lockwood said. "Even Chief Littlejohn thinks so."

Pete Bishop moved closer to the fire so the dancing flames made a fiery mask of his face. "Yeah," he said in a deep voice. "That's what they want you to believe." He laughed under his breath. "The truth of it is that the killer still lives in the woods around here. Lives off the land. They say that a man could live forever out here if he knew how to take care of himself."

"Are they still looking for him?" Jeff Zack asked.

"Naw," Billy Harman said. "Chief Littlejohn gave up on that a coupla years ago even though he says that the killer could still be roaming around the woods up here."

"Wow!"

"What really happened to her?" Lenny Brothers asked. "I heard a whole bunch of different stories. I heard that when they found her she didn't have any—you know—didn't have any things."

"Tits, Lenny. They call them tits," Billy helped. "I heard that one too. And I heard that she was all wrapped up in a bunch of chains when they dropped her in the quarry."

"They?"

"Well, whoever did it," Billy said. "It could have been a couple of guys."

"I heard that it was the fish that bit her things off," Scott contributed.

Pete Bishop rubbed his hands together and leaned closer to the fire. The flames leapt at his jowls and made his eyes sparkle like kindling.

"Stein's right," he said. "By the time they found Melly Zooker, the fish had already gotten to her." His voice was soft and deep and it carried over the lapping of the water and the crackling of the fire. "Her eyes were already gone and they say that Ben Littlejohn looked down into those black holes right into her brain."

Jeff Zack felt his stomach lurch as a ghastly young face floated through his thoughts.

Billy Harman chuckled softly, trying for that eerie kind of laugh that raises goose bumps and stands neck hairs on end. "I heard my father talking about what some guy in Gilly's told him. He said that the grappling hooks stuck right through her skull and that she was slit wide open like a gutted deer."

"Yecccchhhhh!"

The fire sparkled and crackled and a lonesome cloud floated in front of the moon. High overhead an owl hooted a haunting melody and in the underbrush behind the tents something skittered through the dead leaves. Scott Stein's eyes were as wide as saucers. His heart was playing a drum solo in his chest. Chris Lockwood sat with his back to the tents looking through the fire at the lake. He felt unprotected and vulnerable. Lucius Cady let his eyes dart from speaker to speaker, his head cocked dubiously as if he questioned the truth of their statements. The campers had settled into an uneasy silence while, in their imaginations, they each pictured their own haunting version of the mutilated body of Melinda Zooker.

"There are supposed to be creatures around that do that sort of thing to little children." Pete Bishop presented the news in a flat monotone. "There are those who say that one of them lives somewhere in these hills right now and that its spoor's been found as close in as McKechnie's farm and as far away as Hawk Ridge."

The lake where they were camped was the centerpoint between the two sites.

"Farmers hereabout say they sometimes see it roaming their fields on dark nights, not much more than a black shadow against the night sky, and when they come out in the morning they find footprints, not quite like those of an animal but too big and heavy to be those of a man—something in between."

The bushes behind the tents rustled and six pairs of eyes flicked about nervously but no one moved their head.

"Ben Littlejohn has a police report that he'll never show anybody," Bishop continued. "He'll deny that it even exists, but I know that it's there. It describes the condition of Ralph Potter's mare when they found her dead in the barn about two years back. It was stiff as a board, drawn and quartered, with its guts spread all over the floor of the barn in some kind of crazy design. It wasn't until weeks later when somebody was studying a photo of the scene that they realized that the intestines spelled out the word 'kill' and the 'i' was dotted with the poor critter's heart."

Bishop's eyes burned through the darkness into Jeff Zack and he paused while the image worked its frightening magic. In slow, evenly paced words he asked the haunting question. "What kind of a beast could do a thing like that?"

The chilling wail and crashing brush answered Pete Bishop's question. From deep within the woods the haunting scream assaulted their ears. It raced across the lake, ricocheted from the ridge, and attacked them again from the other side. Dead branches were crushed under heavy footfalls and live ones were thrust aside as the bellowing creature roared through the trees, bursting into the open next to Scott Stein's red tent. With a wild sweep of its arm, it grabbed at the rope and yanked the tent peg from the ground. The tent collapsed like a parachute.

"Aaaaarrrrgggghhhhh!"

The cry rumbled from the creature's gut and thrust an icy spike into the campers' stomachs. They were frozen with fear, unable to move, trapped in the fearsome creature's evil stare. It had a face as white as an ice cap and wide, dark holes where its eyes should have been and it crouched by the tent with arms spread wide as if about to envelop the entire campsite in its crushing embrace.

"Aaarrrggggghhhhhh!"

The mighty rumble shook the trees and blew a foul wind into the fire and it flicked its flames in outrage as the beast raised its arms above its glowing head and charged at the ring of campers. In five giant strides it flew into the terrified circle and clamped a large black paw on the neck of Lenny Brothers. Lenny screamed and his heart burst against his chest. In what he was sure were his last seconds on earth, he stared into the dark holes in the white face.

"Haw, haw, haw!"

Wally Fenner grabbed his sides and crumpled to the ground. The blazing fire lapped orange streaks across his whitened face and tears of laughter coursed through the charcoal circles that ringed his eyes.

"Haw, haw, haw!"

He pitched convulsively, his black-gloved hands clutching his stomach where the black pullover had crept up to reveal his creamy waist.

"Haw, haw, haw, haw, haw!"

Lenny Brothers lay on his back and stared blankly at the sky, his own tears rolling unchecked down the sides of his head. None of the boys had the strength to speak and they sat like ashen statues in the fire's glow. Only Lucius Cady seemed unaffected and he studied Wally Fenner's rolling body as one would a raving lunatic.

Pete Bishop sported his biggest smile since leaving Town Hall and he nodded his approval of Fenner's performance.

Billy Harman finally found enough breath for protest. "Keerist, Wally," he chattered. "You scared the livin' crap out of me."

Which started Wally on yet another cycle of rolling haw, haws.

Words served no useful purpose and the Hensleyville Eagles spent the next two or three minutes catching their breath and allowing their heartbeats to stabilize. In the midst of their recovery, a troubled cloud passed across Chris Lockwood's freckled face. He shook his head sadly.

"I wonder if that's how Melinda Zooker felt," he said. A wave of sorrow rolled through his troubled heart for the little girl who he never knew. "I mean if we can get this scared at one of Wally's crazy pranks, can you imagine how that poor little girl must have felt?"

It was a question of significantly more gravity than the Hensleyville Eagles were accustomed to ponder.

"It must have been terrible," Lucius whispered.

It was the first unsolicited contribution that any of the

campers could recall coming from Lucius Cady and it sprang from a well of sensitivity far beyond his years.

"Did you know her?" Chris asked.

"In a way," Lucius said.

Tiring of the solemn topic, Billy Harman tried to move the conversation on a different tack. "Old Melly Zooker was probably scared to death, but do you know what'd be even scarier?"

No one could imagine what Billy had in mind. Wally Fenner had joined the ring and sat in the circle between Pete Bishop and Lenny Brothers. "What are you talking about, Billy?" he challenged.

"Snakes."

Billy uttered the sibilant word with the reverence usually reserved for words like cancer or nuclear fallout.

"Snakes," he repeated. "That gotta be the worst way to die."

"What kind of snakes?" Scott Stein squeaked. His voice, normally in the high treble range, still suffered from the recent scare. It would have shattered crystal.

Harman shook his head in disgust. "Who cares what kind of snakes? Snakes are snakes."

"Yo, Billy, you ain't a'scared of a little bitty garter snake are you?" Wally asked through his white greasepaint.

Billy pushed closer to the fire, trying to effect the play of light on his face that had so enhanced the eeriness of Pete Bishop's earlier monologue.

"Picture this," he said in the deepest voice that his adolescent throat would permit. "You're lying on the bare wooden floor in an empty room. There's a weak light bulb hanging from a wire over your head. You got no clothes on. There's ropes tied around your wrists and ankles and they're pulled real tight and tied onto metal rings in the walls. You're spread-eagled and you can't move an inch. You can only turn your head from side to side."

Billy had the knack, he suddenly discovered, to catch the imagination of his listeners. Each of the boys watched him closely. Lenny Brothers stared across the fire with his elbows on his knees and his chin in the palms of both hands. Jeff Zack's eyes were wide with expectation.

Billy paused for effect and a rustling in the leaves sent a shudder around the campfire. He let his eyes travel from face to face, slowly, tediously turning the pages of his tale.

"You hear a noise like a creaking door. A small door. You twist your head to the side and you see it."

Chris Lockwood felt the acceleration of his heartbeat as he was drawn deeper into Billy's story.

"A little wooden flap opens in the wall. At first all that you can see is the black square of the hole. Then you think that you see something move and you see a little pair of eyes." He paused once again and licked slowly at his lips.

"Come on," Wally urged impatiently.

"It sticks its black head out the door and its little tongue flicks in and out. It's a snake."

"No shit," Wally drawled.

Undeterred, Billy inched closer to the fire and dropped his voice to its lowest octave. "Slowly it crawls into the room. Then comes another—then another—then another. All of a sudden you're lying there with no clothes on and you're surrounded by snakes. Hundreds of them. Black ones. Brown ones. Big and little ones. Slimy ones."

"Snakes ain't slimy, stupid."

"They start crawling over your feet. One of them, a big black one, comes right up to your face and stares at you from only inches away. A fat water moccasin crawls onto your chest and lays its head on your neck."

Scott Stein touched the hollow at the base of his throat and he felt his pulse quicken.

"Suddenly they're all over you, crawling on your legs, your stomach, your face. You can feel their cold bodies on every inch of your skin. A black cobra's lying across your face and you can hardly breathe but you're afraid to shake it off."

What Billy lacked in plot structure he made up in the dramatics of his presentation and he had the Eagles spellbound.

"They're all hissing and the sound is starting to hurt your ears but then all of a sudden they stop."

Another pause, this one accompanied by an expression of gravity.

"They all raise their heads and coil like question marks with their beady eyes staring straight at your face and their little forked tongues flicking in and out. You're terrified. It's worse than a horror movie. A thousand times worse."

Even Wally Fenner seemed to be paying attention and this surprised Billy.

"Then suddenly all of the snakes turn their heads and stare at the small door in the wall. You twist your head to see what they're looking at and the cobra slides off your face. In the black hole in the wall you see the head of another snake, a giant snake with yellow eyes and long white fangs dripping with poison. It's gotta be the biggest snake in the world."

Scott Stein wrapped his arms around his chest and hugged himself protectively.

"The monster snake slithers through the hole. It's so big around that if the hole was any smaller it wouldn't fit. The giant snake oozes across the floor and all the other snakes get out of its way. Slowly, an inch at a time"—Billy paced his words to match the snake's deliberate speed—"it slithers up to you." His eyes lit with excitement and his voice rose. "Then suddenly—"

"It bites you on the pecker. Haw, haw, haw!"

Wally Fenner broke Billy's spell and the boys felt the air rush from the campsite like a punctured balloon.

"Aw yo, Wally," Billy complained. But he was secretly pleased with Fenner's surprise ending since he wasn't sure where the story was going.

The Hensleyville Eagles let out a collective sigh and once again began to breathe normally. The moon was now a glowing ball that streaked a golden trail across the dappled surface of the lake. A soft breeze cooled the bands of sweat that had gathered on their foreheads. A ripple of boyish chatter threatened to completely break the tension but Pete Bishop stepped in before the chill had totally surrendered its icy grip.

"That's an interesting topic," he said.

The boys cut off the gab like a flipped switch and they

waited in patient silence for him to continue, all of them except for Wally Fenner.

"Snakes is an interesting topic?" Fenner said incredulously.

Pete Bishop curled his lip in the firelight and shook his head slowly. "Not snakes, Fenner. Horrible ways to die."

He let his small eyes lope around the circle, catching each young face and holding it in his grip for a second, just long enough for the target to feel a rumble of discomfort.

"Harman thought of it," Bishop went on. "He said that he knew a way to die that was even more horrible than what happened to Melinda Zooker. Now I'd like to hear what the rest of you think would be the most horrible way to die." His even teeth glistened white and wet as his lips spread in a menacing grin.

Pete Bishop wasn't certain what qualities of leadership eluded him. He knew that the boys' parents regarded him as a postadolescent buffoon though he wasn't sure what it was in his makeup that made him come across that way. But he could live with that just as long as he had the attention and respect of the kids and he was sure that he knew how to get that. All it took was a healthy dose of fear and he used the regular campouts and the long dark nights to instill that in the impressionable minds of the Hensleyville Eagles.

"What about it, Brothers?" he ordered. "What do you think would be the scariest way to die?"

Lenny Brothers looked at the leader like a daydreaming student shocked to attention by an unexpected question. "Wh-what do you mean, Mr. Bishop?"

"Think about it, Brothers. Think about poor little Melinda Zooker looking up from her bed and seeing that creature standing over her."

Pete was speaking in the slow, deep voice again, the one that chilled the air and stilled the boys to silence.

"Think how horrible that must have been. Think about the snakes slithering out through the hole in the wall in Harman's story. Can't you picture them? Can't you feel your heart pounding against your chest, your throat going dry? You're too scared to scream and you're sure that you're about to die. Think about it, Brothers."

Lenny Brothers gulped and looked to the other boys for help, but they all seemed intent on studying the fire.

"Can you think of anything scarier than that, Brothers?"

Lenny shifted nervously. "Well, there's drowning," he began. "I always thought that would be an awful way to die."

He wasn't sure if that was what Bishop wanted to hear and he searched the man's face for approval.

"Go on, Brothers. Tell the rest of us how it would feel to drown."

Encouraged, Lenny tried to describe the act of drowning, knowing that Billy Harman had already set the standard with his colorful description of the writhing roomful of reptiles.

"Well, you're swimming in the quarry, you know, the old Blue Rock, the place where they found old Melinda Zooker."

That fact alone, he reasoned, should add a touch of spice to the act of drowning.

"And you're doing the old Australian crawl with your face stuck down in the water and you're looking down into the blackness. Suddenly you see this thing floating up toward you. You don't know what it is. It gets closer. Then you see a leg—and an arm—and a face without eyes."

Lenny lacked Billy Harman's knack for the turned phrase or the pregnant pause and the audience began to fidget in the balcony of the campsite.

"We already know all about Melly Zooker," Wally Fenner groaned. "Tell us about drowning."

"Yeah," Scott Stein piped.

Lenny glanced apologetically at Fenner and angrily at Stein, then he resumed. "Well, when you see this thing floating in the water you gulp real quick and you breathe in a mouthful of quarry water. You try to cough and the water squirts out your nose and it makes you gulp again. Now your neck feels like you're being strangled and your chest hurts because you can't get any air in your lungs and you can't swim anymore and you start sinking feetfirst in the lake."

Unconsciously, the boys stopped breathing.

"It's getting darker and the deeper you go, the colder the water gets. You feel like you have to cough but you're afraid to because you know that when you do you're gonna breathe in another mouthful of water. But you do it anyway because you can't help it."

The boys felt a vise of steel strap around their chests. Jeff Zack's eyes started to water.

"Finally you just gotta give up and you take a giant breath and your lungs fill up with water and now it doesn't feel so bad anymore. Then your feet hit the bottom of the lake and everything goes black and you're dead."

He blew a long breath through pursed lips and smiled triumphantly, glad to be finished and pleased with his performance. He looked hopefully toward the group's leader, anxious for the other man's praise.

Pete Bishop ignored him. He jerked his chin toward the fragile boy with the pretty face. "How about you, Stein? What kind of dying scares you?"

Scott had given the subject a little thought during Lenny's tragic descent into the watery depths of Blue Rock quarry. "I always thought that a car crash would be a bad way to die," he said.

"Jeez, Steiny," Fenner broke in, "anyway that you die is gonna be bad. Mr. Bishop wants to hear the worst way."

"Well, maybe I think a car crash *is* the worst way," Scott said defensively. Then he gritted his teeth and began. "You're in the front seat and you're going down a steep hill. Suddenly there's no brakes and you're speeding out of control. At the bottom of the hill there's a sharp turn but the car's going too fast. And there's a big stone wall."

Wally groaned and rolled his eyes in the firelight. Billy Harman faked a jaw-wrenching yawn.

"The car's doing over a hundred miles an hour when it smashes into the wall. The car stops short but you keep right on going. Your head hits the windshield and squashes like a grapefruit."

"Why didn't the windshield break?" Fenner wondered.

"Why weren't you wearing your seat belt, you miserable little criminal?" Lenny Brothers threw in.

Scott pretended not to hear. "Your chest hits the dashboard and your guts explode all over the place. The motor flies back and crushes your legs against the seat. Gas spills all over the place and it starts to burn and you can feel the heat creeping up your back."

"No way, Steiny. By this time you don't feel nothing. You ain't no more than an blob of strawberry jelly, haw, haw."

The Eagles smiled at Wally's graphic metaphor.

"Anyway," Stein concluded, "I think that would be a horrible way to die."

He glanced around self-consciously. Except for a look of mild approval from Chris Lockwood, his contribution to the campfire storytelling session was met with cold indifference, but he was glad that it was over.

Pete Bishop scanned the anxious faces, stopping momentarily then moving on before finally settling on one of the boys who was studiously looking the other way, as if this ploy would make him invisible and exclude him from the requirement to participate. Pete's steady gaze turned the other heads to the same target until Jeff Zack finally felt the pressure of the group's stare.

"Me?" he asked, pointing a questioning finger at the tip of his own nose.

"You," Bishop announced simply.

Jeff chewed at his lower lip seeking the words that would convey the required level of terror, knowing full well that failure tonight could result in months of insults and ridicule. Such were the unquestionable rules of boyhood. He cocked his head to the side, carefully weighing his opening before diving in.

"Zombies," he finally said.

"What about zombies?" Brothers asked.

"That would be a scary way to die," Jeff replied as if it should be obvious and not subject to dispute. "I mean what if they got in your bedroom closet and came out when you were sleeping."

"So?" Billy Harman challenged.

"So you're lying there half asleep and you hear this creepy kind of noise." Jeff felt that he was doing this all wrong and he questioned his ability to ring the fire with the collective goose bumps of his campmates. But he'd try. "You pull the covers up over your head and you bury your face in the pillow."

"Haw, haw! Is that what you do when you hear a creepy noise?"

"I think he farted under the covers," Lenny Brothers said.

"Creeeeeeek!" Billy Harman screeched.

But Jeff wasn't deterred. "The creepy noise stops. You know it's coming from the closet door but you remember shutting it tight when you hung up your jeans."

Smirks and smiles greeted Jeff's accidental admission of bedroom domesticity.

"You hear a shuffling sound—like something being dragged across the floor. It starts—then it stops. It starts—then it stops. A soft clump, then a slide. Clump, slide. Clump, slide. You turn your head toward the sound. The covers are still pulled over your face so you can't see anything, but the smell gags you. Like deer guts on a hot day that were never buried."

Scott Stein wrinkled his nose and felt his stomach rumble.

"I told you he farted," Lenny Brothers said triumphantly.

"The shuffling sound stops but then you hear another sound, something like breathing but it's different. It sounds something like this."

Jeff mimicked the rasping breaths of an emphysemic pachyderm.

"The sound's coming from right next to your bed. Something's standing there but you're too scared to open your eyes to look at it."

Taking a cue from the earlier storytellers, Jeff inched closer to the fire and let its flames paint his face with their eerie palette of colors. He paused and played his gaze across the ring.

"Slowly"—he let the word ooze from his lips like a phonograph record on a constipated turntable—"slowly you pull the covers down. Over your forehead, over your eyebrows, over your closed eyes."

He cranked up the heavy breathing again.

"The smell is overpowering."

Good word, he thought.

"It stinks like the north end of a southbound skunk."

Fenner moaned.

"You squeeze your eyes open just a little bit, peeking out

of the tiny slit at the bottom. You see something. It's a body but it looks like a pile of rags, all dirty and tattered. You look up and you see that it's all wrapped up in gauze with only two holes where the eyes should be."

Another pause.

"The zombie," he hissed.

"Haw, haw! He don't even know the difference between a mummy and a zombie."

Oh, shit, Jeff thought. Wally was right. "Anyway," he said rapidly, "it reaches down and grabs your neck and strangles you until your face turns blue and your eyes pop out of your head and I think that would be the most horrible way to die."

He took a deep breath and blew it out as a performer might when the curtain finally comes down and he can cast off his stage face.

Pete Bishop shook his head and muttered something inaudible. He had already decided on the next storyteller. "Fenner, besides looking in a mirror and scaring yourself to death, what do you think would be the worst way to die?"

Wally Fenner sat silently for a moment. Physically, he was intimidating to the rest of the Eagles and that helped set him up as a leader of sorts. He would have preferred not to have to compete with any of them on an intellectual level and this storytelling exercise came dangerously close to that. At the very best, his effort might erode his standing. At worst he could look like a smacked ass and have to suffer the hidden snickers that he'd never see. But whatever Wally Fenner was—an oaf, a bully, a teenage tyrant—one thing that he wasn't was a coward.

Shifting his weight, he rocked to his knees and rose to his feet. The group had gotten accustomed to his whitened face and blackened eyes and now, the element of surprise no longer a factor, the once-fearsome face was more reminiscent of a cuddly panda than a bloodthirsty killer. But Wally didn't know that as he stalked around the outside of the ring of campers, planting one foot heavily in front of the other, shifting his eyes, clawing his hands, breathing heavily like his mental image of a forest monster.

"I think—"

He didn't speak the words, he growled them the way someone named Igor might have breakfast conversation with a mad doctor.

"I think that the scariest way to die would be to get yourself eaten alive by spiders."

Pete Bishop shook his head in disappointment, but if the boys were anything less than riveted to Wally's every word, they didn't show it in their expressions. Such was the awesome power of being the biggest kid.

"Spiders crawling over your feet and up your legs and covering your whole body so you look like a hairy gorilla only it ain't hair, it's spider legs."

So far, the image tickled more than it terrified but nobody wanted to be the first to tell Wally.

"They crawl behind your knees and into your armpits."

He kept up his slow rotation around the campfire and half a dozen heads swiveled at his passing. Only Pete Bishop seemed uncaptivated and he chose to watch Wally only when the boy passed within comfortable range.

"They crawl up between your legs and walk all the way down to the tip of your pecker." He stopped his pacing and grinned through the greasepaint. "That'd be a heckuva long walk."

The boys smiled as expected.

"Big, fat, hairy spiders crawling in your ears and up your nose and you swat at them and they pop into green and yellow goo balls. They're all over your face and you open your mouth to yell and a big one, fat as a marble with long hairy legs and pointy pinchers, crawls inside. You try to spit it out but you can't and it keeps on walking back toward your throat."

The other boys listened wide-eyed and closemouthed with their lips pinched together like a quorum of grim-faced elders.

"The spider starts biting that funny-looking thing that hangs down in the back of your throat and you start hacking and coughing and when you do six more spiders crawl in your mouth. Now they're all biting you—your hands, your eyes, your pecker—and some of them are poisonous and your whole body feels like it's on fire."

The campers no longer felt the tickle of tiny feet. A fat ant crawled up Lenny Brothers's pants leg and he swatted wildly until it was no more than a wet spot on his trousers. They all felt like they could use another dip in the lake.

"Now, instead of just making little punctures with their tiny fangs, the spiders start biting off chunks of skin as big as dimes, ripping them off and chewing them up while you start bleedin' to death. You can't even see what they're doin' anymore because your eyes are just big gooey holes in your head but you can hear them munching away. Chomp, chomp, chomp! Then, to end your pain, the spiders insider your mouth crawl down your throat and start eating your heart. For a coupla minutes it feels like there's a blowtorch in your chest and then your heart explodes all over your stomach and you die."

The campers sat quietly for a few moments, cautiously checking the ground around them for any signs of crawling things.

"That was real good, Wally," Billy Harman commended.

"Yeah, neat," Scott chirped.

"Not bad," Pete Bishop added, his first praise of the evening. It was starting to get late and he looked at his watch by the firelight. "We still got a couple to go," he said without enthusiasm. "How about you, Lockwood. Do you have anything new?"

Chris hunched forward and looked earnestly at Pete Bishop. "I had a nightmare once that was about dying. It wasn't really a spooky kind of dream or anything like that but it was scary." He paused as if waiting for permission to continue.

"Well?" Bishop blurted.

Assuming Bishop's blurt to be a go-ahead, Chris told them about his frightening dream. "We were in school. It was winter and Miss Handleman was teaching American history. There was a loud snapping noise and everybody looked up and we all saw a big crack running across the ceiling and then the room started to shake. The blackboards all shattered into tiny pieces like you see car windows do sometimes and then the room started to rock from side to side. Miss Handleman fell out of her chair and a big piece of the ceiling fell on top of her."

"Did it kill her?" Scott asked.

"I don't know."

"It'd serve her right if it did," Wally said. "She gave me a D once."

"What are you complaining about, Wally?" Billy said with a snicker. "That was probably the best grade that you had the whole term."

"Funny man," Wally countered weakly.

It had been a long and trying day and the boys were wearying of Pete's campfire game. That was fine with Chris.

"Anyway," he continued, "I woke up and I was all sweaty and my heart was beating like a jackhammer." He looked across the fire into Pete Bishop's bored face. "I think that it would be real scary to be caught in an earthquake. That's it," he finished.

Pete Bishop absently nodded his agreement. "Earthquakes, snakes, spiders, drowning, car crashes, smelly zombies. You guys have to be the weirdest bunch of campers in the whole state. OK," he said, brushing his hands together with finality, "that wraps it up for the night."

"What about Lucius?" Chris said. "You forgot to ask him."

Lucius sat quietly, his sad face betraying neither anxiety nor a willingness to participate. It didn't appear that he cared one way or the other.

Chris hoped that he had done the right thing but he knew that if Lucius was ever to be accepted as one of the Eagles, he'd eventually have to shuck his shell and join in the activities.

"Haw, haw! How 'bout it, Looshis. You want to tell us about gettin' et alive by killer possums?" Wally jeered.

"Shaddup, Fenner," Bishop said. He turned his small eyes on the towheaded boy by Chris's side. He was unable to keep the sneer from his voice. "OK, Cady. It's your turn. If you want to be one of the Eagles you have to act like one."

His face curled into a mask of hate. It was electric, totally disproportionate to the situation. No man should harbor such loathing for a small child.

"Tell us what you think is the most horrible way to die," Bishop challenged.

Lucius Cady hadn't changed his position since first arriving in the circle. His jeans-clad legs were crossed like a pretzel in front of him and his small white hands were folded in his lap. The fire crackled and popped and its licking flames made yellow buttons of his almond eyes. The rest of the campers waited eagerly, not knowing what to expect from the mysterious child. A few of them wished him success but only one would show it openly.

Chris Lockwood urged him on with a gentle nudge. "Go ahead, Lucius. You can do it."

They watched the firelight flicker on his sad face but there was nothing to indicate that Lucius understood what was expected. His eyes were fixed in the same expressionless gaze that they had worn throughout the evening. All of this made his sudden statement all the more startling. "You all talk about physical pain but that ain't nothin'."

The campers weren't even sure that they saw his lips move but his words rang clear and haunting, like the sound of chimes carried on a chilly wind. Chris felt an icy stab and he shivered. Looking up, he thought that he sensed the other boys experiencing the same wintry gust.

"Horror ain't only in the body," Lucius continued. "It's in the mind too." The voice belonged to Lucius but the words seemed to come from another source, as if someone or something had borrowed his taut vocal chords and his young body to deliver its message.

"The most horrible way to die is to live with the terrors of your own mind and to let them eat away at it a moment at a time."

For the first time, he raised his head and let his gaze sweep the curious faces of Pete Bishop and the Hensleyville Eagles. Then, turning his eyes back to the fire, he uttered, "When you die of fright you die a thousand times."

A wispy breath swept from his narrow chest and he slumped as if a heavy weight had been suddenly removed from his frail shoulders.

For the longest moment no one spoke. They barely breathed as their eyes flicked around the campfire seeking one another out, wondering who would be the first the break the dread silence. As expected, Wally Fenner took the initiative.

"That's real heavy, Looshis," he said as lightly as he could but there was a marked absence of typical Fenner haw, haws.

"Weird," Scott whispered.

Slowly, like a somber mist, the gloomy cloud of Lucius Cady's voice rose through the limbs of the overhanging trees and drifted into the night. Lucius sat unmoving, eyes fixed in a glassy stare on the hypnotic flames. The boys began to stir but none felt the urge to make light of Lucius's contribution.

Lenny Brothers cleared his throat cautiously. "What about you, Mr. Bishop. What do you think would be the most horrible way to die?"

Pete Bishop scanned the expectant faces. "The most horrible way to die," he said without a trace of humor, "would be to spend the might as Lucius's tent mate."

"Haw, haw," Wally Fenner laughed but none of the others joined him.

5

A BLANKET OF uneasiness hung over the darkening campsite, a thinly woven fabric of tension that clouded the usual bedtime merriment. There were no tents caved in, no cherry bombs exploded in the slit trench under a squatting camper, no boisterous farts, no missing sleeping bags. There were no giddy squeals of laughter or roars of outrage. It was as if the campfire revelations had summoned a new entity into their midst, an unwelcome awareness of their mortality, a legacy of Melinda Zooker's violent death.

The organs of the living forest were no longer sources of joy and comfort, they were evil traps waiting to be sprung. The lake became a moon-coated expanse anxious to suck the unwary camper down its silken throat. The chirping insects and skittering night creatures lurked in the darkness, waiting to swarm from the ground and cling to milky skin. The noises of the night, once a comforting maternal heartbeat, became the stomach rumbles of a sleeping demon. The squinting eye of the moon peered relentlessly. The shadows of the grasping branches of the trees encircled them. The muted conversation of the living forest surrounded them with malevolent chatter. The boys of Hensleyville felt trapped and enclosed.

With furtive glances at every click and shadow, the boys executed their methodical nighttime rituals. In the absence of insults and harmless obscenities, bodily functions at the latrine became little more than an embarrassment to be hurriedly completed. Wally Fenner, the exception as usual, loosed a raucous fart that reverberated from the distant ridge, but even that Herculean effort failed to blast away the tensions of the night. Lenny Brothers, returning from the shoreline with a bucket of water, felt certain that he saw a fleeting shadow dart behind a tree but he didn't tell the others. As quickly and as quietly as possible, the boys completed their assignments and hurried to the relative security of their tents and the dim glow of the waning fire.

Jeff Zack was the first camper to be bedded down and zipped up tight. Lenny Brothers was close behind. Pete Bishop's tent glowed in an aura of orange as the group's leader poured over his notes or a magazine or perhaps a stack of dirty pictures. Pete's nocturnal reading habits had always been a source of amused speculation among the Hensleyville Eagles. Wally Fenner, Billy Harman, and Scott Stein were stretched out identically in their individual tents, elbows planted on the ground, chins on hands, heads poked through their tents' front flaps, each of them staring expectantly at the last tent in the curved row where Chris Lockwood and Lucius Cady would soon bed down for the night.

"C'mon, c'mon, c'mon, for crissake," Wally mumbled impatiently.

Chris pulled out another granola bar and this time Lucius accepted a portion, albeit shyly.

"It's kind of a nice night out," Chris said. "How about if we just sit outside the tent for a while." He caught the younger boy's questioning glance. "Unless you're too tired," he hurriedly added.

"No, I'm not tired," Lucius said, and he sat obediently next to the round portal of Chris's tent.

Lucius returned to his cross-legged, hands folded posture, his face a mask of mystery, his gaze fixed blankly on some indistinct point in space. Chris folded himself into a similar pose and looked out across the lake. He was staring in the same direction as his younger companion but he felt certain that they were viewing different scenes.

After what seemed an interminable wait, Chris finally broke

the silence. "What do you like to do, Lucius? I mean when you're not camping or going to school."

What a strange question, Lucius thought. Why should anyone else care? No one ever cared before. Well, his father cared some but then he had a different way of showing it and Festus Cady wasn't much for conversation anyway.

But all of a sudden the question didn't seem so strange after all. Lucius would often sit by himself and wonder what other folks did, didn't he? He spent a lot of time wondering about things like that. He just never realized that other people might have the same kind of curiosity about him. Maybe he wasn't so different from everybody else after all. It was a comforting thought.

What do I like to do? He asked himself the question and wondered why he had trouble coming up with an answer. The truth was that he didn't know what he liked to do because he spent most of his time doing what he had to do.

"I don't know," he finally answered. "I just kind of get my chores done and if it's still not too late I read a little." He turned his sad eyes to Chris's freckled face. "What do you like to do?" His question was charged with an undercurrent of excitement.

"Baseball and going swimming mostly," Chris decided. "And I like the Eagles. They're really a pretty neat bunch of guys," he said almost apologetically. "There's a couple of them that like to pick on people but if you ignore them they'll get bored with it and stop."

Lucius pulled his legs up close and wrapped his arms around his shins. He rested his chin on his knee. "I know that. They don't bother me none," he lied. "What else do you like to do?"

He was anxious to get the focus away from himself and his problems but he was also filled with wide-eyed curiosity. In almost thirteen years he'd never had such a discussion. It pleased him and made him yearn for more.

Chris stopped to think. "Well, I like to watch TV. Do you like to do that?"

"We ain't got no TV. Pa says that TV brings on the devil." He quickly dropped his eyes and turned back toward the lake.

"I don't mean that your TV brings on the devil or anything like that," he hurriedly corrected.

Chris laid an arm across the frail boy's shoulder. "Your pa's probably right, Lucius," he said with a warm smile. "Mostly I just watch sports though. And I like to read about them too. I read the sports page in the paper every day and we get *The Sporting News* and *Sports Illustrated*. They're really neat."

He felt the other boy withdraw and wondered if he had said something wrong.

"My pa don't allow no newspapers or magazines in the house neither. He says they bring on the devil too."

Chris shrugged in the fading firelight. "What do you do then?"

"We got a Bible and some other books."

"Mysteries?" Chris wondered. "I like to read mysteries sometimes."

"Nothing like that," Lucius replied. "Mostly they're books about Jesus. We read them to keep the bad spirits away."

The last was spoken softly, almost in a whisper, and Chris had to strain to hear.

Down the row of tents Wally Fenner growled restlessly. "What are they talking about?"

"I can't hear them," Scott hissed back.

"I wish they'd hurry up," Billy Harman complained. "I'm tired of waiting."

Chris gave his new friend a sidelong glance and decided to change the subject. "That was some trick that you did with the stone," he said cautiously.

Lucius blinked and nodded slightly.

Chris thought that he saw a flash of fear in the boy's eyes but he felt impulsive. "How did you do it?" he asked.

"Do what?" Lucius looked at Chris suspiciously.

"Make Wally think that the rock was hot. I saw a hypnotist do something like that once," Chris said with a lightness that he didn't feel. "He told this guy that his shoes were getting hot and the guy couldn't get them off his feet fast enough." He laughed uneasily.

"I didn't do nothing," Lucius said quietly. His face grew even sadder. "I tried to stop it from happening."

"Stop what?" Chris asked.

Lucius seemed to shrink deep within himself. He had never spoken about the power before except to his father, and on those rare occurrences he was told that it was a family thing, something not to be discussed with strangers. And, to Festus Cady, strangers meant everybody else in the world except himself. But Chris Lockwood seemed like less a stranger now than even his own father. In the past few minutes, Lucius had exchanged more personal information than he had shared with his father in a lifetime.

Fetch some wood. Turn down that lamp. Check the traps. Read the book.

There was little conversation at the Cady home, only short bursts of communication that required no response. Lucius could go for hours without speaking a word and it sometimes felt good just to take the Bible into the woods and sit on a rock and read aloud to himself.

Strangers!

By Festus Cady's definition the whole world was nothing but strangers and right now Lucius felt that world collapsing on top of him. Badgered by his father, ridiculed by Pete Bishop, tormented by the boys in the club—only Chris Lockwood seemed to care a lick about him and it was such a wonderful feeling that Lucius was afraid it might slip from his grasp. But now Chris was asking about some of the most secret things and Lucius was torn between his new friend's curiosity and his father's warning. With a willfulness nurtured by his new friendship he decided.

"I didn't make the stone hot. The bad un' did it."

"The bad one?" Chris echoed. "What do you mean? Who's the bad one?"

"He's a mean spirit," Lucius said simply. "Pa says that he's taken a likin' to me. Pa says that he wants to get inside of me and make me bad like him. That's why we got to pray all the time." He looked at Chris with pleading eyes. "You won't tell nobody about this, will you, Chris? I ain't never told nobody before. Pa says that folks will laugh at us if they know."

"I won't tell anybody," Chris said, trying to hide the

dumbfounded look on his face. Who'd believe it anyway, he wondered.

"You gotta promise," Lucius pressed.

"I promise. But where did you get the stone?"

Lucius blew out a long, slow breath. His face reflected his indecision but he finally decided that he had already entrusted Chris with other secrets—why not go all the way.

"My pa and me prayed for help one night after the bad un' came around. Next morning I went outside and there it was, settin' in front of our house just like an Easter egg."

"Who put it there?" Chris asked.

"Pa says the Lord sent it to help us fight the bad un'. 'The Lord provides' is what Pa said."

Lucius felt relieved. He'd done it. After all these years he'd finally done it. He had told somebody about the bad un' and about the stone and nothing happened, none of the horrible things that his father had warned him about. No licks of fire shooting out of the ground. No bolts of lightning smiting him dead. Festus, in the longest conversation the boy could remember, had sat him down in a dark corner of the shack and told him that the bad un' would go crazy with rage if they ever told anybody about him. But Lucius *did* tell and the bad un' didn't do a thing, not even a little rumble of thunder. Lucius didn't even feel his presence. His father was wrong and this was yet another revelation.

It had been quite a night for the youngster, a new friend, an unburdening, a realization of his father's fallibility.

"How does the bad one do things like that?" Chris asked, working hard to keep the timbre of disbelief from his voice. "How did he make the stone get hot?"

"He has the power," Lucius said simply. "It's an evil power. It talks about it in the Bible. But we can fight him," he said proudly. "We know how."

"How?"

"By not getting angry. That's what he's after. When you get angry you start to think vengeful thoughts and that's just what the bad un' wants you to do." Lucius shook his head as one who knows firsthand about such things. "He jumps on my bad thoughts quicker'n a cat on a june bug. He's a glad un' when I think angry thoughts, that's for sure."

It was pouring out now, a flood of exposition that he had been warned would loose a torrent of the devil's bile. But nothing happened. The moon still beat a burning path across the rippled water. The hoots and chirps and gentle buzzes of the night continued to strike their soothing chords. The fire still sparkled like a friendly beacon. And Lucius Cady felt a wave of relief, vindicated in his decision to unburden himself of his long borne load.

"What kind of things does the bad one do?" Chris asked. He kept his voice low, not wanting to provide the Eagles with any more grist for their mean-spirited mill.

"He killed Red," Lucius answered with an edge of bitterness.

"Red?"

"My dog. We were out a'huntin' and he barked at a noise in the brush and scared off a rabbit. I had a bead on the critter but it bolted when it heard poor Red."

"Then what happened?"

Lucius lowered his eyes in shame. "I shot him." It was barely a whisper. "Shot him right in the head."

Chris was aghast. "Why'd you do that?"

His note of shock erupted louder than he had planned and Lenny Brothers strained to hear.

"Why'd you do that?" he asked again in a hushed tone.

Lucius shouldered a hopeless shrug. "That's just how the bad un' works. That's how he takes you over. He gives you bad thoughts in your head and unless you're real careful you do whatever he wants you to do."

Chris blew out a long breath. "Whew! That's scary, Lucius. Is that what you meant when you told us about the worst way to die? How did you say it?"

Lucius paused as he tried to recall his words. "I said that the worst way to die would be to have the night terrors eat away at your mind." He turned to Chris and fixed him with his almond eyes.

Chris looked into their depths and thought that he saw a wizened old man at war with his own dark terrors.

"But you don't have to worry none, Chris." Lucius made that statement with a sense of purpose. "I'll never let the bad un' do anything to hurt you."

Chris felt a cold shiver ripple down his back. He began to wonder just what kind of a friendship he was getting himself into. It was time to sleep on it. Feigning a yawn and a luxurious stretch he said to his quiet friend, "I think I'm about ready to hit the sack, Lucius. How about you?"

"You go ahead," the boy said. "I'll be right along." Then he gazed across the lake and smiled a peaceful smile, enjoying a rare moment of escape from the monsters of his own mind.

With a backward glance at the boy, Chris parted the canvas flaps and crawled inside the tent.

"There they go," Wally hissed down the line.

Scott Stein inched his head from his tent like a curious turtle. Billy Harman's lips curled into an expectant grin.

Chris Lockwood felt a weighty sense of foreboding and wondered if he had made a mistake by befriending Lucius Cady. Something about the boy touched a raw nerve. It wasn't that he minded siding with him against Wally Fenner or even Pete Bishop—his friends in the Eagles wouldn't hold that against him. They'd expect no less. It was just that Lucius seemed to operate on a different plane than the rest of his friends. The truth of the matter was that the boy spooked him out. That was what was running through his mind when he crawled through the front of his tent and flipped on his flashlight.

Chris's scream ripped the quiet from the night. The hoots and chirps of the forest stopped. One half a mile away, a nibbling doe froze in her tracks, then spun and bolted wildly through the trees. Chris dropped the flashlight and backed out of the tent as if the devil himself was in hot pursuit.

As Chris scrambled backward, Lucius looked with concern into his ashen face and grabbed his arm. "What's the matter, Chris?" he asked urgently.

But Chris was unable to form coherent words. His jaw quivered and his heart beat wildly. Grunting unintelligible noises, he pointed toward the open tent flap.

With no sign of fear, Lucius spun toward the opening and

pushed inside where he scooped up the flashlight and sprayed its yellow beam around the cramped tent. His stomach flipped but held its ground. A few moment's later he pushed his head back into the cool night air and stared up into the fat, grinning face of Wally Fenner.

"Haw, haw," Wally gurgled but Lucius ignored him, crawling with difficulty from the tent while cradling the gory burden under one arm, his blanket in the other.

"Now what the hell's going on," Pete Bishop grumbled, straightening up with difficulty as he clambered from his tent. His gaze fell on Lucius. "What are you up to now, Cady? I told you—" Then he saw the dead, white eyes and the bloody stump of a neck. "What the f—"

Lucius strode past the line of tents and disappeared into the woods. He never looked back as the goat's head left a staggered trail of bloody drops in his wake.

6

CHRIS ROLLED AND tossed through the night, drifting into restless sleep, then jerking wide awake at the slightest woodland murmur. Even during the brief spurts when he was able to doze, he was bedeviled by a flood of torturous images. The abused body of Melinda Zooker floated through inky waters, her milky eyes locked in an obscene stare, her skin flaking off like ancient parchment. A snow-white goat with eyes like fire pranced around the shorelines gushing blood from every orifice and turning the sand a burgundy red. Mottled snakes and hairy spiders and hideous night creatures circled his tent, tugging at the ropes and scratching their pointy claws across the dewy canvas. He thrashed out and knocked them away, but they never failed to return.

When the first dim light of morning finally arrived, it was a welcome grey glow that chased away the monsters of his mind, and for too brief a time, he fell into a restful slumber. When he reawakened, the sun streamed through the trees and the morning rustle and clatter of the campsite restored a sense of reality. Chris's first memories were the events of the previous night and the absence of his tent mate. He brushed aside the tent flap and, with sleep-puffed face, crawled into the sunshine.

Pete Bishop, in brown T-shirt and military dress shorts, stuffed new wood into the red embers of the fire. Billy Harmon, a few tents to Chris's right, poked his head into the sunshine and squinted. Wally Fenner, clad only in sagging jockey shorts, stood in front of his tent, scratching his ballooning stomach with both hands. Catching Chris's eye, he grinned stupidly, put his hands to the side of his head, and extended his index fingers like a pair of horns.

"Baaaa," he rattled.

Chris curled his lips and shook his head. "It's not funny, Wally."

Fenner shrugged. "Did goat boy ever come back?"

"Lucius is still alone out in the woods," Chris answered. "He's out there all alone because of what you did."

"Hey, Lockwood, ain't he supposed to be the great mountain man?" Wally challenged. "He's probably frying up a batch of possum gizzards for breakfast right now."

Wally tilted his head and sniffed into the wind to the amusement of the other campers who by now stretched and scratched in varying degrees of undress.

Scott Stein appeared to be the most prepared for the new day. Being the first camper awake, he had performed his morning ablutions in the grey privacy of the dew-damp forest, then he donned his new hiking gear. He looked like a dressed-up mannequin from a great outdoors catalog.

"I don't know about you guys," he said, "but I had some really weird dreams last night."

"Me too," Jeff Zack volunteered. "That old goat head really grossed me out."

Wally Fenner's attention perked up. "What did you guys dream about?"

"Old Melinda Zooker for one thing," Stein told him. "And I had another dream about a goat."

Lenny Brothers gave Stein a searching look. "That's really weird, Steiny. I dreamed about the same things."

"Me too," Billy admitted.

Then they buzzed among themselves, comparing nightmares of ghostly corpses and bleeding goats, like a group of TV buffs discussing last night's schedule.

"How 'bout you, Mr. Bishop? Did you dream about this stuff too?" Wally asked.

"I slept like a baby," Pete lied.

For the next hour, the Hensleyville Eagles brushed their teeth, straddled the latrine, and went about the business of putting together a campfire breakfast, but the normal chatter and grabass were missing. The campsite seemed visited by a brooding presence that even Wally Fenner's humor couldn't dispel.

"Baaaa," he cackled as Lenny Brothers sunk his teeth into a piece of breakfast meat, but his attempt drew more shudders than chuckles.

"I'm worried about Lucius," Chris told them while stirring a yellow pile of eggs. He searched the others' faces for signs of sympathy but he was unrewarded.

"Hey," Billy Harman answered. "Nobody forced the kid to run into the woods. It was only a joke for gosh sakes."

"Some joke," Chris countered. "He's the youngest kid in the Eagles and he only joined so he could find a friend and you guys make him sorry he ever came along."

Wally snickered without pity. "Hey, we ain't baby-sitters. Ain't that right, Mr. Bishop."

Pete looked disinterested. "He'll turn up," he said, hiding the concern that he felt. But his concern wasn't for the safety of Lucius Cady. He was worried about the skin of Pete Bishop if the parents of the Hensleyville Eagles became critical of his leadership.

"I think we ought to go look for him," Chris said, a challenge to Pete Bishop's indifference. "He might be hurt. He was real upset when he ran off."

Fenner sniffed. "Tough titty." He liked Chris but was getting irritated by his accusations. "If you're so worried, you go looking for him. I don't give a flyin' fart to the moon if he ever shows up."

"Yo, Wally," Lenny Brothers said, "he *is* only a kid."

"Yeah," Jeff Zack agreed. "Nobody wants to see him get hurt out there."

"You don't have to worry none about that," Billy Harman said, and he pointed toward the shoreline. "Goat boy's finally come back."

Every head turned and Chris felt a wave of relief. Lucius stood at the shoreline with his back to the campsite. His head hung down and his hair was a golden sunflower in the slanting rays. Hands sunk deep in his pockets, blanket draped around his neck like a ratty shawl, he seemed to be gazing at the lapping wavelets that washed the pebbles at his feet.

Chris walked to the crest of the gentle slope and looked with pity at the youngster. He seemed so fragile and friendless and Chris grieved for his loneliness.

Not so Pete Bishop. "Cady get your ass up here," he shouted. He stood next to Chris with fists on hips and eyes blazing with anger.

The boy must have heard but he showed no sign of it except that he seemed to shrink even deeper within himself.

"I know a boy named Looshis Cady." Wally Fenner boomed out the taunting chant but none of the others picked it up and he looked about foolishly.

"Cady, if you don't want to spend the rest of the day doing push-ups you'll be here in ten seconds."

Pete's threat seemed hollow even to himself.

"I'll go talk to him," Chris said. He turned a pleading look toward the leader. "I don't think he needs any more teasing or punishment."

"When I want help running this group I'll ask for it," Pete said, but his words lacked conviction. He had been upbraided by a freckle-faced teenager and he tried to hide his confusion in a cloak of authority, but when Chris turned away from him and began walking down the slope, Pete made no effort to call him back. Instead, he shrugged in disgust and turned back to the campfire. "Forget about those two," he ordered. "We have some cleaning up to do."

With cautious glances at Chris Lockwood and Lucius Cady, the Hensleyville Eagles resumed their activities, but Lucius's return did nothing to dispel the ominous gloom that shrouded the campsite. If anything, the feeling of foreboding deepened.

"Lucius, are you all right?" Chris stepped to the boy's side, speaking softly as one does to a friend who has been deeply hurt. The pain in his own voice couldn't be disguised.

"Lucius?"

But the boy showed no sign of recognition. The water lapped at the toes of his battered sneakers and seemed to hypnotize him with its steady rhythm. His face was bleached white, his eyes dead. Lucius was a statue of despair and Chris's pity was mingled with a chill of fear.

"I know a boy named Looshis Cady."

The taunt rolled down the green slope and washed over Lucius's shrunken shoulders, adding to the burden that squeezed any possibility of joy from his slender body. He blinked and a silver tear rolled through the soft down of his cheek.

Chris turned an angry look up the hill but there was no one to be seen. Putting his arm around Lucius's shoulder, he pulled him close. "Just don't pay them any attention," he said softly. "They're just stupid." Being an only child, Chris had never experienced the exquisite simplicity of fraternal love and the outpouring of warmth that surged between the two boys gave him a clue of what he was missing.

But Lucius's forlorn expression didn't change. It remained the catatonic gaze of one separated from reality—or perhaps too close to it.

"Come on," Chris urged. "Let's go up top and get you some breakfast."

Lucius offered no resistance as Chris took him by the hand and turned him around to face the hill.

"Looshis, Looshis," the chant went on.

In choppy little steps, Chris and Lucius worked their way up the gentle slope. "Were you cold last night?" Chris asked.

Lucius trudged at his side but didn't answer.

"Looshis, Looshis."

At each singsong taunt, Chris felt Lucius's grip tighten on his hand. When they were halfway up the hill, Wally Fenner appeared at the crest, his bloated belly hanging over the elastic of his jockey shorts.

"I know a boy named Looshis Cady," he sang.

"I know a boy named Looshis Cady," came the response.

"He's got a crotch just like a lady."

Lucius's grip on Chris's hand became a painful clamp and Chris could feel the angry vibrations from the boy's tense muscles. "Cut it out, Wally," he called. "Why don't you leave him alone?"

Fenner was about to scoff at the demand with yet another chorus but he stopped short when Lucius raised his head and fixed him with an icy stare. The look on the younger boy's face was more than a simple challenge, it was a threat so real that Wally felt its physical force push him away from the crest of the hill. He stumbled over Lenny Brothers's mess kit and fell backward into the weeds.

Billy Harman chuckled at Wally's plight, then decided to try a verse of his own. "I know a boy named Looshis—"

Wally pushed himself to his feet. "Shut up," he stammered, then he stormed through the campsite and pushed Billy roughly aside.

"What's with you?" Billy Harman asked indignantly, but Wally plunged right by, crawled into his tent, and threw the flaps closed.

The rest of the boys exchanged glances but none crashed the silent breach left by Wally's sudden departure.

Except for Pete Bishop.

As Chris and Lucius reached the flat at the top of the slope, Pete turned on them with pent-up rage. "Who the hell do you think you are, Cady? You think you're some damn prima donna who can just go walking off whenever you feel like it? I'm responsible for you, Cady, you remember that. I'm the one who has to take all the crap from your crazy old man if you get yourself killed out here."

Chris tried to steer Lucius toward the tent but Bishop blocked the way with a spread-legged, chest-puffed stance.

"Let me get him something to eat, Mr. Bishop," Chris asked politely.

"Coddling him, that's what you're doing," the leader exploded. He brushed Chris aside with a sweep of his hand and the boy tripped backward and tumbled to the ground. For the second time since he returned, raw emotion burned in Lucius's face.

"You've been a royal pain in the ass since the day you joined the Eagles," Bishop raged on. "We don't need you, Cady. We don't want you or your kind." Bishop had lost all semblance of control and his hate for Lucius Cady boiled to unreasonable proportions.

Chris pushed himself to his feet. "Why are you doing this to him, Mr. Bishop? He's only a kid."

"You snot-nosed little shit," Pete exploded. "Don't tell me what I can't do." His face was beet-red and he grabbed the front of Chris's shirt and twisted it in his hand, bringing his knuckles tightly to the boy's downy chin.

"Let go of my friend," Lucius hissed.

Pete snapped his head to Lucius and released his grip on Chris's shirt. Coughing and shaking, Chris staggered backward.

"You filthy little forest rat," Bishop spat.

He took a step toward Lucius as if to strike him and the Hensleyville Eagles let out a collective gasp. But before Pete could react, Lucius raced around him with more energy than any of them had ever seen. Sprinting to the edge of the campsite, he scrambled up the rounded boulder and stood atop it. Then he turned toward the lake and stared down at the raging man.

"You're finished here, Cady. You're out of the Eagles." Pete jabbed his finger toward the boy, but Lucius looked right through him. "You're crazy as a bedbug just like your loony old man and your no-good mother who walked out on him."

What happened next will never be explained. A blanket of clouds boiled from the clear blue sky, materializing out of nowhere, as if from a magician's hat. A shimmering haze of energy enveloped Lucius Cady, the rock he stood upon, the ground beneath it. An electric hum buzzed like an angry swarm of bees. Pete Bishop looked anxiously toward the sky, and as he did so, an angry bolt shot from the inky blackness. The campsite lit with white heat and the acrid smell of sulphur filled the air. The ground shook, the sky rumbled, the explosion pained the ears of the Hensleyville Eagles. And when their eyes recovered from the flash, the blackened body of Pete Bishop lay smoking on the ground.

7

AT THE MAYOR'S suggestion, the flag over Town Hall flew at half staff although there were those who silently questioned the symbolism. After all, the crowd at Gilly's agreed, Pete Bishop wasn't exactly a war hero, far from it, and his untimely demise, though dramatic in execution, didn't rank with the Challenger explosion or the Mid-East hostage killings. But Mayor Ernest Gumm had few opportunities to make independent decisions so, for the most part, the townsfolk saw no great harm in allowing his patriotic display of grief. It was true that Pete Bishop wouldn't have won any popularity contests but he *was* one of their own, one of the twenty-nine hundred and some odd souls who made the little town of Hensleyville a fine place to live and work.

It was almost noon but grey as dusk and a hint of early fall invaded the summer clime. Across the street from Town Hall, Gilly's was enjoying a better than average Saturday morning as the morbid, the curious, and the just plain thirsty wrote Pete's obit and clucked sympathetically.

"Ah heard he was dang near fried up lak a piece of scrapple forgot in a fry pan."

Timmy Gillespie wrinkled his brow at the grizzled old farmer and slid a shot of bourbon and a short beer across the polished bar.

"It was lak God almighty done struck him down daid." He shook his head and said "tsk, tsk," then he threw the shot in his mouth and washed it down with the beer, leaving a foamy moustache on his weather-beaten lip.

A strapping man in overalls and a blue cap extolling the virtues of organic fertilizer chuckled at the farmer's vivid description. "You just went and spoiled my appetite for scrapple, Caleb."

Across the street, in the Explorer Room of the Town Hall, the topic of conversation was similar though much less colorful. About forty-five townspeople showed up for the hastily called meeting including the parents of the boys who were on the campout, all except Festus Cady, and no one was particularly surprised by his absence. Scott Stein's parents sat near the front, looking conspicuously out of place in their carefully selected ensembles. Ben Littlejohn in crisp police chief's attire sat beside them. Virgil Fenner wore dirty overalls with frayed straps over a Penn State sweatshirt that he had won arm wrestling in Gilly's.

The small gathering milled about drinking coffee and hot cider provided by Ernest Gumm's mousy wife. "It's just terrible about poor Mr. Bishop," she lamented while drawing a steamy cup for Lenny Brothers's father. He accepted the coffee, smiled indulgently, and returned to his seat in the middle of the room.

Sharp-eyed and grey, Father James O'Connor from St. Martin's and Pastor Mallory Whitney, wispy and balding, from First Methodist sat in the rear of the room sipping cider and speaking of the tragedy in hushed tones while a gaggle of younger men lounged near the side door, chuckling over a joke that would have little meaning to anyone not familiar with animal husbandry.

Dr. John Logan checked the street and the anteroom for stragglers. Seeing none, he mounted the stage and approached the wooden podium. He tapped it with the earpiece from his glasses and every head spun in his direction.

"I think everybody's here," the doctor began, checking his watch and seeing that it was already two minutes past the noon starting time. Folks were punctual in Hensleyville.

"As everyone knows," he said while fiddling nervously with

the glasses, "we've had a tragedy. Pete Bishop was killed by lightning while on a camping trip with the boys' club."

As he spoke, the townspeople crept self-consciously to their seats, nodding silent apologies as they passed in front of their neighbors. The people of Hensleyville had high regard for their doctor. It was through his tireless efforts a decade earlier that Memorial Hospital was built so they could now stay close to home for all but the most serious of ailments. The small hospital also brought extra business to the six-unit motel that Minnie Frick ran and the diner and flower shop also benefited.

Dr. John Logan was just shy of sixty but he looked younger. Curly black hair sprinkled with grey framed a swarthy face and a pair of eyes that danced and laughed did as much to ease his patients' suffering as did his professional ministrations. As he looked over the podium at his friends and neighbors, he realized how dependent they were on his skills and wisdom. It humbled him and made him feel deeply responsible but it was also a good feeling and he vowed to live up to their expectations. Three people had contacted him since Pete Bishop's death, each independently suggesting that the town could use his counsel. It wasn't so much Pete's death that bothered them. It was the effect on the children who had witnessed it. Hensleyville was a small town, a close-knit town where everyone watched out for their neighbor so they weren't just seven kids who witnessed Pete's sizzling death. They were "their kids" and now the town wanted Dr. Logan's sage advice. He smiled a pixielike grin at Kathryn Rogers. She smiled back and gave Woody Lockwood's hand a gentle squeeze.

"A few of you have asked that we have this meeting because there seems to be some concern about how this tragedy might affect the boys. Will they have troubled sleep? Will they feel guilty? Will they withdraw? Will they develop unreasonable fears of storms?"

Close to the podium, Scott Stein's mother winced as Logan checked off the litany of potential problems. Dr. Logan caught her eye and flashed a comforting smile.

"The answer to each of these questions," he said with mind-easing assurance, "is no."

The Explorer Room itself seemed to breathe an audible sigh of relief.

"But I understand your concern," he continued. "The newspapers and the TV are full of stories about maladjusted children who are influenced by traumatic events such as Pete Bishop's death. But one thing is important to remember." He scanned the audience and made fleeting eye contact with many of them. "In Hensleyville, we're not dealing with a bunch of neurotic city kids who pass out at the sight of blood. I don't think there's a boy in town, farm family or not, who hasn't birthed a calf, castrated a steer, or slaughtered something or other."

The room nodded its collective agreement.

"There's a whole new industry being born in the cities," Logan said with a wry smile. "Some people call it mind medicine, others call it psychobabble. The more that I read about it, the more I'm convinced that it's the doctors themselves who are creating the disease."

"That's the truth all right," Elmer Partridge agreed, but then no one particularly cared what Elmer Partridge thought.

"My opinion isn't based on scientific research," Logan warned, "but I think the simple truth is that our kids are better equipped to handle this kind of tragedy. You folks saw to that in the way you brought them up."

It was exactly the right thing to say and the assembled townspeople and parents felt good about themselves and less concerned about their children's mental state.

"But then again, I'm only a simple country doctor," he said with an impish grin. "So if any of you do notice the kids having any kind of problem, let's get together and have a chat about it."

"Having a chat about it" was Loganese for making an appointment and visiting him at his office at Memorial. It was all part of his soothing bedside manner. The doctor went on to describe some of the posttrauma symptoms that his city cousins associated with the type of shock that the Eagles experienced and explained that it could be days or even weeks before any such symptom showed itself, but his tone convinced the audience that there was no need for concern.

"Have any of the kids exhibited any kind of unusual behavior?" he asked.

Woody Lockwood sat next to Kathryn Rogers, their knees touching lightly. He raised his hand like a schoolboy and the doctor nodded in his direction. Woody stood and the folding wooden chair scraped noisily.

"Dr. Logan, Chris and I spoke about it last night."

Woody Lockwood was an attorney with an office in York, but he chose the simpler life in Hensleyville and accepted the long commute as the price one had to pay for tranquillity. Widowed for the past five years, he considered the town and its code of ethics as an acceptable substitute parent and this gave him peace of mind. Not that he was totally without words of child-raising advice. Kathryn Rogers, the principal of the Hensleyville Elementary School, was always on call to lend a sympathetic ear or to offer the fruits of her maternal instinct. Some of the older folks smiled at each other when they saw the two together, nodding silently as if biting back a secret.

Woody was in his early thirties, prematurely grey with a wistful look and a soft voice that created an aura of pleasant dignity. Although he was one of the town's wealthier citizens, he didn't flaunt his money, and like his son Chris, he was accepted by his friends and neighbors as somewhat of a reluctant leader. When he stood to speak, they all looked in his direction.

"Chris was upset but no more than I would expect him to be under the circumstances," Woody told the audience. "He was pretty matter-of-fact when he described what happened. He said it all happened so fast that nobody really had time to react. Apparently Pete Bishop was chewing Chris and the Cady boy out for some breach of campout regulation." He swept his gaze around the room. "I never did get the full story on that. And the next thing he knew, a bolt of lightning shot out of a freak thundercloud. It killed Pete instantly."

"How did Chris sleep last night?" the doctor asked.

"Fine as far as I know," Woody replied. "He's sad about Pete Bishop of course, but like you said, Doctor, these boys are pretty well adjusted. They can handle it."

"I heard somethin' different."

Heads spun toward the rear of the room where Virgil Fenner stood with his beefy arms crossed and resting on his bulging stomach.

"What did you hear, Virgil?" Dr. Logan asked.

Virgil wore the sneer of one privileged to very confidential information. "I heard that the Cady kid did somethin' to make it happen."

The few heads that hadn't turned by this time joined the others to stare at Virgil with expressions ranging from amusement to anger.

"Wally told me that the Cady kid gave Bishop something like the evil eye. He said poor ol' Pete glowed like a lightning bug right before he got struck down."

John Logan bit back a smile. Twenty-four hours earlier Virgil Fenner wouldn't have pissed on Pete Bishop if the man was on fire and all of a sudden he's "poor ol' Pete." A tough way to make friends, Logan thought.

"I'm not sure that I get your drift, Virgil," the doctor said, although he was afraid that he did.

"Like hell you don't," Fenner said loudly, and the minister's wife winced and touched her fingers to her lips. "All I'm sayin' is what people been whisperin' all along. There's somethin' funny about them Cadys. Old Festus slinks around like a scarecrow when you see him at all. Hell," Fenner accused, "he ain't even here today."

Heads turned and nodded.

"And that kid of his ain't right neither." Virgil tapped his temple. "Tetched if you ask me. Ain't heard him say two words back to back in his life."

"Dr. Logan." Woody Lockwood shot from his chair, a flush of crimson coloring his face. "Doctor, I think this kind of talk has gone far enough. One of the things that makes Hensleyville such a fine place to live is the way folks help each other out when the need's there and mind their business the rest of the time." He turned and glared at Virgil Fenner. "If I recall, this meeting was called to talk about ways to help our kids, not to make unfounded accusations."

A smattering of applause greeted his speech.

"I don't need no smart-ass lawyer tellin' me what I can say,"

Virgil seethed. "As far as I'm concerned them Cadys can just go to—"

"Fenner." Ben Littlejohn's shout cracked the air like a rifle shot. The police chief rose in the front row and spun to the rear. His gaze burned like lasers over the heads of the startled gathering. "If you have a complaint to make, Fenner, you bring it to me in my office and you sign an affidavit to that effect. Otherwise you keep your big mouth shut, you hear."

Big and loud as he was, Virgil Fenner knew better than to raise the hackles of the chief of police. Even though Ben was fifteen years older and eighty pounds lighter, Virgil knew that the policeman would have him down on his knees screaming for mercy with his wrist twisted behind his back and the chief's finger on a pressure point on his neck.

It had happened before. Twice.

To salvage a little dignity, Fenner glared at the chief as long as he dared before reluctantly dropping back onto his chair.

The confrontation over, the audience turned back to the doctor as if nothing unusual had happened. People minded their own business in Hensleyville.

"Dr. Logan."

Kathryn Rogers raised her hand daintily and the doctor acknowledged her with a grateful smile. Count on the school marm to get the meeting back on track.

"If you think it would be a good idea, John, I can schedule some activities at the school for the boys in the club. If there is any sort of a problem, that might help them take their minds off it."

"Thanks, Kathryn. That's not a bad idea."

Another hand went up—the chief of police.

"Ben," the doctor acknowledged.

Ben Littlejohn stood and faced the gathering. "I think we all agree that Pete Bishop did a fine service to the town when he organized the Eagles and I think it would be a shame to see the club break up due to Pete's unfortunate death. If nobody has any objections, I'd like to volunteer to take over the running of the club." He smiled sheepishly and it drew a thousand laugh lines throughout his ruddy face. "With a little help from a few of the parents of course."

"Hear, hear," Scott Stein's father shouted in approval.

The rest of the parents, except Virgil Fenner, nodded in agreement.

Dr. Logan was pleased with the positive turn of the meeting. "I'm sure that motion won't even need a vote, Ben."

"Well you can count my kid out," Virgil Fenner grumbled, loud enough for those seated nearby but too low for the police chief to hear.

There were a few more questions or suggestions. In a motion of misguided respect for the dead, Elmer Partridge suggested that the Eagles be renamed the Bishops but Father O'Connor and Pastor Whitney led the opposition to that. Lenny Brothers's father thought that it would be a good idea for the boys to go on another campout as soon as possible and Ben agreed and volunteered to organize it. Emma Guilden suggested a special day at the library for the boys and no one had the heart to veto her idea. After a few more minutes, the comments fizzled out.

Logan tucked his glasses in his pocket and smiled pleasantly at his friends and neighbors. "Well, unless somebody else has a question—"

In the middle of the sentence, one of the double doors to the Explorer Room burst open and crashed against the wall.

"Mom, Dad, something's the matter with Jeff."

Little Teddy Zack stood in the doorway, his tiny voice trembling, his eyes searching wildly for his parents. His hands were cupped in front of him as if holding a treasure.

"What is it, honey?" Lorna Zack was out of her chair in an instant and kneeling in front of the sandy-haired first grader.

Tears welled up in his eyes. "Jeff scared me, Mommy. He's saying scary things and he's hollerin' bad words."

Lorna Zack turned worried eyes at her husband who stood by her side. "What kind of scary things?" Jeff's father asked.

Teddy sniffled and his angel lips quivered. "Things about zombies."

Bill Zack smiled indulgently and laid a comforting hand on

the boy's shaking shoulder. Glancing at the attentive audience, he rolled his eyes with a sheepish grin. "You go back home, Teddy, and you tell that big brother of yours to stop scaring you." Then he noticed the boy's cupped hands. "What do you have there, Teddy?"

A new wave of tears broke out in force and streaked down the boy's soft cheeks. "It's—it's something Jeff found right before he started being scary."

Bill Zack looked at the boy's small hands, expecting him to display the hidden object, but Teddy only turned up the flow of tears and trembled more violently. As his wife watched, Bill took the boy's hands in his own and gently peeled back the pudgy fingers.

With a sharp intake of breath, Lorna Zack put her hands to her mouth. Bill Zack's stomach flipped and he jerked his hands away. The startled first grader flinched and the object slipped from his hands.

Amanda Mellon, who was sitting closest to the door, stifled a scream and slumped in her chair, her heart beating wildly in her withered old chest.

"Jesus H. Christ," Billy Harman's father said with a shudder as the eyeball bounced once on the floor before rocking to a stop. It stared grotesquely at the ceiling, a nickel-sized pupil in a veiny cue ball trailing gory tendrils of nerves and muscles.

The little boy choked and sobbed. "I think this is what made Jeff say the scary things. He—he started doing it right after he found it."

"Where did he find it?" Bill Zack asked, trying for the boy's sake to keep the anxiety from his own voice.

"It was on the doorstep," Teddy stammered.

Ben Littlejohn came out of his chair and knelt beside the boy, studying the eyeball as he patted Teddy's back. "It's from some kind of animal," he said with obvious relief. "Maybe from a sheep."

Still trembling from the shock, Lorna Zack breathed deeply and put her arms around the boy and pulled him close. "You go home now, Teddy," she said in a quaking voice. "Wash your hands and tell your brother to behave himself."

The boy gulped and stared into his mother's eyes. "I can't," he sobbed. "I'm afraid."

"Why?" she asked patiently.

"Be-because he's—he's too scary. He's lying on the floor and kicking his feet and—and funny stuff's coming out of his mouth."

8

"YOU HURRY ON home. I'll take care of Teddy." Kathryn
Rogers gathered the frightened boy in her arms as his parents
and Dr. Logan hurried through the door. Before they even
reached the street, Ben Littlejohn managed to have his black
and white patrol car waiting on Main Street.

The Zacks' two-story frame house was less than five blocks
from Town Hall and Ben crunched to a stop at the curb before
any of them had a chance to speak. The house sat on a steep
rise on an elm-shaded street. It was separated from its
neighbors by wide side yards and a white picket fence that
wrapped it in a toothy grin.

But today the grin seemed ominous.

Two flights of concrete steps separated by a flat landing led
to the front door that stood wide open, evidence of Teddy
Zack's hasty departure. With the parents in the lead, Dr. Logan
next, and the police chief at the rear, the worried party raced up
the steps.

Even before they reached the open door, they were struck by
the stench. It was as if the house had devoured rancid meat and
greeted its owners with fetid breath. Lorna Zack stopped in her
tracks and gagged. Then, as suddenly as it hit them, the smell
was gone. Bill glanced at his wife with fear-filled eyes, then
rushed past her into the house.

"Oh, my God."

The living room looked like the aftermath of a small

cyclone. Coffee and end tables were upended, lamps were smashed on the floor, pictures and mirrors were shattered, their crystal shards glowing like gemstones through the thick pile of the carpet. The sofa lay on its back with its legs thrust out like a bloated bovine. The day was warm but the house was cold and a cloud of breath floated from Bill Zack's lips as he shouted.

"Jeff, Jeff, are you OK?" He looked wildly about. "Where are you?"

The response sounded like the throaty purr of a giant jungle cat, one that gradually rose in pitch—a rumble, a grunt, a thundering squawk, finally the mad giggle of a thousand hyenas pounding his ears and stabbing him with a cold finger of fear.

The smell returned.

"Jeff. For God's sake, where are you?"

Maniacal laughter, like the cackle of brew-stirring witches, echoed from the floor above.

"Upstairs," Ben Littlejohn said as he pushed in front of the panic-stricken parents. Shoving aside an overturned chair he stamped up the carpeted stairs. Ben looked to the left, into the pale green master bedroom, as fresh and neat as Lorna Zack herself. Another bedroom, Teddy's, blue and gold with teddy bear and baseball glove atop a messy bed. To the right the third bedroom with the door tightly closed, a DO NOT DISTURB sign tacked at eye level. Ben grabbed the doorknob and recoiled. It was as cold as the handle of a grave digger's shovel in January. Bill Zack was at the chief's side, Lorna and the doctor close behind. Ben glared over his shoulder and saw the fear and trust in the young man's face. He twisted the knob and pushed open the door.

Jeff Zack lay in the center of his unmade bed, his legs rigid, his arms held stiffly at his sides. He was nude and sweating in the chilled room. His skin was chalk white, his eyes staring blankly at the ceiling. His mouth was gaping and twisted in a silent wail.

Lorna clutched her throat, recovered, and raced to the side of the bed. Kneeling, she gripped her son's wrist, wincing at the clammy coolness. Dr. Logan hurried to the other side of the bed and did the same but with more professional purpose. Counting the beats, he looked through bifocals at the pulsing hand of his Timex. Nodding noncommittally, he lowered Jeff's hand. With a penlight the doctor probed the pupil of the boy's eye, and nodded once again before tucking the light back into his shirt pocket.

"Let's get an ambulance," he said without looking up, and Ben Littlejohn turned and pounded down the steps.

Lorna Zack was at the edge of hysteria and Bill laid a firm hand on her shoulder. He looked worriedly at his son, then at the doctor. "What is it?" he asked.

The doctor's was a small-town country practice that dealt in the main with unsophisticated patients and their simple diseases. However, Logan read the new medical journals regularly and traveled to seminars from Boston to Washington, D.C., to keep up with the exotic new diseases and their equally exotic cures. But he had no simple answer to Bill Zack's question.

"I don't know, Bill," he answered honestly. "I want to get him over to Memorial right away where I can run some tests."

Skin cold and clammy, extremities rigid, heart beating rapidly, pupils dilated.

Logan looked up and down Jeff's cool body to check the color of his fingers and toes, noticing as he did the unmistakable sign of sexual arousal. Jeff's parents also stared in embarrassment and disbelief.

"Ha, ha, ha, ha, ha, ha . . ."

With dead eyes still staring blankly, a sickly grin split Jeff Zack's face, matching the hideous cackle that left his lips.

"Ha, ha, ha, ha, ha, ha, ha, ha, ha."

Suddenly his eyes came into focus. They began to dart back and forth from Lorna to Bill to the doctor and back again. Around and around the room they flew, flicking from one frightened face to the next. His body was still stiff and rigid, cold and clammy, but his face was alive, eyes burning like nail heads as they spun about the room.

Then he quivered.

From head to toe, his body shook in tiny tremors, as if electrodes had passed a current through his moist skin. His eyes snapped shut and a shriek left his lips that filled the room with the stench of death. Lorna Zack felt the room begin to spin. When she watched her little boy spurt in sexual relief she closed her eyes and sank to the floor.

Lorna made the ride to Memorial Hospital in thankful oblivion. She had almost recovered by the time Jeff was settled comfortably in a private room. Under the critical eye of the chief of police and Dr. Logan, the hospital's founder, the bureaucracy of admissions had been reduced to a hurried nod of the head, with the boy resting between the clean white sheets in room 514 within twelve minutes of Ben Littlejohn's urgent call.

Lorna slumped wearily in a soft leather chair in the corner of the room. Bill sat in a hard chair at his son's side, head in hands, palms massaging his aching temples. Dr. Logan bent over the boy, holding a stethoscope to his damp chest. A starchy young nurse waited patiently at the foot of the bed with the paraphernalia needed to take a blood sample. The early afternoon sun slanted in the windows, lending a gayness to the room that went unnoticed by its occupants.

"Is it serious?" Bill Zack asked, his voice resigned to a reply that he didn't want to hear.

The doctor straightened and pulled the stethoscope from his ears. Motioning to the nurse to begin her job, he stepped away from the bed and leaned against the window ledge. "I wish I knew, Bill. His signs are a little lower than I'd like. I wouldn't call them weak and they're certainly not critical. But it's curious. Some of Jeff's symptoms point to shock, others don't."

"What do they point to?" Bill asked.

The doctor let his eyes drop to the pale form of young Jeff Zack, then he raised them to the worried father. They were filled with sympathy and understanding. He shook his head slowly. "I don't know, Bill. Let's wait until we see some test results. Then we'll know—"

Without warning, the rank stench of death that they encountered at the Zack house descended once again on the sterile hospital room, carrying in its wake a blast of icy air and a palpable wave of fear. Lorna felt her stomach tumble. The nurse, needle poised, gasped and took a hurried step away from the bed. The boy on the bed clenched and unclenched his fists and his chest rose and fell with each labored breath. A low moan escaped his lips and his sleeping face twisted into a mask of terror. Jeff's eyes snapped open and gazed blankly at the ceiling.

"Don't—let—them—get—me." The words dribbled from the boy's fevered lips.

Dr. Logan stepped back to the side of the bed and laid a soothing hand on Jeff's smooth arm. It felt like the bloated belly of a dead fish.

"Don't—let—them—touch—me."

"He's hallucinating," the doctor said.

Bill Zack stepped to the other side of the bed. Gripping the side rails with both hands, he looked down anxiously at his troubled son. "Can't you do something, John? He looks so—so frightened."

Dr. Logan turned to the nurse who hovered uncertainly beside him. "Get two milligrams of Haldol IM," he ordered.

She nodded and hurried gratefully from the room.

"Oh, God, no. No, don't, don't. Leave me alone. Don't touch me." Another long, low moan escaped Jeff's lips and his breath reeked of spoiled meat.

The doctor wrinkled his nose involuntarily. "What do you see, son?" he asked softly. As he spoke, he gave Jeff's clammy arm a gentle squeeze.

The boy's eyes met his, a slight glimmer of recognition lending a transient spark.

"Zombies, zombies, zombies, zombies, zombies."

The words buzzed from his mouth, tumbling over each other in their frantic effort to escape.

"They want to kill me, kill me, kill me, kill me, kill me."

The litany trailed off, finally disappearing into the ambient white noise of the humming hospital.

"Why is he talking like that?" Lorna Zack leaned back in the soft leather chair, her face ashen, her fingers clutching like claws at the supple material.

The doctor glanced up sympathetically but offered no explanation. The next instant his own heartbeat was frozen in his chest as the boy's scream of pain assaulted the ears of everyone on the entire fifth floor. Beads of icy sweat bubbled on Jeff's forehead. His eyes bulged from his head as if pressured from behind. A fowllike cackle resonated from deep within Jeff's chest and his tongue shot from his mouth and waved grotesquely at his shocked audience. With unmoving lips and his tongue still protruding, a flow of obscenities rumbled from Jeff Zack's mouth. In a deep, unholy voice, like a record on a dragging turntable, the foul suggestions sent his mother to tears and reddened the ears of his father and Dr. Logan. In unmistakable response to his own sexual suggestions, his sheet rose in the center like a pup tent and he gripped himself with both hands through the starchy whiteness.

"Oh, my God," Lorna moaned and her husband stepped in front of her to block her view of her son's frantic manipulation.

"Don't—you—want—to—help—me?" the horrid voice asked, and without warning, his hand shot out and grasped his father's wrist in a viselike grip and pulled it to the throbbing bulge.

"No," Bill Zack shrieked and he tried to pull away, but in a fist like iron, his young son rubbed his father's hand against himself and breathed a fetid sigh of ecstasy.

"Hurry," Dr. Logan cried as the nurse reappeared in the doorway.

With trembling hands, the doctor took the hypodermic needle from the tray. Lorna Zack sobbed and choked. Her husband pulled frantically at his son's unyielding grasp. Jeff Zack's face split in a grin of toothy satisfaction as the sheet above his father's hand darkened. Dr. Logan plunged the needle into the boy's damp shoulder.

Bill and Lorna Zack walked down the corridor leading to the hospital parking lot entrance, hand in hand, heads bowed in grief. Dr. Logan walked on Lorna's other side, trying without success to think of something comforting to tell the distraught couple. The hall was long and colorless and it reeked of the clean yet offensive smell of early death and restored health. It was quiet except for the hum of a generator and the click of Lorna's heels.

"Why?" she murmured and she seemed to hesitate. Dr. Logan quickly grabbed her arm to steady her. She turned to him and tried to smile. "I'm all right, John."

Lorna and Bill Zack were strong, like the town that nurtured them and like the neighbors who were ready to help. But like the town and the neighbors, they were at their best when confronted by an enemy that they knew. Crop blight, tick fever, rainless growing seasons—these were the kinds of inconveniences that stiffened the backbone of Hensleyville and its inhabitants. The tangible roadblocks to community health could be confronted and dealt with. Even on a personal level, the townspeople could deal with broken bones, crushed fingers, and the occasional drunken joyrides of farm boys with their tragic consequences. These were all the kinds of troubles that one grew to expect in a small town in the farm country in the rolling hills of Pennsylvania.

But problems of the mind didn't sit too well. Such fragile ailments were the highly publicized domain of the big city types, brought on no doubt by their own selfish demands for more and more. Bones could be set and mended. Tractors could always be repaired. Rainless fields could be irrigated.

But problems of the mind?

For these the people of Hensleyville had no one to turn to but the good Lord and their friend Dr. Logan, and at the moment, the doctor seemed able to offer the most help. John Logan wished that he felt the same confidence that he saw in the Zacks' eyes.

"I'm going to phone a colleague of mine who has offices in Harrisburg," he told them. "He's a specialist in these types of disorders."

Bill Zack shot him a worried glance. "What type of disorders?" he demanded.

Logan smiled uncomfortably and shook his head. "Nothing specific, Bill. Mental disorders, emotional problems, things like that."

When they reached the door that led to the parking lot, John Logan stopped. The Zacks looked at him hopefully but the doctor's expression offered no solace. "I'm also associated with a center in Philadelphia that might have some other ideas.

They're as up-to-date as can be. They've helped me in the past." He clapped Bill on the shoulder.

The seasoned doctor realized that he was rambling like a frightened intern, building baseless hope, yet he was at a total loss to explain the Zack boy's mental state. On top of the boy's bizarre behavior there was the biting cold and the horrible smell, neither of which had a rational explanation. He quickly dismissed the possibility of supernatural forces from his mind, focusing instead on the possible textbook explanations of Jeff's symptoms.

Shock, stroke, chemical imbalance, head trauma, seizure, pressure—these ailments and the multisyllabic medical terms that described them panned across the screen of the doctor's mind but no single explanation seemed to overlay the boy's apparent symptoms.

"We'll get to the bottom of this," he told them. He looked into the worried faces of the young couple whom he had known for years. Recalling Jeff Zack's simple delivery over a decade earlier and the parents' proud examination of their first child, the doctor smiled reflectively. "We'll get your boy back. Don't worry."

But John Logan was worried. He couldn't shake the chill of the hospital room or the unnatural stench of the boy's breath and his ears still rang with the haunting dirge of Jeff Zack's tortured voice.

"They want to kill me, kill me, kill me, kill me, kill me—"

He shuddered and Bill Zack sensed his discomfort. "We know you'll do your very best," Bill said, and John Logan had to smile at his patient's perception and his bedside manner. In a last gesture of confidence, Logan squeezed Lorna's hand before pushing open the door to the outside.

They heard the siren's faint scream as it careened around the corner of Gorman Street, and by the time it reached the hospital entrance, the wail stunned their ears with its strident message. Crunching to a stop at the Emergency Room entrance, the driver jumped from the van as the back doors swung open and a white-jacketed paramedic leapt to the warm tarmac. Simultaneously the swinging doors of the E.R. burst open and a pair of orderlies rolled a squeaking gurney to the back of the vehicle. Jason Eberhart, the resident on emergency-room duty, was at their side and he rushed ahead, taking an end of the stretcher as it was moved quickly but carefully from the ambulance.

"Excuse me a moment," John Logan said with a motion of his hand that told the Zacks to wait. He hurried across the blacktop, arriving as the cargo was being secured to the top of the gurney.

Hensleyville was a small town and one family's problem was another family's opportunity to help out, so in spite of their own concerns, Bill and Lorna Zack hurried toward the E.R. entrance in the doctor's wake.

"What's happened?" Dr. Logan asked the hovering resident.

Dr. Eberhart looked up quickly from the still form on the gurney. Recognizing the senior physician, he said, "A drowning unless we can shock some life back into him." Then he rushed ahead and the party disappeared into the yawning doors of the emergency-room entrance.

"What's the problem?" Bill Zack asked, arriving on the scene just as the doors swung shut.

"It looks like a drowning," the doctor answered.

"Who?" Lorna asked.

"I don't know," the doctor lied.

He couldn't bring himself to tell the Zacks that the body on the gurney was Lenny Brothers.

9

THE STRIDENT WAIL of sirens was little more than a fading memory, the sun had set within the undulating hills across the valley and Lenny Brothers's stiff body lay in a cool room at Memorial Hospital awaiting transportation to Stieglitz Funeral Home in Albertstown, just this side of York. It had been a sorrowful day in Hensleyville, one of the saddest in memory, and the town absorbed the pain according to its custom. The Ladies Auxiliary of the First Methodist Church, under the direction of Mrs. Mallory Whitney, was busy preparing an avalanche of salads and casseroles to feed the grief-stricken faces of the funeral attendees and to clog Natalie Brothers's freezer long after fresh blades of grass had sprouted over her son's cold coffin.

Anticipating mourners, Father O'Connor had left open the doors of St. Martin's where a handful of parishioners had stopped by to pray for the soul of young Lenny Brothers.

Clutches of neighbors clucked in gayly papered kitchens, on cool porches, and in the mellow darkness of Gilly's Tavern.

"A wading pool, can you believe that. They say it was a kid's wading pool. If that ain't the darnedest. Gimme another cold one will you, Gilly."

Timmy Gillespie dropped the dirty glass into the warm sink, pulled a fresh one from beneath the bar, and drew a long amber brew with a foamy cap. With a bar rag he swept a spot in front of his customer and slid the new glass in front of him.

"I heard the same thing," a voice concurred from the corner of the bar. "They found the boy lying facedown in six inches of water in a plastic wading pool. It was like he just laid down and sniffed up a lungful, but I heard that a person couldn't do that even if he wanted to."

"That's right," an authoritative voice said. "It's an instinct."

"And he was dressed," another patron droned. "It wasn't like he was trying to cool off or nothing like that. He had on jeans and a shirt. He even had his watch on. Seems to me if'n he was gonna try to do hisself in, he'd at leasta taken his watch off."

"Why?" another asked.

"Whole thing don't make no damn sense to me," the first beer drinker said with a sad shake of his head.

"Or me either. Some mighty strange things happening around here if you ask me."

Gilly ran a tray of drinks to two couples in a corner booth, then he ducked back under the bar. "I hear that Ben's called another meeting for tomorrow noon," he said to those at the bar. "Some of the kids' parents are pretty upset. First Pete Bishop gets killed, then the Zack boy gets his problem, and now the Brothers boy drowns."

"I don't blame them none," the customer said. He took a swig of beer and wiped the foamy moustache with the back of his hand. "If I had a kid on that campout, I'd be pretty shook up myself. They're dropping like goddamn flies."

For the second straight day, Town Hall buzzed with an undertone of anxiety. It was noon on Sunday, a time normally reserved for late worship, hearty brunch, or serious newspaper reading. Police Chief Ben Littlejohn's hastily called meeting changed the Sunday routine, bringing together the parents and children of the Hensleyville Eagles and a couple of dozen other interested neighbors. There was no cider but an urn of coffee bubbled into readiness in one corner of the Explorer Room. Woody Lockwood and Kathryn Rogers waited for its final gurgle, then drew two Styrofoam cups. Her hand trembled slightly as she brought the steaming brew to her lips.

"This is all so terrible," she said. "I couldn't sleep at all last night."

"I had a little trouble myself," Woody admitted.

She saw that he was watching her closely; that he sensed her fear and indecision. It made her feel weak and incapacitated, not how a small-town school principal should react in such a crisis. Small-town folks needed sturdy pillars to support their simple needs, reliable people like Dr. John Logan and Police Chief Ben Littlejohn. They filled their roles admirably as should the principal of the town's only elementary school, but Kathryn was riddled with doubt over her ability to carry her share.

Woody sensed her turmoil. He studied her worried face. Crisply chiseled features showed endearing traces of age. Ice-blue eyes, unchanged in the ten years since graduate school, wore tiny lines of worry like a symbol of her occupation much the same as the thick calluses on the hardened thumbs of a bricklayer. Her jet-black hair, now flecked with wisps of grey, framed her features like the curtain that draped the stage of the Explorer Room. Kathryn's was a face filled with doubt and Woody felt a stab of pity for the turmoil she must have felt. It wasn't easy, he suspected, for a single woman from the city to win the confidence of a small town full of traditional folks whose simple upbringing made them ask themselves why she wasn't home baking bread and mending jeans and raising her own children instead of theirs. Not that they weren't willing to give her all of the cooperation and respect that went with the position. They gave that and more without a grudge. They just had to draw it from a deeper well. Woody Lockwood never discussed this with her, sensing incorrectly that it was something she'd rather deal with alone.

"I wonder how the Zack boy is," Kathryn said. "Bill and Lorna must be frantic."

Woody nodded sympathetically and stepped aside as others elbowed their way to the coffee urn.

"It's twelve o'clock," Littlejohn's voice boomed. "How 'bout if we get this meeting under way."

The police chief stood on the elevated stage looking quite handsome, Kathryn thought, in a rough-hewn sort of way. His tan uniform was pressed and crisp and his silver badge shone like a jewel on his breast pocket. The firm set of his jaw established the tone of the meeting.

With Chris between them, Woody Lockwood and Kathryn Rogers sat near the front, to Littlejohn's left as he poised at the podium in the center of the stage. The folding chairs were set up eight across with an aisle running down the middle and the rest of the campers, their parents, the curious, and the concerned filed quickly to their seats. Wally Fenner and Billy Harman stood near their parents at the back of the hall and were among the last to be seated. Noticeably absent were the parents of Jeff Zack and Lenny Brothers.

Ben Littlejohn cleared his throat and the assembly settled into an expectant hush. "I'm sure I don't have to tell you what's happened," he began, "but I guess it's only right to start the meeting by bringing everybody up-to-date."

Heads nodded slightly and the audience shifted in their chairs and crossed their arms and legs into more comfortable listening positions.

"We've had a few sad days," he said, grim-faced. "On Friday, Pete Bishop was killed by lightning while camping with some of our boys. Yesterday while Dr. Logan was chatting about the tragedy with the parents of the boys, we learned that young Jeff Zack was suddenly taken ill."

He met the doctor's eye in confirmation of the fact and John Logan stared back gravely.

"And later yesterday afternoon, the Brothers boy somehow drowned in a little wading pool."

Heads bobbed sympathetically and the mayor's wife touched a lacy handkerchief to the corner of her eye.

The police chief looked around the room and was taken by the intensity of his neighbors' grief. "Like all of us, I'm saddened by each one of these events. We all hurt for the Brotherses and the Zacks and I'm sure that we're all praying hard for them."

More heads greeted the call to sympathy for the two missing sets of parents.

"Late yesterday," he continued, "the mayor's office got a number of phone calls suggesting that it would be a good idea for the parents to get back together today to talk to me about these tragedies." He scratched his head and looked questioningly around the room. "I'm not sure why some of you think that these unfortunate events are police matters, but if it will do some good, I'm all for it."

With eyes opened wide in a questioning stare, Ben looked toward John Logan who sat in the front row and the doctor stood and turned to face the rows of townspeople. "I guess that I'm not too certain either why some of you felt this meeting was necessary. But," he added quickly, "I'm sure that Ben and the mayor, Father O'Connor, Pastor Whitney, myself"—he searched the room for other community leaders—"Kathryn Rogers, Woody Lockwood, all of us will try to discuss any concerns you might have."

A timid hand inched overhead in the middle of the room.

"Do you have a question, Mildred?" the doctor asked the handsome grey-haired woman.

"It's about the Zack boy," she answered hesitantly. "I don't mean to pry but I'm worried for him and feel badly for Lorna and Bill."

The doctor waited for her question. "Yes?" he prodded.

"Well," she continued, looking at the floor as she spoke, "I heard that the poor boy's having some fearsome spells. I'm just wondering if we know what it is that ails him."

Ben Littlejohn sensed the doctor's dilemma and tried to intervene. "Now, Mildred, you might be asking for some confidential medical information that Dr. Logan's not permitted to divulge."

Logan gave the police chief a small smile of thanks. "Ben's partly right, Mildred," he said apologetically. "But I can tell you this much, the boy did suffer from some kind of hallucinations and we're trying our best to find out what's causing them."

Mildred smiled and curtsied imperceptibly before sinking back into her chair.

Another hand went up, big and calloused and stained with the permanent streaks of a half a century in the fields. "I agree with Ben," the farmer said. "The town and some of its families have had a terrible run of luck the last coupla days but we gotta move on."

The man stood ponderously and looked at the chief. In blue overalls and plaid workshirt, the old farmer exemplified the sturdy tradition that was the glue of the small community.

"Folks been living and dying since way back in the Garden of Eden and I suspect they're gonna keep it up that way for some time to come."

Amid his neighbors' puzzled frowns, the farmer nodded gravely at the sagacity of his own words and settled back in his seat.

"Thanks, Eb," the chief said, not sure of the farmer's point and not caring to pursue it.

A sudden shout startled the listeners. "Littlejohn!"

Virgil Fenner rose to his feet without waiting to be acknowledged. Hooking his thumbs in the belt of his baggy jeans he stared hard at the man on the stage. "Why don't you tell us all about what they found in the plastic pool with the Brothers boy?"

Genuinely confused, Ben Littlejohn met Fenner's accusing gaze. "What are you talking about, Virgil?"

"The ear, Ben. Why don't you tell everybody about the ear?" Virgil Fenner crossed his heavy arms across his chest and curled his lips sarcastically. "Unless you don't think we oughta know," he continued in a mocking tone.

Heads that had been turned toward the questioner now swiveled back to the front of the room.

Awareness suddenly lit the chief's face. "You mean the goat ear?" he asked, slightly astonished that the trivial bit of information should be of interest to anyone. "Yes," he admitted with some hesitation. "We found a goat's ear in the pool when we went back to investigate. Why do you ask?"

Fenner grinned smugly. "Don't you think it's a little strange," he said. "First the little Zack boy comes running in here yesterday with a goat's eye and then something strange happens to his brother. Next day you find this goat's ear in the pool where the Brothers kid drowned." Smirking, he waited for Ben's response.

The chief's forehead creased confusedly. "I don't know

what you're driving at, Virgil. In the first place, whoever said that the eye was from a goat? We didn't even look into that as far as I know."

"Maybe you ought to," Fenner said.

Ben Littlejohn stared icicles across the room. "Virgil, if you have something to say why don't you let the rest of us in on it. I don't think anybody here wants to play games with you. Two people are dead and another's very sick and you seem to think that there's something sinister going on."

"That's right, Littlejohn. Something sinister," he echoed.

From near the front of the room, Woody Lockwood rose from his seat and turned to the rear. "Fenner," he said disgustedly, "Ben's too polite to say this so I'll say it for him. Most of us are fed up with your mysterious accusations. If you have something to say, please say it. If not, why don't you just sit down and let the meeting go on."

Grunts of approval and a timid clatter of applause greeted Woody's challenge and most of the men in the room, some of the women too, wished that they'd had the nerve to stand up to the town bully the way the lawyer did. Woody sat down and turned his attention back to the front.

"I guess I'm not too surprised you feel that way," Fenner mocked. "After all, I hear that your kid and the Cady kid are pretty chummy."

Woody started to push himself up once again but a gesture from Ben Littlejohn restrained him. With a look of exasperation, the chief slowly shook his head.

"OK, Virgil. We'll get nowhere until you have your say. Suppose you tell us exactly what you think is the problem."

With a look of triumph, the burly man strutted up the center aisle. Stopping in front of the podium he turned to the townspeople. "There were seven boys on that camping trip with poor Pete Bishop," he began. "One of 'em's dead, another's sick, and four of 'em are here today." He scanned the room and gestured with a grimy finger. "There's Wally back there and Billy Harman." He glanced to the front of the room. "And Scott Stein and Chris Lockwood." A hint of a sneer accompanied the last name. "That leaves one of the campers not accounted for." He made the statement as if it ranked with the discovery of the Dead Sea Scrolls.

"Lucius Cady," someone murmured.

"Damn right," Virgil said with a note of triumph. "The Cady kid ain't here and neither is his old man." He turned and looked up at Ben Littlejohn. "Do you know why the Cady kid ain't here, Littlejohn?" he challenged.

"I couldn't guess," Ben said with a heavy dose of sarcasm.

"Like hell you couldn't," Virgil accused. "He ain't here because he's the one who made all these things happen in the first place, that's why he ain't here and you damn well know it."

Virgil Fenner ignored the mumbles of dissent that rolled through the hall and he stared defiantly at the police chief, but Ben Littlejohn didn't take the bait. "Are you finished, Virgil?" he said evenly.

Virgil's ruddy cheeks flushed, and eyes bulging, he glowered at the lawman. "No, I ain't finished goddammit."

There were a few sharp intakes of breath from the townspeople.

"I ain't gonna be finished till you explain how that ear got in the wading pool."

The chief hovered between anger and exasperation. "You're dying to make a fool out of yourself, aren't you, Fenner? Why don't you just speed things up and tell us how *you* think it got there."

Ignoring the insult, Virgil turned to the room full of curious neighbors. With a glare at Woody Lockwood, he made his accusation. "The Cady kid made the lightning hit Pete Bishop. I don't know how but he did it," he admitted reluctantly. "He also made Jeff Zack go crazy and he made Lenny Brothers drown himself in the swimming pool."

Ben pursed his lips and nodded. "You have proof of this no doubt," he deadpanned.

"No, I ain't got no proof but that don't matter none. I didn't expect none of you to believe me." He looked at Woody Lockwood with disdain. "But when something else happens around here, don't say I didn't warn you."

A chair scraped on the hardwood and heads turned to Dr.

Logan. He was the only one in the room who had seen Jeff Zack's hallucinations in the hospital, who had felt the bitter cold and smelled the foulness. He listened to Virgil Fenner's accusations along with the others but couldn't quite dismiss them as the senseless prattle of the town malcontent. "What makes you think that something else is going to happen, Virgil?" he asked.

"The Cady kid's gonna try to get even," Fenner answered.

"Get even for what?"

Fenner shrugged with a hint of guilt. "A couple of the kids pulled a little prank on him at the campout. They stuck a goat's head in his tent. He didn't take the joke too good and he stomped outta camp. Took the goat's head with him. Ain't that right, Wally?"

"That's right, Pa," Wally called out with a smirk on his round face. "He took that old goat head and went stomping off into the woods. Didn't never come back to camp till breakfast time, but he didn't have the head no more."

Virgil Fenner nodded knowingly. "So where do you suppose the eye and the ear came from," he challenged the audience, and some of them exchanged worried glances. "And that ain't all that's funny," Virgil continued. "Wally," he called to the back of the room, "you tell 'em what Lenny Brothers said he was scared of."

"Drownin'," the boy called back. "He said that would be the worst way in the world to die."

Puzzled, the doctor asked, "Why would he say that?"

Wally snickered and leaned lazily against the wall.

Chris Lockwood raised his hand. "He did say that, Dr. Logan." The boy stood up and briefly explained the exchange of fears around the campfire. "That's what Lenny said he was afraid of," he concluded. "Drowning."

The doctor felt a chill and was afraid to ask the next question. "Do you remember what Jeff Zack said he was afraid of, Chris?"

The lawyer's son pondered for a few moments before answering. "I don't think that Jeff took it very seriously, Dr. Logan." The boy smiled shyly. "Jeff said that the worst way to die would be getting killed by zombies, but I think he was just kidding around."

John Logan felt his stomach do flip-flops and an icy chill ran down his spine.

With a look of victory in his eyes, Fenner turned back toward the podium and pointed his finger angrily at the police chief. "What more evidence do you need, Littlejohn? Are you gonna wait till something else happens before you get off your butt and do your job?"

Ben turned crimson and gripped the edge of the podium with white-knuckled fingers but he held on to his temper. "What are you suggesting that I do, Virgil?" he asked as calmly as he could manage.

"I'm sayin' that you oughta get yourself out to the Cady place and arrest that kid, that's what I'm sayin'."

Murmurs of agreement came from pockets of the audience.

"On what charges, Virgil? I have a good idea what your concept of the law is but civilized people tend to think differently than you."

The chief's temper was getting the best of him but Fenner dismissed the rebuke. He was enjoying this too much. The recent tragedies in the town, even the possibility that there would be more of the same, seemed insignificant to him. He had engineered a confrontation that he couldn't have imagined in his most satisfying daydreams. Virgil Fenner, town joke, had confronted Ben Littlejohn, his lifelong enemy, in front of a jury of his neighbors and Virgil could feel their sentiment shift in his favor.

"I don't care what charge you use, Littlejohn. Why don't you just invent something. You never had a problem trumpin' up charges against me before."

A few snickers rippled through the rows of folding chairs.

Arlen Stein waved his hand softly and Ben Littlejohn acknowledged him.

"Chief," he began apologetically, "I hear what you're saying and I know enough about the law to recognize your dilemma but much as I hate to say it, I think that Virgil has a point."

Scott's father did the books for most of the town's businesses and also did the taxes for most of Hensleyville's important citizens. He was soft-spoken when he spoke at all, but when he did, people usually listened. Ben Littlejohn would have preferred that Arlen hadn't chosen sides in this issue.

Looking at the chief, the accountant continued, "I'm not implying any wrongdoing on the part of the Cady boy, Ben. All I'm saying is that there is something strange going on and we have to get to the bottom of it." His son sat at his side and Arlen laid a protective hand on Scott's shoulder. "My boy was on that campout too." His eyes met Woody Lockwood's and a look of understanding passed between them.

"What would you have me do, Arlen?" the chief asked with a helpless shrug. "I can't go arresting people on this type of evidence." He shook his head angrily. "My God, I don't even like to talk about such a possibility at a public meeting."

Woody Lockwood stood and angled himself so he could see the police chief and most of the gathered townsfolk. "Ben's right," he said. "And I'm sure we don't want our chief of police trampling people's rights or breaking the law."

His statement received a mixed response.

"But I agree with Arlen too," Woody continued. "There's something unusual happening around here and we have to find out what it is."

"May I make a suggestion?"

All heads turned to the town's doctor.

Sensing some kind of breakthrough, Ben Littlejohn said with relief, "Please do, Doctor."

"Perhaps if I visit the Cadys and chat with Festus and his boy we'll learn something."

A puzzled expression crossed the chief's face. "I'm not against it, Doctor, but what could you hope to learn?"

"I wish that I knew," Logan admitted, "but it won't hurt to at least talk to them." He looked at Virgil Fenner and Arlen Stein. "A visit from the town doctor might also be a bit less threatening than a visit by the chief of police."

There seemed to be no disagreement.

"It might not be a bad idea for me to go with you," the lawyer said. He held up his hand defensively. "As a private citizen and a parent, not as a lawyer."

Dr. Logan looked at Woody Lockwood and smiled thankfully.

"And I," the school principal spoke up.

Woody cast a doubtful look at Kathryn Rogers.

"The boy's a student of mine," she reminded him.

"And he's a friend of mine," Chris Lockwood added. "I want to go too."

As the meeting broke up, most of the attendees felt pleased with the outcome. The day was still young and the doctor, principal, father, and son would plan to visit the Cadys later that afternoon. Ben Littlejohn felt powerless in the face of his neighbors' growing fear and was thankful for the help that was volunteered. John Logan tried to shake off the anxious stirrings of his own fear and wondered what was waiting in that forlorn shack in the woods. Virgil Fenner felt robbed of victory as the townsfolk reluctantly picked up his theme only to later turn their backs on him and listen to the doctor, the lawyer, the accountant.

In his muddled subconscious he vowed revenge.

10

Two hours after the town meeting broke up, Woody Lockwood made the circuit of Hensleyville in his station wagon to pick up Kathryn Rogers and Dr. Logan. Kathryn stepped lightly from the neat brick single where she lived with a black Lab named Licorice, a cat of questionable ancestry, and a white cockatoo. Chris held the car door for her as she slid in the back seat next to the doctor.

"What's happened to the sun?" she wondered aloud.

The day's earlier promise of brightness had been blanketed by a layer of rolling clouds that dulled the sun's brilliance and its warmth.

Kathryn wore a knit sweater over her beige blouse, and as was proper when visiting on Sunday, she wore a dark brown skirt in place of the slacks that would have been acceptable the day before. Her question, being rhetorical, was met with acknowledging grins but no answer.

The Cady place was in a stand of forest called Covey's Woods. It was less than four miles from the center of town in a rolling area that stretched as far as the eye could see alongside fertile farmlands. The area was crisscrossed with a spiderweb of nameless streams that roared in the spring and dried up like brittle filaments in the summer heat. A series of rickety wooden bridges forded the dry channels, barely wide enough for a single car. Woody slowed the station wagon as he approached one of them and he could feel the footprint of each ancient board as the tires rolled softly across.

"I love it out here," Kathryn remarked. "It's so peaceful and unspoiled."

Except for the winding gravel road and the occasional wooden bridge there was no evidence of the hand of modern man. The crunch of the tires blended with the gentle forest sounds and the mossy smell of nature's perfume drifted in the open windows. It should have been an idyllic journey but the specter of meeting Festus Cady dampened their mood.

"I think it's just up ahead a little bit," the doctor said, leaning forward and looking over Woody's shoulder.

None of the others had ever been to the Cady place, but Dr. Logan had visited it a few times when the boy was down with a strep infection. Having neither phone nor transportation, Festus had walked to town to report Lucius's condition and Dr. Logan had given him a prescription that Festus filled at the pharmacy before hiking back to Covey's Woods. Concerned, Dr. Logan had twice visited the boy to check on his condition. That had been almost ten years earlier, shortly after Mae Cady hiked to town with a cardboard suitcase, boarded a Trailways in front of the general store, never to be heard from again.

At Dr. Logan's direction, Woody glided to a stop along the side of the road and the four piled out.

"I'm pretty sure it's back there." The doctor indicated a beaten path, about four feet wide, that meandered through the trees before disappearing into a maze of green.

"How on earth did you ever find the place again?" Kathryn asked.

Logan smiled and shook his head. "Boy Scout training and a lot of luck," he admitted.

But the lightness of his answer didn't match their mood as the small group left the relative civilization of the gravel road and entered the well-trod path. Having the experience of his earlier visits, Dr. Logan led the way, followed closely by Chris and Kathryn Rogers. Woody Lockwood was a few paces behind Kathryn at the end of the short column.

The path was narrow, the trees ancient. Their overhanging branches laced together in a green canopy, blocking the light and turning the path into a damp and redolent tunnel that bent with two unnecessary turns before emerging into a clearing that was only slightly brighter.

"Oh, my goodness," Kathryn said sadly when the small structure came into view.

"It's not so bad," Chris said, feeling defensive for a reason he couldn't understand.

The house was square, a peeling box about twenty feet on a side that rested on a row of cinder blocks. The only feature that detracted from its stark cubism was a red brick chimney that poked from the sloping roofline, which fell at a subtle pitch toward the front of the house.

"I think it's kind of neat," he continued, taking in the rope swing that dangled from the limb of a leafy oak.

The yard was a weedy perimeter of perhaps fifteen feet that had been chopped, hacked, and beaten by thousands of footfalls but showed little other care. The group stood at the end of the path where it met the clearing, staring at the forlorn structure as one would look at a box that contained an unpleasant surprise.

"Look at what's over the top of the door," Woody said. "Isn't that a cross?"

"It looks like it. I don't recall that being there before," the doctor answered.

"The windows too," Chris said, slightly above a whisper. "There and there and there."

He pointed at each of the windows visible on the front of the house, one next to the closed front door and two spaced evenly above it. All were closed. All were covered by drawn shades. All had a small black cross nailed clumsily to the peeling yellow siding above them.

Kathryn hugged herself and shivered. "It's been a long time since I went for a stroll in the woods. I forgot how much of a temperature drop there is."

Woody put an arm around her shoulder and pulled her close. "It did get chilly," he agreed.

The doctor felt it also and it reminded him of another chill, one he had felt a day earlier.

"Shouldn't we knock?" Chris asked the hesitant adults.

Woody smiled sheepishly. "I guess we should."

Looking somewhat ludicrous in their Sunday finery, the four crossed the clearing and approached the front door. It was made of wood, thick and solid, protected from the forest elements by countless layers of white paint.

"They must have a very assertive dog," Woody tried the small joke as he pointed to the deep scratches in the lower half of the door. They had been covered by a fresh coat of paint.

"I hope it's tied up," Kathryn said and she hesitated a few steps from the door.

Woody rapped three times, straightened, and took a deep breath. The noise must have startled the myriad forest creatures because an unholy hush descended on the clearing. Until the lawyer's jarring knocks, they hadn't noticed the forest symphony. Only when the instruments were silenced was the music missed.

The absence of sound was unnerving and Woody felt as if the focus of the entire forest was on him and the small party. All of them waited stiffly with their eyes fixed on the metal doorknob, also freshly painted white.

The quiet of the clearing made it possible to hear the noises from within the house. There was no loud barking as they might have expected from the outside evidence, but they did hear a shuffling, an unhurried moving about, but the door remained closed. Woody stepped forward and prepared to knock again but he jumped back as the door suddenly swung inward. His mouth hung open as he stared at the cadaverous form of Festus Cady. The man filled the opening and Lucius stood at his side.

Festus was about as tall as the doorway, sturdy but narrow like the sun-starved trees around the house that stretched for skylight. His dark hair was slicked down except for an unruly patch at the crown that sprouted wildly. The face was drawn and ascetic, hollow cheeks and sunken eyes that made no attempt to hide the sadness behind them. Wrinkled blue jeans stopped far short of his shoe tops and the sleeves of a threadbare suit jacket stretched unsuccessfully for his wrists. A once-white shirt, buttoned to his bulging Adam's apple, completed the ensemble. He wore no tie.

Beside him, Lucius stood like a mannequin displaying a once-fine wardrobe. They were both dressed in their finest and the visitors were touched by the incongruity. Already elevated on the threshold, Festus towered over the four townspeople who looked up and tried to hide their surprise. Neither his lips nor his eyes spoke as he studied them with a bland look. Stepping forward hesitantly and extending his hand in greeting, the doctor finally spoke. "Hello, Mr. Cady. I'm Dr. Logan. I visited you years ago when your boy was sick."

It wasn't so much a statement, more a question seeking the man's recollection.

"I remember, Doctor." The voice was thin and surprisingly gentle. Hesitantly he took the doctor's hand in friendship.

Caught pleasantly off guard, Dr. Logan stammered slightly as he introduced his companions. When he mentioned Chris's name, a tiny spark glowed for a moment in Festus's wary eyes.

"You were kind to Lucius," he said simply, then he turned and stepped inside in a wordless invitation for them to enter.

The three adults exchanged curious glances, shrugged, and followed him into the house.

"Hi, Lucius," Chris said as he entered, and the slight boy smiled shyly and lowered his eyes.

The lower floor was a single open room, broken up only by two supporting posts that were positioned beneath the center joist of the second floor, a fact that was readily apparent because the ceiling was unfinished. A white porcelain sink stood against the wall to their right, next to a wood stove. To their left was a worn sofa surrounded by mismatched coffee and end tables. The back wall was dominated by a wide brick fireplace with a rough-hewn mantel. A picnic table with a pair of benches was placed in the very center of the room. When Festus closed the front door, the room was lit only by the dim glow that filtered through the drawn shades of the four windows. There was no evidence of electricity and the lingering smell of recently extinguished candles bit their nostrils. There was also another odor, vaguely familiar, acrid and spicy.

Incense!

The visitors' eyes were drawn to the picnic table in the center of the room and they took in the candles, the small glass dish leaking a wisp of aromatic smoke, the heavy Bible laid marked and open.

"I'm sorry if we've interrupted something, Mr. Cady," Dr. Logan began.

Festus stood quietly by the window. He didn't seem ill at ease, only patient. The doctor searched for words in the embarrassed silence. No one had been offered a seat. Festus probably never thought of it, being unused to either conversation or company.

"Mr. Cady," the doctor continued, "in light of some recent unfortunate events, I thought—we thought—that it would be a good idea if we could have a chat with you."

Before he could continue, Kathryn edged closer. "Maybe it would be all right for the boys to go outside and play while we talk," she suggested.

"Play?" Festus rolled the word over his tongue and his face grew melancholy, as if the word and the idea had been resurrected from an ancient grave. "Yes, yes. Let the children play," he said softly.

Kathryn assumed her school marm mantle. It came to her quite naturally. "Chris, Lucius." With a wave of her hand she ushered them to the door.

As he crossed the room, Lucius looked at his father queerly and a message passed between them, then Kathryn opened the door and they were gone.

Dr. Logan pushed back his sport coat and jammed his hands into his pants pockets. "Mr. Cady," he started again, "I'm sure you heard about Pete Bishop's unfortunate death during the boy's campout."

Festus nodded slightly without comment.

"Some of the parents got together at Town Hall to discuss it. They were concerned that witnessing such a tragedy might bother the boys, give them nightmares or other problems."

The absent look on Festus's face said absolutely nothing and didn't make the conversation any easier for the doctor.

"Yesterday there was another tragedy," Woody Lockwood broke in.

Festus's eyes shifted to the man who barely came to his chin.

"One of the boys who was with Lucius on the campout drowned," the lawyer said.

Festus Cady's sunken eyes dropped and a look of sadness flooded his gaunt features.

"Another of the boys is very sick," Logan added, and he noticed Festus's hands begin to twitch. "All of the other parents have had a chance to discuss these things, Mr. Cady. Since you haven't been to town since they happened, we thought it would be a good idea to fill you in."

Festus stood like a wilted scarecrow, eyes downcast, bony fingers nervously picking at the seam of his jeans. He raised his head and spoke, his face sad, his eyes filled with unshed tears. "I'll pray for them." A tear overflowed, ran down his cheek, and splattered on the rough floorboards.

"You don't seem surprised," Woody said, his brow furrowed in a curious frown.

"I know about the cruel thing that the other boys did to Lucius," the spindly giant said simply. "Things like that anger the beast." Festus stepped to the table and sat down heavily on the bench in front of the open Bible.

Woody and the doctor looked at each other in dismay. Was this an admission of guilt? Woody decided on a more direct approach.

"Mr. Cady, I know this will sound cruel, but some of the people from town asked us to come out here to talk to you." Woody stepped across from Festus with his hands on the edge of the table. "They're saying some strange things, Mr. Cady. Some of them are superstitious. They think that Lucius might have cast some kind of spell."

Festus raised his head slowly and looked at the lawyer with tear-filled eyes. "Little boys don't cast spells, Mr. Lockwood." He laid his hand on the open Bible and spoke in a voice barely above a whisper. "Demons cast spells."

"The prank that Lucius told you about, it was cruel," Woody said. "They put the head of a goat in his tent. Lucius left the camp and he took the head with him."

Festus looked into the lawyer's eyes and Woody could feel the hurt that they radiated.

"Parts of a goat's head have mysteriously shown up at the Brotherses' and the Zacks' homes," the lawyer said.

Festus lowered his head and placed a knobby finger on the open page, then he moved it slowly back and forth across the worn lines as he read aloud.

" 'When the unclean spirit has gone out of a man, he roams through waterless places in search of rest; and finding none, he says, "I will return to my house which I left." And when he comes to it, he finds the place swept. Then he goes and takes seven other spirits more evil than himself, and they enter in and dwell there; and the last state of that man becomes worse than the first.' "

His hand trembled and he dropped it beneath the table.

Dr. Logan was confused by Festus's strange reaction. "Mr. Cady," he asked, "do you have any knowledge of these tragedies? Does Lucius?"

Festus closed the Bible and rested his hand on the golden cross that was deeply embossed in its maroon cover. "The boy prays for the Lord's protection," Festus intoned. "But the demon still seeks him out. The demon has not succeeded." Festus gazed straight ahead, avoiding the curious stares of his three visitors.

Woody Lockwood seated himself on the bench across from Festus and tried unsuccessfully to meet his eyes. He repeated the question. "Does Lucius have any knowledge of these tragedies, Mr. Cady?"

Festus closed his eyes and spoke in a hushed tone. "The boy knows nothing. The boy is used. The devil waits and watches. The devil never rests."

"Mr. Cady, if you know something, I think you ought to come to town with us and talk to Chief Littlejohn."

"The boy is used," he repeated and he stared blankly, unfocused. "The devil never rests."

"Mr. Cady," Woody said more forcefully, but Kathryn Rogers moved to his side and laid a restraining hand on his arm. He turned to her and saw the look of caution in her eyes and the slight shake of her head. Then he smiled grimly and shook his own head, surprised at himself for taking Festus Cady's idiosyncrasies so seriously. Like so many of his neighbors had long supposed, the man was eccentric, perhaps even deranged. He caught the doctor's eye and motioned toward the door.

"I guess we'll be going now, Mr. Cady." Dr. Logan looked at the man and felt a stab of guilt. "Thank you for giving us your time."

More brightly, Kathryn Rogers said, "We're setting up some summer programs in the school, Mr. Cady. Maybe Lucius would like to attend."

Festus's head shot suddenly up but not in response to the principal's query. The house began to hum softly, like the song of a swarm of honeybees, and a chill crept through the cracks in the wall. Kathryn noticed it first and she crossed her arms and pulled her sweater tightly around her.

"Lucius, Lucius, get inside." Festus yelled the command as he jumped from the bench, shoving it over in his haste to get to the door. Jerking the door open, he shouted hoarsely, "Lucius, get inside. The beast is coming."

But he needn't have bothered. The blond-haired boy was already bursting from the trees, a look of panic on his face. He bolted across the small clearing and into the house.

"Hurry, Chris," he screamed over his shoulder.

Quickly but with a little less urgency, Chris Lockwood ran from the woods. At Lucius's urging he leapt over the threshold and Lucius slammed the door behind him.

"What is it?" Chris puffed. "I didn't see anything."

Lucius put a finger to his lips and leaned his back against the door. Woody pulled Kathryn close and Chris moved next to his father. Lucius put his ear against the door and listened. Festus watched his son closely. Dr. Logan studied the father and son, and was startled by the look of wildness that they suddenly shared. His heart raced and a film of sweat glistened on his forehead.

The low hum became a buzz, the leaky chill became an icy blast, and the stench of death fell over the room. A clatter like a summer hailstorm peppered the roof; there was a tapping at the windows, the thick sound of a large mass rubbing against the sides of the house.

Woody Lockwood wrapped his arms protectively around Kathryn and his son.

"What is that?" the doctor demanded, but the Cadys paid no attention.

As if in ritual procession, Festus and Lucius walked slowly back to the table where Festus relit the candles and opened the Bible. Father and son knelt next to the table. Festus could rest his bony elbows on the stained boards but Lucius's eyes barely peeked over the top. With his hands folded in prayer, Festus began to speak in a low drone.

"Jesus Christ, Son of God, God of Light, Light of the World, repel the beast who would seek harbor in the temple of my son."

"Amen," Lucius murmured.

Festus repeated the plea again and again and at the end of each request, Lucius added his simple punctuation.

For a brief moment there was no sound from outside yet the biting cold and odor persisted. Kathryn Rogers fought the urge to gag and with each trembling gasp she blew a cloud of breath.

Then a new sound began, a clawing at the door, long grinding scratches that froze the blood. Woody held Kathryn tighter. He felt as if he were in the midst of a living nightmare yet it was all too real. The cold, the stench, the ripping of wood, and the monotonous drone of Festus Cady's relentless plea—it was far worse than the worst of nightmares.

"What in God's name is out there?" the doctor demanded, and he took a step toward the heavily shaded window.

"Don't let your eyes behold the beast," Festus screamed. He shot to his feet and pointed a wavering finger at the startled doctor.

Lucius continued to kneel by the table but his eyes were wide with fright.

"Don't let the eyes of the beast behold you lest you be smitten by his evil gaze," Festus warned, and the doctor backed away from the window.

Festus stepped to the door and spread his arms to their rangy width. He leaned against it as if embracing the wall in his magnificent span.

"Jesus Christ, Son of God, God of Light, Light of the

World, repel the beast who would seek harbor in the temple of my son."

He shouted the prayer at the door, his drawn face only inches from its surface, only inches from whatever evil lurked beyond the flimsy wood.

"Amen," Lucius said softly.

Chris clung to his father.

Tears of fright welled up in Kathryn Rogers's eyes.

Then the scratching stopped. As suddenly as it began, it was gone. The tangy smell of incense replaced the rancid stench of death. The shaded windows seemed to glow brighter and the bitter chill gave way to welcome warmth.

"The beast is gone," Festus said simply. "Praise the Lord."

"Praise the Lord," Lucius repeated.

"Praise the Lord," Woody Lockwood whispered under his breath.

Festus walked back to the table. Like a priest at the conclusion of a ceremony, he gently closed the Bible and blew out the candles. As the visitors watched, Lucius took the holy book and rested it upright on a wall shelf next to the fireplace. Then he took the candles and the incense dish and placed them in prearranged locations by the Bible's side. Finished, he stepped to Festus's side and the gaunt scarecrow of a man wrapped a loving hand around the boy's shoulder.

"You must go now," he told the visitors.

"Please, Father. I have something for my friend." Lucius looked up at his father with pleading eyes and Festus nodded.

The boy walked back to the wall shelf that held the Bible and took a blue cardboard box with a tightly fitting lid. With head bowed, he stepped to Chris and offered the gift in the upturned palms of both hands.

"Thank you, Lucius," Chris said uncertainly as he accepted the offering.

"Please go now," Festus insisted. The kindness in his voice was replaced by a note of urgency.

Wordlessly, the four visitors retreated toward the door and Festus swung it open.

"There is nothing to fear," he told them when he noticed their hesitancy. "The beast is gone."

With a last glance at Lucius, Chris jumped across the threshold into the sunlight. The others followed, and without a word of farewell, the door clicked shut behind them.

"Let's get out of here," Dr. Logan urged, and they hurried across the clearing. Before stepping into the shaded woods, they turned for a final glance at the forest shack.

Their eyes were drawn to the white door and the gouges that showed the freshly splintered wood.

11

FEW WORDS WERE spoken during the short ride back to town. A friendly farmer waved a red handkerchief as he leaned against the roadside fence and Woody waved mechanically back. The afternoon sun beat through the windshield of Woody's car but it didn't brighten their mood.

"It's frightening." Kathryn Rogers finally broke the somber silence. "Something was outside that house, something horrible." She shivered and drew her sweater more tightly around her.

Woody Lockwood turned to his son who sat stiffly at his side. "What happened out there, Chris, when you and the Cady boy were playing?"

Chris smiled weakly. "We weren't exactly playing, Dad," he answered like an embarrassed teen. "He was showing me some stuff."

"What kind of stuff?"

"A little creek that runs behind the house. He has a bunch of muskrat traps set along the bank."

"Anything else?"

"He showed me a grave."

"What kind of grave?" Kathryn Rogers asked from the back seat.

Chris turned in his seat to face the school principal who he suspected might someday become his mother, a possibility that brought him joy. "Just a place where he buried his dog," he said matter-of-factly. "His name was Red."

"Oh," she said with a sigh of relief.

Chris frowned. "He's really a lonely kid. I feel kind of sorry for him."

Woody Lockwood saw his son's profile, the concerned wrinkle in his young brow, and he smiled gratefully. "He must think a lot of you. He seemed real happy to see you."

Chris shrugged self-consciously. "I don't think he has a lot of friends."

"What else happened?" Dr. Logan asked. "What made Lucius run to the house?"

"That was really strange," Chris admitted. "We were standing there next to the grave—it's about fifty yards inside the woods, straight out behind the house—and I think Lucius was straightening the cross that he has poked in the ground. All of a sudden he jumped up and said 'We gotta go' and he took off like a rabbit. I just followed him back to the house." He turned to his father. "He must have heard that thing, whatever it is, but I didn't hear a sound, not until we got inside the house." His boyish face turned grave. "What do you suppose it was, Dad?"

Woody took one hand from the wheel and patted his son's knee. "I don't know, Chris. Whatever it is, I'm sure there's a logical explanation."

He made the statement with a sense of confidence that none of them really felt. They reached the edge of town and Woody turned off Main Street toward Kathryn's house.

"What was that that the Cady boy gave you?" Dr. Logan asked.

Chris lifted the lid from the small box and peered inside. The gift was nestled in a pillow of cotton. "It's a special stone. I think it's supposed to be some kind of good-luck charm."

"May I see it?" the doctor asked.

Chris took the stone from the box and passed it back to the doctor who studied it closely.

Kathryn Rogers leaned over and pointed at its polished surface. "There seems to be a mark of some kind."

Logan turned the stone in his hand. "Where?"

"I'm sure I saw something," Kathryn said. "Maybe it was the way the light hit it."

Dr. Logan moved the stone to a beam of sunlight that jiggled with each nuance of the road. He tilted his head back and looked through the moon-shaped lens at the bottom of his glasses.

"There," she said excitedly.

"You're right. There are marks but they seem to be below the surface." He rotated the stone in the ray of light and examined it as a jeweler would study an unusual gemstone.

From beneath the milky gloss, an array of lines and symbols lit like neon, then extinguished when he removed it from the angled light. "Looks like a bunch of hex signs to me," he said cautiously, "but darned if I can figure how the boy put them there."

They came to the Exxon station, the apron of blacktop that drew a line next to the cornfield that was the starting point of what people called town.

"He had it at camp with him," Chris told them. "Or else it was another one that looked just like it."

He went on to describe the incidents with Pete Bishop and Wally Fenner and his conversation with Lucius Cady. The three adults traded worried glances at the mention of yet another unexplained phenomenon.

About the time he ended his narration, Woody rolled the station wagon to a stop in front of Kathryn's house. "I'll call you later tonight," he said as she moved to the door. "I'm going to get together with Ben Littlejohn and tell him what went on out there."

"How about if Chris stays here with me until you're through? We can cook some hamburgers on the grill," she said brightly. "And you can stop by to pick him up when your meeting's over."

"Can I, Dad?" Chris asked hopefully.

"Good idea," Woody agreed and Chris climbed out and Dr. Logan replaced him in the front seat.

The doctor smiled as he watched their departing backs. "If I was only a little younger, I'd consider spooning with a pretty miss like that." That was Logan's way of asking Woody what the hell he was waiting for.

Woody smiled back. "Sometimes I think there are more matchmakers in this town than there are farmers." He watched the screen door slam behind them and he pulled away from the curb.

On the ride to the hospital, where Woody dropped off the doctor, they made their plans for the evening meeting. Ben Littlejohn, always on duty even when his deputy was minding the store, agreed to the 7:00 P.M. agenda as did the Methodist pastor, Mallory Whitney. Father O'Connor was more difficult to track down, but with the grudging help of his cranky housekeeper, they found him at the home of a parishioner. "Mealtime freeloading as befits my station in life," he described his Sunday visit as he reluctantly agreed to leave earlier than planned to attend the meeting.

The others were already assembled in Dr. Logan's comfortable office when Ben Littlejohn finally arrived at five minutes after the hour. He bustled in, checking the watch on his bristly wrist. "Sorry I'm late. I was giving one of Gilly's better patrons a free ride home."

"One of my boys?" Father O'Connor wondered with an impish grin.

Littlejohn smiled and tried to bless himself but got it backward. "I can't reveal that, Father," he said with mock gravity. "The seal of law enforcement you know."

O'Connor nodded gravely. "It's an awesome responsibility," he agreed.

"Grab a seat, Ben," Dr. Logan offered, pointing to a comfortable wingback chair against the wall.

Logan's office was large and ordered, very masculine. He spent a lot of time there, not only in the performance of his healing duties but also free-time hours for research, thinking, or relaxing reading. The walls were paneled and busy with woodland prints and Latin-enscripted diplomas, and except for the desk and chair, the furnishings would seem more at home in a study or den. Logan sat behind the oak-topped desk in a leather swivel chair, the two clergymen sat side by side on an earth-toned couch, and Woody Lockwood sat in a padded armchair across from the doctor.

"I'm sorry to drag you all here to my office," the doctor began. "I thought it would be helpful if we didn't attract attention at your office, Ben."

The police chief nodded.

"Also," the doctor admitted, "I had some rounds to make."

"Speaking of which," Mal Whitney interrupted, "how's the Zack boy?"

A look of pure delight, one of the first for a while, lit the doctor's face. "If watching television, eating a pint of ice cream, and playing blackjack with the nurse are any indication, I'd say the boy is coming along just fine."

"Thank the Lord," Whitney said, and Father O'Connor lowered his head in a brief prayer.

Dr. Logan leaned back in his chair and steepled his fingers under his chin. Searching for the proper words, he closed his eyes and pursed his lips. With a deep breath, he began, "The reason that Woody and I decided to call this particular group together is that we have a—"

He paused and worked his thoughts carefully.

"We have a situation," he decided, "a situation that calls for the expertise of everyone in this room." His eyes bounced from chair to chair. "It has so many implications, so many facets," he said with a sad shake of his head. "Medical, legal, criminal, moral." He met each of their eyes as he ticked off their respective field of expertise.

"Am I to assume," Father O'Connor asked, "that this has something to do with the recent string of tragic events."

"Exactly, Father. More specifically, it has to do with the possibility that more such events might occur unless we decide some course of action. The problem is," he said as he fiddled with a wooden pencil, "that I'm not at all certain what type of action is called for. Let me explain."

Without further prelude, Dr. Logan launched into a description of their earlier meeting with Festus and Lucius Cady, omitting nothing as he recounted the strange events.

Father O'Connor sat forward with his elbows on his knees and his chin resting on his balled fists. He was dressed in green golf slacks and a colorful sport shirt but even this garish display couldn't conceal his priestliness.

"Hanging crosses over entryways served two purposes in early Christianity if I recall," O'Connor told the listeners. "They served as both an invitation to welcome Christ, and at the same time, they were a warning to evil spirits not to darken the portals." He raised his eyebrows and cast an oblique glance at Pastor Whitney.

"I recall such things too," the minister concurred. "I believe that the practice still exists in some parts of the world."

When Logan told them about the picnic table that was set up like an altar complete with Bible, incense, and candles, the two clergymen exchanged worried looks.

Moments later, when he mentioned that Festus didn't seem at all surprised when told about the tragedies in town, the police chief took a turn. "How could he know anything about them? If Cady'd been to town I'd have heard about it. Not too much happens in Hensleyville that I'm not told about. And as far as I know, nobody ever goes out to the Cady place. Until this afternoon," he quickly corrected.

The policeman was leaning forward in his chair, poised for action, until Dr. Logan waved him back. "Hear me out, Ben," he said calmly. "I don't know if Cady knew about Lenny Brothers or Jeff Zack. He just didn't seem surprised, that's all. But that's far from the strangest thing that happened out there today."

The chief settled back in his chair but his hands held a firm grip on the armrests.

Logan reminded them about the boys' prank with the goat head and Littlejohn sat forward again. "That would be Mr. McKechnie's goat," he said accusingly. Then he told the others about the strange crime that had been reported by the farmer a few nights earlier. "That Fenner kid's growing up to be just like his old man."

"The acorn doesn't fall far from the tree," Mallory Whitney intoned and Father O'Connor looked at him quizzically.

Logan moved ahead with his story. "Then Festus suddenly got a faraway look in his eyes and started to read something from his Bible. It was about seven evil spirits. I'm not sure what that was supposed to mean."

"Luke, chapter eleven, verse twenty-four," the pastor mumbled under his breath, and O'Connor grinned covertly and rolled his eyes.

Ben Littlejohn leaned forward impatiently. "John, what's this all about? Does Cady know something about these things or doesn't he? And what's all this about there being more of the same?"

The chief of police was uncharacteristically on edge. He was a gentle bear of a man who spoke softly and infrequently and was renowned for his control under pressure but the rapid-fire chain of events of the past few days, coupled with the threat of more of the same, had jangled his sensibilities.

John Logan held up his hands apologetically. "I'm almost through, Ben. Woody and I discussed this and we decided that it would be best to tell you and Father O'Connor and Pastor Whitney exactly what happened, exactly what we saw out at the Cady place. I can't explain it. The only thing that I can do is describe it and let you draw your own conclusions."

The chief held up his hands in surrender. "Sorry, Doctor. It's your show." He settled back, crossed his legs, and laced his fingers together in his lap, but he couldn't conceal his restlessness as his toe tapped a tattoo on the floor.

Once the police chief settled back, the doctor became more animated. He stood, and with head lowered, thumbs hooked behind his back, he paced around the room as he described, in minute detail, the sounds and the smells that they had experienced in their last few minutes at the Cady place. He told them about Festus's frantic call to his son—their prayerful plea—the bitter cold—the foul smell—the terrifying clawing at the door. He told the story well, reliving each frightening moment and dragging his listeners along the same heart-pounding path. Finally finished, he blew out a long, exhausted breath, circled his desk, and fell heavily into his chair. Sitting silently for a full minute, he met their troubled eyes one at a time.

"That, gentlemen," he concluded, "is why I asked you here tonight." He leaned back in his chair and waited.

Littlejohn finally broke the stubborn silence. "It could have been an animal," he tried without conviction.

"Yes," the doctor agreed with a polite nod of his curly head. "It could have been."

The uncomfortable silence that followed seemed endless. Father O'Connor finally took the initiative to break it. "I'll volunteer to make a fool of myself and say aloud what's on everybody's mind."

Woody Lockwood gave him a hint of a grateful grin.

"What's probably running through each of our minds is the possibility that something evil and perhaps supernatural is lurking around the Cady cottage."

Without being aware of it, Woody and the doctor nodded their agreement.

The pastor sat in a corner of the couch with his arms folded stiffly across his chest. His expression displayed neither belief nor rejection of the supposition.

Ben Littlejohn made no secret of his feelings. "With all due respect, Father, I wasn't thinking anything of the sort. I've been chasing after strange events in this town for more years than I care to remember and no matter how queer things seem at first, they usually end up having a simple explanation." His piece being said, the chief leaned back and waited for words of support but none were forthcoming, only another spell of embarrassed silence. Sensing that the ball was still in his court, Littlejohn added with finality, "Anyway, even if what you're suggesting is true, there's not a law on the books that would allow me to act on it."

Woody Lockwood entered the discussion for the first time. "John and I aren't suggesting anything at all, Ben. We're only telling you what we saw and what we heard in Covey's Woods. We were both terrified."

The admission added a stark note of reality to the astonishing tale.

Mal Whitney coughed lightly for their attention. "But the fact that you asked Father O'Connor and me to attend carries with it the implication that you suspect that supernatural forces might be at work."

"It certainly entered our minds," Woody Lockwood understated. "And I fully understand where Ben's coming from." He turned to face the lawman. "There's not a person in town who would want you to think any differently. But all the same," he said, "I for one would be very interested to hear how the clergy feels about it."

"And I," the doctor agreed.

"I guess I would too," Ben Littlejohn admitted self-consciously.

Three pairs of eyes turned expectantly to the earth-toned couch. The pastor raised his hands defensively. "While the good father and I worship the same God and read from the same holy book, I'll defer to him on this matter." He grinned sheepishly. "If I recall, we breezed through this chapter rather quickly in divinity school."

The minister's deferral focused the attention on the ruddy old priest. He leaned back comfortably, crossed his legs, and wrapped his entwined hands around his knee. Chewing pensively on his lip, he closed his eyes as if reflecting from the pulpit before launching into a fire and brimstone sermon. He removed his glasses, toyed with them for a few moments while gathering his thoughts, then he spoke slowly and thoughtfully.

"We're talking about Satan here. I think we're all agreed on that." He put his glasses back on and peered over their top at his listeners. "More specifically," he continued, "we're talking about him in a very tangible and deadly form, a form capable of causing tragic events."

The looks that greeted his statement told him that while they might not all be believers, they were all curious about his thoughts on the subject.

O'Connor nodded to the man sitting stiffly at the other end of the couch. "I have to admit to a few years on my good friend the pastor. That means that my years in—er—divinity school are perhaps even a bit more remote in my memory."

Pastor Whitney smiled blandly.

"So," the priest went on, "I ask your forbearance if I seem a bit rusty on the topic. With that caveat in mind, it seems to me that your description of the events at the Cady place doesn't bear much resemblance to the currently popular notions about demonic possession. The more familiar situations seem to involve individuals who become possessed by a very tenacious spirit, and once under its spell, they're forced to dance to its evil tune."

"Like the little girl in the movie that was around a couple of years ago," Ben Littlejohn said.

"Probably," the priest said drolly, "I didn't have the pleasure. Anyway, from the description you've given, if the devil is involved in this, he seems to be making a real botch of it. At least he doesn't seem to have gotten his claws too firmly into the Cady boy or his father."

"*If*"—Dr. Logan emphasized the word—"*if* there is something supernatural involved, the Cadys appear to be fighting it."

He could still hear the rasping scratches on the door and smell the rank presence, and the picture of the father and son kneeling at the picnic table flashed across his mind.

"And like I said, I'm not trying to make a case for either the supernatural or for something very explainable. All that I'll swear to is that there was something outside the Cadys' door, something big and something smelly."

"And I'll second that," Woody Lockwood said.

"There are other forms of demonic activity besides actual physical possession," the priest continued, peering at his audience over the top of his spectacles.

The others straightened and waited expectantly.

"I don't recall the exact names of the phenomena, if indeed there are names, but I do recall reading of some rather bizarre affairs where our friend Beelzebub was a prime suspect."

He winked impishly at the police chief, proud of his use of the lawman's lexicon.

"There's the old story about a young fellow from somewhere up in New England, Rhode Island if I recall. He was never one to have a temper but others quickly learned not to cross his path. Even the slightest offense brought severe punishment." He glanced in John Logan's direction. "The village doctor had the misfortune of unintentionally causing the man some pain while lancing a boil or some such medieval malady and the poor doctor was thrown from his horse the same day. Died of a broken neck if I recall." He paused thoughtfully, then continued, "The same man's barber nicked his ear while shaving him and that poor man then committed suicide by drinking a shelf full of hair tonic. To top it off, the grocer sold him a rotten potato and was struck down by a bolt of lightning from a clear blue sky."

"Sounds like the same M.O.," the police chief said.

It was a natural reaction for the lawman, not one meant to inject levity into the situation, but it drew smiles nonetheless.

"When did all this take place?" Ben asked.

"I believe it was in the early part of the last century," the priest said. "It's all very well documented. Satan was a much feared presence in those days, much more so than he is today." His tone indicated that he didn't condone contemporary thought on the subject.

"What's this story supposed to tell us?" Ben asked, trying not to exhibit a scoffing attitude toward the priest's convictions.

Father O'Connor shrugged. "Maybe nothing at all," he admitted. "All that I'm trying to point out is that in the mind of the Church, there are ways for the devil to manifest himself other than physical possession. If the case I just described can be attributed to Satan, then it seems that the old boy sometimes has the penchant for doing his version of good deeds for those who don't even ask for them."

Woody Lockwood rubbed his jaw thoughtfully. "So the doctor, the barber, and the grocer in your story were the victims of the devil's revenge even though the young man himself wasn't necessarily vengeful."

"If one can believe the reports," the priest agreed.

"And," the lawyer went on, "the victim's modern-day counterparts would be Pete Bishop and Lenny Brothers."

"And perhaps the Zack boy," O'Connor said regretfully.

"Except that he seems to be recovering completely," the doctor said.

"Let us pray that's so," Mallory Whitney offered.

"There are more current incidents," O'Connor continued. "Some are very similar to the Rhode Island story but most of the cases are your garden variety possession with a lot of cussing and bouncing furniture and the like."

Littlejohn crossed his arms across his chest. "No disrespect intended, Father, but you seem to take the existence of such phenomena lightly."

"And why shouldn't I?" the priest protested with a smile. "The existence of Satan is the reason for my own existence. It gives folks like Mallory and me steady employment."

The pastor winced at the priest's rationale.

"Satan is to the priesthood what disease is to the medical profession or what crime is to the police force," the priest explained. "They're the filthy facts that make us useful. For me to deny the works of the devil would be like Dr. Logan to deny the existence of cancer and the two aren't all that dissimilar. People don't really believe in cancer until it strikes close to home. Oh, they know that it's out there, but it's always someone else's problem. The same thing applies to Satan. I'd guess that most of us haven't given him a second thought in quite a while and now we have five educated men sitting in a circle talking about him." He raised his eyes and cast a knowing glance at the audience.

"Well put," Woody Lockwood acknowledged. "Tell me, Father, what's the frequency of these events?"

"And the cure rate?" the doctor added.

"I don't think we keep score," the priest answered. "In fact I suspect that it's one of those things the less said the better." His usually cheery face saddened. "There are those who consider the devil and possession and exorcism as modern-day examples of hocus-pocus. They belittle the belief and use it to cast doubt on religion in general, the Catholic Church in particular."

Woody Lockwood smiled grimly. "Sounds a little like being a lawyer. People tend to blame you for the crimes of the people you're trying to defend."

"An apt analogy," the priest congratulated.

John Logan folded his hands and rested them on the edge of the oak desk. Looking around his office at the semicircle of faces he said, "Now that we've had this meeting, where do we go from here? As I said at the start, there could be medical, legal, criminal, or religious implications, depending on what you want to believe. I for one don't know what to make of it but if there's the slightest threat of more tragedies occurring, I think that some sort of action needs to be taken."

"I feel the same way," the lawyer agreed, "but I'm stumped. I don't know what to do."

The police chief shrugged his large shoulders and shook his head. "An hour ago if someone told me that the devil was behind Bishop's and Brothers's deaths, I would have said they'd spent too much time at Gilly's. Now, I must admit, I'm not so sure." He grinned and held up his hands. "Don't get me wrong, I'm not totally converted." He lowered his hands. "It's just that you've given me some food for thought," the last addressed to the old priest. "But even so, what does it really change?" he asked helplessly. "Even if I believed that the devil was drag racing down Main Street, I couldn't arrest him without hard evidence."

The others smiled at the allusion.

"It seems then," the priest said, "that the proverbial ball is in the clergy's court. If there's anything to be done at all, it's going to be up to us to do it. Don't you agree, Pastor?"

Mallory Whitney apparently didn't feel that way at all and his face betrayed his dismay at being made an unwilling party to such a suggestion.

Woody Lockwood came to his aid. "I don't think that there's necessarily any action that can be taken by any of us," he said. "It's just important that we have all the facts."

"And the suppositions," O'Connor added.

"Oh, I almost forgot." Woody Lockwood dug into his jacket pocket and pulled out a small cardboard box. Handing it to the priest, he explained, "The Cady boy gave this to Chris."

Father O'Connor lifted the lid from the box and peered curiously inside. Shrugging, he looked questioningly at the lawyer. "Is there some significance?" he asked.

"I was hoping you might be able to tell me," the lawyer said. Woody retold Chris's account of the stone's effect on Pete Bishop and Wally Fenner and the old priest raised his eyebrows with interest. He also told him Lucius's explanation of where the stone came from.

His curiosity aroused, Father O'Connor lifted the shiny object from the box and studied it closely. "He uses it to keep

away the bad un', does he?" the priest said with no suggestion
of humor or doubt. Turning it in his fingers he admired the
workmanship. "A fine job of polishing," he said. "I used to do
a bit of this myself."

"Look more closely, Father. Spin it under the light," Woody
suggested.

The priest grunted and leaned laboriously to the left, toward
the shaded floor lamp. With the stone in his outstretched arm
and his head tilted back he studied it through the bottom of his
glasses. "Interesting," he admitted when he finally caught the
proper angle and the markings glowed like ivory veins sunken
under translucent skin. With each slight twist of his wrist, some
of them would fade to nothingness and new ones would pulse
to life. "It's very symbolic but the symbolism seems confused
as if the artist couldn't come to grips with where he wanted to
commit his loyalty."

"How so?" Ben Littlejohn asked. He was on more comfortable ground now, discussing a piece of hard evidence with an
expert witness.

The priest winced as he shifted into a more comfortable
position away from the lamp. Still studying the stone, he
answered. "There are some Christian signs here," the priest
explained. "Christ's cross being the most obvious, but there
are some other things too. I'll have to do a little checking but
I think I recognize some ancient Druid symbols." A look of
worry briefly clouded his pixie features. "And then there's that
number."

"What number?" the chief questioned.

"A Satanic reference," the priest told him. "It shows up a
few times. I'd wager that the good pastor could answer your
question without benefit of studying the stone."

He turned to his right and Mal Whitney nodded knowingly.
"Six-six-six," he predicted.

"Right on the money," O'Connor congratulated. Then,
bouncing the stone playfully from hand to hand, he tried to
lighten the growing tension. "Probably nothing more than a
superstitious trinket from a clever artisan."

The next instant the stone landed in his white palm and there
was a soft hiss and the priest yelped in pain and let it tumble to

the carpet. He looked at his stinging hand, then at the stone. It looked pretty and harmless, propped up on the thick pile like an egg on a rich lawn. "Maybe I spoke too soon," he admitted.

The others stared at the inanimate object in shocked silence, unwittingly leaning back in their chairs to lengthen the distance that separated them from it. The harsh buzz of the phone startled them.

Without taking his eyes from the glossy stone, Dr. Logan lifted the receiver to his ear. "He's what?" he shot into the mouthpiece. After listening for a few seconds, the doctor lowered the phone quickly to the cradle.

"The Zack boy," he said while staring at the stone. "Something's happening to him."

12

THEY MOVED SWIFTLY and drew curious stares from shuffling patients in colorless robes who were inching down hallways for their evening exercise. One of the nurses waited like a traffic cop at the duty desk, indicating the direction of room 514.

"What is that smell?" Pastor Whitney asked as they rounded a corner in the pale yellow corridor.

Of the group racing down the hallway, only the pastor and the priest hadn't experienced the cloying stench. As they neared room 514, they heard the echo of a haunting wail and felt the first chilling bite of wintry air. A nurse in starchy white stood frozen in the doorway and Dr. Logan moved her gently aside.

"They want to kill me, kill me, kill me, kill me, kill me." Jeff Zack was sitting against the back of the hospital bed, chin resting on drawn-up knees, his arms tightly hugging his legs. Drops of blood trickled from his ears and his nose. Despite the chill, he was bathed with sweat and it mingled with the rich red blood to form a pink rivulet on his chin.

An orderly leaned heavily against the wall, pressing a bloody tissue to the deep scratch that gouged his black cheek.

"He's gone crazy, Dr. Logan," the man accused, gesturing toward the bed with his free hand. "All I done was come in to change some towels and he jumps outta bed and tries to claw my eyes out."

Logan nodded sympathetically and approached the bed. Jeff

dug his heels into the sheets and pushed back against the headboard. Drops of pink sweat rolled down his face and spotted the front of his white hospital gown. His ñostrils opened and closed like a panting racehorse and his eyes were blotched with red where tiny capillaries had exploded. He hardly looked like the boy who the doctor had visited on evening rounds.

"Make them go away, away, away, away, away," he wailed, and as he did so, a gout of blood burst from his throat and landed in a gory puddle near the footboard.

"Jeff, Jeff, listen to me." Logan drew close and the boy squeezed more tightly against the headboard. "Nothing here is going to hurt you, Jeff. We're all your friends. We're here to help you."

"What is that horrible smell and where is that cold coming from?" Mallory Whitney complained. He was looking around the room, seeking the mysterious source, a bewildered frown creasing his bland face.

Father O'Connor also winced at the smell and shivered at the cold but he was aware of something else, the unmistakable presence of evil. "Our Father," he began, "who art in Heaven . . ."

The priest stood near the foot of the bed with trembling fists and frightened eyes. He felt like a boxer who had trained all of his life for the one big fight only to have his legs turn to jelly when he finally stepped into the ring with his most formidable opponent.

Logan tried to check the pupils of Jeff's eyes but the boy turned his face away and wrapped his arms protectively around his head.

"Don't kill me," he shrieked, then he flailed his arms wildly and the doctor backed away.

Jeff's eyes blazed with hate and his face contorted into a mask of rage. Pink froth bubbled at the corners of his mouth. "They want to kill me," he raged, and he jumped to his feet and sank into a defensive crouch with knees bent, legs spread, arms extended and bent at the elbow with his hands opening and closing like predatory talons. "They won't get me. I won't let them." He shifted like a prizefighter, snapping his head from side to side so he wouldn't be caught by surprise. He swung wildly at a phantom to his right and smashed the wall lamp, sending a shower of broken glass raining down on the utility table by the bedside.

"You," Logan shouted at the orderly, "help me get him down."

After a moment's hesitation, the orderly stepped closer.

Dr. Logan spoke calmly. "I want you to lay down now, Jeff. Everything's going to be all right. Just take it easy."

Without being asked, Ben Littlejohn eased Dr. Logan to the side and reached for the arm of the crazed young boy. Jeff recoiled at the touch, and while he was distracted, the orderly grabbed his other wrist with both hands. Startled patients peered in the door, then hurried on as the boy shrieked obscenities and wailed. He tugged helplessly at the iron grips that drew him down to the damp sheets.

"He's burnin' up," the orderly grunted as he struggled with the boy's surprising strength.

Ben said nothing but he looked strangely at the dark-faced man across from him. The arm that the police chief held wasn't burning up at all. It was clammy and cold.

"Give us this day our daily bread and forgive us our trespasses . . ." the priest droned.

Woody Lockwood and Mal Whitney hovered uncertainly in the corner. The nurse, who had raced from the room, hurried back with a hypodermic needle. Like a preoccupied surgeon, Dr. Logan extended his arm while closely watching his writhing patient and the nurse placed the hypo carefully in the palm of his hand. She walked around the bed, lifted Jeff's loose sleeve, and swabbed a spot just below his shoulder. Ben Littlejohn leaned his hairy hand on Jeff Zack's bony chest as the doctor plunged the needle home. Logan stepped back and blew out a slow breath. Shaking his head wearily he said, "So much for miracle recoveries."

Woody came cautiously forward. "Same as yesterday only worse," he lamented.

Jeff's eyes closed and his head sank into the pillow.

The police chief straightened and wiped his forehead with the back of his hand. Then he pulled a tissue from a box on the night table and dabbed gently at the boy's sweat-and-blood-streaked face. "What the hell could it be?" he wondered aloud.

"I'm glad Bill and Lorna weren't here to see that," Woody remarked. "They've already been through enough."

At the foot of the bed, Pastor Whitney had joined Father O'Connor, and as the two recited familiar prayers, the huddled people gazed down with a blend of fear and pity at the drugged boy.

Ben's iron jaw softened and his hard eyes filled with the love of a caring adult for a stricken child, any child. He was wearing his tan uniform, slightly rumpled now, his service revolver snugged into the supple leather of the holster that laid against his hip.

"He looks like a normal little kid again," the chief observed. "For a minute there he looked more like a wild animal."

Dr. Logan leaned over and pulled back Jeff's eyelid. Peering into the dark pool of the pupil, he assured the others, "He'll stay like this until lunchtime tomorrow. That shot that I gave him would knock out a horse."

Pausing in his prayers, Father O'Connor observed, "Now I understand why you called this group together, John. There's much more to this than meets the eye."

The doctor nodded.

"But we're still left with the same question," the priest continued. "What force is at work here?"

"And," Woody Lockwood added, "are the events connected?"

The noxious odor had disappeared and the penetrating chill had been replaced by the hospital's cozy warmth. The pastor noted this. "At least that terrible smell is gone."

Father O'Connor nodded his agreement but his normally placid face was etched with concern. The aroma of evil may have disappeared but he couldn't dismiss its presence. The air was sterile, the room comfortably warm, the boy sleeping peacefully, but the evil persisted nonetheless. In the rush from Dr. Logan's office, the priest had hurriedly stuffed the strange stone in his pocket. He touched it now and was rewarded with a warm tingle that, for an instant, seemed to break the grip of fear in which the room was held hostage.

"The only thing that I know how to do," he admitted, "is to pray. I'm afraid that I can't contribute to the medical or legal solutions."

Ben Littlejohn shoved his hands in his pockets and shrugged. "That's more than I can do, Father. Even if I believed in some evil force, there's not a thing that I can do about it until somebody breaks the law and the only law that's been broken—"

What happened next was almost too quick to be seen. One moment Jeff Zack had been sleeping like a newborn, out of touch with the rest of the world and its horrible realities. Then, in the next instant, he moved like a cat, rolling to his right on the damp sheets and shooting his hand toward Ben Littlejohn's girded waist. By the time the police chief realized what had happened, Jeff Zack had grabbed his revolver, snapped off the safety, and shot to his feet in the middle of the bed.

Ben started to make a move in the boy's direction but immediately thought better of it, which was wise because before the veteran policeman even completed his thought, he was staring into the working end of his own weapon.

Jeff started to laugh the frantic giggle of a maniac and he shoved the gun to within an inch of Littlejohn's weathered forehead. "I'll kill you, you fucking zombie," he screamed. Waving the pistol in a sweeping arc, he shouted at the others. "I'll kill every fucking one of you." Again the laugh and it washed the walls with icy fear.

The nurse put her hand to her mouth and began to whimper. The pastor felt his knees grow weak. Father O'Connor began reciting fervent prayers under his breath. Jeff threw his head back and roared like an outraged animal, once, twice, all the time waving the revolver in loose circles.

And the smell returned.

And the cold.

The sudden crash turned all their heads and they gaped at the shards of glass surrounding the picture that had fallen from the wall. The water pitcher went next. At first it rattled and danced on the hard surface of the side table, then it leapt into the air and showered Dr. Logan before crashing in crystal splinters at his feet. This touched a chord of humor in the pistol-waving

patient and Jeff bounced up and down on the bed like a playful
chimp, alternating between shrieks of joy and wails of dispair.
A straight-backed wooden chair stood beneath a wide window
that let in the faint glow of the street five stories below. First
it rocked lightly from side to side, then it changed direction and
tilted forward, then backward, faster and faster until it rattled
like a tap dancer on the hard floor.

"They're going to kill me, kill me, kill me," Jeff shouted,
and the pink foam oozed from his mouth and the blood ran
freely from his ears.

The foot of the bed rose an inch and then dropped. It did it
again. Then the stuffed leather chair skidded across the room
and slammed the terrified nurse into the wall. Finally reaching
her breaking point, the young woman screamed and buried her
face in her hands so she never saw the flash of the gun but she
heard the explosion. The impact of the bullet boring into her
shoulder spun her like a top before she crumpled like a rag doll
to the floor.

In a heroic but misguided rush, the orderly lunged toward
the bed, but before reaching it a second bullet shattered his
skull and sprayed the wall with the grey pulp of his brains.

Mallory Whitney fainted when the third shot whistled past
his ear.

"Stop," the priest shouted foolishly.

With mind-numbing slowness, the froth-mouthed boy lowered the gun until its warm barrel was pointed unnervingly at
the man's white head. Ben Littlejohn was dismayed by his own
inaction but couldn't fault himself. Sound police methods
suggested that type of passive behavior. But two people had
already been shot and a third was threatened.

The chief was about to leap but the old priest preempted
him. Pulling the stone from his pocket, Father O'Connor thrust
it forward in his outstretched hand.

"Begone, Satan," he shrieked, and a stench like the bowels
of death sucked the air from the room.

Jeff Zack staggered backward and crashed into the wall
behind the bed. "Don't let them," he cried and he shielded
himself with his open hands.

The pistol dropped harmlessly from his grip and the police chief snatched it from the mattress.

"Keep them away," the boy wailed.

Suddenly the air was still and the boy's shouts for help echoed as if in a vacuum. There was a muffled roar and Woody Lockwood's ears screamed with pain and he covered them with his hands. The wall behind the lawyer frosted with a billion crystals and through it marched a ragged file of creatures, wrapped in frayed ribbons and gazing at Jeff Zack through black holes in the filthy bandages. With trembling hands Ben Littlejohn pointed the pistol at the misty leader but he had no strength to pull the trigger. Father O'Connor shielded his eyes and dropped to his knees in prayer.

The others watched helplessly as Jeff Zack leapt from the bed and crashed headfirst through the dark window. His high-pitched cry of freedom echoed through the night and then all was still.

13

THE FIRST LIGHT of the new day trickled in the window and laid a radiant stripe across Ben's desk. He snored and grunted, raised his head from the hard desk, and rubbed bristly knuckles into his reddened eyes. Then the memories began to flood back. It had been a long night, the longest in Ben's life—and the worst.

Ben Littlejohn had been the town cop when Bill Zack and Lorna Heplēy were still a pair of high school kids, groping and panting in the front seat of Bill's '58 Chevy. He had caught them at it on Horny Hill—that's what the kids called the place, still do for that matter—and he had turned his back while they hastily buttoned up. Years later, he had driven the young couple to the hospital on the night that Jeff was born because Bill couldn't get his car started. The final chapter, last night with the help of John Logan, was to tell the couple that the boy who they had all helped into the world was now a broken heap lying under a white sheet in the basement of Memorial Hospital. It had been a long night. A bad night.

When Dr. Logan had finally settled the parents down, Ben returned to his office on Main Street and began to fill in the blanks on the terrible forms that would make Jeff Zack's death official if not acceptable. Sometime in the early morning hours, he must have surrendered to the demands of exhaustion. He hacked a foul cough and rubbed his palm over the stubble of his jaw. "Nobody ever said it would be easy," he lamented aloud. Then he spun around in the swivel chair so the sun was less bothersome, closed his eyes, and fell into another dead sleep.

The squeal of brakes and the crunch of gravel jolted him back to his senses. Littlejohn didn't know how long he had slept, but the sun had risen to a more respectable height and didn't intrude its painful rays through the slats of the dusty blinds. Spinning his chair toward the door, he tried to look the role of the natty police chief, alert and primed for business. He needn't have bothered.

Virgil Fenner and Dick Harman burst into his small office, their eyes bloodshot from drink and anger, their faces twisted into scowls of indignation.

"We heard about what happened last night at the hospital," Fenner growled, "and we want to know what the hell you're gonna do about it."

Littlejohn looked up from his desk and studied his adversary through his own reddened eyes. There had been, for as long as Ben could remember, a natural enmity between the two men, one that ran deeper than the normal conflict between lawman and lawbreaker. Ben, for his part, resented Fenner's callous indifference to the feelings of others, his mindless bully instinct. And Fenner hated the policeman because he knew that Ben read him like a book, thought of him as stupid, and, worst of all, had absolutely no fear of him. It was the last that rankled most.

But now Fenner had the upper hand. He had warned the chief that if he didn't take action against the Cadys, still more tragedies would visit the small farm community. His prediction had been deadly accurate.

"Good morning, Virgil," the policeman drawled with weary sarcasm. "Nice of you to drop in."

"Don't give us that shit," Fenner shot back. "We want some action and we want it now."

Ben turned to the other man, ignoring Virgil in the process. "Morning, Dick. Are you the other half of the 'we' that Virgil's mouthing off about?"

Billy Harman's father, never one to be decisive or independent, had walked in Virgil's lumbering shadow since childhood and their boys were proof of the breed. "Damn right, I am," he stammered, trapped between his fear of both men. "We're worried about our boys."

Ben was worried about them also but what could he do? Never in his career as a lawman had he felt so powerless. There was an enemy out there, an evil power. After what he had seen in Jeff Zack's room at Memorial, he had no doubt about it. He had felt its cold and rancid breath and he had pulled the sheets over the cool faces of its victims, but how could he stop it? What guarantees could he give Dick Harman and Virgil Fenner that their sons wouldn't be the next victims?

"If it will make you feel any better," he said, "there will be an investigation into the shooting by the Attorney General's office. It's automatic. You can tell them what you want the law to do if you aren't satisfied with me." He shrugged helplessly. "I'm worried too," he admitted. "I'm worried for your boys. I'm worried for the town."

"Well that ain't good enough, Littlejohn," Fenner growled. "That ain't good enough at all." With his hands on the front of Ben's desk, he leaned toward the lawman until their faces were only inches apart. "You're gonna do somethin' damn quick or me and some of my friends are gonna do your fuckin' job for you."

Ben had tried to be civil and understanding, even in the face of Fenner's abuse, but after a night that left one man's head blown apart, one boy's body shattered on the sidewalk, and one young woman painfully wounded, his reservoir of patience was finally exhausted. Lashing out his hand, he grabbed the front of Fenner's shirt and twisted it under his chin until the bully's eyes bulged. Fenner gasped and clawed at Ben's iron grip. Fortunately for both men, the jangle of the phone jarred the chief to his senses.

Ben Littlejohn loosened his grip and looked in shock at the hand that had reacted so violently. The phone rang again and Virgil Fenner rubbed his throat and glared at the chief with hate-filled eyes. Trembling with anger and fatigue, Ben lifted the phone. "Hensleyville Police," he said with a raspy catch to his voice.

The voice on the other end of the line was on the thin edge

of hysteria. Arlen Stein was calling to report the finding of an eye when he unrolled the morning newspaper.

"It was horrible, Ben. I opened the paper and there was this—this thing stuck to the front page."

Ben could hear the man's short, clutching breaths.

"Thank God, Jennifer didn't open it," he gasped. "She would have—would have—"

"Try to get hold of yourself, Arlen. Nothing's happened. Nobody's hurt. It's probably somebody's idea of a practical joke." How the chief wished that he could believe that. "How about if I stop right over and we can talk about it?"

"No," Arlen Stein answered firmly. Then, after a moment's hesitation, he said, "I heard about what happened last night at the hospital, Ben."

The police chief didn't look up as the door slammed angrily in the wake of Fenner and Harman's departure. "What do you plan to do?" Ben asked quietly.

"We're getting out of town for a while, Ben. It's a slow time for me anyway. Summer isn't tax time," he joked weakly. "We're going to visit Jenny's folks at their place in Ocean City. It'll be nice to get away," he added with a false note of optimism.

"Yes," Ben agreed. "I suppose it will." They said good-bye and Ben laid the phone softly in the cradle and frowned as Virgil squealed recklessly down the street.

Arlen Stein carefully fitted the matched suitcases in the trunk of the Mercedes and he slammed the lid closed. "Buckle up," he ordered with a forced smile. "We want to get there in one piece."

They looked like a page out of the Sears's catalog with colorful pullovers, trendy slacks, an assortment of Pumas and Adidas. Arlen nestled behind the wheel and pulled the woven strap across his chest and clicked it home. Jenny sat beside him, twisting to the rear to watch the children perform the same ritual before adjusting her own belt. Arlen had told her of his gruesome find and it took all of her will to keep the fear and revulsion from her voice.

"Your grandma and grandpa were so excited to hear that we

were coming to visit," she said brightly. "They can't wait for us to get there." Her voice cracked but neither Scott nor eight-year-old Caroline seemed to notice.

"What's the big rush all of a sudden?" Scott wanted to know. "I thought we were going to the shore right before school starts."

Arlen turned to the back seat. "I was pretty well caught up at the office," he lied, "and the weather's so great. It just seemed like a good idea to go now. Don't you think so?" he asked.

"Sure," Scott agreed dubiously.

"Well, let's get going then," and Arlen tooted the horn three times and backed out of the drive. "See you later, Hensleyville," he shouted as they started down the street.

In the back seat, Scott and his younger sister rolled their eyes at each other.

They turned onto Main Street and passed the hardware store. "See you later, Coast to Coast," Arlen shouted and the kids picked up the echo.

"See you later, Town Hall."

"See you later, Gilly's."

By the time they reached the Exxon station at the edge of town they were all in the spirit of vacation. Even Arlen could feel some of the tension draining from his pores. They drove in silence for the next fifteen minutes, and by the time he looked down the steep slope into the river valley, the last vestiges of foreboding were erased.

"Let's play the alphabet game," he shouted above the hum of the motor.

"A for Appaloosa," Jenny said immediately, pointing to a spotted animal in a passing field.

"That's only a horse," Carolyn complained.

"It's an Appaloosa horse," her mother told her.

"Vote, vote," Scott demanded. "All for Appaloosa raise your hand."

Two hands went up in the front seat.

"Tie wins," Jenny said triumphantly.

"B for barn," Carolyn chirped, and they followed her tiny

finger to the derelict structure nestled next to a stand of evergreen.

"Good one, Carolyn," her father praised.

The slope fell sharply toward the river. To the right was a sheer facing of granite where the road was carved from the hardened hillside. To the left was a metal guardrail that separated the two-lane road from a sheer drop of ninety feet to the valley floor.

"C for curve," Scott yelled at the same time that his father pumped lightly on the brake pedal.

But there was no resistance and Arlen's foot shot to the floorboards. Panicked, he slammed his foot against the useless pedal.

"What is it, honey?" Jenny asked.

He didn't answer and the car rolled faster, now less than one hundred yards from the sharp curve that wound like a goat path toward the river. A large orange and black sign advised the unwary driver of the approaching peril but Arlen didn't need the warning. He had driven the road countless times.

"Wheeee," Carolyn squealed as the wall of rock whistled by to their right.

Arlen Stein's last conscious act was to yank on the emergency brake. The handle snapped off in his grip as the car ripped through the guardrail and tumbled end over end before landing in a fiery heap on the valley floor.

14

SHORTLY AFTER THE accident, the clouds rolled in and the skies over Chester County opened with a vengeance. Lightning rocketed into the fields, splitting trees like matchsticks and shooing trembling pets into sheltered corners. Almost an hour had elapsed before an alert citizen noticed the flattened guardrail and peered over the edge of the precipice. He did this at the risk of his own health since the rain was still pelting down and the road was treacherous. It was another forty-five minutes before a Pennsylvania State trooper worked his way down the steep slope to the steaming wreckage and quickly determined that no one could have walked away from the mass of charred metal.

By the time the news finally leaked back to Hensleyville, over three inches of rain had doused the countryside and most of the town's businesses had shut their doors for the lunch hour. The bad news had first reached Ben Littlejohn who told his deputy, Nils Larsen. Nils let it slip to Eb Sawyer who carried it to Minnie Frick's diner and from there it raced through town like a brushfire in August. The lunch crowd at Gilly's was dumbstruck.

"Kee-riiist, what's gonna happen next?"

"Damned if I know. It's gettin' so's I'm afraid to ask 'what's new?' anymore."

"It's spooky as all get out, that's what it is. First Pete Bishop gets hisself hit by lightning, then the Brothers kid ups'n drowns, next the Zack boy jumps outta the hospital window, and now the whole Stein family gets itself wiped out. It's enough to make you cry."

"It's enough to make you pray, that's what it is. Do you know what I heard? I heard that up on that there campout where the lightning got ol' Pete, the Brothers boy said that he was a'scared of drownin' and that the Stein boy said he was a'scared of gettin' hisself killed in a smashup. It's dang near like these kids predicted how they was gonna get themselves killed."

"No shit?"

"No shit. And I heard that old Virgil Fenner thinks the whole shootin' match is the Cady boy's fault. Says he's casting a spell or somethin' like that."

"Fenner's an asshole."

"No shit."

"Anyway, him and Dick Harman are makin' noises around town like they aim to do somethin' about it if ol' Ben don't."

"Fenner's an asshole."

"You already said that."

"It bears repeatin'."

Ben Littlejohn rubbed the heels of his hands into his burning eyes. He felt useless—worse than useless—he felt that he was betraying the trust of the town that pinned the silver badge on his breast pocket. Eight people were already dead and the brawny chief had the uneasy premonition that he hadn't seen the end of it. He looked with pleading eyes at his visitor.

"Jesus, Woody, when is enough enough? You're the lawyer, isn't there something I can do?"

Given the tragic events of the past weekend, Woody Lockwood had chosen to work at home today, to be close to Chris and Kathryn should they need him. He was doubly glad that he had taken the precaution when Ben Littlejohn called for his advice. The police chief had provided no details during the short phone conversation, saving them until Woody arrived at his office. Now, sitting in the Spartan surroundings, the lawyer listened to the account of the recent car accident with an expression of shocked resignation. He pondered Ben's question before answering.

"As a lawyer, I'm obligated to say that there's nothing you can legally do, Ben. There's no hard evidence that any of the deaths was willfully caused. Nor is there any evidence of complicity or conspiracy."

"How about the goat's eyes?" Ben tried. "We know that the Cady boy had a goat head and we've determined that the parts that keep showing up are from a goat. Couldn't we bring them in on that?"

The lawyer thought about that for a moment. "You know, Ben, I'll grasp at any straw to stop these tragedies. Remember, Chris was along on that campout too."

The chief nodded grimly.

Woody continued, "The problem isn't so much that we have no evidence. The problem is that we have no crime. Even if we could prove that one of the Cadys delivered the goat's eyes or caused those apparitions at the hospital, there's absolutely no crime to accuse them of. Nobody shot Pete Bishop with a bolt of lightning. Nobody held Lenny Brothers's head in the water. Nobody pushed Jeff Zack out of that window. We know that for a fact. We were there."

"So what are we supposed to do, Ben?" he asked. "Do we wait for more accidents? Do we look the other way and let Virgil Fenner and his bunch solve it their way? Or do we sit still like the law-abiding creatures that we are and hope that Father O'Connor can pray it away?"

"You want to know what I think, Ben? I think that, for a moment, we just have to put aside all of the great rules that guide law and order. You stop being a cop and I'll stop being a lawyer. We can't use either one of them in this situation. Why don't you just be a concerned neighbor and I'll be a worried father."

"How will that help?" Littlejohn asked.

"It simply means that we pay another call on the Cadys only this time we don't leave before we know exactly what's going on out there. I don't care what kind of abomination is scratching at the door," Woody said, his voice and jaw firm, "but if it's endangering Chris or anybody else in this town, I don't plan to leave Covey's Woods without knowing exactly what it is and how to deal with it."

"Mr. Lawyer," Ben said with a ray of hope, "I like the way you think."

15

THE RAIN POUNDED down from the cloud-blackened sky, lashed by a wind that ripped leafy branches from the trees and made telephone wires hum like banjo strings. Ben hunched over the wheel, catching a moment's visibility with each squeal of the wiper blade. He suddenly jerked the wheel to the left, barely missing a tree limb that had blown across the rain-washed blacktop.

"This is crazy," the lawman said. "I don't think I've ever seen it rain this hard."

"I just hope we're able to find the path," Woody said. Like the police chief, Woody Lockwood leaned close to the windshield and squinted into the squall. "I can just about see the hood ornament."

With his sleeved forearm, Ben smeared the mist from a spot on the windshield in front of his face. "I think it's just around the next bend."

A jagged scar of lightning crackled and encased the car in a luminescent glow.

"But I can't even see the next bend," he said with a fumbling attempt at humor.

Littlejohn pulled as close to the right side of the road as he dared and Woody rolled the window down about an inch and peered into the downpour.

"You just creep ahead," the lawyer said, "and I'll let you know when we come to the path."

"Let me know when I'm about to run into a tree too," Littlejohn said and he rolled along so slowly that it didn't nudge the needle on the speedometer.

"Here we are," Woody announced suddenly and Littlejohn shifted into neutral and let the black and white patrol car roll to a soft stop. The two looked at each other uncertainly, wondering whether to wait out the downpour or brave it down the soaked path.

"If we give it a couple more minutes, it might ease up," Woody said with little conviction.

Ben gave him a doubtful look. "Or it might get worse."

As they speculated, their decision was made easy. Hailstones, at first no bigger than green peas, grew into marbles, then golf balls, and they pelted the car with a tommy-gun chatter that brought the two men's hands protectively to their ears. Then, as quickly as it began, the hailstorm stopped, but before the weather released them from its intimidating grip, it rung down the curtain with a deafening bolt of lightning that assaulted their eyes and ears and rattled the police car like a flimsy matchbox.

"My God, that was close," Woody said when he finally caught his breath.

It took a few seconds for their senses to recover from the shock and they realized with relief that the rain had stopped.

"It looks like you were right after all," Littlejohn told the lawyer, and he pushed open his door and stepped onto the hail-strewn roadway.

"This must be how a Brazilian rain forest feels," Littlejohn mused. The two stood next to the car at the confluence of the blacktop road and the beaten footpath. Water-laden leaves gleamed like emeralds in the newborn shafts of sunlight that dappled the ground. Wisps of steam rose from dying embers of hail. A damp coolness and the fresh, clean smell of nature enveloped them. Large drips continued to fall as the trees shook off their refreshing burden.

But the sensual treats were wasted on Woody Lockwood. His thoughts returned to the day before when he beat a hasty retreat down the same path in the wake of some unseen horror. It was hard for him to believe that so much had happened in so little time, so many innocent lives snuffed out in unexplainable ways for unknown reasons. But he couldn't escape the reality of it, nor could he elude the gnawing fear that ate at his gut when he took the first cautious step down the same soggy path. Something roamed these woods, something diabolical, and though there was neither spoor nor scent, the lawyer was as certain of its evil presence as he was of his own fragile mortality, and for the first time, he began to fear for that. Whatever was preying on the good folks of Hensleyville had walked the same narrow path.

"They're really out in the boonies, aren't they?" the chief remarked. He led the way, his hand unconsciously close to the leather holster that bobbed on his hip.

"The house is about one hundred yards in," Woody told him. "It backs up to a little creek."

They trod deliberately down the path, the heavy drips splashing cool reminders of nature's rage on their unprotected heads. Each footfall erupted in a tiny fountain and released a new burst of fresh green scent into the damp air.

But something was missing.

There was no sound. Except for the patter of spent raindrops, the woods were as quiet as a tomb. Not a chirp, a whistle, or the slightest rustle of leaves signaled warm-blooded existence.

Ben Littlejohn's antennae for trouble must have picked up some unheard signal and he stopped in his tracks and held up his hand for Woody to halt.

"Something's not right," he whispered over his shoulder.

Woody moved alongside him on the narrow path. "I feel it too, Ben, but I'm not surprised. I felt the same thing yesterday." He pointed to the trees that lined the path. "Let's go. It's just around that clump of evergreens."

Woody was anxious to get to the house even though he had no idea what he was going to say to Festus and Lucius Cady if they were even there.

The policeman was more cautious, preferring to be in control and to minimize surprises. He began to move once again, but now the heel of his hand rested on the butt of his revolver. They traveled the rest of the path in silence and arrived moments later at the narrow clearing that separated the woods from the home of Festus and Lucius Cady.

"What the hell is going on?" Littlejohn exclaimed as they rounded the copse and the house came into view.

The clearing around the house was firm and dry as an August drought, the sun-baked weeds as brittle as desert sage.

"It looks like it didn't even rain around here."

His leading foot scuffed at the parched weeds while the trailing foot sank in the swampy loam. The Cady house was still and silent, a bleak box sitting in the center of the clearing like a tombstone waiting for a name to be chiseled into its cold face.

"Look at the house," Ben said under his breath. "It's as dry as a bone."

Woody *was* looking at the house but his focus wasn't on the moisture content of the peeling wood. He was gazing at a spot above the door where there existed the faint outline of a cross, yellow on yellow, a fading symbol of man's indestructibility. The shades were drawn, the door slightly ajar. A chill worked its way from the ground to the top of his head and he could feel the short hairs of his body rise in response. On the concrete step in the front of the door lay the shattered pieces of the cross amid the fresh wood chips of recent, frantic clawing.

Ben pointed at the broken symbol. "What do you suppose that means," he whispered.

"Nothing good," Woody answered.

Ben nodded and took a deep breath. "Let's get this over with," he said. Taking a brave step forward onto the arid perimeter he called out, "Festus, Festus Cady, are you in there?"

He realized that his hand was wrapped around his gun butt and he quickly moved it away.

"Festus, it's Ben Littlejohn and Woody Lockwood. We came from town to talk to you."

The echo of his own voice was all that broke the deathly silence. He turned and met Woody's eyes and he realized that the lawyer was filled with the same sense of foreboding that held him in its grip. He turned back to the house and stiffened. There was a noise, not from the house, but from the woods to his right. Dropping his hand to his holster, he unsnapped the leather flap and eased the shiny weapon from its sheath.

Footfalls, heavy and moving away, felt more than heard. Breathing, rasping and phlegmy. A movement through the trees, a flash of dirty white amid the sumptuous green, then it was gone.

Woody exhaled in long, spasmodic breaths. "It was just an animal," he whispered.

"It's gone, whatever it was," Ben answered, and he slid the pistol back in place.

The policeman shuddered inwardly. Except for cleaning and oiling, the weapon hadn't been out of the holster in over two years—until last night. Since then, it had killed one man, wounded a woman, and been drawn in dubious self-defense, all in the span of less than twenty-four hours.

Woody stepped to the lawman's side. "Festus, Lucius," he called. "It's me, Woody Lockwood. I want to talk to you. I'm coming to the door."

Why are we acting like this, Woody wondered. It wasn't as if they were approaching a houseful of armed gangsters, and in spite of Festus Cady's glaring eccentricity, there was no reason to believe him to be dangerous. In fact, yesterday's visit was proof that the man was marginally hospitable. Woody met Ben's hooded gaze, shrugged resignedly, and stepped to the door, stopping on the way to pick up the fragments of the cross. Shoving them in his pocket, he peered through the darkened crack where the door stood ajar. He could see nothing but the dimness of the sparsely furnished room.

"Festus," he called.

There was no answer. Cautiously he laid his hand against the wood, careful not to touch the fresh claw marks, and pushed inward. The door groaned on rusted hinges and swung away, sending a slice of light knifing across the room.

Woody stared inside and gasped.

"Oh, my God," Littlejohn moaned as they saw the lanky body swinging from the rafter like a grotesque puppet.

Festus was staring directly at them with his eyes bulging from their sockets, his tongue sticking out like a ghastly sausage. The noose around his neck had cocked his head at a bizarre angle so that his ear almost rested on his sloping shoulder.

Ben was the first to action and he bolted through the door, already fumbling with the catch on the razor-sharp pocket-knife. Dragging the bench from the table, he clambered atop it and slashed the taut rope. The body of Festus Cady crumpled to the bare wood floor. Woody knelt beside him and felt for a pulse. The bony wrist was warm but still. They were too late.

"The boy," Littlejohn said, "where's the boy?"

They turned to the corner of the room and both men saw him at the same time. Lucius Cady huddled in the dimness. His eyes were wide with fright. He was trembling uncontrollably.

"Help me," he whimpered. "Please help me."

16

AFTER THE DELUGE, the sun had finally broken through and begun to bake away the soggy residue. Now, in the early evening, it still shone brightly but its brilliance had little effect on the murky dimness of Gilly's Tavern. In this gloomy atmosphere sat more than the usual complement of evening patrons, an outlet, no doubt, for their grief, their fears, or perhaps only their morbid curiosity about the mounting plague of tragedies to visit their normally predictable existence. Gilly worked behind the bar while Fannie Setzer lumbered back and forth to the row of booths that lined the walls across from it.

Gilly's decor was a questionable tribute to the taste of his patrons. The ceiling was hung with an eclectic collection of antiques and miscellaneous paraphernalia that had been ransomed from estate sales and trash piles to be reborn for the artistic edification of the farmers and mechanics who even bothered to notice them. There was a battle-scarred Flexible Flyer with rusty runners, a dented spittoon, numerous tea and cookie tins, and a flintlock rifle that saw duty in the county over two centuries earlier. A faded poster of the 1960 Philadelphia Eagles, personally autographed by Chuck Bednarik, was thumbtacked above the cash register next to a pair of red boxing gloves, brittle with age. In the end booth, under a precariously suspended washtub, Virgil Fenner and Dick Harman worked on their second pitcher of beer.

"Watcha thinka that, Virgil?"

The man who sought Virgil Fenner's opinion leaned his back against the bar and hooked his thumbs into the straps of his greasy coveralls. A shock of dirty blond hair fell over his forehead and his teeth were blackened stumps.

"I heard that ol' Festus was strung up in that ol' shack o' his like a scarecrow. He was deader'n a doornail by the time ol' Ben showed up and cut him down."

Virgil chugged half a glass and burped resonantly. "Good riddance."

The man at the bar scratched an itchy armpit. "Hear tell you think it was ol' Festus that was causin' all the ruckus in the first place."

"Why don't you shut the fuck up," Virgil called back.

Gilly wheeled and banged a mug loudly on the bar top. "That'll be enough of that kind of language, Virgil. There are ladies in here."

"Fuck 'em," Virgil mumbled under his breath and Dick Harman grinned approvingly.

Customs die hard in Chester County and one such was respect for the delicacy of womanhood. Undaunted by Virgil's lack of interest, the man at the bar turned from Virgil and continued his discussion with the patron standing next to him. "That boy of his—Lucius they call him—he's gonna be just as crazy as his old man someday, mark my words."

The other man nodded a grudging response, not wanting to get entangled in conversation.

"Ol' Ben's got the boy holed up in the hospital right now as if that'll do him any good." He turned back to the booth. "Didja know that, Virgil? Ol' Ben got the Cady kid locked in a hospital room like he's some kinda criminal. Even got ol' Nils settin' outside his door like a guard."

Fenner ignored him and poured another beer, then he waved at Fannie to bring a fresh pitcher, but another customer picked up on the conversation.

"Nils Larsen couldn't guard a garbage can," the new entry slurred.

"Now why would you want to say that?" Gilly challenged. Nils was a home-grown boy, not destined to be a corporate executive or a rocket scientist but certainly deserving of more consideration than he was getting tonight at Gilly's.

The customer shrugged sheepishly and sipped at his whiskey.

"It seems to me," Gilly continued, "that we ought to be trying to heal our wounds instead of opening new ones."

Given his standing in the town's social structure, Gilly could get away with that sort of scolding.

Except Virgil Fenner wasn't buying it. "Listen to Father fuckin' Gillespie," he said loudly, no question about the challenge in his voice.

Gilly wiped his hands on his apron and moved down the bar across from Virgil's booth. He wasn't a big man but he'd handled trouble often enough, and if things got too rowdy, Littlejohn was only a short phone call away. "You don't hear too well, do you, Fenner?"

Virgil just leered back at him, saying nothing.

"You open your dirty mouth like that one more time and you're outta here and I don't mean just for tonight, Fenner, I mean for good."

Gilly fixed the booth with an angry stare but Virgil just sneered and sipped at his beer. Fannie Setzer waddled over with a fresh pitcher and she looked to Gilly for approval. The owner thought for a moment, finally nodded reluctantly, and, with a last warning glare, walked away to refill the glass of a thirsty patron.

"You gonna take that kinda shit?" Dick Harman asked, secretly pleased at the dose of comeuppance that Gilly had dished out.

"Fuck him," Virgil mumbled as the combination of anger and alcohol began to take its toll.

"Did you know that they had the Cady kid at the hospital like Mel said?" Harman asked.

"Lot of good that'll do if there's still some kinda spell out there," Virgil said.

"Do you really believe in that stuff?" Harman wondered. His sallow face was creased with wonder.

"Fuckin' right," Virgil answered, loud enough to be heard in the next booth but not so loud that Gilly caught it.

Harman looked surprised. "Well, if there really was a curse and Festus did put it on, maybe now that he's dead it won't work anymore."

"Maybe," Virgil agreed. "But maybe not. Anyway, I ain't gonna take the chance." He looked across the booth with alcohol-hooded eyes. "I'm tired of waiting for Littlejohn to do something about it. I'll do it myself."

"Waddya mean?"

"The kid, stupid. We take the kid. We let him know that if anybody else gets hurt, his ass is done for."

"Christ, Virgil, the kid'll squeal on us, then it'll be our ass."

Virgil muffled a burp. "He won't even know it was us. I got it all figured out."

"Dick Harman wasn't thrilled to be included in Virgil's plans but he lacked the stomach to extricate himself. He shrugged helplessly. "When are you gonna do it?"

"When are *we* gonna do it?" Fenner corrected. "We're gonna do it tonight."

Forgetting his earlier rebuff, the man at the bar turned back to Virgil's booth. He weaved from side to side and a wave of whiskey sloshed over the edge of his glass. Slurring noticeably, he asked, "Are you going to Festus's funeral, Virgil?"

Virgil slammed his glass on the table and shouted, "Will you shut the fuck up."

"That does it." Gilly ducked under the bar and stormed down to Virgil's booth. "Out, Fenner," he ordered, and he jerked his thumb toward the door.

Virgil studied him sullenly. "I ain't finished my beer yet."

"Get out," Gilly repeated, "or I call Littlejohn and he'll whip your butt so bad you won't be able to walk for a week."

Virgil sneered at the threat. "I'll go, Gillespie, but not 'cause I'm scared of Littlejohn." He pushed himself heavily from the booth and bumped the smaller man with his bloated belly. "I'll go 'cause I don't like your fuckin' face. C'mon, Harman, let's get outta here."

As his cohort started to rise, Virgil lifted the half-full pitcher from the table and dumped it deliberately at Gilly's feet.

"Haw, haw," he laughed as he staggered toward the door.

17

WITH EACH PASSING moment, Dick Harman felt the faint stirrings of panic. Getting drunk with Virgil and tagging along with him when he pulled some of his juvenile antics was one thing, but kidnapping—that was a serious crime. It was more than Harman had bargained for. They sat in Virgil's old Chevy at the far end of the hospital parking lot, watching the evening sky turn a prism of color before finally succumbing to the pitch of night.

"There's got to be another way, Virgil. I mean what if we get caught. We can go to jail," Harman whined.

"We ain't gettin' caught and we ain't goin' to no jail." Virgil popped the top of a can of Bud and turned angrily to his unwilling partner. "You want your kid to get killed by snakes, Harman? That's what he said he was afraid of."

Harman sucked moodily on his beer can.

"Well, do you?" Virgil insisted.

" 'Course I don't, Virgil."

"Then stop your goddamn bellyachin'."

Dick Harman breathed a sigh of resignation and looked at the hospital lights across the dark parking lot.

"Now let's go over the plan one more time," Virgil said. "You do just exactly what I say and everything's gonna work out just fine."

"What do you think, John? Will he be OK?"

The priest and the doctor stood over the bed looking down on the sleeping boy.

"Physically there doesn't seem to be anything wrong with him," Dr. Logan observed. "But he's in a state of shock and so far he isn't responding. He's mildly sedated right now. I'll be able to get a better idea of his condition when he comes out of it."

The doctor picked up Lucius's limp arm and checked his pulse, looking at the count on his watch through the bottom of his bifocals. "So much for the medical diagnosis," he said. "What's the latest from your side?"

"It's a puzzler," the priest admitted, "but one has to look at the facts, and to my way of thinking, there's simply too many of them to be coincidence."

"Meaning?"

"Meaning it's hard to dispute the presence of something evil."

"And unexplainable," the doctor added.

"I'm not going to agree to that, John. To a scientific mind like your own it might be unexplainable but to me it's as real as cancer. The difference is that you're able to see your cancer and you can slice it out with a sharp knife. The disease that Lucius has isn't so obvious and my weapons aren't so sharp."

"So in your opinion, the boy's possessed."

"Not exactly possessed, but for whatever reason, the demon's always near him."

"Father O'Connor," the doctor said, taking off his glasses and cleaning them with a cloth, "I may have a scientific mind but that doesn't mean that I have to put my fingers in the wound to believe. You'll be surprised to hear that I'm half tempted to agree with your diagnosis." He glanced out the second-floor window into the dark parking lot. "Now the question is, what can be done about it?"

"When all else fails we can always pray," the old priest said.

"I'm all for that, Father, but if you don't mind I'll do it in the privacy of my own bedroom. I'm bushed."

"As well you should be, John. If there's nothing more to be done here, I'll be on my way too."

With a final glance at the sleeping boy, the priest and the doctor softly left the room and closed the door.

Nils Larsen sat in the corridor staying alert with a Louis L'Amour western.

"Night, Nils," the doctor said. "The boy's out like a light. I don't think you'll be hearing from him on this shift."

"I'll be here just the same, Doctor." He flashed a wary grin. "I don't know for sure what I'm supposed to be looking for, but Ben told me to stay awake and keep my eyes open." He flipped the cover of his book at them. "Not much chance of me going to sleep with this to read."

"Night, Nils."

"Night, Doctor. Night, Father."

With visiting hours finally over, the parking lot emptied quickly, and one by one, the windows darkened across the brick face of the hospital. Driving without headlights, Virgil quietly crossed the lot, stopping next to a metal fire door that blended easily with the red brick.

"See that window right up there?" he said.

Virgil pointed to a window one floor above and slightly to the left of the door and Dick Harman nodded.

"That's where he is. See the bars on the window?"

Harman looked up and nodded once again.

"They call it the prisoner's room. It's for when they want to keep an eye on somebody who's dangerous."

"How do you know so much about the hospital?" Harman wondered.

"I helped build the place, remember? I know every brick and stairwell in the whole fuckin' hospital. That's why the plan's gonna work. Now you go do exactly what I told you."

Harman nodded reluctantly and stepped from the car.

Virgil got out also and walked to the metal fire door. It opened easily since he had earlier entered the hospital with visitors, slipped unseen into the stairwell, and walked down to the ground floor where he strapped a strong piece of filament tape across the spring-loaded latch. He was in and out in less than two minutes. Now, back in the stairwell, he climbed quietly to the second floor, his soft-soled shoes silent on the metal stair treads.

The metal door that faced him was painted a drab beige and

windowless. It had the number two stenciled six inches high at eye level. A bare bulb in a wire cage provided the only illumination. Twisting the doorknob slowly so as not to cause a click, he pushed gently until a narrow gap opened onto the second-floor corridor.

Virgil pressed his head to the door and caught a glimpse of the long hallway. Seated in a straight-backed metal chair about twenty feet away was Nils Larsen, decked out officiously in his crisp tans and browns and totally engrossed in a dog-eared paperback. So far so good, Virgil thought.

"Will Deputy Larsen please come to the main desk for a phone call. Deputy Nils Larsen, please come to the main desk for a phone call."

The page echoed through the hallway and the policeman looked up startled, then he dropped the book beside the chair and started down the hallway. Passing the elevator, he walked down the stairway and arrived half a minute later at the desk.

The receptionist looked up at him and pointed to a white phone on the counter. "You can take it there, Nils."

"Larsen," he said as he lifted the phone from the cradle.

But all he heard on the other end was an insistent dial tone.

"Nobody's there," he told the white-haired woman. "Just a dial tone."

"That's funny," she said. "He was there a minute ago."

"How come you didn't transfer it up to the nurses' desk," Nils asked, curious about the procedure. "I could have got to it quicker up there."

"I would have," the nurse told him, "but he said to ask you to come down here. Something about security."

"Was it Chief Littlejohn?"

"I don't think so. I'd have recognized his voice."

"Hmm. That's strange."

She gave him a smile and a shrug. "If he calls back, I'll try again—unless you want to wait a bit."

"Better not," Nils said. "Ben wants me to stay close to that room."

A startled look crossed his face as he was shocked to action by his own words.

"Oh, shit," he barked. He spun around and sprinted to the stairs.

As soon as the deputy disappeared around the corner, Virgil pushed open the door and stepped into the corridor. It was empty and quiet except for the lingering echo of Larsen's footsteps. Wasting no time, he hurried the few steps to the door beside the folding chair. Hanging from his back pocket was a small burlap bag with a drawstring to pull over the boy's head. He pushed open the door and peered inside.

A dim night-light cast an eerie glow across the room. Lucius Cady lay flat on his back, breathing deeply, sleeping the sleep of the drugged. With little need for stealth, Virgil hurried to the bedside and, in a quick and brutal move, lifted the blond head from the pillow, pulled on the bag and jerked on the drawstring, at the same time clamping his hand over the small face to stifle any shouts of alarm.

He needn't have bothered. Lucius Cady was limp and lifeless, numbed in a dreamless stupor. It didn't really matter to Virgil Fenner. He would just as soon have chopped the boy on the jaw but this did make it easier. He looked at his watch. It had been less than sixty seconds since the page drew Nils Larsen from his western fantasy. Good—even better than planned. He jerked down the crisp white sheet and hoisted the boy over his shoulder. He seemed weightless. Hurrying back to the door he poked his head outside and looked to the left, then to the right. It was clear. He stepped into the hall and hurried to the fire door.

As Virgil reached the door, he heard the racing footsteps behind him. He stopped and glanced back.

"Stop," Larsen shouted.

Virgil pushed quickly into the stairwell and thrust the limp boy into Dick Harman's waiting arms. The man was still out of breath since his jog from the corner telephone booth.

"Get him in the trunk. Now," Virgil snapped, and with a frightened look at Lucius's burlap-covered head, Dick Harman clanged down the flight of stairs and pushed into the night.

The ground-level door had barely clicked shut when the second-floor fire door burst open. The young deputy never saw

Virgil's foot shoot out. He launched headfirst down the metal stairway, finally touching down on the next to the bottom step where his head smashed into the metal tread with a hollow thud. He rolled to the bottom, then lay motionless, his head cocked unnaturally, his eyes staring blindly at the bare bulb in the ceiling.

Virgil Fenner stared down and grinned. "Fuck you, cop," he said, and he reached into his pocket, pulled out a small object, and dropped it on the deputy's breathless chest. Then he hurried through the fire door, jumped into the waiting car, and gunned it out of the parking lot.

18

THE NURSE ON duty that night, Edith Porter, had nodded coyly to young Nils Larsen when he passed her station on the way downstairs to the main desk. She glanced up anxiously when he raced by a minute or two later. Curious, she left her station to follow him, reaching the corner that turned onto the south corridor in time to see him disappear through a fire exit near the end of the hallway. She had noticed something in Nils's face as he passed that spoke of more than usual trouble. Reluctant to leave her duty, she stood at the intersection of the corridors for a full minute, waiting for Nils to reemerge and take up his post by the door to the "prisoner's" room. But as the seconds ticked by and he still didn't reappear, Edith grew concerned. Moving quickly in her rubber-soled shoes, she walked to the fire exit and pushed it open. She stepped onto the landing, looked down the stairs, and threw a hand to her mouth to stifle a gasp.

Nils Larsen lay at the bottom of the stairs, his feet on the steps, his back on the landing. His arms were flung out to his sides and his dead eyes stared at the ceiling. She raced down the steps, saw the goat's ear lying on his chest, and gagged.

Virgil drove cautiously, avoiding Main Street by looping around the back side of town on the way to Ridge Road. He knew that he should feel worried but he wasn't. He felt exhilarated. Killing Nils Larsen wasn't part of his plan but it didn't matter. He had intended to leave the goat's ear in the stairwell from the start, to make it look like Lucius's escape was more of the evil at work. Leaving it with the dead deputy made it all the more effective. He grinned as he turned onto Ridge Road, thinking of the ruckus the goat made when he snipped off its ear with a pair of hedge clippers.

Dick Harman hadn't spoken since Virgil had handed the boy to him. As ordered, he had placed the night-shirted bundle in the trunk and climbed into the passenger seat. Moments later, Virgil had appeared and jumped behind the wheel.

"What happened in there?" Harman asked shakily.

Virgil squinted into the headlights of an oncoming car. "Just a little trouble. Nothing serious."

He gave Harman a smile as they left the fading lights of Hensleyville behind them. Five minutes later, after a few turns on country roads, he slowed to a crawl, then pulled off the main road onto an almost-invisible path that trailed into the woods.

The old Chevy bounced and bumped and leafy branches raked its sides as they moved slowly ahead. The trail was barely more than a footpath, but it was clear of trees and passable. They had gone about three hundred bumpy yards straight in from the road when the headlights finally picked up Virgil's destination.

One could hardly call it a shack. Shed would be more like it. It had been there for as long as Virgil could remember. Local lore spun the tale that some long-forgotten moonshiner once called the place home while he was fermenting his illegal brew. When Virgil had come upon it as a kid, he had used it as a clubhouse. Apparently nobody had stumbled onto it since. That suited Virgil perfectly.

The structure was a ten-by-eight box with a sloping roof. It was about the same size as the fishing shacks that popped up on Lizard Lake in the dead of winter. A door with four pane windows, all smashed and boarded, was the only break in the tar-paper-covered walls. It was bleak and foreboding.

"You're not gonna put him here, are you?" Dick Harman said incredulously.

"Why not? We spent a lot of nights here, didn't we? Didn't hurt us none."

Fenner walked to the back of the car and opened the trunk.
The inside light was broken so he shone a flashlight on the
white bundle. Except for the bouncing from the rough ride,
Lucius lay just as Harman had left him, hooded head resting on
a pile of greasy rags. His hospital gown was pulled over his
knees revealing thin white legs stretched over the spare tire.

Harman moved to his side and followed the beam of light.
"What are you gonna do now, Virgil?"

"Don't use my name goddammit," Fenner hissed. "Hold
this." He shoved the light at Harman, then, none too gently, he
lifted the boy from the trunk and moved through the knee-high
weeds to the shed.

"Open the door," he ordered.

There was no doorknob, only a rotting hole where one used
to be, and Harman creaked the door open. Shining the
flashlight inside, boyhood memories flooded his troubled mind
as he saw the open studs, the blackened walls, the spindly chair
flipped over on the rotting planks of the floor. Two beer cans,
years old but remarkably preserved, sat upright in the corner.
Cobwebs crisscrossed the corners where walls and ceiling met.
A cot mattress, filthy with use and age, was rolled up against
the wall to his right.

"Get outta the way," Fenner ordered, and using Lucius's
outstretched feet as a ram, he nudged Harman to the side. "Get
the rope. It's under the seat."

Mechanically, Harman trudged to the car while Virgil
carried Lucius into the shed. When he returned, Lucius was
propped up in the chair stirring lightly as the powerful effects
of shock and the sedative began to wear off.

"Keep the light on him while I tie him," Virgil said, and
while Dick Harman watched with mounting concern, Fenner
looped the strong rope around Lucius and the chair, finishing
the job by tying his wrists and ankles to the rungs.

Lucius moaned softly then, finally realizing his predicament, his head snapped from side to side as he tried to shake
off the smothering burlap. "Where am I?" he gasped. "Why
am I tied up?"

His thin voice was on the edge of panic. He had no idea

where he was, his last lucid thought being an image of his dead father dangling from the rafter.

The earlier effect of the alcohol was evaporating and the full realization of what he had done began to dawn on Virgil. Not that he felt any guilt about it, but he knew he'd better be cautious.

"You're the reason everybody's gettin' killed around here all of a sudden, ain't you?" Virgil rasped a throaty whisper designed to both disguise his voice and intimidate his captive. He heard the hooded boy take a deep and faltering breath.

"It's not me," the boy said, an edge of resignation in his muffled voice.

"Oh, then who is it?" Virgil rasped.

Lucius didn't answer.

Dick Harman stood next to the trussed and hooded boy, listening with apprehension. He kept the light trained on the burlap mask.

"My arms hurt," the boy complained.

"Tough shit," Virgil hissed. "Tell me what you do that's makin' everybody die."

Lucius turned his head slowly from side to side as if in pondering a response he was checking the attentiveness of an unseen audience. He mumbled something unintelligible.

"I can't hear you," Virgil whispered harshly, and he gripped the front of the hospital gown and twisted the material under Lucius's chin.

Lucius's fear-filled voice croaked a response that loosened Virgil's grip and sent an icy chill through Dick Harman's spine. "It's an evil beast," he managed to say amid a flood of hidden tears. "I don't tell it to do nothin'. I don't even want it. It just comes," he told them in a choking voice. "It just comes."

His voice trailed off and his slight shoulders heaved in tiny convulsions.

"It just comes, does it," Virgil hissed sarcastically. Then his voice rose, and forgetting any need for anonymity he roared, "It just comes when you cast one of your goddamn spells, that's when it comes," and he lashed out viciously at the burlap with his balled-up fist.

Lucius's hidden head snapped to the side as Virgil's blow

landed on his cheekbone. Once again, he was mercifully unconscious. He never felt the second or the third openhanded blows that jarred his head from side to side.

"Stop hitting him, Virgil. For Christ's sake, you'll kill him," Harman whined.

"So what if I do," Fenner snapped. "Ain't he killed half the town already." He looked with undisguised malice at the trussed-up boy. "He'll get whatever's comin' to him." Virgil did a final check on the knots that bound the boy to the chair. Satisfied, he went to the door. "Move your ass, Harman. We ain't got all day."

Before he pulled the door shut, Harman flashed the beam inside one last time. Bare feet and thin white legs protruded from beneath the hospital gown. Boyish arms were pulled painfully around the back of the wooden chair. A burlap sack hid the sad eyes and youthful face that hung toward his chest. A premonition of disaster roiled in Harman's stomach and he flicked off the light and trudged to the car.

"What are we gonna do now, Virgil?" Harman worried as they bounced along the rutted path on the way to the small wooded road.

As far as Harman was concerned, the whole affair had gotten monstrously out of hand. Getting drunk and taking potshots at mailboxes—those kind of Virgil Fenner antics he could go along with, even enjoy. But snatching the Cady kid from the hospital? He hadn't counted on that. As far as the wave of Hensleyville tragedies was concerned, Dick Harman wasn't sure what to believe. Until Virgil's accusations and his violent plan, Harman hadn't connected Lucius Cady to any of the deaths. That would have taken a thought process that included deductive reasoning and Dick Harman preferred to limp through life mindlessly. That's what made him Virgil Fenner's logical cohort and accomplice. No thinking adult would seek out the company of an asshole like Virgil Fenner. The pair just naturally fell in together. But now, after years of drunken sprees and childish vandalism, Dick Harman was finally afraid and it wasn't only the threat of getting caught, it was the undefinable grip of terror brought on by Lucius Cady's words.

"It's an evil beast," the boy had said and the thoughts that conjured up made Dick Harman shiver.

Virgil ignored Harman's question, watching for the deeper ruts as they jolted the last few yards to the gravel country road.

"What are we gonna do now?" Harman repeated.

"We're gonna go back to town and act just like nothin' ever happened," Virgil answered. He kicked the gas pedal and they roared down the road.

"What if somebody saw us leavin'? Maybe Nils saw the car in the parking lot—or maybe one of the patients was looking out of a window."

"Nils didn't see shit," Virgil said with a chuckle. "Gimme a beer."

Dick Harman obediently popped the tops off two cans of Bud. Virgil emptied his can by the time they reached the filling station at the edge of town. He arced the empty in a left-handed hook over the roof of the car. It clattered on the apron in front of the unleaded pump. Dick Harman was still sipping when they saw the glow of flashing lights.

"That's comin' from somewhere near the hospital."

"Do tell," Virgil said, unconcerned, and he belched in Harman's face. "Let's go and have us a look see."

Ben Littlejohn's patrol car was nosed against the curb at the edge of the hospital parking lot. It was near the metal fire door. Off to the side a cluster of citizens talked, their grim faces glowing like psychedelic posters in the spinning orange light. Room lights were unnaturally ablaze as curious patients craned their necks against the windows.

Virgil bounced into the lot and rolled the old Chevy to a stop behind the group. "What's happenin', Barney?" he called through the rolled-down window.

Barney Eller broke from the pack and strode to Virgil's car. But for the good fortune to have married a good woman, Barney might have been another of Virgil's cronies much the same as Dick Harman. He leaned down next to the window.

"It's Nils Larsen," he said excitedly. "He went and got hisself killed. They think he was chasin' that Cady kid when it happened."

"K-k-k-killed!" Dick Harman's eyes popped open and he

stared at Virgil in disbelief. "Did you hear what he said, Virgil? Nils Larsen got killed."

Out of sight of Barney Eller, Virgil reached across the seat and grabbed the panicked man by the shirt. "I ain't deaf," he said pleasantly. "How did it happen, Barney?"

"Ain't sure, Virgil. Littlejohn won't say too much. He got the door shut and the whole area roped off."

Virgil pushed open the car door without warning and Eller had to jump back to keep from being hit. Walking around the bunched-up crowd, he approached the police car. He stopped at the orange tape that hung at waist height in a semicircle around the metal door.

Barney Eller shuffled along behind him. "See what I mean," he said.

Dick Harman had also left the car and stood on Virgil's other side. "What's gonna happen now, Virgil?" he said, his voice cracking with the effort.

"Know what else I heard?" Barney asked, leaning toward Virgil conspiratorially.

Virgil gave him an amused look. "No, Barney. What else did you hear?" he asked, washing the man in his beery breath.

"They found somethin' funny on Nils's body."

With a growing sense of dread, Dick Harman asked impatiently, "What are you talking about, Barney? What the hell did they find?"

Eller grinned and his teeth glinted orange in the spinning light. "Part of a goat," he said, leaning close and wide-eyed. "They found another part of a goat."

Dick Harman felt his stomach churn and he had to swallow hard to keep from getting sick on the spot. As Barney Eller wandered back to the pack of onlookers, Harman grabbed Virgil's sleeve. "He's dead, Virgil. Did you hear what Barney said? Nils Larsen is dead. What the hell did you do to him?"

Virgil roughly shrugged Harman's hand away. "I didn't do nothin' to him. He tripped. It ain't my fault if the cops around here are clumsy, is it?"

"Then it was an accident?" Harman asked with a ray of hope.

Fenner smiled grimly at the frightened man. "Yeah, Harman, that's what it was, an accident." Then, chuckling to himself, he walked to the edge of the curious crowd. With his hands triumphantly on his hips he faced the gathering. "What did I tell you?" he announced. "I told Littlejohn that somethin' like this was going to happen but nobody wanted to listen to me."

"We're going looking for the Cady kid," someone in the group called out. "Ben wants to bring him in."

"It's kinda like a posse," another man volunteered. "Ben figures that the kid can't get too far on foot and he wants to find him. We're gonna comb the area. He figures the kid's hiding in one of the buildings or maybe he's lying low in one of the cornfields."

" 'Bout time he's doin' something." Then, sensing an opportunity, Virgil said, "Me and Harman will go along with you." He turned to Dick Harman who stood by his side in stunned silence. "How about it, Dick? Wanna go?" Without waiting for Harman's reply he turned back to the crowd and said, "We're gonna go home first and get our guns."

"Unh, unh," Barney Eller warned. "Ben says there ain't to be no guns. All he wants to do is find the kid. He ain't armed or anything like that."

Looking at the group, Virgil noticed a few of the town teenagers. "OK," he agreed reluctantly. "I'm gonna go home and get my kid then. He can help. Besides, it ain't safe for him to be sittin' all alone at home. He was one of the kids with Pete Bishop, you know."

A few of the people nodded sympathetically.

"Better get a move on, Virgil," Barney warned. "Ben says we're leavin' in a half hour."

Virgil looked at his watch. It was almost eleven o'clock. "Then we better hustle, right, Harman?" Then he took the man by the arm and led him to the Chevy.

19

VIRGIL BOUNCED FROM the lot with a screech of tires and a loud haw, haw. Before he reached the corner he had the top popped from a fresh can of Bud. "What a bunch of goddamn jerks," he said with a sneer.

"I don't like it, Virgil. I don't like it one bit." Dick Harman had told his wife that he was going out for a couple of laughs and a beer with Virgil Fenner, which was true enough, but he didn't bargain on a kidnapping and a deputy's death. He wished now that he had stayed at home. Maybe he should quit drinking so much, quit running around at night. At the very least he should spend less time with Virgil Fenner. The man was trouble with a capital T. But all the hindsight in the world couldn't change his predicament now.

"We could be in real trouble. Goddammit, Virgil, you never told me somethin' happened to Nils Larsen."

Virgil tromped harder on the gas pedal and shrugged. "Accidents happen, Harman. Them's the breaks. Besides, if I'd a'known you was gonna be such a goddamn crybaby, I wouldn't have asked you to come along."

Harman's sallow face grew even longer at the rebuke.

"Haw, haw. I'm just kiddin'." Fenner pulled another sweaty can from the floor and shoved it at his contrite friend.

Harman shook his head and smiled a lopsided grin. "I guess everything'll be OK," he said.

"You bet it will," Virgil roared and he dropped into a lower gear and popped the clutch. The car shuddered, then leapt ahead. "Haw, haw."

"Why'd you want to go on the hunt for the Cady kid?" Harman asked.

"Simple. Nobody's gonna suspect anybody that's helpin' out. If we weren't there they might get suspicious."

Dick Harman mulled Virgil's explanation. "Makes sense," he admitted.

"Makes damn good sense," Fenner corrected.

Fenner squealed around a corner, spinning the wheel with one hand while the other tried to balance the can of beer. A fountain of foam washed over his hand.

"That was a good idea you had about gettin' the kids to go along," Harman said. He sipped at his beer and nodded appreciatively. "Too much crazy shit goin' on in this town to leave them home alone. I mean them bein' on the campout and everything."

Virgil snorted derisively. "Don't be such an asshole, Harman. There ain't nothin' gonna happen to them. Them accidents were just bad luck, pure and simple."

Harman turned to the driver, his eyes wide with surprise. "That ain't what you said at the town meeting," he accused. "You was the one blamin' it all on the Cady kid. Then you even snatched him outta the hospital." Harman toyed with the top of the can. "Christ, Virgil, if you didn't believe none of that stuff, why'd you go and do that?"

Virgil took a last swig and flung the empty can through the window. Turning to Harman he grinned at his own cleverness. "To make an ass out of Littlejohn," he said. "Haw, haw. It worked, didn't it? He looks like a jerk already and when they don't find the Cady kid tonight he'll really look like an idiot." Fenner giggled and banged his fist on the steering wheel. "I wish I coulda seen his face when he seen that goat's ear."

Harman wrinkled his brow. "Yeah. I was wonderin' about that. Where'd that come from anyway?"

"A real pissed-off goat. Haw, haw, haw."

Fenner pulled the top from another can and drained a third of it off in one quick gulp. A river of amber rolled down his chin and stained the front of his shirt.

"I got the idea this afternoon," he bragged. "I wasn't sure what I was gonna do with it but I figured it'd come in handy sometime. Haw, haw." He banged gleefully on the wheel again. "I bet it scared the shit out of 'em. And now they'll really figure that the Cady kid made all those other things happen."

A frown suddenly clouded Dick Harman's sallow face. "But when the Cady kid shows up in town again, he's gonna tell everybody what really happened and some of 'em might believe him. Then what'll happen?"

Virgil drove along silently as if Harman hadn't asked the question. He pulled another beer from the floor and popped the top.

"What'll happen then, Virgil?" Harman insisted.

Virgil Fenner sucked deeply on the fresh can. He burped and wiped the back of this hand across his lips, allowing the old car to careen untended down the street. Finally he clamped his hand back on the wheel and answered, "What makes you think he'll ever show up in town again?"

"Whaddya mean? Where the hell else does the kid have to go? His old man's dead. He ain't gonna live in that old shack all alone."

"What makes you think he's gonna live anywhere?" Virgil asked.

A sudden fear, boiling like nothing he had ever experienced, caught a painful hook on Dick Harman's gut. Could Virgil mean what Harman thought he meant? He looked cautiously to his left, searching for the glint of mischief in Virgil's eye that presaged a lusty haw, haw. There was none. Virgil stared with icy eyes at the street that flew by. There was not a trace of humor in his gaze.

"Now wait j-just a minute, Virgil." Harman's face paled in the darkness, a sheen of sweat reflected in the lights of a passing car. "It's one thing to snatch the kid outta the hospital and stick him in that old shed. I mean I'll go along with that. But if you're sayin' what I think you're sayin', I'm gonna—"

His whiny voice faltered in mid-threat. He had never stood up to Virgil before and his current infusion of fear-induced courage slowed to a trickle.

"You ain't gonna do shit," Virgil said with a sneer. "If you open your fuckin' mouth, I'm gonna tell 'em that snatching the kid was your idea, then what'll you do?"

"But it wasn't my idea, Virg, I didn't know—"

"And I'll tell 'em it was you who tripped Larsen and got him killed."

"Tripped?" Harman said, his eyes suddenly wide with understanding. "I thought you said it was an accident."

Virgil jerked the car to a stop in front of Harman's house. His own house was only one street over. Both homes were somewhat shabby compared to their well-kept neighbors. "You go and get your kid," he ordered. "I'm goin' home to pick up Wally. I'll be back in five minutes. Tonight we're goin' out like good citizens to try to find poor little Lucius Cady. Tomorrow we got a job to do."

Reluctantly, Dick Harman stepped from the car. His stomach ached and his head pounded. Even his moral sense, poorly developed as it was, had a hard time contemplating murder—especially that of an innocent child. But balancing the scales with that moral sense was a finely tuned instinct for survival. Dick Harman didn't want to go to jail for either kidnapping or for murder, and if he spoke up now, the kidnapping charge was a certainty. On the other hand, if he went along with Virgil's heinous plan, a murder might never be discovered.

As Virgil squealed away, Harman trudged wearily to the cracked concrete path leading to his front door. Downstairs lights were still burning, unusual for so late at night. As he pushed on the picket gate, he saw something on the porch, something dark in the yellow gloom. It wasn't until he reached the bottom step that he realized he was looking at the lower jaw of a goat.

Virgil circled the block and rolled to a stop in front of his own house, a frame two-story lacking both care and pride. Weeds flourished on the sloping lawn. A bald tire leaned against the side of the house next to an upturned wheelbarrow. Beer can in hand, he shouldered open the door and lurched drunkenly up the walk, kicking idly at the encroaching weeds as he passed.

"Wally," he shouted even before he reached the door. "Get

off your butt and get out here. We're goin' huntin'." He tripped on the top step but caught his balance before reaching the door. "Wally," he shouted again, pushing through the doorway, "where the hell are you?"

Becky Fenner's voice pierced the night like an ice pick and stabbed at his ears. "Virgil," she shrieked, "hurry!"

The call came from the kitchen and Virgil was shocked to a numbed sense of alertness. Stumbling down the narrow hall-way, he knocked over the telephone stand and his shoulder cocked askew a family portrait.

Becky stood barefoot in the kitchen doorway, dressed in a shabby nightgown, hair in curlers, mouth working uselessly as she pointed into the room. Her whole body trembled. "That— that thing is after Wally," she finally managed to say.

Virgil studied her strangely through beer-clouded eyes, annoyed at how she looked and at how his ears still rung with her strident alarm. "What the fuck are you talkin' about?" he blurted with a burp.

"In there." As she pointed, she backed out of the kitchen so Virgil could see.

Virgil poked his head around the doorway and his eyes were drawn to the far corner where Wally huddled in terror. The boy was backed up against the wall and staring at the floor, but the object of his fear was hidden from Virgil's view by the corner of the kitchen table. He took a leaden step through the doorway for a better view and was jolted sober.

A bloody ear, dark and hairy, lay on the worn pattern of the kitchen floor. Crouched next to it, taking occasional bites that flipped the ear from side to side, was the most disgusting creature that Virgil had ever seen. It resembled a spider but could a spider be so huge? Maybe in Africa or Brazil, but in Hensleyville? Its furry legs shot up from its fist-sized body at sharp angles before bending at a pointed joint to reach the floor. The head was as big as a plum with a pair of shiny pincers that squeezed in and out obscenely as it pierced the ear, dropped it, then pierced it once again. The hideous thing crouched by the table leg, a mere four feet from where Wally stood trembling, sweaty and ashen-faced, in the corner.

"G-g-g-get it away from me," he pleaded.

He was one with the wall, pushing helplessly into the safety of the corner. His eyes were locked on the grotesque creature, his face was a sweaty mask of terror. "Pl-please, Dad. Don't let it get me."

Virgil felt his knees tremble. His legs barely supported him but he found the strength to stumble from the room, disappearing down the hallway as Becky watched helplessly.

"Virgil," she screamed, "don't go. Don't leave that thing there."

Charging up the steps two at a time, Virgil burst into the bedroom where he threw open the closet door and grabbed at the shotgun. It was a matter of principle for Virgil to keep the weapon at the ready, loaded with enough shot and powder to blow a hole of deadly proportions through the chest of the first prowler who violated the shabby sanctity of his home. He itched to use it but never intended to vent its fury on a crawling insect. With his finger on the trigger and his left hand clutching the barrel, he thudded back down the stairs.

Becky, Wally, and the creature were exactly as he had left them. He brushed past his wife, and barrel pointed at the floor, he inched into the kitchen.

"Sh-shoot it, Dad. Kill it," Wally begged.

Virgil moved cautiously into the room, a sheen of perspiration covering his face. His eyes and the barrel of the shotgun were trained unerringly on the spider. With his back to the counter, Virgil inched sideways, maintaining a safe distance from the creature as he worked his way to the corner where Wally shook in fright.

The spider clamped its pincers on the leathery treat and snapped its head from side to side, finally releasing the ear and sending it skidding a foot across the floor. The rapid movement spooked Virgil and he jerked the gun, coming within a speck of pressure of blowing the tattered ear into oblivion. In that instant, the spider crouched deeper, as if loading its legs for an explosive leap. Virgil swung the gun back and jerked at the trigger, blowing a hole through the floorboards and scattering shot into the basement below.

The gaping hole was at the exact spot where the spider had been an instant before, but in the flash from the muzzle, Virgil had seen the furry blur shoot into the air. Wally's tortured scream was almost lost in the echo of the blast. The creature, with legs spread wide, clamped onto the front of Wally Fenner's T-shirt.

With its hairy legs outstretched, the spider spanned an area from nipple to nipple, sternum to belt buckle. Clinging like a thirsty leech, the animal cocked its head and spread its pincers, ready to puncture the puffy flesh of Wally's chest and inject its juices.

Becky Fenner put her hands to her mouth and screeched, "Help him."

Wally's mouth opened but his vocal chords wouldn't function. He slumped against the wall and the blood drained from his face. In a paternal reflex, uncharacteristically courageous, Virgil swiped at the clinging creature with a closed fist. His stomach turned when the spider's body melded to his fist, but his reaction was quicker than the spider's and it was ripped from Wally's shirt. It landed on its back with a sickening sound, then flipped upright with disgusting agility.

About eight feet separated Virgil and the animal and he filled some of the space with the warm barrel of his shotgun. Virgil trusted his skill and he knew the size of the shot pattern at the distance. He knew he couldn't miss and he felt elated and in charge.

"Shoot it, Dad. Quick, before it jumps again."

"It ain't jumpin' nowhere again," Virgil said and he sighted down the barrel and tightened his finger on the trigger.

A moment before the blast, Virgil would have sworn that the animal gave him an insolent stare but he'd never really know for sure. Where the body had been there was now a wet hole surrounded by eight hairy legs that twitched and scurried, stopped, twitched again before finally accepting the rude reality of their death.

As if fearful of its resurrection, Virgil and Wally inched around the hairy mess, their backs pressed tightly against the counter, their eyes glued to the creature's remains. A leg twitched again, a last grasp at life, and the father and son darted toward the kitchen door where Becky Fenner stood trembling, hands to mouth, drained of color.

"Get in the car," Virgil ordered, herding his family down the hallway with a warm barrel of the shotgun.

Becky didn't protest, and clad in her nightgown, she hurried down the path. With his family aboard, Virgil screeched from the curb. He no longer scoffed at Lucius Cady's powers but he was more certain than ever of his course of action.

20

BEN LITTLEJOHN LOOKED on sadly as Nils Larsen's body was removed from the stairwell, to be relocated to some cool, dark spot in the hospital awaiting the pitiless knives and buzzing saws of the autopsy. Shaking his head, he asked Dr. Logan, "When's it going to end, John? How many is it now? How many people have died?"

"I'm afraid I've lost count," the doctor admitted.

Woody Lockwood fought to keep his voice under control. "There was a time when I chalked these tragedies off to coincidence. Pete Bishop—no one thought twice about that. I mean no one suspected anything unusual other than Pete being in the wrong place at the wrong time."

He searched Ben's face for agreement and the police chief nodded.

"Even after Jeff Zack took sick and Lenny Brothers drowned I wasn't ready to accept a supernatural explanation. I mean we're in the twentieth century and this is Hensleyville, not Transylvania."

From the flat top of the newel post in the stairwell he picked up the sealed plastic bag where Littlejohn had placed the evidence. The three men looked at the ear but none ventured an explanation for its presence.

The lawyer continued, "Eyes, ears, apparitions, bad dreams, accidents—and all of it tied together by a bunch of kids telling scary stories around a campfire." He turned to John

Logan. "I'm afraid I've run out of coincidences, Doctor. I like to think of myself as a man of logic but this defies all logic." A frown clouded his features as he held the plastic bag up for closer inspection. "There's something evil in this community and I don't know how we're going to stop it." Turning to Ben he shrugged helplessly. "Guns and bullets aren't going to help. We're chasing shadows."

John Logan laid a calming hand on his friend's shoulder. "I know that you're worried for Chris, and I don't blame you. But he'll be safe. He's with Kathryn and she's not going to let anything happen to your boy."

Woody turned to the doctor and smiled gratefully. "I know, John."

But none of them knew. They didn't know where the evil was or how to stop it. All they knew was that it lurked near Lucius Cady. Now he was missing and they all felt an urgent need to find him before the terror struck again.

Ben Littlejohn pulled on the knob of the fire door that opened to the parking lot where the townspeople were gathered to help in the search. "Let's get this group organized," he said. "There's a little boy wandering around out there somewhere and my guess is that he's as scared as we are."

Becky Fenner huddled in the corner of the back seat, her eyes glazed, her arms wrapped around her chest, hugging tightly to still the tremors that convulsed her. Wally sat up front next to his father, still too terrified to speak. With jaws clenched resolutely, a sober Virgil Fenner screeched around the corner and ground to a stop in front of the Harman house. In violation of the quiet of the night, he leaned on the horn. At the insistent blare, a few lights popped on in surrounding houses but there was no response from the Harmans.

"Hurry, goddammit," he mumbled under his breath and he blasted the horn again.

"Shuddup out there," a voice howled from an upstairs window across the street.

With his left arm thrust out the window, Virgil answered with an unseen obscenity in the darkness.

Crack! Crack! Crack!

No boy grows up among the hills and farms of southeastern Pennsylvania without knowing the difference between gunshots and backfires. "What the f——" Virgil growled as he heaved open the door, grabbed his shotgun from the seat, and ran up the path toward the open front door. When he reached the porch, he uttered a sharp yelp of alarm at the sight of the jaw but his momentum carried him past. He was inside the house before he had time to consider the implications.

"Harman," he shouted as he burst through the door.

The crack of another shot directed him to the dining room where he froze in the doorway at the shocking scene. Billy Harman stood atop the dining-room table, bent over like a hunchback under the ceiling, hanging on to the brass light fixture as if, without its support, he'd crumble to the tabletop. The shattered remnants of its frosted globes were sprinkled on the gleaming mahogany along with the debris of a terrarium that had been kicked over in the boy's panic. Billy stared down at the floor, his face grey with fear, his knuckles white in their urgent clutch on the brass chain.

On the colorful oval rug next to the table lay Marilee Harman. She was a pretty little woman and Virgil often fantasized about her. Now she lay on her back apparently passed out, arms and legs akimbo, nightgown lying open to reveal her tempting body, so appealing compared to Becky's dumpy frame. But the sight did nothing to stir Virgil's imagination. It was filled with too many other horrors.

Like a crawling mass, the floor writhed with the shiny bodies of countless snakes. They wound over and around each other, glistening browns and blacks, camouflaged splotches, most smooth and sleek, some bloody and bent at sharp angles where Dick Harman's bullets had destroyed their fluid symmetry. The floor was a constantly moving mass, weaving itself into changing knots and patterns.

A fat black snake with flicking tongue spiraled up the table leg and arched its pointed head over the edge of the surface. Billy lurched away from it and the ceiling ripped open. A shower of plaster rained down amid the shards of frosted glass. He backed off to the farthest corner, one hand tugging on the chain, the other on the ceiling, unable to cry in alarm as his eyes met the tiny black beads in the snake's face.

Crack! Crack!

Click!

Dick Harman squeezed off two more rounds before the hammer fell on an empty chamber. Its spine shattered, the snake's head thudded to the floor, its body still wound tightly around the splintered table leg. Harman stood near the doorway, his back to the wall. With arm outstretched, he aimed the empty weapon at the wriggling mass of flesh.

Click. Click. Click.

Click followed harmless click as Billy's father sought to save his son from the undulating serpents. Another snake, this one brown and black with gemlike patches of green, had almost reached the tabletop. Virgil leveled his shotgun from his hip and pulled the trigger. The blast rang through the small house. It atomized the snake's head and the stump wavered back and forth like a spellbound cobra before slumping to the floor like a discarded garden hose.

"Look." Dick Harman thrust his finger toward his unconscious wife. A snake, no more than eighteen inches long and as fat as a finger, slithered over her shoulder, wound between her breasts, then slipped through the puff of hair where her legs met. Her right arm was stretched above her head, close to where Virgil stood with his smoking shotgun. Only a small snake was between him and the pleading hand. In a move he seemed to enjoy, he brought the gun butt down on the serpent's head, crushing it like a grape. The snake was tying itself into a knot as Virgil grabbed Marilee's hand and dragged her limp body through the swarm and into the next room. So relieved was Dick Harman that he didn't notice Virgil's twisted grin as he watched the flimsy garment fall completely away.

With his wife lying safely on the living-room floor, moaning softly as she slowly regained her wits, Dick Harman turned back to the dining room. The squirming mass of black and brown was focusing on the table's vulnerable legs. Each of the four underpinnings was now encircled by one or more of the creatures, working their way steadily to the edge. Two of the snakes were within inches of making the turn onto the flat surface.

Virgil reloaded and leveled his shotgun at the nearest leg, then quickly reconsidered. His earlier shot had blown a hole in the wall the size of a grapefruit and a similar blast at the table leg would surely topple it, sending Billy Harman into the serpents' crawling midst.

"Billy," he called, "you got to jump."

Billy's eyes were wide as saucers. His knees quivered and each shake brought down a fine shower of plaster from the crumbling ceiling. From the edge of the table to the farthest snake was no more than four or five feet, a simple stride for the teenager, but his legs were boneless and the short step seemed a gaping chasm.

"For Christ's sake, kid, jump. It's only a coupla feet," Virgil exhorted.

Billy Harman took a tentative step toward the edge, arriving there at the same moment that a green head with beady eyes and flashing tongue peered over it.

"Eeeee," he shrieked. He lashed out with his foot, but in the fine white dust that coated the tabletop, his other foot shot from beneath him. He crashed to the table, jerking the fixture from the ceiling in a cloud of dust and a shower of sparks. Stunned from the fall, Billy coughed in the choking cloud of dust. One foot hung over the edge of the table and a thick snake stretched at an angle from the table leg and coiled around his ankle. Two more snakes, using the first one as a bridge, slithered quickly across.

Billy lay on his back, coughing and shaking the dust from his eyes and mind. Looking up, he saw the advancing snakes. One was already beside him on the table, another zigzagged smoothly across his chest. As his father and Virgil watched helplessly, the teenager's eyes rolled back and his head thunked against the mahogany.

"What'll we do?" his father cried in panic.

Fenner looked wildly about him. "I got an idea," he said suddenly and he leaned his gun against the doorjamb and edged along the wall to the bureau, a matching piece of mahogany about six feet long and flush with the floor. With an eye on the carpet of snakes, he eased around it, then he lifted one end and slid it easily along the wall. The piece of furniture was now positioned in front of the dining-room doorway, separated from the table by about six feet.

"All we got to do now," Fenner said, "is clear a path. We'll slide this sucker across the floor to the table. Then we can grab Billy."

"Yeah," Harman agreed, "that'll work."

With a simple shove, the bureau would clear a six-foot swath, enough to open a path to the table and the unconscious boy. Fenner and Harman stood in the doorway behind the heavy piece. With a sweep of his arm, Virgil cleared the top of a few framed pictures and other Harman family heirlooms but Harman didn't seem to notice. He was in a semistupor like the rest of his family.

"Wake up, for Christ's sake," Virgil snapped as he swatted the back of the man's head.

A flicker of life returned to Harman's eyes but they filled with fear when he saw the snakes crawling over his dazed son.

"On three we shove," Fenner ordered. "One, two, heave."

The bureau was old and heavy but the two men underestimated the explosive power of the adrenaline that surged through their veins. The bureau shot forward, but after sliding about a foot, it caught the edge of the oval rug. Before the two could change its course, the heavy piece tilted on its back legs, wavered uncertainly, then crashed down on the squirming mass of reptiles.

The outraged hissing sounded like cold water poured on hot rocks. Heads and tails wriggled helplessly beneath the fallen bureau, curling unnaturally, twisting at sharp angles in their struggle for freedom.

"Grab your kid," Virgil ordered as he spun around and grabbed his gun.

Harman reached for Billy's ankle, the one not enclosed in shiny coils. Hooking his fingers in the cuff of Billy's pants, he pulled viciously and his son's limp body slid across the table, crashed on top of the upturned bureau, then bounced to the floor. Only one snake still clung to him, the large brown serpent on his ankle, and it raised its head and hissed in outrage an instant before Fenner squeezed the trigger and turned it into a headless hose, gushing blood over Billy Harman's crumpled form. Dick Harman paled and wavered from side to side, on the verge of collapsing across his son until Virgil's hand exploded on his cheek like a rifle shot.

"Don't faint now, you asshole. Pick up your kid and let's get the hell outta here."

Snapped from his trance, Dick Harman grabbed Billy's wrists and dragged him toward the hallway. The snakes hissed their resentment and turned en masse, an angry carpet flowing like an ebb tide around the upturned bureau. Virgil lumbered into the living room where Marilee was sitting in the middle of the floor, mumbling incoherently as she fumbled with the buttons of her nightgown.

Fenner rested his gun against the sofa and grabbed her under the arms and flung her effortlessly over his shoulder. She offered no resistance as his fingers closed over her buttocks. With his free hand, he grabbed the barrel of the gun and stepped toward the door. Harman was struggling to lift his son as the hissing swarm closed the gap.

"Here," Fenner ordered and he thrust Marilee into Harman's arms. Looping his arm around Billy's waist, he hoisted the boy like a sack of grain, and carrying their burdens, the two men burst through the front door with the swarm of snakes hissing angrily at their heels.

21

THE OLD CHEVY spun away from the curb, spitting dirt and gravel as it fishtailed down the street. Usually dark and deserted, tonight the neighborhood shone in the dim glow of a dozen porch lights as curious neighbors in nightclothes clustered on the sidewalk muttering among themselves and pointing fingers at Dick and Marilee Harman's house, wondering what new tragedy was about to befall their once-peaceful farm town.

Virgil Fenner was frightened and angry, both emotions directed at the young boy who was only a few miles away, tied helplessly to a straight-backed chair in the midnight dark moonshiner's shed. He was also angry at the muffled blubbering coming from the back seat where Billy Harman and the two wives took gasping breaths between sobs. Wally Fenner sat up front, squeezed between the two dads, not fully recovered from his ordeal but acting the brave role with an occasional pitying grimace at the back seat hysteria.

"Will you shut the hell up back there," Virgil growled as they hurtled toward the hospital.

By the time they bounced into the parking area, the flashing police lights had been put to rest and the lot was illuminated by a few pairs of headlights. A crowd of citizens, larger now than before, mingled near the metal door and Virgil wheeled to a stop beside them, noticing as he did that they were ringed tightly around the police chief. Littlejohn stepped from among them and directed his gaze at Virgil's car.

"What do you want, Fenner?" he asked, making no effort to mask his hostility.

"Do I got to want somethin'?" Virgil shot back, matching tit for tat.

Littlejohn set his hands on his hips and spoke for all to hear. "We have work to do, Fenner, and we don't have time for any of your nonsense."

Virgil stepped closer. He scanned the anxious faces in the crowd and sneered. "I thought you was makin' up a posse, Littlejohn." He smiled maliciously. "I mean it's kind of fittin' ain't it, you bein' dressed up like some goddamn cowboy sheriff and all."

"Go home, Fenner. You're drunk." Ben turned his back on Virgil and tried to pick up where he had left off.

"Whyn't you go fuck yourself, Littlejohn?"

Ben ignored the challenge but turned when he heard another of the Chevy's doors slam.

Dick Harman rounded the front of the car on shaky legs. His eyes were wild as he approached the crowd. "You shoulda seen it," he raved. "Snakes. Just like Billy talked about at the campout. They were everywhere."

Ben Littlejohn held up a calming hand. "Hold up a second, Dick. What are you talking about?"

With rolling eyes and gestures like a boastful fisherman, Dick Harman went on to describe the serpentine invasion of his home. "And there was a goat's jaw on the porch when I got there," he concluded.

The townspeople mumbled among themselves, shaking their heads in disbelief.

"It's true," Harman swore with a raised hand, "every last word of it. Ask Virgil." He looked hopefully at his ostracized ally who stood nearby with his arms folded scornfully across his chest.

"Well, Virgil," someone shouted, "is it?"

Arms still crossed, Virgil lumbered forward. "Damn straight. It happened just like Harman said." His eyes roamed the anxious faces, daring anyone to challenge him. "Not only that," he continued, "I had somethin' happen to me too." He described the spider and the ear and his prowess with the shotgun that dispatched the horrid creature. To dramatically conclude, he reached in his jeans pocket and pulled out the ear. The crowd recoiled and gasped.

Littlejohn stood off to the side and allowed Virgil his say. The information added some new evidence, nothing incriminating, but more pieces to the edgeless puzzle that terrorized and confounded him.

"Wasn't it a spider that your Wally was a'scared of?" a farmer asked.

Virgil nodded.

"Yo, Virgil," another said, "ain't no spiders like that around these here parts."

Virgil glared angrily, then he jerked his thumb at his car. "You callin' me a liar? Ask Wally. Ask Becky. She still can't hardly talk she's so damn shook. C'mere, Wally," he shouted toward the Chevy.

Wally Fenner slid from the seat, and at the same time, the back doors of the Chevy swung open. Trancelike, the sons and wives of Virgil Fenner and Dick Harman emerged from the car. With glazed eyes and blank faces they stood by its side. Marilee Harman's nightgown hung wide open and some in the crowd gaped, but she made no effort to cover herself. Seeing her exposed, Dick Harman hurried to her side and stood in front of her while she fumbled with the buttons.

Dr. Logan was at the police chief's side and he stepped in businesslike strides to Becky Fenner and Marilee Harman. A quick look at their shock-induced stupor moved him to action.

"Get them inside," he ordered. "They need attention." Another look at the two boys drew a worried frown and the same conclusion. He addressed Fenner and Harman. "Get them back in the car and drive to the emergency entrance." It was just around the corner of the building. "Check them in overnight. Tell the admission's nurse that I said it was all right and to come out here to see me if she has any questions."

He rattled his orders with the efficiency of one accustomed to command and the police chief eyed him admiringly.

"Tell the resident that I'll be in later to take a look at them."

Fenner and Harman stood dumbly on the tarmac under the barrage of the staccato orders.

"Well, don't just stand there, man," Logan exploded. "Get moving."

Harman's eyes lit and he sprung to action, urging Marilee and Billy into the back seat. Fenner was slower but only slightly, requiring a few moments of purposeful slowness to demonstrate his disdain for authority. He finally got his family inside, then he spun off, kicking gravel at the crowd who awaited Ben Littlejohn's next directions.

When the disruption was over, the police chief resumed his organization of the search teams. "Remember," he warned, "we're not looking for a dangerous fugitive or an escaped convict. We're only looking for a little boy who's all alone and probably very frightened."

"That may well be," someone in the crowd challenged, "but just the same, I wouldn't want to catch up with him if I was all alone."

Murmurs of agreement rumbled through the crowd.

"Nobody's going to be alone if you do what I tell you," Ben told the worried gathering.

Teaming them in groups of threes and fours, he sent them in the directions where a little boy on foot would most likely choose. Eb Hetter's cornfield, the outbuildings on the nearby farms, the nooks and crevasses of the tiny town. It was a long, shot, he knew that, but he had to take some sort of action and the people of Hensleyville felt the same way. And, regardless of Lucius Cady's guilt or innocence, there was no longer any doubt in the chief's mind that trouble clung to the boy like a bloated tick, and since he was the key to the town's problems, young Lucius Cady had to be run to ground.

"Where should I go, Chief Littlejohn?"

Ben looked down into the anxious eyes of Chris Lockwood, then at Woody.

The boy's father stepped forward. "I think you're best off with Kathryn until we get back, Chris."

The disappointment showed on the boy's freckled face.

"Your dad's right, Chris," Ben said. "You'd be as good a

man as I have here but we have Miss Rogers to think of. Somebody should stay with her."

That compliment lifted the cloud of disappointment and the boy nodded sagely. "I'll go right over there," he volunteered.

Woody put his hands on the boy's shoulders. "It's already pretty late. The two of you go to bed and I'll be by in the morning to pick you up."

Chris hurried off on foot, Kathryn's house being only a few blocks from Memorial Hospital. The teams went in their appointed directions leaving the police chief, Dr. Logan, and Woody Lockwood standing beside the patrol car.

"What's that leave for us, Ben?" the lawyer asked.

Ben shrugged his heavy shoulders in a helpless gesture. "Hell, we might as well go home and watch the Late Show for all the good it will do," he admitted. "That boy has probably spent more nights under the stars than he has under a roof. He could be just about anywhere." Then, seeing the disappointment in the lawyer's face, he tried a more hopeful tone. "The road out of town," he said. "If he's heading back to the woods, he'll go north along County Line Road. We'll just sit alongside it and watch for him."

"How will we know if one of the other teams find him first?" Logan asked. He had missed part of the chief's instructions to the volunteers while he finalized some paperwork about the deputy's death.

"I told them to phone my office. The dispatcher will radio me here in the car and I can be anywhere in town within minutes." Ben hiked up his belt and straightened his wide-brimmed hat. "Well, we're not getting any closer to Lucius just standing around here and gabbing."

Ben climbed behind the wheel of the black and white patrol car. Woody sat next to him and Dr. Logan slid into the back seat and they drove out of town, checking every movement and shadow as they cruised down Main Street toward County Line Road.

Virgil leaned against the desk and resentfully answered the nurse's questions. "Dr. Logan said you weren't supposed to give us any crap," he told her. "If you got any questions, go ask him." He jerked his thumb toward the exit sign.

"Is there a problem?" The resident poked his head from an open door leading to a treatment room. Seeing two men, two women dressed for bed, and two teenage boys, none with apparent injuries, he cocked his head to the side and asked, "Is someone hurt?"

Between Virgil's blustering and Dick Harman's frantic narration, the young doctor was able to piece together enough of the story to presume that the women and the boys were suffering from some form of mental shock although the rantings about snakes and spiders left him cloudy about the cause. Besides it was late, already past midnight, he had extra beds, Dr. Logan presumably approved their admittance, and the women and boys did seem disturbed.

He nodded at the nurse, rolling his eyes in bewilderment out of sight of his patients. "Let's get them bedded down," he ordered. Turning back to the group he wondered, "How many of you are checking in?" A hint of a grin crossed his face as he reminded himself of a motel desk clerk.

"Just the wives and kids," Virgil answered.

"Yo, Dad," Wally protested. "There ain't nothin' wrong with me."

"And there ain't gonna be neither," Virgil responded. "You just shut your mouth and do what the doctor tells you." He gave the young resident a comradely glance indicating, the doctor supposed, some sort of mutual dedication to the boy's welfare.

"Why don't you go and check 'em all in, Doc, while we slip out for a smoke."

"I suppose that'll be all right," the resident said, "but you're welcome to come along if you'd like to."

Dick Harman made a move and said, "Yeah, I'd . . ." but a jab from Virgil's elbow stifled his enthusiasm.

"How long's it gonna take, Doc?" Virgil asked, fumbling as he spoke for a crumpled pack of cigarettes.

The resident looked at his watch. "It's twelve-fifteen." He smiled good-naturedly. "You can come in and kiss them good night at about quarter to one. They'll be as peaceful as angels by that time."

Virgil nodded at the resident, then shot a warning glance at Wally. "You don't give the doctor no crap, you hear?"

Of the four being admitted, only Wally resisted. The two women and Billy Harman were dazed and submissive.

"C'mon, Harman," Virgil said as he tugged on his arm, "let's go grab us a smoke."

With a worried glance at Billy and Marilee, Harman followed Virgil through the door.

"Why didn't you want to go along with them?" Harman asked when they were out of earshot of the doctor.

Virgil smiled a crooked grin. "It's too goddamn perfect," he gloated, slamming his fist into his meaty palm. "It couldn't work out any better if we planned it."

"I don't know what the hell you're talking about," Harman complained.

"I'll tell you all about it in the car," and Virgil pushed through the doors and walked to the parking lot with a pace that made Harman trot to keep up.

"What's the rush?"

"It's a perfect alibi," Fenner answered while backing recklessly before dropping into a forward gear.

They shot into the street and sped away from the hospital. Virgil held the wheel in an iron grip and stared with determination through the windshield.

"What do we need an alibi for?" Harman whined.

"For what's gonna happen to Lucius Cady," Virgil answered.

Harman gaped at the driver and felt a surge of fear as he watched Virgil's face glow with malice. "Wait a minute, Virgil. We never said nothin' about doin' anything to the kid. I thought all you wanted to do was scare him."

"Sure," Fenner said. "We'll scare him. We'll scare him like he scared Jeff Zack. Like he drowned Lenny Brothers. Like he filled your fuckin' house with snakes for chrissakes." Virgil was shouting and pounding the steering wheel for emphasis as he recounted the tragedies. "You don't get the picture yet, do you, Harman? I don't know how the hell he does it but I know that this kid is makin' all these things happen and if we don't get him first, he's gonna get us." He paused in his tirade, looked to his right, and said calmly, "We got to get rid of him, Harman. It's as simple as that."

Turning back to the street, he went over his plan. "As far as anybody knows, we're both still back at the hospital havin' a smoke in the parking lot. The doctor and the nurse will swear to it. All we got to do now is kill the kid, then get back to the hospital before we're missed. It's goddamn perfect."

"Shit," was the only reply that Dick Harman could manage to come up with.

"We make it look like an accident," Virgil continued. "I'll bust his neck like a chicken, then we'll just toss him out of the car on the way back to town. After he bounces on the street a coupla times it'll look like a hit and run."

Harman's mouth went dry and he continued to stare straight ahead.

"We'll dump him where somebody is sure to find him real quick. That way they'll know that it just happened. They'll think the kid was walkin' along the road to get away." He chuckled to himself and his jowls quivered. "I got another idea. I got an old Plymouth hubcap in the trunk. Musta found it a coupla years ago. We'll toss it down the road from the kid and send the cops on a wild-goose chase. We'll get rid of the kid and make an ass out of Littlejohn at the same time. Haw, haw."

They passed through the last lights at the edge of Hensleyville and sped down the dark road leading to Covey's Woods.

Ben Littlejohn tapped a broken rhythm on the steering wheel, impatient with the futility of the search. The patrol car huddled in a leafy shelter only a few yards off County Line Road but invisible to the speeders who saw the straight line of emptiness as an opportunity to clear the clogged throats of their lusty engines. It was the chief's favorite speed trap but tonight it was just a handy place to sit out the search while keeping an eye out for a little boy trudging disconsolately into loneliness.

"We'll find him," Ben said. "It might not be tonight but it's just a matter of time. A little kid like that can't hide out forever, I don't care how well he knows the woods."

Woody Lockwood sat beside the chief with the window rolled down, peering through the trees, watching for the slightest movement, listening for the scuffle of small feet. "That still doesn't solve the problem of what to do with Lucius when we finally do find him." He swiveled to the rear and looked into Dr. Logan's worried face. "Do you have any ideas, John?"

In the dim interior, John Logan shook his head. "Maybe we could have him committed somewhere, a place where he could be talked to and examined. Until we know what the problem is we can't find a solution," he said wearily.

"I thought we already pretty much agreed on what the problem was," the police chief said in the darkness. "As far as I'm concerned, we're dealing with something unexplainable, something supernatural. That may not be a very professional conclusion, but it will have to do until somebody comes up with something better." He laughed softly and shook his head. "I can't believe that I'm saying this."

"What do you make of what Fenner and Harman told you?" Woody asked the policeman, more for conversation than for enlightenment.

They sensed more than they saw the shrug of Ben's strong shoulders. "It's just more of the same," he answered resignedly. "What else could I think? It's the same M.O. Parts of a goat and more of those damn campfire predictions coming true."

Woody Lockwood shuddered. "All that's left now is an earthquake."

"Huh?" the policeman grunted.

"An earthquake," Woody repeated in a strained voice. "That's what Chris said he was afraid of."

"I wonder where he got that," the doctor said.

Woody shook his head slowly. "Beats me. Maybe they were trying to outdo one another. The boy's always had a good imagination."

"Maybe he'll be a writer someday," Logan offered, trying to brighten the mood with the promise of a hopeful future.

"He sure won't have to look far for a plot," Littlejohn added. "Enough's been happening around Hensleyville to last a writer a lifetime."

The policeman saw the first flicker of headlights through the maze of leaves and branches and he knew instinctively that the vehicle was moving too quick but tonight Ben wasn't in the mood for a speeding bust. You're lucky this time, he thought to himself as the lights raced toward them, then flew by. "Son of a gun," Ben mumbled aloud. "I wonder what the hell he's up to."

"Who?" the lawyer asked.

"That was Virgil Fenner's car," Littlejohn said.

Woody shook his head and smiled with amazement. "All I saw was a pair of lights," he admitted.

Ben turned the key and the motor kicked to life. The black and white rolled from its hideaway onto the dark road. "If you sat in the woods squinting at cars as long as I have, you'd know a Ford from a Chevy at a quarter mile," he boasted jokingly.

With headlights still out, he picked up speed, racing down the darkened road with only a pair of fading taillights as a target. Lifting the mike from its hook on the dashboard he called up the dispatcher. "Milly," he said with practiced authority, "patch me into the switchboard at Memorial Hospital."

"Sure thing, Ben," she answered.

"Memorial Hospital," the pleasant voice chirped.

"Chief Littlejohn here," Ben announced without introduction. "Connect me with emergency."

"E.R. desk." The new voice was crisp and efficient.

"This is Chief Littlejohn. Who's got the duty tonight?"

"Dr. Menard."

"Let me talk to him."

Ben briefed Menard. At the chief's suggestion, the doctor looked for Fenner in the parking lot. After about a thirty-second wait he returned to the phone.

"He's not out there," Menard said, mildly surprised. "He told me that's where he'd be. He and his buddy were going outside to have a cigarette while the wives and the kids were checked in."

Ben paused with the mike to his lips. "I guess he must have changed his mind," he mused. "Thanks, Doc."

Ben hung up the mike and glanced at Woody. "Sounds to me like Virgil's trying to pull some kind of fast one but damned if I can figure out what it is."

"Do you suppose it has anything to do with the troubles?" Woody wondered.

"Nothing would surprise me anymore," the chief answered, and in the dim light of the moon and stars, the patrol car sped down County Line Road.

22

THE DOCTOR AND the lawyer winced as the police car flew through the darkness but Ben Littlejohn held the wheel with the casual assurance of a Sunday sightseer. Less than a quarter of a mile separated the cars but the chances of Virgil seeing them were remote as long as Ben could manage without headlights. This became more difficult once Virgil left County Line Road and turned right onto Covey Road, a narrow strip of blacktop that bisected Covey's Woods.

"Where could he be going?" Dr. Logan wondered aloud. He had resigned himself to Ben's night-driving skill and he leaned his elbows on the back of the seat, watching the red dots of Virgil's taillights.

Before anyone could even hazard a guess, Virgil took another sharp right, this time onto Ridge Road, an all but abandoned stretch of blacktop whose original purpose was to connect a creekside gristmill with what was then considered civilization. The mill had been a pile of rubble for half of a century but the county still maintained the road simply because it was there.

"I don't think I've ever been back here before," Dr. Logan said.

"I have," Ben said ominously, "and if my guess is right you'll see him turn off just around the next curve."

The narrow lane bent gently to the left, then straightened. Ben seemed to keep to the road by conforming to the arc of

Fenner's lights because, under the thick foliage, the night was dark as the bottom of a coal mine. As Ben had predicted, Virgil's car began to slow, its brake lights blazing like flames in the blackness.

"Now where's he going?" Woody asked as Virgil's car lurched from the road and disappeared into the woods.

"The old moonshiner's hut," Ben said. "I haven't been back here in years." As he coasted to a quiet stop by the barely visible path, he briefly told them some of the lore about the old abandoned shed.

"Are you thinking what I'm thinking?" the doctor asked.

But no one wanted to answer the question and they quietly left the car.

Woody was impressed by the chief's thoroughness when he noticed Ben's hand hooding the dome light until the two right side doors clicked shut, then he quickly withdrew his arm before gently closing the driver's door. The chief held a powerful flashlight in his hand but kept it off. Groping blindly, they met in front of the car.

"Keep your hand on my shoulder," Ben told Woody. "John, you keep your hand on Woody's." He chuckled low. "That way if somebody walks into a tree it will be me and I get paid for it." Single file, they left the road and entered the utter blackness of the forest.

The night was still, the forest unnaturally quiet. There were no twitters, clicks, or rustles to mar the unearthly mood, only their own nervous breathing. Somewhere ahead of them a car door slammed and the glow of distant headlights gave them direction. The muted echo of conversation filtered through the trees.

The dampness from the earlier downpour lent an extra chill to the air but not enough to cause the icy atmosphere that they stepped into when they were halfway down the path. It was like stepping over an invisible line and into a walk-in freezer, so swiftly did the temperature drop, and with it came the smell.

Littlejohn stopped short and the others felt the movement through their arm-to-shoulder contact. The chief turned to them, but in the blackness, they couldn't see the lines of worry that etched his face. "I'm the cop here," he told them, "I get paid for doing things like this. There's no need for the two of you to come any farther. In fact," he whispered, "I'd be shirking my duty to expose you to danger."

"Nice try, Ben," the doctor whispered back.

"Yeah," Woody added. "We appreciate the thought. Now let's keep moving before we freeze to death."

They could sense the crooked smile on the lawman's face as he clapped their shoulders in the darkness, then they re-formed their single line.

Ben walked through the night in small, choppy steps, carefully placing each foot in front of the other to avoid ruts or brittle branches, his left arm extended in front of him like a blind man without a cane. Foot by foot they neared the moonshiner's shed.

"This could be real big trouble, Virgil. Ain't there some other way?" Dick Harman stood by the car, arms wrapped around himself as he tried to still the trembling. Whether it was brought on by the cold or by his icy fear, he couldn't say. With each worried plea, he blew a puff of steam into the air.

Virgil had pulled the car to within twenty feet of the shed and left the headlights on. The blazing beams violated the night and bathed the tacky structure in their fierce glow. Tendrils of steam curled from the damp foliage and laid down a blanket of fog at the level of their knees. The air was biting, the stench overpowering.

"You're so goddamn scared you shit in your pants, didn't you, Harman?" Virgil chided.

"Damn right I'm scared," Harman countered with uncharacteristic vehemence. "Shit, Virgil, we could go to jail for the rest of our lives if we get caught. Besides," he protested, "it just ain't right."

Fenner walked around the front of the car and came face-to-face with his terrified and unwilling accomplice. "It just ain't right," Virgil mimicked in a singsong parody.

Fenner shoved Harman against the car, then twisted a handful of his shirt and jerked him back until their faces were only inches apart. In the misty glare, Harman could see the fire of hate burning in Virgil's eyes. His breath was sour and rank.

"Well, like it or not, Harman, you're in this with me all the way."

He released his grip, reached into his pocket, and pulled out an ugly switchblade. He snapped the catch and the blade shot out. The click echoed through the twining mist like the crack of a whip.

"Wh-what are you gonna do with that?"

"Cut the ropes, stupid. Remember, this got to look like an accident." Virgil snorted derisively. "You wait here and try not to shit your pants anymore. I'm gonna get the kid."

With Dick Harman shivering with cold and fear, Virgil stepped into the brilliant beam and walked to the door of the moonshiner's shed.

A little over one hundred yards away, the policeman, the lawyer, and the doctor cautiously picked their way through the darkness. Guided by the luminescent glow of Virgil's head-lights, they neared the rickety shed, each of them lost in their own thoughts. Ben Littlejohn didn't need the overpowering stench to smell the danger. But how could the law combat such an evil? The desire to unholster his pistol was fierce but he clenched his jaw and resisted the urge. There had been too much death, too many grieving friends and family. Ben didn't want to add to the count. With a surge of will, he moved his hand from his holster and inched toward the glow.

Behind him, Woody Lockwood felt the mixed rumblings of fear and fatherhood. Ahead lay the dark unknown. Back in town were the two people he loved most, chatting happily over a bowl of buttered popcorn as they watched an oft-repeated video. They felt safe in their togetherness, confident that whatever evil terrorized the town would be held at bay by the sheer goodness of life. With a tingle, Woody realized that the only fear he harbored was for the safety of these two special people and the knowledge braced his courage.

John Logan's fear wasn't of the evil presence itself. It was of the doubt that it cast on the logic and order of things that ruled his world.

Bound together arm to shoulder, united yet separated by their fears, the three men were less than sixty yards from the shed when the stillness was shattered by a nerve-grinding shriek. Instinctively, the police chief flicked on his flashlight, drew his weapon, and broke into a trot down the weed-ridden path. After a moment's hesitation, Woody and the doctor jogged behind him, arriving by the dimly lit taillights of the Chevy a few seconds after Ben.

The scene was surreal. A wooden shed, an overgrown outhouse that would be comical under most circumstances, shone in the glow of the headlights like a monument to depravity. It was the face of death with a complexion of rotting planks.

"What happened?" Ben asked. "Who screamed?" His flashlight lit Dick Harman's panicked face and shrunk his pupils to pinheads.

"It was Vi-Virgil," he stammered. "He's in th-there." With trembling hand he pointed to the moonshiner's shed.

Woody tramped to a stop at Ben's side. "What was it?" he echoed.

Ben waved the pistol in the direction of the shed. "It was Fenner. He's in there." Turning back to Harman the chief asked, "Is anybody else in there with him?"

Harman winced.

"Damn it, Harman, answer me. Is Fenner alone?"

A grimace of guilt flashed across the mask of terror. "The boy's in there too," he mumbled. "The Cady boy."

Ben pushed the man roughly aside and made a move toward the shed. As he did, the door began to creak open and the policeman braked to a stop and leveled his pistol on the hole where the knob should be. In the blaze of the headlights, with clouds of mist hovering at its base, the door slowly inched outward.

Ben Littlejohn stood rock solid, about ten feet from the structure. His legs were spread widely, his feet planted firmly on the damp ground, his pistol thrust out in front of him and held in two hands. Woody Lockwood and John Logan moved gamely forward, standing slightly behind Ben and to his left.

Inch by inch, the door creaked outward, releasing, as it opened, an odor so powerful and corrupt that it brought bile to their throats and made their eyes water. Ben Littlejohn recoiled and brought one hand protectively to his face. Woody retched silently. Dick Harman bent over the hood of Virgil's car and loosed a flood of curdled beer. Then, as quickly as the horrible smell had engulfed them, it dissipated.

The men's eyes were fixed on the flimsy door. It moved steadily outward, rasping indignantly on its tired hinges. Wide-eyed and trembling, Dick Harman cowered against the car, oblivious to the vile liquid that soaked his shirt. Woody and the doctor stayed their ground, their hearts pounding, waiting to finally have revealed to them the source of the town's terror. Ben was closest to the door, steadying his weapon like a rock, ready—almost anxious—to blast the evil back into the world it came from.

A movement, slight but undeniable, flashed inside the shed. An object, black and shiny, a spot of white, a pair of black eyes peering around the corner of the door and blazing back the reflected brilliance of the headlights. With head held high, strutting proud as a gamecock, it stepped through the narrow opening and landed lightly on the misty ground. Turning its head toward the police chief, it stared with indignation into the gaping hole at the end of the barrel.

"Baaaaaa," it protested.

The kid stood barely a foot and a half at the shoulder, its dirty white coat all but invisible in the camouflaging mist.

"Baaaaa," it repeated, meeting the eyes of each of the men in a quick survey of its surroundings.

"Jesus Christ," Ben muttered as he lowered the pistol in hands just beginning to tremble from the blast of adrenaline.

At the sound of Ben's unconscious oath, the small goat yelped. It shrank back against the wall of the shed then. With its lips curling like a rabid dog, it crouched low to the ground and hissed like a cornered reptile. Startled, Ben raised the pistol once again but before he could react, the goat sprung to its left and bounded into the darkness like a frightened jackrabbit.

The icy chill that had enveloped them seemed to lift with the animal's departure. The hint of a fresh breeze brought with it the fertile smell of the valley and the warmth of summer. As one, the four men blew out a long, low breath, proclaiming their release from fear while their throbbing chests sought a return to normalcy. Surprised that he had allowed himself the small luxury of relief, Ben took the final few steps to the shed. The others breathed deeply and braced themselves for the revelation.

The policeman wrapped his hand around the edge of the door and pulled it open on reluctant hinges, flooding the interior with the glare from the car's headlights. A hooded figure sat slumped in a straight-backed chair against the back wall, arms and legs bound tightly to the rungs and braces.

"Lucius," Dr. Logan muttered as he recognized the hospital gown, the boyish feet.

Before the chief stepped boldly inside and blocked their view, Logan and Woody saw the look of raw terror on Virgil Fenner's face. The man sat on the floor next to Lucius, his back against the wall, his legs thrust out in front of him. His mouth was twisted in a frozen wail. A runnel of blood coursed down his cheek. The black hilt of a switchblade protruded from his eye.

23

BEN WASTED NO time. He radioed his office and instructed Millie to send a backup to stand guard at the death scene, catching himself at the last moment before asking for Nils Larsen. Woody Lockwood had volunteered to stay behind but the police chief waved him off.

"All of us have more important things to do in town," Ben told him. "Somebody will be here soon enough, and in the meantime, Virgil won't be lonely."

He felt a little guilty for the flip remark but excused himself by blaming it on the tragic set of circumstances. Cruising down Covey Road he had another thought and radioed once again, this time instructing the operator to call in the searchers and alert Memorial Hospital to their impending arrival.

"Tell 'em that Lucius is coming home and to get his room shaped up." He gave the sad-eyed boy a fatherly wink and a pat on the knee.

Lucius was groggy but alert. He huddled between the chief and Dr. Logan while Woody and Dick Harman shared the back seat. Things had happened too fast to permit much of a reaction. The three searchers were thankful that Lucius was located so quickly and that he was safe and unharmed, but the circumstances of Nils Larsen's death were still unresolved. At least they were until Dick Harman began to blubber like a baby in the back seat.

"I didn't want to do it. It was all Virgil's idea. He's only a

little kid. Why would anybody want to hurt a little kid?" he
blurted before surrendering to a fit of shoulder-wracking sobs.

If Harman had been Woody Lockwood's client, the lawyer
would have felt obliged to put a halt to the confession but he
felt no such compulsion.

"What was Virgil's idea?" the chief asked casually over his
shoulder.

"You know, to snatch the kid outta the hospital"—more sobs
and tears—"I didn't know that anybody got hurt. He didn't
even tell me about Nils's accident till later."

Ben realized that the man was on the thin edge of hysteria
and experience told him that if he was ever going to get at the
truth, now was the time to go for it. So what if it spoiled a case.
Virgil Fenner was beyond trying in a court of law and Ben's
immediate concern was to find out what was going on. With no
prodding, Dick Harman blubbered the entire story, and although it still left some doubt whether the deputy's death was
premeditated or accidental, it at least cleared Lucius of any
complicity.

"I didn't want to do any of it," Harman moaned. "You got
to believe me."

If they did, none showed it as they drove the rest of the way
in silence.

When they pulled up to the hospital, Dr. Menard waited in
the thin yellow glare beneath the overhang at the emergency
entrance. A single orderly with a wheelchair stood at his side.
The resident seemed shaken when he greeted them and was
barely civil to Lucius as he transferred him to the care of the
orderly.

"Put him back in the same room and stay with him," Dr.
Logan ordered. "I'll be along in a few minutes to look him
over."

Woody Lockwood crouched next to the wheelchair as Lucius
was made comfortable. Searching the boy's sad eyes, he saw
only a frightened little boy, for all practical purposes a
homeless orphan. Missing entirely from Lucius's stare were the
wild eyes of a maniac or the taint of evil. Woody's heart ached
for Lucius Cady and he imagined his own son sitting helplessly
in the chair, his head reeling from the traumatic battering. Then

he noticed signs of other kinds of abuse on the boy's swollen face.

"Did he hurt you, Lucius?" Woody asked, gently touching the boy's bruised cheekbone.

"It don't hurt much," Lucius said. Then he turned to the lawyer urgently. "How's Chris, Mr. Lockwood. He's all right, ain't he?"

"He's fine, Lucius."

"The stone. Make sure he keeps that stone with him."

The orderly started to wheel the boy away and Lucius twisted and peered around the back of the chair. "Don't never let him forget it," he called as the doors closed behind him.

"I won't," Woody whispered to himself. "You can bet that I won't."

At the chief's order, Dick Harman waited in the police car, watching the scene like a captured criminal. Ben wasn't sure what to do with Virgil's hapless accomplice. There was no doubt that he participated in a kidnapping although the extent of his involvement was in question. Ben opened the back door and stared at him uncertainly.

"You're in some kind of trouble, Dick, only I'm not sure just how much."

Harman stared at his folded hands shamefully.

"I'm short on help right now or I'd take you to my office and book you."

The town had two holding cells behind Ben's office that hosted more drunks than criminals and Dick Harman was no stranger to their Spartan accommodations.

"Why don't you hike on over to my office and tell Millie that you're spending the night. I'll be along later to figure out what we're going to do with you."

Harman nodded and slouched from the car. "Can I say good night to Marilee first?" he asked the policeman hopefully.

Dr. Menard stepped forward. His voice shook. "Your wife's asleep," he croaked. "She's had a sedative."

"Oh," Dick Harman said, nodding his head in resignation, then he turned toward the center of town and slinked contritely into the darkness.

Dr. Logan gave the resident a worried glance. "Is everything all right, Doctor. You seem on edge."

The resident shook his head evenly. "Everything's not all right, Dr. Logan."

Logan studied the man. Joe Menard was a promising young physician, controlled and in charge. Logan couldn't recall ever seeing him upset.

"I checked the four of them in," Menard explained, "the two boys and their mothers."

Woody and Ben moved closer to the conversation and Menard looked at the older doctor apprehensively.

"It's OK, Joe, you can talk freely," Logan told him.

The younger doctor continued, "All four of them were shaken up but none of them were hurt. They were rattled like anybody would be after a bad scare."

Logan nodded that he understood.

"Actually," Menard said with a shrug, "under normal circumstances I would have given them each a Valium and sent them home but you suggested—"

"I know, Joe," Logan acknowledged. "I told you to check them in. Then what happened." He was impatient with the young doctor's delivery but sensed that the man needed to tell the story in his own way.

"I gave each of them sixty milligrams of phenobarbital," Menard continued. "Just enough to help them sleep."

John Logan again nodded professionally. "Exactly what I would have done, Joe," he said.

The young doctor's face clouded with doubt and he wrung his hands nervously. "I tucked them in, then I went to the desk to fill in their charts."

Logan nodded a third time but worried wrinkles began to crease his forehead.

"I went back five minutes later. The two women were sleeping peacefully."

Littlejohn breathed a sigh of relief.

"But the two boys were dead."

Woody felt the bottom drop from his stomach.

"Oh, my God," Logan uttered.

"I tried everything I knew," Menard pleaded. He wiped

away a tear that creased his cheek. "Shock paddles, adrenaline—everything known to medicine."

Woody Lockwood spoke up. "I don't think we're dealing with anything known to medicine," he said consolingly. He thought about Lucius Cady's warning as he was being wheeled through the door. "I don't think either one of those boys ever had a chance."

The young doctor looked at him queerly. "How can you say that. All they had was a bad scare. There was no reason for them to die."

"There was no reason for Jeff Zack to die either," the police chief reminded him. "Or Pete Bishop or Lenny Brothers or the entire Stein family."

Dr. Logan shook his head. "How many times have we asked when it's all going to end?"

"Somebody should tell Dick Harman," Woody remembered. "It wouldn't be fair to have him spend the night in jail with his son lying dead in the hospital."

With each new tragedy, his thoughts went back to Chris, reminding him how devastated he would be if his boy got caught up in the same web of terror. But before anyone could solve Dick Harman's problem, the E.R. doors burst open and Woody felt the worst of his fears materialize. Ashen-faced, Kathryn Rogers stumbled in, towing a frightened Chris Lockwood by the hand.

"Thank God you're here," she cried.

With a fresh jolt of apprehension, Woody crossed the lobby to her side. "What is it? Are you OK?" He looked at his watch. It was after 1:00 A.M.

Kathryn stammered, "We were in the parlor watching a video when we heard a—"

"There was something outside, Dad," Chris interrupted. "We heard it."

"Bisquit heard it first," Kathryn said. "She ran to the door and started barking."

"And when I looked outside," Chris continued, "there was nobody there but there was something lying on the porch."

Kathryn shuddered and Woody put his hands on her shoulders. "What was it?" he asked, fearing the answer he knew was to come.

Ben and Dr. Logan had drifted to the edge of the conversation, anxious about the new development.

Chris looked up at the three men, his frightened eyes seemingly misplaced on the freckled, boyish face. "It was the rest of the goat's head."

"I'm going to be sick," Kathryn mumbled and she bolted across the lobby.

Helplessly, Woody watched Kathryn disappear into the ladies' room, then squatting in front of the boy, he rested his hands on his thin shoulders. "Do you feel OK?" he asked, thinking of Jeff Zack and the horrible atrocities that were played on his mind.

"I'm fine, Dad. I really am. But Kathryn's pretty shook up. You know how ladies are."

Woody nodded solemnly. Turning his head to the police chief, his pleading eyes asked the question that his lips couldn't form.

Ben looked at the freckle-faced boy sympathetically, then at the worried father. "I swear to you, Woody, I'm not going to let this boy out of my sight until this thing is over. I'm calling for help," he decided. "I don't care if it takes the National Guard, I'm not going to watch one more person get hurt. We're going to get to the bottom of this if I have to call in the F.B.I."

"I don't think that will be necessary."

In the intensity of their discussion, none of them had noticed the lobby doors swing open and they spun at the sound of the voice.

Father O'Connor stood at the threshold. He was dressed in striped pajama tops and rumpled chinos. His white hair bristled wildly and his eyes were still blurred from his midnight awakening. But the priest's appearance wasn't the focus of their surprise.

Standing next to Father O'Connor was a ghostly specter of a woman. Her hair was grey and frazzled, combed straight back without style and flowing to her waist. She wore mourning black, an ebony robe that covered her shriveled body from her mottled neck to bony wrists. Pale white hands with clawlike fingers protruded from the black folds and worried at each other, scratching and jerking in nervous twitches. The woman's features betrayed the fragile structure of former beauty, high cheekbones and a classic nose under a pair of pale blue eyes. But now, whatever appeal had once existed, was forever lost in a tortured face coursed with deep creases and ablaze with purplish scales.

Speechless, the cluster of startled people stared at the newcomers, stunned to silence by the sudden apparition.

Ben Littlejohn looked into the woman's troubled eyes and he felt a stab of recall. There was something about the pain that they reflected that dredged up a long buried memory, another time of sadness and of horror. It came to him in a charged bolt of recollection.

Father O'Connor placed his hand on the woman's elbow and gently moved her forward. "Gentlemen," he proclaimed solemnly, "I'd like you to meet an old friend, Leticia Zooker."

24

EXPRESSIONS RANGING FROM shock to confusion greeted Leticia Zooker's introduction. There were some such as John Logan who had once known her well but failed to recognize her and there was Dr. Menard who didn't even recognize her name.

Ben Littlejohn's mind raced like a printout chattering from a computer. *Zooker, Leticia, white, female, age 34, medium height, slender, dark hair, blue eyes, wife of Horace Zooker who was killed in 1978 in farm accident, mother of Melinda Zooker who was born just before the death of her father, who herself died violently but whether it was murder or suicide was never established, disappeared without a trace after Melinda's funeral, current whereabouts unknown.*

Until now.

The woman looked into the startled faces of her former neighbors seeking recognition, understanding—perhaps a little friendship. She was ill at ease and shaken. Noticing Dr. Logan's probing eyes, she nodded slightly and forced a distant smile, and for an instant, the once-charming face of Leticia Zooker glowed through the damaged skin.

The priest released her elbow and took her bony hand in his. "Leticia has something to tell us," he began. "She's come a long way to do so." He squeezed her hand and gave her a comforting smile. "She arrived unannounced at the rectory a little after midnight so I hope you'll pardon my appearance."

John Logan stepped forward. "Welcome home, Leticia," he said, coating his words with kindness.

"Thank you, Doctor," she answered, and the voice was the same soft purr that once charmed the strapping young farm boys from Hensleyville.

Logan turned to the priest. "Let's go to the doctors' lounge," he suggested. "It's more comfortable than standing here and there's coffee brewing."

"An excellent idea," the priest said brightly, trying to lift the pall that hung over the lobby. He wasn't yet aware of the four recent deaths and he blamed the somber mood of the others on the earlier tragedies.

The lounge was bright and cheery with soft, colorful furniture that had been donated by the Women's Auxiliary. A pair of Currier and Ives prints entertained from either side of the long couch and stacks of well-read magazines littered the tops of coffee tables and other strategically placed furniture. Father O'Connor steered Leticia toward a comfortable recliner, but she shook her head and chose a stern-looking wingback.

The group, including Kathryn Rogers who had returned during the exodus from the lobby, poured Styrofoam cups of steaming coffee from a silver urn and found seats. Woody steered Kathryn and Chris to the couch, making concerned inquiries about her health. With a pained smile, she told him that she felt better, and with the bitter taste of sickness still acid in her throat, she sunk into the soft cushion of the sofa.

Dr. Menard excused himself and went to look in on Lucius.

When the rest were situated, Father O'Connor stepped to the side of Leticia's chair as if to give a preface to her talk but Ben Littlejohn raised a delaying hand.

"Before you begin, Father, I think there's something you ought to know."

The priest's shoulders slumped, his eyes filling with sadness as Ben reviewed the sorrowful events of the night, and he said silent prayers as each new death was ticked off.

Nils Larsen, Wally Fenner, Billy Harman, Virgil Fenner.

How many was it now? He didn't try to count. It was much too painful.

Chris Lockwood's eyes filled with tears. "Billy and Wally too?" he said in a choked voice.

Ben looked at the boy apologetically. "I'm sorry you had to hear it like that, Chris. I forgot that you didn't know. Everything's happening so fast."

"Yes it is," the priest agreed, "much too fast. And that's precisely the reason that Leticia has come to visit us."

He looked down at the woman and saw new pain in the face that seemed to have grown even older as it absorbed the recent tragic news. Leticia sat stiffly, knees together under the black robe, hands folded tightly in her lap. The muscles of her jaw quivered under the harsh purple scales of her cheeks, but her eyes blazed with determination.

"Leticia came to me tonight to confess her sins," the priest told them. "That's unusual in some respects," he continued, "not the least of which is the fact that Leticia isn't Catholic."

Kathryn nodded as she recalled the woman's infrequent attendance at Mal Whitney's Sunday services.

"She told me a very sad and strange tale," Father O'Connor went on, "one that I feel certain is the key to the horrors we've witnessed in the past few days."

He rested a gentle hand on her shoulder and almost recoiled at its skeletal hardness.

"Leticia lives far from here and I'm sure that neither her journey nor her decision to make it came easily, but she felt compelled to do it. You must understand that, until she arrived at the rectory an hour ago, she knew nothing of our recent problems." He looked at the group sternly. "You must also realize that Leticia in no way caused any of these problems. Like us, she is a victim."

He moved away from her and settled into the soft chair to her right. "I'd like her to now repeat the story that she told me earlier so we'll all know what we're dealing with and, more importantly, why tragedy has come to Hensleyville."

He settled back, steepled his fingers, and urged softly, "Please begin, Leticia."

The soft hum of the air conditioner sounded like a roar in the deathly anticipation that shrouded the doctors' lounge. Hearts and minds raced. Sitting between the two he loved, Woody Lockwood tightly gripped the hand of each.

Like a specter, Leticia rose from her chair. Her eyes, blue and piercing, sought the soul of each of the anxious listeners. With her hands lost in the folds of her robe, only her tortured face protruding from its blackness, she told her story.

"I was once considered very pretty," she began simply, the words not sounding boastful, coming as they did from a visage of such horror. "I was pretty and I was happy. I was on the threshold of an idyllic life with a caring husband who worked hard and who loved me dearly as I loved him."

She paused to allow the listeners to picture her former self, to focus on who she once was.

"And I was blessed even beyond that," she said, "because I carried within me the blossoming seed that would one day be Melinda."

Her voice was soft yet firm. She was telling a story that ripped her soul, but the fierceness of her need to tell the tale stilled the tremor that should accompany her words and stopped the tears that should be shed.

"Those of you who knew me then might recall the happy young bride that I was."

Her eyes rested briefly on John Logan and Ben Littlejohn and they nodded imperceptibly.

"But sometimes it seemed that Hensleyville moved too slowly to suit me."

A look of melancholy clouded the blueness of her eyes.

"Why should that be?" she wondered aloud. "I was no different from the others. And I was still happy. Bored, perhaps, but happy. There were things for a young bride to do."

She paused again, remembering. "We used to go to the church basement to quilt with the preacher's wife," she said, referring to Mrs. Whitney. "And we'd drive in to York every Wednesday morning for shopping and sometimes we'd go to a movie." A flicker of a smile crossed her tired face. "Once or twice we'd have lunch and a cocktail at the Wagon Wheel. There were things to do," she concluded, "but most of all we read." Her hands moved nervously beneath the gown. "That's what started the troubles."

The listeners looked surprised at that revelation, but they sat patiently, sensing the woman's need to spin the story out in her own way.

Chris Lockwood began to fidget, and his father gave his hand a loving squeeze.

"There was a group of us," she went on, "who met every second Friday of the month. We usually met in the library but sometimes we'd get together at someone's home. We called ourselves the Hensleyville Book Club."

An affirmative nod or two among the listeners indicated that some of them recalled the group.

Leticia spoke softly and deliberately and her eyes punctuated each point as she made it. Together, her eyes and voice were sensual, a contradiction when viewed in the context of her overall appearance.

"Usually we would each read a different book and report on it at our monthly meeting. It was interesting," she admitted, "but I had an idea that would add spice to the meetings. I suggested to the group that, every so often, we all read different books on similar subjects and that we demonstrate our new knowledge at the monthly meeting."

She began to pace slowly back and forth, with her eyes fixed on the floor, as if the activity aided her recollection or perhaps made it less painful.

"The first time that we tried it, some of the members were against it. They were comfortable with the old format and were reluctant to try something new. But we chose gardening for the first meeting, something that we all liked, and it was a huge success as each of us arrived with samples of our skills to show and tell like schoolchildren."

She stopped pacing and resumed her original stance in front of her chair.

"We decided to tackle new topics, things that were outside our current interests, things that we'd never delve into on our own. Since the original idea had been mine, I was asked to select the next subject."

Her voice trailed off and she breathed deeply, the type of

breath one takes to gather strength before delivering bad news.

"I chose the occult."

The word released a tide of apprehension. It confirmed suspicions but it left unanswered the many questions that still plagued the listeners.

"It wasn't a popular choice by any means," she continued. "Some of the members felt that it was sacrilegious. All felt uncomfortable with it. One woman stopped short of accusing me of consorting with the devil."

John Logan vaguely recalled the controversy, one of the minor tempests that blew through the town to be quickly forgotten by the time of the next farm accident or church social.

"But I stuck to my guns and set the rules for the meeting," Leticia said. "I had already read one novel that dealt with the subject, a frivolous paperback, but it intrigued me and gave me a superficial idea of what the occult was all about. And I had already chosen a list of books for the other members to read. I was well prepared," she said ruefully. "I even had in mind a guest speaker."

Ben Littlejohn felt the power of Leticia Zooker's pointed gaze.

"I invited Daphne Monet."

"The witch?" Ben whispered.

"Yes," Leticia said. "We all called her the witch."

"Who was she?" Kathryn asked, relieved by the break in Leticia's monologue.

Leticia didn't answer. With her look she let the police chief know that the question was his to field.

"She was a strange old lady who lived alone in the apartment over the hardware store," Ben answered.

"The place where Ollie Ahrens lives now?" Chris wondered.

Ben looked at the boy and nodded. "She always kept to herself," Ben continued, "and she was very eccentric. She always wore black dresses and her hair was long and stringy."

Ben winced when he realized that he had just described Leticia Zooker, but she showed no offense.

"She spoke to no one unless it was absolutely necessary and

then she'd snap at them. It was the kids who named her the witch."

"Where did she come from?" Kathryn asked.

"It seems like she was always here," Ben answered. "She was a farm wife if I recall, until her husband died and her kids grew up and left town. It seems that I was just a kid myself when she first moved into the apartment over the store." The chief looked pensive for a long moment. "Given the way she looked and acted, I guess it was natural for the kids to call her a witch but she seemed harmless enough. She finally died about ten years ago. Must have been close to a hundred years old."

"It was thirteen years ago," Leticia corrected, "and she was one hundred and one years old and she wasn't at all harmless. She was a horrible old woman."

For the first time since beginning her story, Leticia showed anger. Her face became even more appalling, and Chris shrunk back in the cushions of the sofa.

"But I suppose I have only myself to blame," Leticia said. "I was the one who invited her to join the group."

"Why did you do that?" Woody asked. "You said yourself that she was a difficult old woman."

Leticia shrugged. "I ask myself that same question every day. I ran into her quite by accident one day in the market. I felt sorry for her and tried to strike up a conversation. She wasn't very responsive but I persisted. When I told her about our book club her ears perked up. And when I told her that the occult was the topic of our next discussion group, she became very excited, almost agitated. She insisted on knowing the details and seemed obsessed with learning how many people would be there."

"That's strange," Woody observed.

"I thought so too," Leticia said. "It was even stranger when she learned that our group numbered an even dozen and that her participation would bring the number to thirteen. I thought she'd have a stroke. She started shivering and jabbering like a crazy woman. She insisted on joining. I recall that I was amused by her at the time but later, when I had a chance to think about it, I became quite frightened. It wasn't natural. She wasn't natural."

"Was she really a witch?" Chris blurted.

Leticia smiled indulgently. "I'll let you decide that," she said. "On the day of the meeting, Daphne Monet arrived more than forty minutes early. I was still in the shower and had to quickly wrap a robe around myself to answer the door. She didn't seem at all concerned that she might have inconvenienced me. When I opened the door she asked me which room the meeting would be held in, and when I pointed to the living room, she just brushed past me, lugging a canvas sack."

She paused for breath and Ben Littlejohn broke the silence. "Like I said, she was very eccentric."

"I was too busy to object," Leticia went on, "so I went back to my room and finished dressing. When I finally got back to the living room, I couldn't believe my eyes when I saw what she had done."

Although it was unclear what connection Leticia's tale had with the terrible events of the past few days, she had her audience spellbound. Chris Lockwood leaned forward on the couch with his elbows on his knees and his chin resting on his hands. Even Ben Littlejohn, accustomed to unusual stories, was caught up in the mystery.

Leticia held her arms about a yard apart, palms facing each other. "She had set up a wooden table about this big, a clever device that folded into a compact package. On top of it she had arranged a pair of crystal cruets, a small goblet, a few small statuettes that looked like crude replicas of animals, and a brass tray that held a granular powder. She was holding a match to the tray when I got there."

"Incense," Chris guessed and Kathryn Rogers nodded her concurrence.

Leticia pulled a clawlike hand from the folds of her robe and scratched at an angry pustule on her neck, then, embarrassed, she quickly buried her hand once again. "Yes, it was incense," she said, "and I was angry with the old woman for lighting it without my permission, but if my anger showed, she didn't seem to notice it. She ignored me and bustled around the room like a cyclone, angling chairs this way and that, closing drapes.

I must have been stunned speechless because I didn't say a word to her, and before I realized the time, the other women began to arrive. You can imagine their surprise when they walked in and saw Daphne Monet."

"I bet they were scared," Chris ventured.

"Some of them were, child."

Chris wrinkled his brow, not sure that he appreciated being called a child.

"Some of them were frightened, most were just startled." She grinned ruefully. "They were even more surprised when she turned out to be charming."

"I bet they were," Kathryn agreed. Even though she had never before heard of the old woman, she had formed an accurate mental picture.

"Daphne went from person to person, greeting them warmly," Leticia said. "I remember it all so clearly. She went up to them one at a time and took their hand between her two. She was shorter than any of them and she looked up at them with her eyes sparkling and introduced herself in a sweet little voice. 'I'm so pleased to finally meet you,' she said. 'We must get together more often.' The ladies were so taken back, they didn't know what to make of it."

Leticia's face hardened.

"At first I thought that it was cute, but eventually I realized her purpose. She was a shrewd old woman who was trying to take control of the meeting.

Leticia's voice had been rising steadily, adding a pinch of volume for every trace of anger. Realizing this, she paused to fight the impulse. Leticia looked at the priest who had been sitting silently to her right since the onset of the story. "I almost forgot," she said. "As the ladies entered, Daphne seemed to be keeping count. One of the members was late. She was eight months pregnant like I was, and while we waited, Daphne flitted about from lady to lady asking about their families as if she was a long-lost friend. It was only after Mae finally arrived, when all twelve of the original group were there, that Daphne got agitated and wanted to start."

"Mae?" Kathryn asked. "I don't recall anyone named Mae in Hensleyville."

"You probably wouldn't," Leticia said. There was a haunting melancholy to her voice as if the topic dredged up painful memories. "She left Hensleyville even before I did. Her last name was Cady."

The name fell like a boulder amid the listeners.

"Lucius's mom," Chris said with a gasp.

Leticia studied the stunned faces of her audience. "She was to become the mother of Lucius Cady," she replied. "As I said, we were both very pregnant. I was due to give birth in four weeks. Mae's date was less than three weeks away."

She began to pace again, walking from side to side with a flowing grace, a counterpoint that made her facial appearance all the more obscene.

"Once Mae arrived, Daphne's attitude changed dramatically. She suddenly became all business, shuffling the chairs around and telling the ladies where they were to sit. I started to object but each time that I did, I became nauseous and I felt the baby kicking uncomfortably inside me. That, plus the fact that the ladies didn't seem to mind being bossed around, made it difficult not to go along with her wishes."

Leticia walked slowly back to her chair and sat down. The others were ringed around her, caught up in the tale as she peeled away the mystery layer by layer. Each of the listeners had their own idea of the story's direction but none, except the priest who had already heard it, could predict the final chapter.

The woman seemed to slump within the dark folds of her robe and her strength appeared to drain from her body with every word. "Finally, even I did as I was told," she said wearily. "Daphne seated us all in a circle around the table with the statuettes and the other objects. Then she went to her sack and took out a stack of black felt squares. Each of them was about a foot on a side and she laid these around the outside of the ring of chairs. I recall that she was very deliberate about where she placed them. Each of the squares had an image drawn on it in red paint. Some I recognized, like signs from the zodiac, others made no sense to me at all." She leaned back into the soft cushion of the chair and took a deep breath.

Dr. Logan leaned forward. "Are you feeling well?" he asked.

Leticia smiled weakly and nodded. "I'll be all right," she said but the firmness was gone from her voice.

With an effort, she sat up straighter and continued.

"Daphne had been dressed in a proper skirt and blouse, quite appropriate for the occasion, but as we watched, she reached again into her sack and pulled out a beautiful vestment, white with threads of gold brocade running through it. She pulled it on over her head and it hung to her knees."

The toll of Leticia's journey combined with the effort of telling the story was having a formidable effect on the woman. The eyes that earlier had been the only source of beauty in the scaly face had lost their luster. The voice, once soft and throaty, was degenerating to a raspy whisper. With considerable effort, Leticia continued.

"Daphne proceeded to give the ladies a very interesting lecture on the study of the occult. She began by explaining that during her early schooling she became interested in Eastern European customs and that this led to the study of early tribal religions and from there, quite naturally, she became a student of their superstitions. The way she unfolded it, it all seemed quite harmless to us. She demystified it, and in doing so, she made it acceptable. I was amazed. Instead of being disgusted by some of the abominations that she described, the ladies hung on her every word, asking questions and delving deeper into the unknown. So when she innocently asked if any of them would be interested in seeing a demonstration of one of the ancient rituals, they all jumped at the chance." She looked to Father O'Connor through a veil of grief. "I among them," she admitted sadly.

"What did she do next?" Chris blurted. He had almost forgotten the circumstances of their gathering, so absorbed was he at the drama of the story.

Leticia coughed lightly and a gurgling sound fluttered from her chest. "Daphne went back to her sack and pulled out a handful of necklaces. They were leather thongs with small carved images, like the brass ones she had set up on the table. She gave one to each of us and we hung them around our necks. Then she threw a handful of powder on the incense dish and a cloud of smoke blossomed. It had a funny smell, not unpleasant, and all of a sudden I found myself no longer resenting her intrusion. In fact I was thankful for it and anxious for the demonstration to begin."

Ben Littlejohn met Dr. Logan's eye as they arrived at similar conclusions.

Leticia continued, "Daphne Monet told us that the key to the ancient rituals of the occult was sacrifice." With an apologetic glance at Father O'Connor, she explained, "She compared it to the Mass at a Catholic church except I remember that she winked to remind us that it was all just pretend, that this was only a demonstration to show us how the ancient superstitions were acted out. Then Daphne Monet asked the question that has haunted me for the last thirteen years."

Tears welled in her eyes, finally overflowing and zigzagging down the canyons of her face.

"She asked each of us what we would like to sacrifice."

Leticia worked her hands beneath the robe and paced nervously in spite of her exhaustion. She had told the story only once before, an hour earlier, when she confessed to Father O'Connor, and the strain of repeating it bore down on her bony shoulders like a mighty weight. But she had to tell her story and she had to tell it now. It might already be too late.

"By this time we were all getting giddy. I think it was something that Daphne mixed with the incense. She started at one end of the circle and worked her way around it, asking each member in turn what she'd like to sacrifice. I was the last one in the ring and Mae Cady was right before me. The ladies were being silly, each one trying to outdo the other by the outrageousness of their answer. One volunteered to bake a pie as if it was for a church social. Another offered her husband's bowling ball. It went on like that, one silly sacrifice after the other, working all the way around the ring until it got to be Mae Cady's turn."

She was racing through her story now, almost devoid of emotion, as if to smile or shed a tear would cause the momentum to be lost, perhaps never to be regained.

"As I told you, Mae and I were each eight months pregnant, bloated like cows and suffering miserably in the summer heat.

Her idea seemed funny at the time. So funny, in fact, that I imitated her. I offered the same sacrifice."

This time, Leticia did pause and she let her eyes make painful contact with each of the listeners. They burned with the anguish of thirteen years.

"We offered to sacrifice our unborn children."

Kathryn Rogers's hand shot to her mouth in horror. "Oh, no," she gasped.

"You have to picture it," Leticia pleaded, leaning toward the listeners clasping and unclasping her withered hands. "You had to be there. A dozen bored women were letting their hair down and a haggard old crone was holding court. The situation invited silliness and that's what we thought we were being."

She swallowed hard, shook her head, and whispered, "We thought we were just being silly."

New tears followed the weathered course of old ones. She was upset and weary but determined to tell the story. It would explain the town's recent string of tragedies and it might help to prevent others.

"Daphne seemed very pleased with herself when we were through making our suggestions. She continued performing the ritual, making strange sounds, holding up one statuette after another. Finally she grew very serious. I remember thinking at the time, My God, she really believes this. But I dismissed the thought as quickly as it came. With great care, she poured the liquid from the cruets into the goblet and she drank from it. Then she asked each of us to take a sip. Our mood was still high so no one objected. She started at my end of the circle this time. Being first in line, I might have refused, but that would have dampened the mood and I remember being pleased with the meeting's success. I sipped the liquid, not knowing what to expect and hardly caring. I remember that the taste was bitter. Then I passed it to Mae Cady. For some reason, after Mae and I each took a sip, Daphne suddenly decided that would be enough. She became very brusque and officious and she told us that the demonstration was over. Then, without a word, she gathered up her paraphernalia, stuffed it into her sack, and walked out the door.

"She dropped dead on my doorstep." Even after thirteen years, Leticia couldn't conceal the surprise in her voice.

In the deathly silence, Father O'Connor stood. "Might I suggest," he offered, "that we refill our cups. Leticia has more to tell you, much more, and we have much to discuss."

Dumbstruck and with the startling echo of her words still ringing in their ears, the listeners filed past the silver urn and refilled their cups. Chris shook the drops from a can of Pepsi that he took from a small refrigerator tucked in the corner of the room. An honor box requesting fifty cents lay on top of it and he dug in his jeans and came up with a pair of quarters. As they mingled silently, Leticia once again sat down, turning down offers of refreshment with a shake of her head. With the quiet reverence reserved for a wake, they returned to their seats and turned to their weary visitor with expectant faces. She didn't disappoint them.

"There was no great fuss made over the passing of Daphne Monet. She had lived her later years in self-imposed isolation, and except for the burst of activity in the hour preceding her death, she departed the same way. The ambulance arrived minutes after I phoned, and less than five minutes later, Daphne Monet and her bag of statues were gone forever."

She turned her head slowly around the circle of listeners, fixing each with the intensity of her gaze before moving on. "But she left behind a legacy of death and destruction that exists till this day."

"She *was* a witch," Chris whispered.

Leticia ignored the interruption. "That same night I went into labor, and at six o'clock in the morning, Melinda was born."

At the dead girl's name, the police chief winced and felt a pang of sorrow.

"At the same moment," Leticia continued, "Mae Cady gave birth to Lucius."

Dr. Logan recalled the coincidence of thirteen years earlier and nodded his head knowingly. "I had almost forgotten about that," he admitted. "Melinda and Lucius are exactly the same age." A look of curiosity crossed his face. Leaning toward her he asked, "When is their birthday?"

Leticia pulled a scrawny hand from beneath the robe and looked at her watch. "Had Melinda lived, her thirteenth birthday would occur in less than two hours."

At the announcement, the listeners sat startled, but not only from the impact of Leticia's words. A deep rumbling shook the group into silence. They looked at each other for the assurance that they weren't alone and the puzzled faces of the others satisfied their doubt.

"What was that?" Kathryn Rogers finally asked.

Though he didn't trust his answer, Ben Littlejohn replied, "Probably an eighteen wheeler rumbling down a street where he doesn't belong."

To test his theory, the chief cocked an ear toward the outside wall and the others listened and waited.

"Just a truck," Ben concluded.

Dismissing the interruption, the group refocused their attention on Leticia's most recent revelation, so absorbed that none of them, not even Woody or Kathryn, noticed the dread that masked Chris's freckled face.

In a rush of words, Leticia described the year that followed. Less than six months after Melinda's birth, her husband was crushed beneath a tractor, leaving the grieving mother to care for the baby girl. Also within the year, Mae Cady disappeared without a trace, taking off on a Trailways bus and leaving the stoic Festus to care as best he could for the baby boy. By unspoken consent, the book club never met again and Leticia drew within herself, feeling her health slip, along with her fragile grip on reality, as the agonizing weeks became months, the months years.

"I have dreams constantly," she told them. "They're always the same. I see Melly on the verge of womanhood. She is beautiful in a long white dress with a red sash snugged around her waist as she carries a bouquet of roses. She is standing at the head of a long table and there are happy little children seated all around it. Lucius Cady stands at the other end, also dressed in white like it is the day of his First Communion. He has a red flower in his lapel and his hair is slicked back like a school picture. In the very center of the table is a large round cake, white with fat red candles. Written across it in bold red icing is the number thirteen."

Recovered from his earlier shock, Chris asked, "What happens then?"

"That's when Daphne Monet returns," she said simply. "She wears the same simple skirt and blouse that she wore at the meeting of the book club. I never see her enter. All of a sudden she's just there. In the dream, it's always the same. She smiles sweetly and raises her arms above her head like a choir director and the children begin to sing. It sounds like a symphony, sweet young voices singing "Happy Birthday." Then, halfway through the song, the words and the voices suddenly change. The words make no sense at all. They're hardly more than noises, and the children's sweet voices become like the gruntings of pigs. The horrible noise swells to a din and a knife suddenly materializes in Daphne's hand. The sweet smile disappears from her face and she raises the knife above the birthday cake and bellows a long, low wail. The children echo the wail and suddenly they're no longer little children, they're horrible, misshapen beings screaming in pain."

Leticia's own agony glared through the narration but her condition didn't slow the torrent of words.

"Melinda and Lucius both stand and they meet at the center of the table. The creatures scuttle out of their way and the two children stand across the table from Daphne Monet, the birthday cake between them. They join hands as if in a wedding ceremony, then with a horrible shriek, Daphne plunges the knife into the cake."

Leticia closed her eyes and spoke in an emotionless monotone. "The last thing I always recall before I wake up is a loud squeal, a horrible smell, and the sight of grey liquid gushing from the wound in the cake."

She took a long breath and sunk into the deep cushion of her chair, physically shrinking as she did so.

"Melinda had the same dream," she whispered, "over and over again. It preyed on her nerves. We were both tense and irritable. We fought all the time. One day I—I—"

Leticia brought her hands to her face and finally broke down and sobbed freely.

"One day I hit her," she blurted, "and she ran crying from the house."

With an effort of will, she braced herself and met the pitying stares of her audience.

"I never saw my little girl alive again."

25

SHE WAS SO distraught that it took a full five minutes before Leticia Zooker could resume her story. For the years since Melinda's death, the woman had been heaping blame on herself for not doing more to ease her daughter's anguish, for not protecting her from the mind monsters that were eroding what little joy life held for her.

The corners of her mouth turned down in an ugly frown. "I did nothing to help her," she said between sobs. Turning to Father O'Connor, she shook her head sadly. "I could have tried to call on God. I could have at least brought her to church."

The priest nodded thoughtfully. "Yes, you could have done those things," he agreed, "but don't blame yourself. Remember, you had formidable opposition. You had the prince of evil opposing your every good intention."

But O'Connor's kindness did little to console her. "Festus Cady tried to fight it," she continued. "I think he knew what was happening. He tried to protect Lucius by bringing the power of God into his house." She ground her hands together beneath the robe.

"And look at what happened to him," the priest said with a rueful shake of his head. "The devil turned him against himself in the worst way under God's law." O'Connor sighed and blessed himself. "He was murdered by the beast the same as Jeff Zack and the others."

"Festus knew more than he told us," Ben Littlejohn agreed,

"and it killed him. But why now?" he wondered. "Why should this evil all of a sudden become so—so murderous? Why, after it's been dormant for all these years, has it finally decided to show its power."

Leticia swallowed hard, pulling herself together with an act of will. She must warn them. This is why she had come. "I see the plan in my dream," she told the chief of police. "Since the day after Daphne Monet's death, the dream has always been the same. When Daphne plunged the knife into the cake, she released the evil and it captured the souls of Lucius Cady and my Melinda." Her blue eyes hardened and a hint of steel entered her voice. "It happened on their thirteenth birthday."

"If indeed that is the devil's plan," Father O'Connor said, "the pieces of this sad puzzle fall neatly into place. He's waited thirteen years for this moment, not a lot of time by his calendar but certainly a significant portion of the time we humans have on earth."

He glanced at the police chief. "Speaking in modern-day terms, the suspect, in this case we'll call him Satan, has laid very intricate plans for an abduction." He shrugged apologetically. "Perhaps not a physical abduction but a spiritual one, sinful and criminal nonetheless."

He addressed the group like a lawyer making closing comments to a rapt jury. "The timing of his plan is crucial, in this case Lucius Cady's thirteenth birthday."

"What's so important about that?" John Logan asked.

The priest shrugged once again. "I'm not privy to all the rules and rituals that govern the forces of darkness," he admitted, "but I do recall that the number thirteen has some significance in the practice of the black religion. My guess is that by coming forward at that particular time, Satan will exert a more powerful influence on the boy, perhaps making him an acolyte, a modern-day apostle of evil."

"That's precisely right," Leticia said. She didn't know why she was so certain but there wasn't an ounce of doubt in her mind.

The priest continued, "Festus Cady endangered the plan. By trying to protect Lucius, he became a potential hindrance." He laid a gentle hand on Leticia's sharp shoulder. "I think Leticia's correct when she says that Festus recognized the danger. He tried to stop it." Father O'Connor made a weak sign of the cross in the air in front of him. "God knows he tried."

Ben Littlejohn raised his hand and spoke. "But how does this theory explain all the other deaths? What purpose was served by murdering Pete Bishop or Lenny Brothers or the entire Stein family?"

The priest smiled grimly. "Forget for a moment the so-called supernatural aspects of this case, Ben. Pretend that you're just dealing with one of your run-of-the-mill criminals. We're talking about mischief here and mischief is only a matter of degree."

The chief's expression showed that he didn't understand what O'Connor was getting at.

"This is only conjecture," the priest continued, "but let's try it on for size. When a little boy gets angry and upset, he has a range of options in which he can show his emotion. It's a very narrow range," he said, holding his hands about six inches apart as if bragging about a baby bass, "and in the worst case, he might sass his parents."

He let that sink in for a moment and the others nodded.

"That's a young lad's level of mischief. Now let's raise the stakes and go to the other end of the spectrum. If sassing his parents is the kind of mischief you can expect from a nice little boy, what do you suppose constitutes mischief for the most malicious mind in the universe?"

"Murder," Kathryn Rogers whispered.

"I'd hate to see him get really mad," Ben quipped without humor.

"You might just get that chance if he doesn't get his way," the priest warned.

Kathryn squeezed Chris's hand until the boy's fingers hurt. "There were seven boys on the camping trip," she said. "Only Chris and Lucius are alive today."

The potent reality of her words chilled Woody Lockwood's heart.

"We have to protect them," Leticia said with the fierceness of a mother watching over her young.

Protection was Ben's job and he looked to the priest and

Leticia for help. "Does your theory hold that if we can keep the boys from harm until Lucius's birthday is over, they'll be safe?"

"It's possible," the priest said, but his voice was filled with doubt.

"What can we do?" Woody asked.

As his words trailed off, the rumbling vibrations began again and their eyes met in apprehension.

"What *is* that?" Kathryn asked.

Father O'Connor looked across the room at the youngster huddled on the couch. "Each of the boys on that ill-fated camping trip spoke of a terrible fear that they had, didn't they, Chris?"

The boy nodded.

The priest was a rumpled mess but his eyes were sharp as tacks as he spoke to Chris softly. "Suppose you remind us of what you said your fear was," he urged.

Embarrassed, Chris looked at the ring of searching faces. "It was no big deal," he said. "We had to say something. I just picked something that nobody else said."

"And what was that, Chris?" O'Connor prodded.

The boy shrugged in resignation. "Earthquakes," he told the anxious adults. "I told Pete Bishop that I was afraid of getting killed in an earthquake."

The rumble, at first no more than a deep vibration, rolled to a new intensity, not sufficient to set pictures askew but enough to make the lampshade tremble with respect. Then it stopped once again. In eerie silence, a wave of recognition floated over the room.

With a brave young smile, Chris admitted, "I think I'm getting scared."

Woody and Kathryn moved closer to him, their own safety forgotten in their need to protect him.

"There was a special stone," Ben Littlejohn recalled. "What happened to it?"

Father O'Connor dug into the pocket of his chinos. "Here it is." He held it like a fragile egg, thumb on one end, forefinger on the other.

Leticia looked up at it, then she laughed bitterly. "That's a toy," she told them with a sad shake of her head. "It couldn't blunt a curse, let along stop the devil."

The priest recalled its effect on Jeff Zack moments before he plunged through the window to his death. "But it does have some strange power," he said, his brow furrowed with worry and wonder.

"Enough to stop an earthquake?" Leticia scoffed.

Chris turned to the woman, his face full of indignation. "Lucius believes in it," he said defensively. "He gave it to me to protect myself."

Leticia's face softened and she shook her head sadly. "Lucius Cady probably knows more about evil than any other twelve-year-old on the face of the earth but he hasn't a clue of the depths of Satan's evil or the heights of his power."

Her eyes filled with tears, and for a moment, it was possible to see her former beauty as maternal love clouded the horrid scales.

"I'm sure that Lucius meant well," she said softly. "There *are* powers in the stone to be sure, but they come from Lucius himself, not from a pretty piece of granite. His love can deflect evil, a little bit of it, and that's what you have in your stone, a little love and a lot of hope."

Father O'Connor nodded in understanding. "It was very brave of you to come to us tonight, Leticia. You've confirmed our worst fears and now we know what we're up against and why Satan has chosen our small town to wreak his destruction. What we still don't know is how we're going to stop him."

While the group pondered the problem, the door to the doctors' lounge swung open. A worried Dr. Menard stood framed in the rectangle with Lucius Cady by his side.

"He wouldn't stay in his room," the doctor apologized. "He said he had to come down to be with you."

"Lucius," Chris called out, "are you all right?"

"Are you?" Lucius echoed.

His sweet young face was bruised and purple from Virgil Fenner's abuse and it wore lines of fear that should be reserved for one who was five times his age. He wore a fresh hospital gown and the dirt and grease of the trunk of Virgil's car had been bathed from his pale legs.

Chris smiled. "You look funny, Lucius, like Wee Willy Winkie."

Lucius didn't return the smile. "The beast is near," he said. "It is time. It will try to win now."

His voice held a note of finality but not of surrender. He stood erect, like a diminutive general on a field of battle, prepared for the worst but willing to fight to the death. He gazed around the room and met the eyes of Leticia Zooker.

"I still see Melly in my dreams," he said without preface. "I don't think we'll ever have the dream again."

Her eyes clouded as she pictured the boy of her dream in the white suit with the red rose pinned to the lapel. "No, we won't," she agreed.

The rumbling returned, more intense now, and this time the pictures did rattle against the wall and the metal ashtray danced across the coffee table with a tinny clatter.

Lucius stepped across the room to his friend. "We're stronger when we're together. It might not be enough but we have to try." He moved the coffee table from in front of the couch and pulled a chair into its place.

The rumbling was constant now but not yet destructive. Lampshades jiggled and ashtrays danced but nothing broke. Amid the trembling, Lucius sat across from Chris and took his hand. "I wish I had my Bible," he said. Then a sudden thought struck him. "You still have the stone, don't you?"

"I do, Lucius," Father O'Connor said, holding it as he did before between thumb and forefinger. "It's full of your power."

"Not my power. It's the power of God," Lucius corrected, not recognizing the priest, particularly in his state of dress.

"Yes," Father O'Connor agreed, "it's surely the power of God. But might I suggest that we retire to another place where I think our dark visitor might find himself even more unwelcome."

Lucius looked at him curiously.

The priest extended his hand in greeting. "I'm John O'Connor, Lucius, and I've some experience in dealing with evil. I'm the priest at St. Martin's."

Recognition lit the boy's face. "Yes," he said, "we should go to your church. It will be better there."

A sudden jolt rocked the room and a jagged scar split the ceiling, showering the lounge in a mist of dust. A table lamp tumbled to the floor and the bulb exploded.

"The patients," Dr. Logan said, "I've got to make sure they're all right."

"The best thing we can do for the patients is to leave the hospital," Leticia said. She stood and moved toward the door. "Let's hurry to the church."

"I have the parish van," the priest said. "We can all fit."

Amid the screams of startled patients and the frantic shouts of the night staff, the group raced from the hospital.

26

THE VAN WAS old and, like its owner, it creaked from years of good deeds. The clock on the dash read 4:30. The priest threw it into gear and it lurched from the lot and Leticia, who sat in the middle seat next to Lucius Cady, had to grab the back of the driver's seat for stability. Eight people crowded into the van, and if the earth still shook, it wasn't evident during the wild seven-block ride from Memorial Hospital to Father O'Connor's church.

St. Martin's was a small country church trying to look stately and gothic like its European ancestors. Never did it succeed so well as it did in the false dawn of this misty morning. The grey luminescence that preceded the first flash of dawn hung over St. Martin's twin spires like a ghostly halo, giving a false impression of its size but the true magnitude of its majesty.

Father O'Connor stared up at the structure as if seeing it for the first time, feeling unlike ever before the strength of its character. If a building can gulp a breath, square its shoulders, and flex its muscles, St. Martin's did so as the van rattled to a stop in front of it.

"Come quickly," the priest ordered as he shouldered open the door and stepped down to the street.

They clambered out behind him but Father O'Connor didn't wait. He raced up the steep flight of stone steps, grasping the iron railing for support. By the time Leticia joined the group on the sidewalk, the priest was already fumbling the key into the lock of the massive wooden doors.

"Hurry," he shouted through the grey mist. He felt a growing urgency to reach the sanctity and protection of St. Martin's and his relief was tangible when the doors swung open and the familiar smells enveloped him.

Obedient to the priest's command, Chris and Lucius sprinted up the steps at his heels, taking the risers three at a time as they felt the cold breath of evil creeping up their backs. They scurried through the door and skidded to a stop in the darkened vestibule while the priest groped at a switch box in the corner.

The snap of each toggle brought to life a section of the towering ceiling, the yellow glow bathing the dark oak pews beneath it as the light worked its way from back to front on the bride's side, then repeated the sequence on the groom's. By the time that the farthest corner of the church felt the breath of light, the last of the group had passed across the threshold. With a glance at the light-streaked sky, Father O'Connor pulled the heavy doors closed. They thudded shut with a comforting finality, enclosing the frightened group in the bosom of St. Martin's goodness while barring the forces that would destroy them.

Then why, the priest wondered, didn't he feel the strength of his patron's protection?

He twisted the key in the lock and the dead bolt clicked home with a comforting snap.

The vestibule ran the width of the church, a grey flagstone floor worn smooth by millions of reverent steps. Last Sunday's church bulletins sprouted from a literature rack and stacks of dog-eared song books were piled high on the last pew.

Lucius Cady took a cautious step toward the front of the church, stopping where the center aisle met the vestibule. With wonder in his almond eyes, he took measure of St. Martin's mysteries. The place wasn't bright and cheery like he remembered the Methodist church that he used to attend before his father developed his own home liturgy. St. Martin's was cloaked in funereal dimness, cavernous and hollow. It flooded his overburdened senses with messages that should have brought peace, but instead pierced him with a fresh stab of fear.

To be sure, St. Martin's was the house of God but the message it sent to Lucius Cady was tainted by another presence.

The others sensed it too and some wondered if they had brought it inside with them, as if the smell of evil clung to their clothes like the musk of a dank cellar or the smoky breath of Gilly's. Chris moved to Lucius's side.

The somber atmosphere weighed heavily in the boys' imagination. It was a midnight excursion through a dark cemetery. It was awakening from a nightmare only to find yourself locked in a sepulcher with the heavy breath of evil panting at the bolted door.

Lucius shuddered and Chris laid a brotherly hand on his shoulder. Together, their eyes locked on St. Martin's only contemporary touch, a stylized wooden cross suspended above the altar by three taut cords, one at the head and two where the hands would be except that there was no crucified Savior, only the two plain shafts, intersected and carved to arrowheads that aimed left and right, up and down like points on a compass. The lines of the wooden cross were a breath of freshness amid the reminders of a more somber time.

Lucius looked up at Chris thankfully, feeling the strength of his innocence mingle with the austere power of the church.

The silence was thick and foreboding, assaulting their ears. The echo of the dead bolt and their own heartbeats gave the only proof of life. Even Father O'Connor was moved by the spell, and he felt, for a moment, like a stranger in his own home. He cocked an ear, listening for an echo of the tremors that sent them scrambling from Memorial Hospital, but the slate underfoot was firm and steady. Glancing anxiously at the suspended cross, the old priest blessed himself with uncharacteristic care and began to walk down the aisle.

"I think it's time that we should pray," he said and his words reverberated from every corner of the church.

Taking his cue, Chris and Lucius fell in behind him and the others followed. As he neared the altar, a thick slab of granite atop heavy stone legs, the priest gestured to the kneeling pad that ran along the altar rail. Chris led and the others filed across behind him, finally kneeling on the soft pad with their elbows or wrists resting on the polished rail. As they settled in, Father

O'Connor disappeared through a small door to the side of the altar, reappearing a minute later in vestments more appropriate to the occasion.

He wore a gleaming white alb covered by a golden chasuble with a fiery red cross blazing across its breast. He had brushed his thin white hair in place.

"We combat darkness with light," he told them, indicating his selection of vestments, "and we defeat the voice of evil with the word of God. Our Father," he began.

"Who art in Heaven," Lucius picked up.

"Hallowed be thy name," they all said.

Their voices swelled like a chorus and the church seemed suddenly brighter and alive. They finished the prayer together, except for Leticia Zooker who trailed the others by a few soft words.

"I'm an old-fashioned kind of minister," Father O'Connor admitted from behind the slanted lectern, "and we're coming to grips with an old-fashioned kind of evil." His fingers curled around the edge of the lectern and he met the determined eyes of Lucius Cady. "I'm going to use the strongest weapon that I have in my arsenal. I'm going to say Mass." He looked at the cloudy crystal of his watch. "It's just after five o'clock. Leticia has advised us that the greatest danger will be past by six. I'll pray in my special way and I ask each of you to pray in yours. Together we possess great strength, and with the help of God, we will focus it and drive away the evil that threatens us."

The white-haired priest turned to the altar and bowed in a manner reminiscent of an earlier time, a time when women wore veils and men wore suits and the faithful would sprint the last mile to church rather than walk in late. With the reverence of one whose faith is solid, Father O'Connor made the sign of the cross.

"*In nomine Patris, et Filii, et Spiritus Sanctus,*" he intoned in a language lost for the second time.

He was facing the altar, saying the mass of his youth, the mass of his training and of his early years as a priest. He was glad to be in possession of the weapons in his ancient arsenal.

He raised his eyes to the gold cross on the altar. "*Introibo ad altare Dei,*" he said.

"Ad Deum qui laetificat juventutem meam," came the answer.

The response sounded natural enough, two youthful voices mechanically chirping the Latin words, but today he had no altar boys and he doubted that there was a lad in Hensleyville under the age of forty who could follow the old liturgy. Turning slowly, his brow furrowed with lines of curiosity, he sought the source of the response and found the equally startled faces of Chris Lockwood and Lucius Cady. Neither boy was Catholic, neither to his knowledge had any earthly reason to know the words they had just recited.

"I will go to the altar of God," Father O'Connor had said and the boys had answered, "To God, the joy of my youth."

How he missed it, he suddenly realized, shaken by the thin voices of these two special boys. They stared back at him, confused by their unwitting response yet fortified by its meaning.

Were they getting help? Were their prayers being answered?

Father O'Connor certainly thought so. Turning slightly so he could catch them in the corner of his view he continued, this time in English but still using the words of the older liturgy.

"Give judgment for me, O God, and decide my cause against an unholy people, from unjust and deceitful men deliver me."

Chris and Lucius were kneeling stiffly against the rail, their hands folded, chins raised, eyes locked on the golden cross.

"Quia tu es, Deus, fortituda mea: quare me repulisti, et quare tristin incedo, dum affligit me inimicus."

Woody Lockwood leaned forward and looked down the rail at his son, hardly able to believe the boy capable of the sounds coming from his young throat. Dr. Logan was lost in thought, a hint of a smile touching the corners of his mouth. The words had sounded familiar but why? And then he recalled the dark script in the glass frames that hung on the walls of his office.

Latin!

The ancient language of medicine. Logan the healer of bodies. O'Connor the healer of souls. It came together in a flash of intuition and he felt a surge of confidence that the vile attack on the town was still treatable. Help was on the way.

O'Connor paused, as if taking stock, counting the members of his team and weighing the strength of the opposition. The field of battle was turning in his favor—in their favor. He craned his neck to look overhead. The cross that hung above him shone with the strength of the oak from which it was hewn. The row of people kneeling at the altar rail followed his eyes and they felt the same wave of strength.

"Do you feel it?" Woody whispered excitedly to Kathryn Rogers.

She nodded and radiated confidence. "I've never felt anything like this before," she whispered back. "It feels like we're ganging up on it, like it can't possibly win."

And it continued in that vein through the Confiteor and the Introit. By the time that O'Connor reached the Kyrie, they were all singing out the Latin responses only it no longer seemed strange. Their voices rang through the church as one, growing in strength with each new volley.

"*Kyrie, eleison,*" the priest said.

"*Christe, eleison,*" they responded.

"*Gloria in excelcis Deo,*" they all sang out, praising God in words they had never heard before but understanding their meaning as if they'd spoken the language for a millennium.

To a bystander it would have been a remarkable scene. Leticia Zooker, missing these many months, angel eyes peering from a ghoulish face, mouthing the rhythmic words of a language whose antiquity matched her own appearance.

Ben Littlejohn with stubbly jaw and rumpled uniform, staring at the wooden cross with the devotion of a third grader, his gun hanging lazily on his hip.

The town doctor, lawyer, school principal, the intelligentsia if such exists in an unpretentious place as Hensleyville, all huddled to the railing of Father O'Connor's altar, talking to God in a language of the past, pulling together their strength to crush the evil of a power that, a few days earlier, would have brought bemused smiles to their suntanned faces. And the two youngsters whose upturned faces glowed with the goodness of trusting innocence.

The assembly even amazed the old priest, not only in its diversity, but also in the fervor of its devotion. He walked to

the right side of the altar and opened the tome that rested on a
wooden stand. Like the others, he was lost in the flush of the
hypnotic moment.

Leticia was the first to see the movement and she gasped a
short breath of surprise.

It had only been a subtle shadow for these many minutes but
suddenly it twitched. It had been lying beneath the granite slab
of the altar, huddled inconspicuously against the great stone
leg, a dark blur that blended invisibly with the shadowed slate
until it squirmed awake and blinked in surprise at the equally
startled audience.

The cat's eyes shone like vigil candles and its pointy teeth
gleamed as it arched its back and pointed its tail in a luxurious
stretch. Leticia breathed a low sigh of relief when it slunk from
its hideaway and strode righteously to the front of the lectern
where, unconcerned with the prying eyes, it bared its teeth,
yawned, bathed a foot with a small pink tongue, and curled up
once again, safely removed from the shuffling feet of the old
man at the altar. Closing its eyes, the cat tensed for a second
and a column of stiff hair rode its back like a wave until it
finally settled into a satisfied sleep.

Lucius eyed it warily.

"*Dominus vobiscum*," the priest prayed.

"*Et cum spiritu tuo*," the kneeling row of worshipers
responded.

O'Connor read the gospel to himself and waived the homily,
a rarity, he mused and he allowed himself a small, unseen
smile. He was praying the Mass slowly, with the fervor of the
recently ordained, hearing once again the mysteries and the
prayers that had, over the years, become rambling words
strung together in a mechanical flow. Facing the golden cross,
he prayed, "*Credo in unum Deum*."

I believe in one God.

How the familiar words suddenly made sense.

He prayed the Creed piously, genuflecting when the Word
was made flesh by the Holy Ghost, and as he spoke the words,
the cat bared its razor teeth and hissed softly, unseen by all but
Leticia Zooker and Lucius Cady who both felt a mild chill,
barely noticeable.

And the Mass proceeded.

Through the offertory, the animal slept uneasily, as if bothered by fleeting dreams that made it shiver and twitch. Through the ritual of the washing of fingers, it settled back to a peaceful rest, its dark whiskers flicking fitfully as tiny smiles like a baby's gas pains sporadically crossed its black face.

"*Sanctus, Sanctus, Sanctus,*" the priest intoned, ringing a brass bell with a flick of his wrist as he did so.

The tinkle ricocheted through the cavernous church, seeking out hidden corners and wrapping around wooden beams before floating back to the ears of the black cat and it unsheathed its claws and pawed angrily at the air before resuming its peaceful vigil.

Kathryn Rogers noted the look of concern on Lucius's face and she followed his eyes to the resting animal, then she too felt the mild bite of ice on the air and goose bumps raised the fine hairs on her arms.

Father O'Connor stood at the center of the altar, his back to the rail. Before him, on the cold stone of the altar, was the chalice of wine and a round silver plate containing circles of unconsecrated bread. He spread his hands over the offerings and deliberately recited the prayers of sacrifice. At this new display of worship, the cat's tail jerked and another hiss steamed from its mouth. Its eyes snapped open as if in discovery and it glared at those lining the altar rail with yellow eyes filled with venom.

Leticia gasped.

At the altar, Father O'Connor genuflected devoutly. His white head was bowed low and he held a host at the edge of the altar with thumb and forefinger of both hands.

"For this is My Body," he prayed, but before he could rise from his knee, a tremor jolted the church and the cat pawed at the air and roared a jungle cry of outrage that joined with the quake to announce that the evil had returned.

Startled, the priest turned his head. He was still on one knee, still raising the host, but his look of piety had been dampened by a mask of fear. His old face blanched as the blood raced away and his eyes widened when they met the yellow eyes with the black slits that poured out such a torrent of hate. So evil was the look that for the moment the threat of the quake was forgotten. With host raised in adoration, the cat and the priest locked eyes and the two engaged in a war of wills.

It was a short battle. The cat opened its mouth to roar again. Wide.

Too wide.

The jaws came unhinged and from deep within its throat another pair of eyes appeared and an earsplitting shriek split the air that now was bone cold and filled with wisps of acrid smoke. From the animal's gaping jaws, a new face emerged, like the birthing of a disgusting baby, tugging the cat inside out with a howl of pain. The determined eyes of the new face met those of the old priest. As if it was part of the ceremony, O'Connor let the host fall lightly to the altar, then he brought both hands to his chest and croaked, "My Lord and my God."

His eyes bulged like a toad's, a purple vein throbbed on his temple, and he tumbled slowly to the side. His breath was a clutch of halting gasps as he lay on his back and stared blankly at the ceiling.

The row of onlookers was stunned into helplessness. Even the police chief was paralyzed by an unearthly fear. Clouds of steam puffed from his lips as he watched the unfolding obscenity and his gun hand drooped uselessly on the wooden railing.

"Happy birthday, Lucius," the creature from inside the cat wailed.

As they stared in horror, a grotesque little beast with wrinkled, stubby legs stood where the cat had been. It was blue and naked with grossly large male parts and a concave face with a piglike nose that puffed vapor that, even from the distance, had the foul smell of raw sewage.

"Happy, happy birthday," it screeched. And then it grew. It took shape, lost the sick blue hue and transformed into something from the gates of hell. As they stared in horror, the devilish monstrosity changed slowly until it became the sickening incarnation of Daphne Monet.

She stood by the lectern straight as a rule and naked as a newborn. Her skin was grey and wrinkled and her breasts hung like empty sacks from her bony chest. The head of a serpent showed itself from the scraggy grey hairs where her blue-veined thighs came together, then with a wet sound it quickly disappeared.

"It's your birthday, little boy. It's time for the party. We've waited so long."

Her eyes blazed like embers and her voice was shrill and strong. A carpet of mist roiled about her ankles and she emanated the putrefied stench of death. As Daphne Monet turned toward the altar, wisps of reddish smoke began to curl up the granite legs. The stone platform lost its grey coldness and began to glow from the light of the thirteen candles that sprouted from the cake that suddenly materialized where the bread and wine had once been. The happy giggles of little children filled the church and a dozen of them appeared around the altar, clapping their little hands and bouncing up and down on springy legs. They all wore white, some in short-sleeved shirts with long pants, some in tiny white jackets with short pants that showed their milky legs and socks and shoes.

Daphne Monet approached the happy celebration and they all turned to greet her, their faces blank, their eyes rolled back and white as eggshells. They smiled at her and drooled through blackened teeth.

Daphne stepped up to the party, detouring slightly to avoid the sprawled form of Father O'Connor. The children gurgled in delight and their tiny white coats and pants disintegrated into motes of dust revealing stubby blue legs, gross organs, malformed joints, and running pustules.

"Happy birthday, Lucius," they barked and they danced around the altar like a gaggle of grotesque dwarfs, waving their stunted arms and leaving in their wake a musty smell of decay.

Daphne stood facing the altar and the troll-like creatures wound closely around her, stopping to sniff at her like dogs seeking a mate. Her back was a map of veins and wrinkles, the cheeks of her buttocks a pair of deflated balloons. Her head pivoted on her shoulders as if her neck had no bones and her eyes sought out the birthday boy.

"It's your party, Lucius. Don't you want to join the other children?" The voice was deep and hollow, like it rose from the depths of a bottomless well.

Lucius met her stare and didn't shrink. With his hands on the altar rail, he pushed himself shakily to his feet. "Jesus Christ, Son of God, God of Light, Light of the World, protect me from Satan and his evils."

He raised his head and locked his eyes on the wooden cross suspended above the altar. His plea bounced from the walls and ceiling and floor and it filled the church with his urgent prayer.

Daphne Monet laughed sharply and the partying trolls grunted their approval. "It's almost time to cut the cake, Lucius. Do you want to help?"

The boy raised his arms to the hanging cross, palms up in supplication. "Jesus Christ, Son of God, God of Light, Light of the World, protect me from Satan and his evils."

Daphne forced a pitying smile. "Very well," she told him, "I'll just have to do it without you." With a shrug of her naked shoulders she turned back to the altar and raised the gleaming knife above the cake.

"Happy birthday, Lucius," she cried.

"Happy birthday, Lucius," the creatures shouted back, and she plunged the knife into the center of the cake.

The cake burst like a bloated tick, spraying Daphne Monet and her creatures with a putrid grey juice.

A phosphorescent flash exploded above the altar.

Ben Littlejohn groped at his holster and pulled out his pistol but he didn't know what to shoot. There was a naked old crone, twelve ghoulish trolls, and now, from the center of the cake, there stepped a miniature goat with spindly legs, hair like silk, and a face something less than human but more than animal. A pair of horns protruded from its forehead. It smiled at Lucius.

Without warning, the church was battered by a mighty jolt. Littlejohn rocked on his feet and Chris hugged the railing to keep from falling. Motes of dust exploded in the sunbeams that suddenly streaked through the windows. Jagged cracks like bolts of lightning raced across the walls. The bank of candles shook and rattled before crashing to the slate floor, scattering shards of bloodred glass in every direction. The church was coming apart, but the altar remained an island of calm.

Shaking like rag dolls, the group at the rail grabbed at one another for support while gaping in horror at the mutation on the altar.

The small goat began to grow. Its silky hair grew long and shaggy, coarse and matted, darker. Spindly front legs mutated into hairy arms. In bursts of flesh and hair, the kid became a man/beast standing upright on muscular legs with cloven hooves. It not only grew, it expanded in every direction until it towered above them, a goat, a man, a mammoth incarnation of all that was evil.

The blue creatures loved it. They danced around the altar as it rose steadily above them, whirling faster and faster and whipping up a storm until a spinning vortex reached from the ceiling and sucked them into its cone. Daphne Monet raised her arms above her head and joined them, drawn into the maelstrom that rose from the foot of the altar, spiraled to the ceiling, then burst through the roof of St. Martin's, leaving the monstrous creature standing on the altar, alone but for the motionless body of Father John O'Connor.

The beast snorted and a billious cloud shot toward Lucius, enveloped him, and made him reel and gag.

"It's time, Lucius," a disembodied voice bellowed from every corner of the church.

A fresh jolt battered the old building. A plaster statue of St. Martin tottered on its pedestal, then toppled to the floor where it crumbled to marbled fragments. The building began to sway, ceiling timbers shuddered, the wooden cross above the altar swung from front to back on its thin cables like a trapeze artist playing before a doomed audience. A massive beam above the altar rail torqued and twisted. Like champagne corks, its bolts exploded from their moorings and it ripped from the ceiling. One foot square and stained with age, the heavy beam lost its grip on the rustic joists and, with a loud crack, began its murderous plunge.

As if aware of her own death sentence and the tool of her execution, Leticia Zooker pushed from her scaly knees. With a strength born of faith, she dove through the air. Her weight was meaningless but the force of her thrust into Chris Lockwood jarred the breath from his body and sent him sprawling to the floor an instant before the timber crashed into his vacated space. The altar rail was smashed to useless splinters as the beam landed on the repentant mother of Melinda Zooker, crushing her at the waist before coming to rest on her lifeless body.

The creature's black lips curled back. It leapt from the altar and laughed at the mangled woman. Another beam fell in the back of the church, pews buckled, and Ben Littlejohn was knocked from his feet by the shifting floor. In a gesture of pure love, Kathryn Rogers threw herself over Chris Lockwood's trembling body and Woody threw himself on top of her.

Dr. Logan had tumbled backward and sat in a daze on the cold slate floor, his back at rest against the wooden wall that fronted the first pew.

Littlejohn crawled on hands and knees, hooked a hand over the altar rail, and fired blindly toward the towering beast. It laughed derisively, spraying the policeman with its fetid breath. Littlejohn jerked at the trigger, piercing the beast with round after round of harmless lead until, at the hollow click of the hammer, he hurled the useless weapon across the altar.

The beast took a ponderous step toward Lucius who managed to stagger once again to his feet.

"Jesus Christ," he shouted, "Son of God, God of Light, Light of the World, protect me from Satan and his evils."

The beast rocked back and roared with laughter. Then it looked down at its feet and saw the old priest.

With one hand still clutching his chest, O'Connor stretched the other toward the monster. Between thumb and forefinger he held the shiny stone.

The beast took a half step back, a startled expression on its ageless face. Then it drew its furry lips over black gums, revealing teeth as big as a child's hand and as yellow as corn. Its eyes grew red as molten nail heads and they shot a laser of light through the dust, focusing their evil power on the shiny stone. With a crack like a whiplash, the stone exploded in a shower of chips, leaving the priest staring at the stream of blood running down his arm.

Another tremor rocked the church. A portion of a side wall caved in, sending statues flying, crushing the pews in its path and boiling a wave of dust across the slate. The massive

wooden doors screamed in outrage and twisted from their
hinges. The cross above the altar swung wildly, soaring from
front to back, then jerking up and down like a puppet on a
string.

With the minor inconvenience of the stone removed, the
creature sneered disdainfully at the wounded priest. With a
massive hoof, it kicked him aside, lifting him off the ground
and flipping him to the side like a child's stuffed toy. Then it
lost interest in the old man and took another step toward Lucius
Cady. A distance of less than fifteen feet now separated them.

"You belong to me, Lucius Cady," a dark voice rumbled
from the beast's throat. "You have been promised."

It took another step, closing the gap farther. The beast
smelled like the cesspool of a zoo, and on its matted coat nests
of insects writhed and crawled.

"Jesus Christ," Lucius shouted.

"Son of God," Chris joined in from beneath the pile of
humanity.

"God of Light," the rest poured out.

"Light of the World, protect us from Satan and his evils."

Ben Littlejohn stood on shaking legs and shouted louder than
any of them. From the dusty slate, Dr. Logan raised his long
silent voice in prayer. The mingled pleas of Chris, Woody, and
Kathryn carried a powerful message.

About to take a final step, the beast was stopped in its tracks
by the invisible wall of prayer. It recoiled and tottered
backward, then it bellowed a roar of anger that sent a violent
shudder through the shell of the church.

Behind the loathsome creature, buoyed by the same power
that had slowed it, Father O'Connor struggled to his knees.
Scrabbling like a wounded crab, he scuttled painfully to the
marble pedestal of the baptismal font. As the beast gathered its
strength for a final assault, O'Connor rose slowly to his feet
and slid his arms beneath the shallow brass dish containing the
waters of baptism. With the final ounce of his physical and
spiritual strength he turned to the wooden cross.

"My Lord my God," he shouted and he flung the tray at the
creature's back.

The wail of pain sent new tremors through the walls and

loosed a shower of plaster from the ceiling. Turning on one black hoof, the beast roared with the anguish of hellfire and it raised its arms above its head to deliver a crushing blow to the waiting apostle of God.

"Jesus Christ," Lucius shouted above the din.

"Son of God," the others joined.

Crack.

Crack.

Crack.

The metal cables were taut as bowstrings and they snapped like rifle shots. The wooden cross seemed suspended by nothing but faith, but then it plunged downward.

The beast sensed the danger. It stalled its lethal blow and looked up. The pointed foot of the cross pierced the side of its throat, ripped through its body, and erupted with a gush of pus and blood from the bloated belly. The creature's eyes bulged and the mouth gaped in a silent scream. It staggered backward, clawing at the cross at its neck and belly.

"Begone, Satan," Lucius screamed and an explosion rocked the church. The air sucked through the holes in the church, drawing walls and ceilings and floors together. A glow like the core of the sun blinded them, then all was silent.

Lucius woke first and stared dumbly at the scene surrounding him. The others opened their eyes moments later.

"This is My Body," Father O'Connor prayed evenly, standing at the altar and raising the host reverently overhead.

Ben Littlejohn looked wildly about him, meeting the startled faces of the others at they surveyed the peaceful church. As one, they glanced overhead and their eyes locked on the heavy wooden cross suspended above them. Then their searching gazes raced about the walls, the ceilings, the floors. St. Martin's church shone in the beams of morning sunlight that pierced the stained-glass windows. The church was as they had found it an eternity ago.

"This is My Blood," the priest intoned and the white eyes of the plaster St. Martin bathed the worshipers with pride and love.

EPILOGUE

IT HAD BEEN exactly one year since "the bad week" as the days of tragedy had come to be called when they were discussed at all.

Which wasn't often.

Not that the people of Hensleyville felt that ignoring the dark days would make them go away. That wasn't it at all. It was more a fear that talking about them would make them come back.

There were a handful of people who knew exactly what had ailed the town during those horrid days but they never spoke of it, not even among themselves, although it was often in their thoughts and always in their prayers.

A slight correction, one of them did bring it up. Father O'Connor described the events to the bishop who felt that it was time for the old priest to hang it up, which he did. He died six months later, a contented man at peace with the world. Leticia Zooker stood at his side and held his gnarled old hand when he sighed his last breath and his final vision was of her beautiful face.

John Logan had marveled at Leticia's recovery, and even though he doctored her back to health, he didn't feel that he could take full credit for her creamy complexion or her youthful bounce.

Ben Littlejohn hired a new deputy, a young fellow from Marietta who used to ask questions about "the bad week" but finally gave up after countless stony silences. There were times when Ben wished he could tell someone about it but who would believe it anyway.

Higher authorities had a hard time understanding how a pious man like Festus Cady could hang himself or how a coward like Virgil Fenner could drive a knife through his own brain. They asked Ben for his opinion but he just shook his square head and said it was a mystery to him.

Some things were better left to rest.

"What time's dinner, Mom?"

Calling Kathryn Lockwood "Mom" came easily to Lucius but calling Woody "Dad" brought back a flood of painful memories.

Woody understood.

Lucius had come home with Woody and Chris right after that Mass. He stayed over that night and never left. On a sizzling day in the fall, Kathryn joined them in the house on the hill after a quiet wedding with Mal Whitney presiding. John Logan and Leticia Zooker were proud to witness the event. Ben Littlejohn would have been there but some goofy teenager with too much beer flipped his Trans Am on County Line Road.

"Dinner's at six," Kathryn called through the kitchen window. "Don't be late."

"We won't. See you, Mom."

Her eyes misted as she watched her two new sons pedal off to do whatever it was that young boys did on a hot summer day.